A Counterfeit Wife

THE SIRENS

PAULLETT GOLDEN

Cover Design by Fiona Jayde Media
Interior Design by The Deliberate Page

Also by Paullett Golden

To all who traverse "through dangers untold and hardships unnumbered." This book is for you.

Praise for Golden's Books

"Paullett Golden isn't afraid to weave complex family matters into her historical romance... The author's strong points are her ability to reveal the vulnerability of her characters while showing you how they work through their differences."

— *Readers' Favorites Reviewer*

"There are rare occasions when a plot, characters, dialogue, and backdrop align to make an inspiring book. This is one of those times. This book was a tumultuous, all-encompassing love story. I fell in love with every aspect of this book... The author created a world that I want to visit again and again."

— Jenna of *Reading Rebel Reviews*

"Character development is wonderful, and it is interesting to follow two young people as they defy the odds to be together. Paullett Golden's novel is compelling and a stellar work that is skillfully crafted."

—Sheri Hoyte of *Reader Views*

"It's thoughtfulness about issues of social class, birth-rights, gender disparities, and city versus country concerns add provocative emotional layers. Strong, complex characterizations, nuanced family dynamics, insightful social commentary, and a vibrant sense of time and place both geographically and emotionally make this a poignant read."

— Cardyn Brooks of *InD'tale Magazine*

"The author adds a few extra ingredients to the romantic formula, with pleasing results. An engaging and unconventional love story."

— *Kirkus Reviews*

"The well-written prose is a delight, the author's voice compelling readers and drawing them into the story with an endearing, captivating plot and genuine, authentic settings. From the uncompromising social conventions of the era to the permissible attitudes and behaviors within each class, it's a first-class journey back in time."

— *Reader Views*

"[The Enchantresses] by Paullett Golden easily ranks as one of the best historical romances I have read in some time and I highly recommend it to fans of romance, history, and the regency era. Fabulous reading!"

— *Sheri Hoyte*

"The author Paullett Golden has a gift for creating memorable characters that have depth."

"What I loved about the author was her knowledge of the era! Her descriptions are fresh and rich. Her writing is strong and emotionally driven. An author to follow."

"I enjoy the way Golden smartly sprinkles wit and satire throughout her story to highlight the absurdity of the British comedy of manners."

"With complex characters and a backstory with amazing depth, the story … is fantastic from start to finish."

"Paullett Golden specializes in creating charmingly flawed characters and she did not disappoint in this latest enchantress novel."

"…a modern sensibility about the theme of self-realization, and a fresh take on romance make the foundation of Golden's latest Georgian-era romance."

"I thoroughly enjoyed meeting and getting to know all of the characters. Each character was fully developed, robust and very relatable."

— *Flippin' Pages Book Reviews*

"This is one of the best books I've read EVER! It made me smile, it made me laugh, it made me angry and then it made me very happy."

— *FH Denny Reviews*

"One of the best historical romances I have ever read. Everything about this book is empowering and heart touching."

— *SR.EE Vine Voice*

Prologue

July 1795

Tidwell Hall, Lincolnshire

"I've taken the liberty of assembling a list of candidates, my lord." Mr. Lloyd Barmby, Jr. inched the parchment across the desk.

Silence stretched as the marquess considered the names.

A longcase clock struck the hour. Eleven pendulum strikes. The sound resonated through the paneled study.

"If I may be so bold," Mr. Barmby added after the final chime, "I could offer my top recommendations."

He pinned his solicitor with a penetrating stare. "That is, Mr. Barmby, why I put you to the task."

"Not for my plucky comic relief?"

His reply, a granite expression.

"Right." Mr. Barmby's chuckle turned to a cough. "I recommend Miss Whittington, Miss Carpenter, or Miss Ironwood."

"Tell me which one is to be Lady Pickering, and then see to the settlement." The Marquess of Pickering dismissed the list with a flick across the desk.

The solicitor cleared his throat. "Miss Whittington, then."

"She is the wealthiest, I presume?"

"Yes, my lord." Mr. Barmby rubbed the side of his nose then busied his hands by rolling the parchment.

"What are you not telling me?"

His man of business tightened the scroll, tapped its edge, then wrapped it with twine. "You might not like how she came by the dowry."

"If you believe Miss Whittington is the best candidate, then I trust you." The marquess rested his elbows on the desk, steepling his fingers. "Now, tell me your hesitancy."

"The Textile King of London," Mr. Barmby mumbled.

He arched a brow.

"He would be your father-in-law."

The words hung in the air.

When he did not protest, Mr. Barmby explained, "Miss Whittington is the daughter of the textile merchant, you see. She may be of undesirable descent, but she is the wealthiest filly in the stable and the most attractive, or so they say; I've not seen her myself to confirm."

"If having a cit for an in-law is the only sacrifice, I do not see a problem with the match." The marquess laced his fingers and rested his chin on his knuckles. "I assume I needn't reiterate; the dowry is what's important."

"Should be an easy deal, all cards being in your favor, as it were, at least with this gel," the solicitor assured his client. "The others may be skittish about a fortune hunter, but not Miss Whittington. Rumor has it her father is angling for a titled connection, using the dowry as bait. Trouble is, not many are willing to associate with industry. *Nouveau-riche* is what they call him, although I doubt we'll ever find that in a Johnson's lexicon, vulgar as it is."

"I don't care from whence the dowry comes as long as it comes." Flattening his hands against the desk, he rose from his chair. "I'm for Sladesbridge Court in the morning. I'll see to the license. The nuptials are to be within a day of her arrival. The sooner we have the dowry, the sooner we lighten the millstone about my neck. I'll leave the details to you."

Chapter 1

Phoebe Whittington threw the bottle with such force it shattered against the Arabesque wallpaper, scenting the dressing room with lilac.

Her lady's maid dropped the hairbrush and leapt out of harm's way.

"I refuse to marry him!" Phoebe screeched, glaring at her father's reflection in the *poudreuse* mirror.

The portly merchant shouldered the maid aside to reach his daughter. "This is our chance, lovey. You'll be a marchioness, and I'll have the connections to be voted Lord Mayor of London by next Michaelmas."

"I refuse to marry an impoverished ogre!" She grabbed for another perfume bottle, but Mr. Whittington stayed her hand.

"It's either the Marquess of Pickering or the Earl of Collumby. I like the marquess for you, but if you've a change of heart... Collumby instead?"

"You shan't make me choose between a recluse and a septuagenarian. Unequivocally not Collumby — do we know what happened to Lord Collumby's previous four wives?"

"Unimportant." He leaned over her shoulder to address her reflection. "You'll spend more time in

London than tending to your husband. Balls! Soirees! Think of the invitations you'll receive." Taking her hand in his, he added, "Don't forget your papa in the diversion. With the right word in the prince's ear about the future of textiles, you could triple our wealth."

"I won't be coerced. I will marry Mr. Wilkins or no other." She struggled to free her hand from his grasp. "Go find your own bride amongst the nobs if you want their influence. I will marry no one except Freddy. He's my true love!"

Wrenching her hand free, she sent the second bottle of perfume sailing, narrowly missing the maid shadowed in the corner.

Mr. Whittington's face reddened. He puffed his cheeks, good humor gone.

Taking his daughter by the shoulders, he shook her and bellowed, "You will stay away from that rogue. Don't risk my wrath." Huffing, he loosened his grip and softened his tone. "I want trunks packed and you on the coach within a fortnight. I've arranged to sign the settlement with the marquess' solicitor on the morrow. Last chance for a change of heart. Are you to be the Marchioness of Pickering at Sladesbridge Court in Yorkshire or the Countess of Collumby at Lobelia Hall in Shropshire?"

Eyes lowered, Phoebe acquiesced. "Pickering."

"That's my girl." He patted her arm, and then about-faced. Eyes widening to see the maid, who attempted to blend into the wallpaper, he pointed with a bloated, gold-ringed finger. "You. Maid. Have bags packed by the end of the week. You'll be accompanying my lovey."

Although the lady's maid curtsied, Mr. Whittington did not stay long enough to notice, door slamming behind him.

The maid closed her eyes, wishing she were anywhere except in the dressing room of Miss Phoebe Whittington.

"I'll not marry him," Phoebe muttered. "Freddy will find a way. He loves me, you know."

Without replying, the maid retrieved the hairbrush and resumed styling her mistress' hair. While Miss Whittington may protest, a one-way trip to Yorkshire did not sound the least unpleasant to her. London left much to be desired with its noisy streets and foul air. She missed the starry nights and slow pace of country life. Besides, she had never been that far north.

Feeling Miss Whittington's eyes trained on her, the maid braved a glance to the mirror. Her reward, a mischievous grin reflected in the glass.

In a whisper, her mistress said, "Ensure no one comes to my room tonight, J'non. I'm meeting Freddy. Tell anyone who asks I have the megrims. Oh, and pack the portmanteau as Papa ordered, but between the two of us, we will *not* be going to Yorkshire."

J'non Butler nodded. While not as confident as her mistress that Mr. Whittington's word could be defied, she did not doubt Miss Whittington would concoct a scheme. But then, what would become of J'non?

Chapter 2

The hired coach lurched, and along with it, J'non's stomach. She sat with her back to the horses, nauseated, while Phoebe Whittington fidgeted across from her. J'non's eyes remained closed more than open, yet she could not miss the fervent darting of Miss Whittington's gaze, searching the horizon from the window. At their most recent stop, those hungry eyes had scoured the innyard. Anxious to meet the Marquess of Pickering? Although they had already traveled for a week since leaving London, there remained anywhere between three and five days. Too early to be fretting about meeting the marquess in J'non's opinion, but then, she had never been in Miss Whittington's shoes before, traveling across the country to meet one's betrothed, a stranger and a nobleman to boot.

Their next stop would be Doncaster where they would retire for the evening. The journey would resume at daybreak, but by way of a new carriage. The marquess' own coachman would see them the remaining distance to Sladesbridge Court in the North York Moors.

J'non shifted her attention to the window.

A river flowed parallel to the road with what looked to be extensive wetlands in the distance. Traveling sickness aside, she was hopeful, the future full of promises. She would be in the country again, living safe at the court, far away from London and the roving eyes of Mr. Whittington, and even farther from — no, best not think on the past. She shuddered.

Whatever reservations her mistress felt about the arranged marriage, J'non had none. Easy sentiment to feel when she had not committed herself to marrying a stranger, yet why the reluctance for the match? A life of security awaited Miss Whittington. Did that not fill her with confidence as it would J'non in the same situation? Few women understood what it was like not to have a home, a family, someone to turn to in a time of crisis. J'non knew. This journey meant more to her than pampered Miss Whittington could fathom.

A dip in the road brought her attention back to her fellow passenger.

"Excited?" J'non asked.

Miss Whittington spared a glance, then pretended not to hear the question. Her dark curls flounced with the sway of the carriage, thick lashes framing doe eyes, distinguished against alabaster skin. Even her dress was the height of fashion, a perk of having a textile merchant for a father. Without doubt, the marquess would be pleased with his bride, at least in appearances. The young lady's petulance was another matter, but that was not J'non's concern.

A tightening in her chest, a dull ache. Not envious so much as wistful. Never in her life had she possessed beauty or wealth, and yet at one time, she might have secured a good match. Had it not been for their death. Had it not been for the scandal.

She looked now, wistfully, on Miss Whittington's journey and wished it were her own.

Trying again, J'non said, "You must be excited to see him."

Miss Whittington turned from the window with a start. "How did you know?"

"Is that not the purpose of our trip? To see your betrothed?" J'non studied her companion.

"Oh, him." She waved a gloved hand and returned her gaze to the passing countryside.

They rode in silence, Miss Whittington fidgeting with increased agitation. She knotted the ribbon at her waist, unknotted it, then knotted it again. She plucked at her curls, wrapped them around her fingers, one finger at a time, then released them with a spring. With each passing mile, her hands busied and her body shifted. J'non observed it all from her periphery. For her part, she rested against the seat, her sweaty palms pressed to her stomach, trying not to move. In hindsight, attempting conversation had been a terrible idea.

As though reading her mind but misinterpreting, Miss Whittington said, "This isn't going to work." She tugged at the ribbon until it unknotted. "Not unless you help."

"I'm certain his lordship will favor you," said J'non, assuming her mistress referred to the situation rather than the ribbon. "You will come to like him over time, as well. Familiarity has that effect." After a moment's thought, she added with an encouraging smile, "Even if he is an impoverished ogre."

Miss Whittington reached for J'non's hand, clasping it between her own. "My dearest, dearest J'non. You're going to do me the teeniest favor."

Her limbs tingled with apprehension, mixing uncomfortably with the travel sickness.

"I've worked it out. Or rather Freddy has. He's to meet us in Doncaster," Miss Whittington confessed, massaging J'non's hand, chafing more like. "Together, we're going to Scotland, or maybe France, or maybe Spain. The future is ours! If we dare. And, oh, I dare!"

Edging her hand free, J'non said, "I'm not sure I understand you."

On the contrary. She understood perfectly. Miss Whittington had arranged to elope with Mr. Wilkins—a rogue and fortune hunter, according to Mr. Whittington. If true, where did that leave J'non? Returning her hand to her stomach, she closed her eyes, afraid she would be sick in the carriage after all.

Fear wrapped a heavy hand around her throat. She could not return to London alone, not without her charge. Mr. Whittington's wrath would be severe, after which she would lose her job without a character. What would she do then? Where would she go? Not yet a month had she held this post. If she were turned out, the agency would not offer her another position. It had been made clear she only received this position because the Whittingtons, being of industry, would not know a qualified lady's maid from a chimney sweep. Their ignorance was her luck. Luck did not offer second chances, however.

Jumping to conclusions, J'non. It will not be as bad as that.

Miss Whittington would take her with her, of course. Life with a libertine as he escorted his bride to Scotland or the continent was not the security for which J'non hoped, but with a roof over her head and bread in her bowl, she would not complain.

Then, was Mr. Wilkins not penniless? So had said Mr. Whittington.

Every bone in her body ached the truth. She was to be turned out. Again.

J'non focused on breathing. In, then out. In, then out.

Miss Whittington, oblivious to J'non's mounting panic, said, "I wish we had found a way to secure the dowry, and I think we still may find a way, but Freddy insists we can manage without it. He's to inherit, you see. Any day now, he'll inherit. With or without money, he wants *me*. He loves me to distraction, J'non! Never again will I be a pawn of the greedy. Please say you'll help me. You must! Once the marquess discovers he's been deceived, he'll hunt me like a fox."

"I don't see how I can help."

"My plan is so brilliant you'll wish you had thought of it yourself. It's the only way I'll escape unnoticed. Even Papa won't find out." She tittered before continuing, "I've been planning this all week, and I believe I've worked it to perfection. I'll leave with Freddy, but you'll continue to Sladesbridge Court."

Her breathing shallow, J'non stuttered in protest. "But I can't arrive without you!"

"That's the brilliant part, my dearest J'non. You *will* arrive with me."

J'non mouthed her confusion but could not form the words.

"You'll show up *as* me," her mistress said. "Brilliant, yes? The marquess doesn't know me, so he will be none the wiser. Show up, introduce yourself as me, as Miss Phoebe Whittington, and then the marriage will take place as planned. All will be well. Papa will think I've married the marquess, and the marquess will think he's married me. You'll have the marriage of a lifetime, as will I. With Freddy and I starting a new life in Scotland or France or wherever we choose, our paths will never cross. Go on, thank me for making all your dreams come true, from maid to marchioness."

"No! I can't take part in this." J'non trembled, cold despite the beads of sweat at the base of her spine. "Besides, the marquess will know I'm not you."

"Nonsense. He's never seen me. I never met his solicitor either. Papa handled everything, as he always does." Miss Whittington regarded J'non from head to toe. "We both have brown hair. We're close in age, I think. See, we're not dissimilar. I contest it doesn't matter; Papa won't expect a letter, nor will he ever be in company with the marquess. He wanted bragging rights, nothing more, a feather in his cap for the election to say he has the ear of the nobility. Honestly, J'non, once you've married the marquess, who will care?"

J'non closed her eyes and breathed. Inhale, exhale. "Someone would find out." Inhale, exhale. "It's deceitful and treacherous." Inhale, exhale. "I want no part of it." Opening her eyes, she fixed her mistress with a resolute stare. *Maid to marchioness… I want no part of it.*

Miss Whittington's smile slipped. "It *will* work. You need only cooperate." She wet her lips, rouging them with venom. "You are my maid. You must obey."

"I will not pretend to be you," J'non stated with more confidence than she felt. *Maid to marchioness...*

Eyes narrowed, Miss Whittington turned back to the window.

J'non rested her head against the seatback until the pounding of her heart quieted.

As seconds turned to minutes, Miss Whittington's anger dissipated into resignation, or so J'non assumed from the relaxation of her posture and ghost of a smile. She must be realizing, now that the plan had been verbalized, how foolish was the scheme. The best choice, the only choice, was for Miss Whittington to continue to Sladesbridge Court and marry the marquess as contracted. Yes, she must be realizing that now.

It had been a madcap scheme. Maid to marchioness indeed. Preposterous!

Then, had they not died... Had there not been the scandal... No, not even then.

They exchanged not a word until the coach stopped at Doncaster.

Only after they stepped into the inn did Miss Whittington turn to her with an endearing smile. "All is forgiven, my dearest J'non. You're right, of course. It never would have worked. Now, let's hope the accommodations are satisfactory because I'm fit to be knackered. I'm sure every bone in my body has been rattled out of place."

J'non trailed behind her mistress.

Noises from the taproom filtered into their room, but it was fear rather than noise that kept her awake, fear of being left behind. J'non's truckle bed stood sentry at the foot of her mistress' sleeping form. Should Miss Whittington toss or turn, J'non would know. Should she pad across the room to escape in the night, J'non would know. That did not keep her from peering over the bedframe throughout the night. For reassurance.

During the stretches of sleeplessness, J'non counted water spots on the ceiling, each elongated by the moonlight. Too hot, she kicked off the coverlet. Too cold, she pulled it over her head.

In hindsight, how naïve to have panicked over Miss Whittington's plan when it had been so absurd a scheme. Miss Whittington must have intended to mock J'non. A humbling thought. Although mockery was superior to sincerity in this case. To imagine, J'non arriving at the estate claiming to be a wealthy and reputable beauty. The marquess would laugh at best or have her committed at worst.

Then, was that the worst? Returning to London to face Mr. Whittington could be worse. Being jailed or transported for fraud would be worse. Was impersonation a hanging offense or finable? Not that she had coin to pay a fine. J'non rubbed her neck.

Pushing away morose thoughts, she allowed her mind to wander in the direction of the mysterious marquess, the "impoverished ogre." What sort of man contracted marriage with a woman he had never met? A desperate man. A risky gambler. But was it about the dowry? Mr. Whittington had called the man a recluse. Was he too monstrous to court a woman by traditional means?

It was a good thing, then, J'non would not have to face him alone.

She sat up to check on her mistress. For peace of mind.

The blanketed curves of Miss Whittington reassured her. Settling against the straw-filled pillow, J'non humored herself with the composition of a play in three parts, a foxhunt wherein her mistress starred as the fox, Mr. Wilkins the hound, and the marquess the hunter.

Sleep took her with a far more vivid dream. A dream not of foxhunting but of the Marquess of Pickering's wedding. *Maid to marchioness...*

Chapter 3

T he Marquess of Pickering strode through the entrance hall of Sladesbridge Court with Gunner trotting at his side. At the edge of the vestibule, his brindle Lurcher — part Irish wolfhound, part greyhound — stopped to rest on his haunches, tail thumping, awaiting command.

The butler opened the front door, saying as Pickering passed, "The staff will assemble in the vestibule momentarily, my lord."

"Excellent, Hawkins," Pickering barked without breaking stride.

His coachman had been spotted traversing the drive — a grueling ascent riddled with dips and holes — the length of which needed resurfacing. Not the most auspicious welcome for his betrothed and her maid, but she would learn soon enough the straits of the estate, far and above a few ruts in a driveway.

Crossing the courtyard, he side-stepped protruding stones, stones that at one time had been cut and painted to display his family's coat of arms. The courtyard, as with the drive, needed refinishing. The courtyard, as with the drive, was the least of his concerns. He reached the edge where stone met earth as the carriage crested the hill and passed the gatehouse. Feet apart, hands clasped behind his back, he stood at ease, observing the vehicle's progress.

Pickering had planned the arrival with meticulous timing so as not to unduly burden his schedule. He and his betrothed would exchange pleasantries in the vestibule before Hawkins would escort her to the lady's chamber. He would return to his study. Three hours his betrothed would have to rest, for three hours hence, they would dine together. Following supper, he would retire for the evening to the inn in the dale. He did not want her discomfited by sharing a roof with a bachelor, betrothed or not.

The carriage rocked to a halt. Pickering watched with detached interest, keen to complete this task and move to the next.

A groom jumped to attention. He set the steps, opened the door, and offered a hand to assist the occupants in their descent. The lady's maid, in a drab traveling dress and unadorned straw bonnet, stepped down, looked about her, then turned to consider the lord of the manor. Ignoring her, he eyed the carriage door for his betrothed to appear.

He waited.

Too nervous to descend?

He waited longer.

An act of defiance?

He furled and unfurled his fingers.

The groom closed the carriage door, returned the steps, and climbed onto the box with the coachman, the carriage rocking forward to head to the stables.

Pickering turned his attention to the woman standing before him, patience personified, her eyes lowered, her fingers laced. Realization dawned. He took her in fully with a mixture of indignation, confusion, and — relief.

Indignation paramount and primary.

How dare *that cit*, he thought.

How *dare* he send his daughter unchaperoned across the country when the threat of highwaymen and any number of unsavory characters lurked along the roads. How *dare* he dress her in rags while he rolled in textile riches. How *dare* he force her to face a tedious journey to meet a stranger without companionship.

Although she may not be Pickering's wife yet, she had entered his protection the moment he signed the settlement, at least from his perspective. This young lady, in all appearance a gentlewoman's poor relation rather than the daughter of the wealthiest merchant in London, would find her situation improved under his care, even if the roof leaked.

His indignation aside, he could now admit he had dreaded the arrival of the buxom beauty Mr. Barmby had described. Yes, he needed the dowry, but he had cringed to think of life with an attention-seeking wife who preferred shopping and fashion to country living. More than once, he entertained the possibility of her living at the London house while he resided in the north. The heavens favored him today, for the young lady rumored to be of curvaceous figure and disarming eyes was the antithesis of the woman standing before him. Wisps of mousy hair framed a teardrop-shaped face.

This woman was far more to his taste: subdued, petite, and plain.

When she looked up, however, so that he might see beneath her bonnet, he confirmed one rumor true—disarming eyes. He faltered, arrested by her eyes. The nondescript brown of her irises was inconsequential to the depth of expression within. These were not the eyes of an idle lady affecting ennui, rather the eyes of a young woman who had seen too much of life in too short a time.

Taking one step forward, he bowed. "Welcome to Sladesbridge Court, Miss Whittington," he said.

She hesitated.

Was she displeased with him? Did he disappoint her expectations?

Her hand crept towards him, as though uncertain how to greet him, but the corners of her mouth lifted into a shy smile.

Enclosing her fingers in his, he inclined his head over her hand. "Lord Pickering," he said, "at your service."

Another hesitation, and then with eyes lowered, she replied, "Thank you, my lord. It is a pleasure to be here."

Surrey, he thought with mingled solace and curiosity. Her accent was unmistakably of Surrey. As with his expectations of her figure and personality, he had dreaded her pronunciation, anticipating a bourgeois London inflection or a faux cut-glass intonation, exaggerated for effect.

Stepping to her side, he offered his arm. She laid a hand on his forearm with featherlight touch and with, what he could not help but notice, worn gloves. Should she turn her hand, would he find the fingertips threadbare? Pursing his lips against resurfacing anger at her father's thoughtlessness and neglect, he escorted her across the courtyard, navigating her around the ruins of the family crest.

"You'll pardon the state of the courtyard, Miss Whittington. Much work is to be done. You will want a tour, of course, but it must wait until the day after tomorrow, that is if you wish for me to serve as guide. Today, you will wish to rest. Tomorrow, we wed."

"So soon?" she asked with a sharp intake of breath.

Pickering led her up the steps into the vestibule where Hawkins waited, door held in one hand, the other indicating the line of staff.

"The wedding? Yes, it would be inconvenient to delay the vows. This evening should be enough time for you to rest from the journey."

Miss Whittington favored him with a quiet smile before he directed her to the liveried servants. Did she realize this skeleton crew consisted of all employees at the estate save the stable hands? Employing staff on a paltry budget was not easy. His mind wandered to the moldy study where an ever-increasing pile of correspondences, mostly from bill collectors, awaited his attention, likely procreating on his desk, multiplying by the dozen with each passing second. Any reservations he held to have arranged a marriage through his solicitor was quelled by the condition of said study. Damp. Stale. Using the dowry, he could patch the roof and repair the window casement; the study, however, as with the courtyard and the drive, was the least of his concerns.

One final introduction remained, the most important of all. A pat to his thigh preceded the clicking of nails against wood flooring. Miss Whittington gasped as Pickering's dog marched from behind the line of staff to sit on his rump before her, tail thumping.

"May I introduce to you Gunner? Gunner, this is Miss Whittington, your soon-to-be mistress."

The dog looked from the young lady to his master and back before raising a paw. Miss Whittington hesitated, much as she had done moments ago when meeting him in the courtyard.

Pickering said, "This is where you shake his paw."

The shy smile returned before she leaned to offer the pup her hand, not that she had to lean down far given her petite stature and the Lurcher's large build. Had the dog stood on hind legs, he would have been a head taller than Miss Whittington. The visual tickled one corner of Pickering's lips.

A hand to her elbow, he said, "Hawkins will see you to your suite where your belongings should be waiting." He turned to the butler. "Miss Whittington will need a maid."

"Very well, my lord," replied Hawkins.

"We dine at five sharp," Pickering clarified for his betrothed. "At a quarter to five, Hawkins will show you to the dining room."

With a bow, he left her in the capable hands of the butler, Gunner heeling at his side.

Chapter 4

J'non collapsed against the bedchamber door, hand to pounding heart.

What had she done?

Or rather, what had she *not* done? Like a fool, she had stood in silence.

Sinking to the floor, she wrapped her arms around her shins and rested her forehead on her knees. Her eyes stung with unshed tears.

It began when she woke at the inn. Not for some time had she realized herself alone, but she had undeniably been alone. She rose to Miss Whittington's shapely form still sleeping under the bedcovers, a pillow snug over her head to muffle noise and blot out daylight. Seeing her mistress still asleep, J'non busied herself by washing in the basin and dressing, checking that the traveling dress she had set aside the night before for Miss Whittington was still wrinkle free, and then slipping into the taproom for breakfast. She brought up a plate for her mistress. Time passed, but still the young lady slept. J'non became antsy, not wanting to be late. After letting her sleep for as long as possible, J'non approached the bed.

Pillows and wadded clothing. That was what she found beneath the sheets. J'non had never felt so naïve in her life.

How long had Miss Whittington been gone? An hour? Five hours? All evening? Had she departed before J'non retired for the evening, sometime in the night, or when J'non slipped out for breakfast? Not that it mattered. The point was she had gone.

During the carriage ride to Sladesbridge Court, J'non had rehearsed her speech a thousand and one times. She would explain the situation rationally, after which time, she would beg for mercy, and perhaps employment, or at least enough money to return to London and face her fate. By the time the carriage left York, she had convinced herself the marquess would thank her forthrightness by accepting her plea and offering her employment.

But when the time came, she panicked. She descended from the carriage ready to confess and fall on his good graces. Her moment's hesitation tumulted into his mistaking her for Miss Whittington. What was she to do? Interrupt a marquess' introduction? How was she to convey the inconvenient truth that she was not, in point of fact, Miss Whittington, but rather the inept maid who allowed his betrothed to run away with another man?

The situation escalated before she could correct him. He introduced her to the staff. He introduced her to his dog! How was she to contradict the lord of the manor in front of his staff or after shaking paws with the dog?

And now… The wedding was tomorrow.

It was not too late. It could not be too late. She had time to confess. At supper. Yes, supper. She would explain how her fatigue and distress caused a momentarily lapse in which she found herself embroiled in a misunderstanding that did not, at the time, seem appropriate to rectify.

Yes, she would tell him at supper.

It would all have been easier if he had turned out to be an ogre. The trouble was, he was far from being an ogre. From the moment she laid eyes on him, her heart had been in her throat. However impossible the situation, however plain her appearance, however distinguished his air, in that moment, she wanted more than anything to be Lady Pickering. *Maid to marchioness*.

He could not be older than thirty. He intimidated in height with long, powerful legs and haughty visage with lean face, angular nose, and brown hair cropped in a Brutus style. His hazel eyes had weakened her knees, along with her resolve. Rather than speak when she had the chance, she had admired, lost in wonder and longing.

Supper would not be too late. If she confessed then, the marquess would be relieved to learn the truth. Once he calmed his fury, that was. Regardless of whether the truth meant a mad search for his betrothed or a new bride, he would be relieved to learn J'non was not his intended. His displeasure with her had been evident at first glance. He had swept his gaze over her with pursed lips, clenched jaw, and steely eyes. She could read his thoughts in his expression—duped, misled, sent a discarded nobody. While she admired, he judged.

She knew beyond question he needed money. Not only did he plan to move forward with the wedding, even after meeting her, but the home was deteriorating around his ears. The ivy on the front of the Tudor mansion strangled three stories of windows and red brick. A stale odor permeated the vestibule. The grand oak staircase, although freshly polished, creaked and groaned on the ascent to the west wing. While a great deal of time and care had gone into cleaning her bedchamber, it showed signs of disrepair no amount of beeswax or perfume could mask. Threadbare furniture, peeling wallpaper, a draft from the window. The room must have been breathtaking at one time, with its Gothic fireplace hugging one wall, gilded furnishings, and an ornate plaster ceiling heralding a hand-painted mural — cracked and faded.

The marquess had bargained for a bride for the sole purpose of redecorating his house. What sort of man was so proud he would commit two people to marriage to restore a home he had already destroyed through neglect? An arrogant man. One born into nobility without a care for anyone but himself. A gambler no doubt, spoiled by family fortune.

Conceited nobles were easy to dislike. If she disliked him, she could walk away from temptation.

A knock broke her reverie. Rather than a rapping at the chamber door behind her, the knock came from an adjoining room — the dressing room, she presumed. A swipe to her cheeks reassured her no tears had fallen. She stood, straightened her dress, and prompted the person to enter.

A young maid stepped over the threshold, curtsying, her eyes downcast as she waited to be acknowledged.

"Mr. Hawkins sent you," J'non said, aware one lady's maid addressed another. "Whom do I have the pleasure of addressing?"

"Edith, miss," she said, eyes remaining downcast. "I've unpacked your trunk. Shall I help you change for a rest?"

"I don't believe I could relax if I tried. I would value company, however. Shall we settle on getting to know each other instead?" When her response was little more than a flush from the maid, J'non prompted, "You could show me which dress you think best for dinner."

Edith curtsied again, then led J'non into the dressing room. Indicating a blue dress already hanging from a dressing screen, she said, "I've set this aside for you, Miss Whittington. Did I choose well?"

J'non wondered what Edith made of the dismal contents of the solitary trunk. Aside from the waded dresses her mistress left at the inn, which would all be too large in the bust and too long in the hem without alterations, J'non only owned a few articles of clothing. The dress in question was the least plain, only because of the embroidery at the hem and bodice, adornment J'non had added herself during the long nights as Miss Whittington's maid.

"Yes, thank you, Edith. That will do."

Only three hours until supper. Three hours was longer than she needed to refresh, change clothes, and style her hair, but not long enough to rehearse a new speech to rectify the misunderstanding.

At a quarter to five, Pickering and Gunner strode from the east wing library towards the dining room in the Elizabethan center block of the house.

He descended the stairs—Gunner bounding two steps at a time—his mood foul after sifting through bills from creditors who erroneously thought hounding him would pay them faster.

The click of his boots echoed through the hallway. While he did not wish to offend Miss Whittington by wearing boots to supper, he nevertheless opted for convenience given he would depart for the inn after they dined. It would take him longer to change clothes than to ride to the inn, or so he justified his bad manners, manners that would have him uninvited from every household of his acquaintance. But then, this was his house, and more to the point, he doubted a woman of an industry background would know respectable dining attire.

For the remaining paces to the dining room, he composed a lecture on timeliness. To respect the lord of the manor meant to be punctual. He would accept nothing less. She would be late. He knew it. He expected it.

Thus, when he entered the room to find Miss Whittington waiting for him, he halted in his tracks, a startled Gunner heeling at his side.

From the moment he had realized he must sacrifice his life's plans to make a fast match, he had considered the arrangement inconvenient. His original marital plans could not be more different or further in the future, yet life had dealt him a discourteous hand. Nothing about this situation had been to his liking.

Until now.

Would wonders never cease? A punctual woman.

He clicked his heels together and bowed.

"Good evening, Lord Pickering." She curtsied, then stepped forward.

"Miss Whittington." He signaled his dog to the fireplace where a bowl of sumptuous delights awaited the Lurcher. Turning back to his intended, he commended, "You're early."

"Yes. I hoped we could have a private word." Her brows knitted.

Establishing intimacy was not yet on his schedule. Supper was. He walked to the head of the table where a footman readied his chair.

Standing next to the seat, he waited for her to join. "The purpose of supper, Miss Whittington, is to share company and, I hope, exchange conversation for the duration of the meal."

She flicked her eyes to the footman holding her chair. "I had hoped for a *private* word, my lord."

"Ah. You are unaccustomed to how gentility lives. We are, for all intents and purposes, alone. You may feel at ease to speak candidly. But first, are we to eat standing?"

With pinkened cheeks, she accepted her chair.

Once seated, he nodded to signal the commencement of supper.

Rather than speak, as he expected, his bride fidgeted, touching the cutlery until it moved askew, then straightening said cutlery again. Nervous? Yes, he believed she was. The private word she had desired must be to do with the marriage, a confession of her shyness to take vows with a stranger.

"Say not a word," he reassured, "I know what you wish to discuss and take it upon myself to right the wrong. As difficult as you might find this, I sympathize with your predicament. I'm not insensitive and am chagrined to be to blame for your discomfiture."

Eyes widening, she asked, "You know why I wanted a private word?"

"Because you're nervous about the wedding." He studied her expression for confirmation of his intuition, then added, "It is only natural. You don't know me any better than I know you. You are far from home, family, and friends. What woman would not be nervous under these circumstances?"

He had been no less anxious when awaiting her arrival, but now, having met her, he felt the first ray of hope since finding himself in his current plight. A quiet, dutiful woman who respected his time and person would suit him perfectly. With minimal effort, he could ensure her comfort.

Ah, food at last. A bowl of white soup appeared before him.

"From this supper onward," he said, "I wish you to think of Sladesbridge as your home. The sooner you settle, the more contented we both shall be." He tasted his soup and closed his eyes briefly to savor the flavor. Cook had outdone herself to impress the new mistress. Spoon poised, he paused, humbled by another thought. "Am I mistaken?" he ventured. "Are you, instead, displeased with the bridegroom?"

"Oh, no! You mustn't think that," she rushed to answer. "You're... that is to say... no. I'm not displeased." Studying her soup bowl, she caught her bottom lip between her teeth.

However pleasing her reassurance, he wondered at what sort of father was Mr. Whittington for his daughter to be so meek and timid. The kind of father who dressed his daughter in rags despite a factory full of fabrics. The kind of father who sent his daughter across the country without protection or companionship.

Her downcast eyes allowed him an opportunity to admire her without appearing rude. Although she still bore the air of a discarded relation, her dinner dress hugged her figure pleasingly, a welcome change from the dour traveling dress. Some sort of feminine stitching drew attention to her décolletage. Without the bonnet, he had full view of her hair, cut fashionably short to expose the slope of her neck. The color showed to advantage in the waning sun filtered through aged windows. He corrected himself for thinking her hair dull. Light brown, yes, but with a silken sheen that promised softness to the touch.

Never would he have thought this at first glance, but now, he could see she possessed an understated beauty, nay, a suppressed beauty, hidden beneath timorous eyelashes and worn clothing. With the right modiste, her best features could be accentuated.

Scowling at the thought of spending money on clothing before imperative estate expenses and debts, but realizing the necessity, he said, "You'll need a new wardrobe. I'll send for a modiste."

"I beg you not to trouble yourself," she said, her voice soft, her eyes still trained on the soup.

"I will not allow the Marchioness of Pickering to wear rags."

Almost as a whisper, she breathed, "But I'm not the Marchioness of Pickering."

"Not yet. Tomorrow morning, however, you will be. I'll not have you dressed as a maid, and I'll not hear another word to the contrary." He spoke more gruffly than he intended, his thoughts again on her father's ill treatment not to have dressed her in the finest his merchandise had to offer. In an attempt to soften the conversation, he asked, "Have you found your accommodations satisfactory?"

"Thank you for the room and the maid, my lord, but I really can't remain—"

"Say no more." He held up a staying hand. "I'm aware of the dampness of your room and offer apologies. All will be remedied in good time, as your comfort will be seen to before any other repairs. After the wedding ceremony, I'll begin the most necessary renovations, namely repairing the window casement in the lady's chamber."

Pickering leaned back in his chair, ready for the next course.

Hoping to steer the topic to one that would not make her as anxious as their upcoming nuptials, he said, "I look forward to showing you the estate. I hope you have an eye for detail, as I plan to leave most of the house to your good opinion while I focus my attentions to the home farm." Thinking about her new home should set her more at ease, he thought. Women loved to decorate and entertain. "During the tour, I encourage you to take notes of how you might see the house improved." Noticing she had not touched her plate, he inclined his head. "Is the fish not to your liking?"

"It is," she squeaked.

When she made no effort to continue, he tried again for conversation, prompting more pointedly. "What do you make of what you've seen so far?"

His little mouse studied him for a time, then looked about the dining room. "The fireplace is unique."

He followed her gaze to the monstrosity of black marble with scagliola columns and overmantel engraved with the family crest, contrasting with the Tudor-Gothic room wallpapered in crimson between timber beams.

He grunted, then said, "I prefer the inglenook fireplace in the lord's chamber. With such a fireplace, I may retire confidently each night knowing I will never go hungry, for in a pinch I could roast a pig on the spit."

Miss Whittington cast an arrested expression.

Was he about to marry a humorless woman?

He caught her eye, frowned, and barked, "You have permission to laugh."

One corner of her mouth twitched into a shadow of a smile before she turned her attention back to the plate.

He was eager for her to sate her appetite, for bread pudding of some sort was for dessert, and the sooner she finished her fish, the sooner they could move closer to the bread pudding. Spooning a helping from his plate, he nonchalantly lowered it below the table. Not as subtly, Gunner rose and snuffled over, shoving chairs to reach the proffered bite. Did Miss Whittington like dogs?

"The ceremony will begin at nine in the chapel. Hawkins will arrive at half past eight to escort you. You'll find it a short walk on estate grounds."

"Oh, but I can't—"

"Marry without a wedding dress?" Pickering offered with a knowing nod. "Judging from your wardrobe thus far, I'm not surprised. The only guests will be the two obligatory witnesses, so you needn't concern yourself. Your dress this evening will suffice."

Returning to his place before the hearth, Gunner gave a howl of a yawn, letting his satisfaction with the fish be known.

Chapter 5

J'non woke the next morning determined to put an end to the charade.

Lord Pickering was a self-absorbed noble who expressed his displeasure with her in his every movement and every word. He scowled. He insulted. He made disparaging remarks about her wardrobe and table manners and judged her from beneath pinched brows. So intent on autocracy, he never permitted her to speak. How was she supposed to tell so dominating a man anything?

Something had to be done to stop the wedding. She had no business being here, no business allowing Edith to curl the fringe around her face and across her forehead, no business dressing in her wedding attire, which to her chagrin was the same dress she had worn for supper. She needed to be assertive. She could not allow herself to be cowed.

With the truth out at last, she could return to London, face Mr. Whittington, be turned away by the employment agency, and choose a corner of London on which to set up residence for a lifetime of homeless starvation.

No, that would not do.

The minutes in which she could confess ticked by, her fate sealing with each move of the clock hand. Conflicted, she left her dressing room and followed the butler. Too agitated to take in the sublime weather, the expanse of the estate grounds, or the vistas overlooking the vale, she trudged down a half-mile avenue of lime trees towards a Palladian chapel in far better condition than the house.

The trouble was, by telling him, she would be turning her back on safety and comfort. With lips sealed, however, she would be safe. The assumptions were already made due to no effort on her part. She need only maintain the secret. But how could she live a lie? This was not a temporary fib. This was a life sentence of being someone else.

The closer she drew to the chapel, the heavier her steps, more leaden her shoes.

A lie for security or the truth for destitution?

An exaggeration to say she would be living as someone else, was it not? Aside from the signature, she would not *be* Phoebe Whittington. Not really. She would be herself, and her name would be his. The only lie would be the register signature. Would it be so tragic to sign the name, the work of a second, and then move forward? It was not as though she had chosen this or set out to deceive. The situation had forced her hand. *He* forced her hand by insisting they continue with the ceremony despite his disappointment at seeing she would be the bride. Would it not be foolhardy, injudicious, daft even, to turn away from security? In a curious way, it was as though this route had been prepared for her, gifted to her.

Miss Whittington had vowed never to set foot on England's soil again. Why should she? Phoebe hated her father and wanted to be free of dominating men, a hopeless romantic who wanted love at any cost. With Mr. Wilkins, it would seem she had found that love. This was, then, a gift to J'non.

The more she thought about it, the more certain she believed the plan foolproof. Her path would never cross with Mr. Whittington's, and those few people in London who knew Miss Whittington would never be in company with the marquess. J'non was a world apart from all she left behind.

This was her chance. Her only chance. The chance of a lifetime.

In that moment, she spied the Marquess of Pickering. He stood in the portico of the chapel, hands clasped, stone-faced, immaculate in dress, and with eyes fixed on her.

On her approach, he bowed. "Are you prepared to become Lady Pickering?"

"I am." Her words did not falter.

J'non Gaines, Marchioness of Pickering, wife of Trevor Gaines, Marquess of Pickering, stood in her bedchamber that evening.

No longer was she Miss J'non Butler, unwanted nobody, or Miss Phoebe Whittington, imposter. The new name, and with it a new identity, brought euphoria. It was done. There was no turning back.

She twisted the gold band on her finger.

Phoebe's ring. No, Lady Pickering's ring, and she was Lady Pickering.

J'non was Lady Pickering.

Undeniably, it had been *she* standing before the vicar, not Phoebe Whittington. Lord Pickering looked into *her* eyes, not Phoebe Whittington's. He made vows to *her*, not to Phoebe Whittington. That name might have been spoken, true, but the name represented a dowry, not a person.

J'non was Lady Pickering.

She twisted the gold band.

With it being a summer month, there was no fire in the hearth. The room was, instead, brightened by dusk's glow, still visible through one of the windows, J'non having begged Edith not to close the drapes or light the candles. She had wanted to cling to the daylight, the remaining vestals, the last rays of her life as J'non Butler.

Edith had been in the room only minutes before, readying J'non for the wedding night. The night-dresses in the trunk were all modest and plain, much like the day dresses, and so her chosen night-dress was a long-sleeved, high-necked, ankle-length shroud. J'non, no, Lady Pickering, stood next to the four-poster bed, uncertain where to stand or what to do. Should she crawl into bed? Should she feign sleep? Should she don a robe and sit by the fireplace, reading a book? She did not have a book. Steadying herself with a hand against a post, she waited, eyes unfocused, mind muddled.

At supper, he warned — promised? — he would come to her at eight sharp. The clock had not yet chimed. Her ears perked at every sound, awaiting the knock, awaiting the sight of him walking into her private chamber to claim what was rightfully his by marriage.

Intimacy with a stranger — did all brides feel as she did now? The length of their acquaintance was two suppers.

The first supper involved scowls and insults to her wardrobe, however warranted. The second, tonight's supper, was more complicated. Although he paid more attention to his dog than to her, she was aware of his every movement. *Her husband.* She hardly ate a bite. How could she when the wedding night loomed?

As handsome as she found him, he was all hauteur from the arch of his brows to the manicure of his nails. He was imposing and… large. Not the type of largeness of Mr. Whittington with his rotund girth or the largeness of a farmhand. Pickering was not unlike his Lurcher, formidable in height, lean and lithe when standing, towering above her. When seated, he was no less intimidating with his air of authority and his aristocratic presence.

They were opposites in all ways. How were they to be… intimate?

The chime.

J'non's breath hitched. She gripped the bedpost, afraid to let go should her knees fold. On the eighth strike, she heard the knock. There was no mistaking who knocked, for the knuckles rapped on the door separating her room from the lord's chamber.

She was to be his, body and soul. This was not a moment to fear. This moment meant security. From this moment forward, she had a home.

Lord Pickering opened the door, stepped over the threshold, and shut the door behind him. *Thump*. He carried a lone candlestick, the flame wavering as he moved. Her gaze followed him. He set the candleholder on the fireplace mantel. *Clink*. His lordship then walked to the window and drew closed the curtains. *Swish*. Darkness enshrouded the room.

J'non blinked to accustom her vision to the flickering of the solitary flame. His face, cast in shadow, was sinister, hawkish. Her knees trembled.

He stepped closer, no less intimidating in his banyan.

When he took another step towards her, she could see he wore a nightshirt beneath the banyan. In the open vee at the neck, a light dusting of hair could be seen. Had she not been afraid to move, she would have smiled. Only a bit of hair, but it humanized him somehow.

His voice husky, he commanded, "Get into bed."

J'non obeyed, lying with her palms against the cool sheets. No sooner had she returned her gaze to him than he extinguished the candle flame, plunging the room into black.

The sound of fabric rustled, a flutter, silk falling to the rug. The mattress dipped under his weight. Eyes squeezed shut, she breathed deeply to steady her nerves. The effect was anything but steadying. With each inhalation, she became more aware of him, of the essence of Pickering. His scent was a cologne musk, masculine, heady, an aromatic reminder of her decision.

Hot tears stung her eyes, not to be mistaken for tears of sadness, fear, or pain. They were tears of joy. Never had she been a *somebody*. This night would change everything. No longer plain. No longer unwanted. No longer futureless. Never again would she be a *nobody*.

She was Lady Pickering.

Lord Pickering rose from the comfort of his bed before dawn, grey light streaming through his window, along with a view of low-lying clouds. Despite the morning fog, the promise of another bright day lay ahead. It had not rained since his move to the estate a month ago, a far cry from the wet Yorkshire weather he expected.

The weather was not the only perfection of the morning. Pickering took pride in the efficiency of his household, the staff knowing what he wanted and when he wanted it, a feat indeed given the limited servants employed. His valet made quick work of dressing him, already having the attire laid out and the wash basin readied. The butler likewise had at the ready an appetizing plate of boiled eggs and soldiers with an ample selection of meats and endless availability of black coffee. Even a groomsman had his horse warmed, saddled, and ready to ride when Pickering arrived at the stables with Gunner at his side.

A reader of Jean Jacques Rousseau, Pickering believed if the body was to obey the soul, it must be vigorous. A strong body obeys, whereas a weak body commands. His Lurcher agreed. Gunner darted about the yard, as eager as his master for a morning of hardy exercise.

Patting the horse in welcome, Pickering mounted the thoroughbred, adjusted his seat, then flicked the reins. They set off at a trot, steady and straight, then into a canter, the trio of horse, man, and dog champing at the bit for the inevitable third stage. With a click of Pickering's tongue, they pressed into a gallop, riding neck-or-nothing against the wind. Gunner raced ahead, giving the horse a spirited chase. One day, Pickering vowed, he would win a horse race against his dog. Today was not that day. The Lurcher took a clear lead after jumping a hedgerow, leaving master and horse behind to regain speed post hurdle jumping. By the time Pickering reached the lake, his dog lounged under the willows, greeting him with a wide yawn, as if to scold him for taking too long.

Dismounting, he foraged in the saddle bag. If he were the only aristocrat of his acquaintance to equip his horse with saddle bags for a leisure ride, then so be it. Utility surpassed fashion.

"Now, where did I put your breakfast?" He teased his companion.

Tail wagging and nose snuffling, Gunner bounded to the horse.

Out of the bag, Pickering pulled a rabbit, prepared in advance by Cook. Allowing Gunner a quick sniff, he tossed fluffy at an arc. The Lurcher leapt to catch the meat then dragged it beneath a solitary tree to devour. Reaching into the opposite bag, Pickering pulled out a handful of oats for his horse before encouraging the beast to graze in the surrounding pasture.

Having the moment to himself at last, he stretched his legs—quads, hams, and calves taut after the vigorous ride. Although a morning chill hung in the air, he was sweaty from the exertion of the ride. Layers of clothes, including boots and stockings were peeled off and tossed to the ground. Leaving only his breeches, he set off at a run towards the lake. Without hesitation, he dove into the still water.

Only after touching the lakebed did he propel upward, breaking the surface with a splash and shake of his head. Running a hand over his face to dispel excess droplets, he kicked off for the far end, swimming with smooth, even strokes. The far end was weedy but still deep. After diving down to touch bottom once more, he resurfaced to spy Gunner at the opposite shore, prancing to and fro. Pickering waved him to join, then treaded water until his companion had covered the length of the lake. Together, they made several laps, swimming alongside each other. The Lurcher paddled, his own body slicing through the water, each moving with silent grace, Gunner only breaking the rhythm in the shallows to bounce and frolic.

Half an hour later, Pickering lay lakeside, drying his breeches. Part of him enjoyed the idle lounging, while the other part fretted about wasted time. Slades-bridge Court's oversized pond could not rival the ten-acre lake at Tidwell Hall, where both Pickering and Gunner had learned to swim, but it served its purpose, greeting them each day for their morning constitutional. 'Twas not a waste of morning hours if spent strengthening the body, even if lounging was part of that ritual. Drying one's breeches was import-ant, after all, but there was more to it than that, for he did not hold to the fashion of depriving one's body of sunlight and favoring powdered skin, pale and sickly pallor the desired complexion. If the sun was good enough for the Navy, it was good enough for Pickering. His idle time was to be longer than usual today, however. He would typically have followed his swim with a bout of boxing, but his pugilist partner was on holiday, spending time with family.

It was just as well. Sparring took concentration, concentration he did not have this morning. He need only think of his wife to lose focus. As much as he had tried last night to think of their consummation as only a duty, he could not deny he had enjoyed bedding her.

Begetting an heir was of the utmost importance, for he was living proof of the difficulties incurred by heirs derelict in their duties. The line would not be broken by him, however weighty the responsibility given he was the last of the line. To his chagrin, that sense of responsibility had not been the reason he had counted down the hours between signing the wedding register and his eight o'clock appointment with Lady Pickering. The reason had been his desire for his bride. He did not fancy himself the only bride-groom to anticipate enjoyment in his wife's bed, but it surprised him, nevertheless. He had married only out of necessity. That there could be more from the marriage was bewildering.

How *she* had perceived their consummation, he could not say, but he hoped her docility was indicative of her attraction to him and anticipation of receiving pleasure rather than any duplicity of a bride trained for servility. Considering her background, he would wager there had not been any artifice to her meekness.

A wicked and heretofore unexplored desire had him wanting to keep the candle lit tonight when he went to her again at eight o'clock, to undress her fully this time, to—but no, he would not risk embarrassing or disrespecting her. He vowed to protect her, to honor her. Thus, he would show her respect during their joining. Somewhat distressing to him was his desire for her in the early hours, even after coupling. He had awoken in his own bedchamber wishing he had remained in hers. Never had he shared a bed before, nor could he imagine doing so, but from the moment he had slipped between his sheets, he had wished to return to her. A selfishness he was unaccustomed to experiencing. Then, he was unaccustomed to being a newlywed, and that alone ought to excuse him.

Did it excuse his lingering gaze at the dinner table, as well? The merest glimpse of her bare wrist had captivated him, so slender and delicate. In silence he had admired her. However subdued, she epitomized grace. She would think him a brute if she knew how difficult it had been for him to avert his eyes or press conversation when all he wished to do was regard her.

A brute indeed. His wife had entered this arrangement with the promise of a comfortable and content life, not a marriage of romantic demands with a needy husband who wanted her affection as well as her duty. The renovations to Sladesbridge should distract his focus. With dowry in hand, he could now repair the most immediate problems and prepare the march for self-sustainability. Yes, focusing on the estate was his best course of action.

All week, his mind had skirted the word *farming*. No longer could he procrastinate the inevitable, not if the estate were to thrive. The people of the march depended on him to rescue the estate from the depths of bankruptcy. The crux was that while he knew estate management given his experience as Lord Tidwell of Tidwell Hall, he had never dealt with agriculture. He needed a steward, but the interview process could take weeks, valuable time wasted. Until he could secure a steward with agricultural experience, he was on his own.

Bloody intimidating. He had devoted years to learning how to manage his barony, which earned its keep through tenantry. No tenant farmers or home farm, only homes to let. The march, however, would not survive on tenant rents alone. His knowledge base was useless. Fleetingly, he had thought of expanding the nearest village with terraced housing to attract new tenants, but the location was poorly situated for generating rental income. If he could turn it into a prosperous market town to draw new tenants and shopkeepers, he could make it thrive just as well as the Tidwell barony, but unlike Tidwell, it was not near enough to another town to make it convenient, nor was it on or near the mail route for stagecoaches.

Farming was the only way. The footprint of the march was that of farms, both in tenant farming and a home farm. Unfortunately, the fields had been left fallow for too long. With the sloping and rocky terrain, he could not fathom the conduciveness to any farming techniques he was aware of, however limited his knowledge. The estate had thrived on farming since the reign of Queen Elizabeth I, so someone had found a way, but his predecessor's disinterest and irresponsibility left the lands in too sorry of a state to hint at how it had been possible. The ninth marquess, devil take him, had devoted his time to being the quintessential gentleman: idle, wealthy, and of the opinion his pockets were bottomless. If Pickering could reach into the man's grave and choke him, he would. Not the most Christian thought, but he fancied it would do them both a world of good—what man did not need a good shake to set him right, even beyond the grave?

It was only August, he consoled himself. By that same token, it was mid-August, September two weeks away. Whatever farming plan he devised needed to be implemented post haste to sow before the winter months. His first goal was to clear the fields of the overgrowth. Sheep would be a perfect solution. He could move the sheep from the dale up to the slopes to graze. Quick and brilliant as far as solutions went.

Breeches dried, he dressed, whistled for his horse and dog, and prepared to return to the house.

Chapter 6

Morning twilight shone through the window as Edith drew back the curtains and presented her mistress with a cup of chocolate. "Thank you, Edith," J'non said before sipping the holiest of beverages. However accustomed to this ritual, she would never take her morning hot chocolate for granted. "Since I'm expecting my first guests today, I'd like to break my fast with more than chocolate. How might I make that dream come true?"

Even after being lady of the manor for a full week, she cringed inwardly at having asked, no matter how simple the question. She had maintained as much invisibility as she could muster thus far, both from nerves and habit. Being an early riser, far earlier than any sensible person, she had never wanted to inconvenience the staff by requesting food, nor had she wanted to intrude in a house she could not yet accept as her own. Today, hunger won over guilt. She was more than a touch peckish; she was famished.

Edith took the empty cup, helped her mistress out of the nightgown, and wet a cloth in the basin. "We will prepare a plate of anything you like, my lady.

Should I bring the tray, or do you wish to eat in the morning room?"

"Oh! There's a morning room?" J'non flushed, embarrassed by her ignorance.

The maid helped her mistress into a morning dress. J'non loved each new dress. Her husband had promised to hire a modiste, but to bide time, he ordered a modest wardrobe of store-purchased, albeit altered for her figure, dresses. Pre-made and restitched though they may be, they hid her plainness, as if by magic. When wearing one of the new dresses, she felt like Lady Pickering rather than ugly J'non.

Oh, there was no denying her ugliness. Her aunt had oft reminded her of her too short stature, her boyish figure, her longish face, her unbecomingly straight brows, and her lifeless hair that could not hold a curl beyond a half hour. The marquess did not need to extinguish the candle each night to show he recognized these traits, for she already knew herself to be ugly. The dresses, however, changed everything. The bodices framed her insignificant bosom, boosted by stays. The slight flair at the hips emphasized the slimness of her waist, giving her a woman's figure. The embroidery at the hem created the illusion of height. Despite the reality of her plainness, she felt almost pretty in her new dresses.

Today, J'non added *confident* to her *almost pretty* descriptor. Hosting friends—for what more could she ask?

J'non trembled with anticipation. *Friends* would call on her today.

With little to do, given she only saw Lord Pickering during supper and his evening visitation, she had spent a good deal of time in the village making the acquaintance of Mrs. Gwen Harvey, the vicar's wife. Mrs. Harvey had been one of the witnesses at the perfunctory wedding ceremony and had taken it upon her shoulders to introduce J'non to the parishioners whom she felt a newcomer and wife of the marquess ought to know. The two women, after taking tea together nearly every day since the wedding, decided to establish a sewing group.

J'non was not to join as a member rather to serve as hostess. *She*! A *hostess*! Not in her wildest dreams could she have conjured such a delightful role. Since her formative years, she had shadowed the corners of drawing rooms, ignored, invisible. *Friends at last.*

With her hair trussed in a bandeau, and blue muslin hugging her frame, she made for the morning room on the directions from Edith and the additional guidance of a helpful footman.

Not far from her mind, paramount to the day's promises, was the curiosity of Lord Pickering's morning habits. She suspected he slept late and ate in his chamber. After a week, he remained a mystery. From the little she had gathered from the staff, he spent most of his time in his study or on estate grounds. The only tasks of his day she knew well were his five o'clock supper and his eight o'clock conjugal visits, the former never lasting beyond an hour, and the latter rarely lasting longer than a quarter of an hour.

However irrational, she counted down from supper until eight o'clock, wishing each day he would come earlier or stay later. Despite feeling bereft when he left for the lord's chamber, she longed for the intimacy, clinging each evening to the lingering scent of his cologne. He was a stranger, and yet...

She nearly tripped over her feet as she entered the morning room. Lord Pickering sat at the table, dipping toast into his egg.

He stood so abruptly, his chair tipped backwards, caught by the butler's swift reflexes.

"Pardon me, my lord." J'non's cheeks burned. "I didn't mean to disturb you." She turned to leave.

"Stay," he barked. "Join me."

Hesitant, she took a step into the room. A genuine invitation or one of polite obligation?

One more step, then another. She approached the table.

Buckskins, boots, utilitarian coat and waistcoat. He was dressed for riding. Was it the train of her thoughts, or was his appeal enhanced by the smooth cheeks of a fresh shave? Before he caught her staring at his bare throat, left naked by the missing neckerchief, she turned to the butler, requesting the same meal as Lord Pickering.

No sooner had she said the request then she chided herself. She hated coffee and did not care for boiled eggs, but when confounded by his presence, she could not think rationally. Before supper, she always steeled herself for his granite expressions, gruff interruptions, and even his appeal. There had been no opportunity to steel herself before this encounter. The only positive of this moment was his presence assuaged her guilt of requesting food and service from the staff at so early an hour.

Lord Pickering stared at her, still holding a forgotten piece of toast.

Were other women as awed by him as she? He did not seem Miss Whittington's type nor her cousins' type. With his height, hooked nose, and furrowed brows, he was more forbidding than handsome. No, she wagered that other women were not as awed as she. But then, she was not other women, and she found him exceedingly attractive, unquestionably more attractive than—no, she had promised not to think of the past.

Before either of them could stare overlong, her plate and coffee arrived. Relieved, she took her seat, Lord Pickering following suit.

He broke the silence first. "Is anything wrong? Why did you rise this early?"

"I always wake before dawn." She gulped the bitter tar in her cup.

His eyebrows rose. "But women don't rise early."

J'non pursed her lips. "I do."

He harrumphed, then recalled the toast in his hand. A dip into the egg. A bite. A sip of his coffee. "An impertinent assumption. My apologies," he said, coffee cup still in hand. "I ask because I'm surprised. I rise at five every morning, yet I've never met a woman who wakes before ten."

"Cook wakes earlier than five to prepare your breakfast. My maid wakes earlier than five to prepare my chocolate and choose my morning dress. I'm certain if you questioned the staff, you would find all the women in this household rise before ten," she braved, feeling a surge of courage—perhaps because of the coffee, although it could be the missing cravat.

Knowing what he meant, especially given neither her aunt and cousins nor Miss Whittington ever woke before ten, and wanting to antagonize him were separate facts. Yes, it must be the coffee. She took another sip.

"That's not what I meant," he said. "Servants aren't —" His words suspended.

Was he about to say servants were not women, as in thinking, feeling, rational women who knew their own mind? He had not the slightest he was talking *to* a servant, not the slightest he shared a bed with a servant for a quarter of an hour every night, not the slightest a servant wore his wedding band. She stared into her cup but did not drink.

"Servants aren't," he continued, "at leisure to sleep late. They rise early because their job requires it. Women of my acquaintance, ladies that is, are at leisure to sleep late, wasting the better part of the day in idleness. Pardon my bluntness, but I do not find that an admirable quality." His gaze locked with hers. "I do, however, admire your resolve to rise early."

Oh.

Oh!

A compliment. Not a veiled insult? No, indubitably a compliment.

When she did not reply, he divulged, "I've risen early for as long as I can remember. I ensure every day begins with corporal exercise. My father instilled in me the teachings of George Turnbull and John Locke, both believers in exercise's ability to invigorate the body and the soul."

Well, that explained his solidness, she thought, stealing a glance at his person, his coat fitting like a second skin with no need for padding. Lean and lithe indeed.

For a week, she had hoped for a glimpse into the private life of her husband, some opportunity to know him, yet she had never been invited to do so. She had thought it because he did not want her to be part of his life—either because of the nature of the marriage or because of his displeasure with the bride—but could it be he had thought the reverse, that she did not wish to be part of his life?

She could not turn timidity into temerity in a single meal, but with time, she could turn shy J'non into assertive Lady Pickering. Life had required she change roles twice before. At this stage, it was difficult to recall who she had once been. With certainty, she could say she had not always been a submissive mouse, but had she been destined for the role of Lady Pickering? Had circumstances not changed, that was.

She ventured, "I take it you enjoy a morning ride to remain… vigorous."

He drained his cup, then leaned back in his chair, studying her. "I do. I follow with a swim. Do you ride, Lady Pickering, or swim?"

"Neither," she confessed.

"By choice?"

"I've not had the opportunity to develop a taste for either." Averting her eyes, she added, "being a—a merchant's daughter."

"We must remedy that." He crossed his legs and folded his hands over one knee. "Both riding and swimming are too important for me not to wish my wife to enjoy them, as well. We will schedule time in the coming weeks to ride and swim. Together. My morning regimen is an important part of my day, albeit too rigorous for a lady. A brisk ride, followed by an enduring swim, and then a competitive bout of boxing. My father was a military man, you see, and trained me in preparation for war with warlike discipline."

Over a simple meal, he was becoming less of a stranger. Curious they had never spoken this candidly over supper. She fought the urge to smile and reveal her fascination. "Did he expect you to purchase a commission?"

Lord Pickering's expression hardened before he said, "My father anticipated his sons would follow in his footsteps by joining the Royal Navy. As it happens, I am an only child. You see the conflict."

She did not immediately follow. Her blank stare must have given her away.

Clearing his throat, he clarified, "When it became clear he would only have one son with no hope of future sons, he could not risk his heir dying in battle. He preserved me to continue the line, you see."

"Yes, I understand, but he must have been proud to have you as his heir."

"Quite the contrary, my lady. I believe I was his greatest disappointment."

J'non studied her husband's marble expression. He spoke in much the same way as he might have announced the splendid weather forecasted for the day. For an unjustified and heartless moment, she thought he might be right, for any father who could see the state of the house and lands would be ashamed of his heir.

"My father's life was war," he continued. "You must understand this. He spent a lifetime making a career of war. Upon his promotion to Admiral, the

King granted him a barony. His life's work ended when his tendon was severed. He retired to the barony. His remaining years were spent wanting nothing more than to live vicariously through his sons. Plural. In the end, there was only me."

"It doesn't follow he would be disappointed with you," she argued.

"It does. He believed in *earning* honor. I have earned nothing. As the heir, I inherited, never proving myself on a battlefield or even an estate field. I firmly believe he would be ashamed to see me now."

"But he would be proud to see you restoring Sladesbridge, would he not?"

"My father was not a marquess, Lady Pickering. My father *earned* his invitation to the peerage through his service to the Crown. He was the youngest son of a younger son and so on for five generations. No, my dear wife, I inherited the Tidwell barony from my father and lived there quite happily until this summer when my life plans and my contentment were shattered. I am now responsible for this unexpected inheritance, but I have not earned it."

As she was about to reply, the clock chimed, echoing through the hallway beyond.

Lord Pickering pushed back his chair and stood. "My morning regimen awaits. Good day, my lady." He bowed, then pivoted and left the room.

After finishing what remained of her breakfast, J'non escaped her thoughts through the double doors into the garden. But then, that was the trouble with thoughts, was it not? One could not escape them.

Rows of parterres, overgrown with flowers, herbs, and weeds, formed what once must have been a majestic Elizabethan knot garden. Inhaling the country air, fresh and aromatized by the herbs, she ran a hand through one of the beds, her fingers combing the soft tips of rosemary.

The personal tone of breakfast surprised her. Lord Pickering was a stranger to her, yet in a single conversation, she gained more than a glimpse of the man. If she were to live here as his wife for the rest of her life, and especially given her attraction to him, she ought to know him as a person rather than a formidable noble who overshadowed her. She longed for genuine conversation void of haughty interruptions and polite topics. The circumstances of the marriage gave her pause. Would it not be safer if their marriage stayed as it was? There was safety in distance.

With anonymity, there was little risk of revealing her identity, little opportunity to suffer a slip of the tongue. This man was a means of security, nothing more, and that security was precarious even without her taking unnecessary risks. Instead of living as a wife, she needed to live for herself, doing what she enjoyed. After all, she did have ideas for improving the estate, including the land. It was best, then, she maintain distance. If she stayed busy on the areas of the estate that would bring her the most happiness, she could help restore the house and make herself a comfortable home without risking discovery.

There were many things she would like to do, starting with befriending more villagers to encourage their invested interest in the estate, and in doing so, have a hand in the restoration from dilapidation. The first renovations should be the gardens and drawing room since those were not only the two places in which she spent most of her time, but the two best places to entertain guests, including the hosting of the sewing circle.

At one time, her father had — oh! Yes! This could be the needed incentive.

She pressed her fist to her mouth with a squeak, then dashed back through the double doors into the morning room where the butler was overseeing the tidying of the table.

"Mr. Hawkins, would you be so good as to accompany me to the gardens?"

He bowed.

"Will you walk with me the length of the gardens, help me envision what each area would look like if manicured to original majesty?" She had a specific question to put to him, but first, she wanted his companionship, not only so he could see with her the expanse of the needs, but so she could assess the same, for she had yet to explore the walled gardens.

Hawkins followed her to the kitchen garden and walked with her along tall-grassed paths surrounded by beds of herbs, some now dried weeds and others growing unchecked. However brimming with excitement to share her idea, she remained calm and pointed out the plants she recognized, asking questions of him along the way. They moved then into the apple and pear orchards to the back of the house. Hawkins shared what little knowledge he had of the orchards, then they struggled past a rusted gate to enter the walled garden, now a desolate wasteland. Through yet another rusted gate beyond, this one detached from the wall and buried in overgrowth, they found what would have been a water garden. A pond that looked to be part of an old moat stretched the length of the house. Stately fountains with broken statues littered the landscape, along with an unkempt hedge labyrinth in the center that might have been a child's delight had it not been overgrown.

Looking up at the house, she realized they had walked around the corner to one of the wings she had not explored — the gentlemen's wing with billiard room, bachelor suites, and study. This would be Pickering's view from his study, then. Hawkins confirmed her suspicion. If this was what he looked onto every day, it was no wonder he saw circumstances as desperate. For all her ideas, after seeing the expanse of gardens and the amount of work needed, she felt overwhelmed and disheartened, as he must feel as well. There was too much to do. Having already gone through the trouble of leading the butler about the property when he undoubtedly had more important tasks of his own, she owed him her thoughts, but after seeing the situation, how was she to voice them without him thinking she was away with the fairies? The labor. The supplies. The time. The cost.

This is no way to think. You're the one they're supposed to trust. If you're motivated, they will be also. The exterior of the house was more important than the interior because it could give the impression of a prosperous march, and it would inspire the villagers to invest time and devotion in the estate. Prosperity, even in illusion, inspired confidence. *Do not be quelled, J'non. You've faced tougher beasts.*

Taking a moment to gather her optimism, she first inwardly railed at the previous marquess for being so reckless, so fueled by vanity to allow this disrepair to occur. Until breakfast, she had thought that man to be Lord Pickering, but he had been Baron Tidwell, living elsewhere until the inheritance, not in the least responsible for this mayhem. A relief, that, at least. She ought not think ill of the dead, she reminded herself. There were more important matters at hand than to be angry about the past, something she knew all too well already. There was only forward momentum.

There. With anger at the unjust entertained then tossed aside, she could push forward.

Shoulders back, head held high, she turned to her companion. "Do you know any local horticulturalists, Mr. Hawkins? Someone or a few someones who might be interested in breathing life into the gardens. A head gardener would be ideal, but anyone willing to get their hands dirty would do for a start."

"You might inquire for references from Lord and Lady —"

"No, no, no," she interrupted. "I want someone from the village. We need to work together. All of us. This is *our* march, and if we work together, we will *all* be invested in the land prospering. I have in mind to recruit the help not of contractors but of locals, you see, not for one-sided labor, either. Symbiosis. For instance, and tell me if I'm overthinking; what would you say to turning the kitchen garden into a community garden? Anyone from the village who wishes to take items for their own cooking may, but on the condition they help maintain the garden, offering whatever help they can."

The butler gaped. "I don't know, my lady. I suppose it could work."

"Too much too soon?" She implored him with her gaze, willing him to join forces in her radical idea. "Yes, well, let's begin with a village gardener."

He took a step back, looked around as if searching for answers, then said, "I might know a potential candidate for head gardener."

"Yes, Mr. Hawkins? Tell me."

"My cousin, an Army pensioner, fought in the insurrection, or what some call the American War of Independence." He hesitated before adding, "He returned in a sorry state, my lady. Did his duty for Crown and Country, but paid the price. I regret to say he has not had work since returning. Shame. A finer gardener you would not find, if I'm at liberty to say."

"He hasn't worked in all this time?" J'non pressed her hand to her bosom. The war had ended ages ago.

"He's not found work," was all the butler offered.

"Does he have family?" she pressed, unable to abstain. "How does he support himself—surely not only with the pension?" This was a situation she knew personally, even if the circumstances were different.

"Truth be told, I send him a portion of my pay. To help with the wee ones."

"Oh, Mr. Hawkins." She groaned for the kindness of the butler to share his salary and the shame his cousin must feel not to be able to support his own children. "Tell me. Be honest. Why can't he find employment?"

He grimaced. "My apologies, my lady, but it would be inappropriate to say."

But if she were to employ him, she needed to know the truth, the full truth. If he drank, she would be as hesitant as others to hire him, regardless of her good intentions. She shuddered at the memory of Mr. Whittington when he was in his cups. If not drink, could it be that he was not in his right mind?

"Please tell me. Consider me a friend rather than an employer."

He stared at one of the toppled statues. "The truth is, my lady, he is a hard worker, always has been. Only has the one arm now. And there's the scarring. Scars don't affect the work, but when one's not fit to be seen by employer or guest… You'll understand why no one will employ him."

She could not have cared less about scarring, but could a man with only one arm garden?

Hoping she was making the right decision, she said, "The way I see it, Mr. Hawkins, is that *you* must have faith he can do the work, or you would not have recommended him."

"He is as hard a worker as ever you'll see, my lady. With a few lads from the village, apprenticing, like, he could make the gardens fit for the Queen."

"Would he want to be a gardener, though, or does he aspire to another calling?" J'non crossed her fingers.

"He has a love for the land, my lady. Always has. Tends to his home garden with some enthusiasm. Never liked farming but has a way with flowers and herbs. He used to work here, by gum, as a gardener, until the war."

"Let us extend a formal invitation for an interview. Have him bring a few of those lads you think, or should I say that he thinks, would be willing to help."

Hawkins nodded. "Yes, my lady."

With new purpose and an ungenteel skip in her step, she returned to the house to inspect the drawing room where the sewing group would meet in a few hours.

Chapter 7

The ladies group proved so successful that when she hosted the second sewing circle a few days later, five new members joined. No fewer than ten women were in attendance.

J'non looked about the drawing room with a swelling heart. She was surrounded by *friends*. The women ranged in age and gentility, but they were all goodhearted souls who reminded her of home and happiness, life before smallpox, before her aunt, and before the scandal.

The blacksmith's wife, plump with a mob cap covering frizzy red curls, announced with a broad Yorkshire accent, "I hope I speak for everyone when I thank her ladyship for inviting us. This is a reet grand do. I were expecting her to invite gentlefolk, but here we are, sharing a brew with her ladyship. Eee, tha's a reet gradly brew tha'. A treat, innit?"

Nods accompanied a chorus of agreement. J'non smiled sheepishly.

Not that she had met the local gentry, but she imagined taking tea with that sort would involve talking of the weather and looking down long noses. Lord Pickering had made mention during supper of their need to call on the neighbors. She dreaded it. While he had not seen through her charade, heaven knew how, she feared others would and point an accusing finger. *Imposter!* that finger would exclaim. Although she knew how to behave as a gentlewoman just as well as a maid, it had been a long time since she played that role, not to mention neither role, gentlewoman nor maid, fit the supposed merchant background of Lord Pickering's wife. But then, what did she expect them to see? If she were sensible, she would ask herself how many locals would know enough about a London merchant to judge her behavior. By her reckoning, none.

The draper's wife, a mere slip of a woman, interrupted J'non's thoughts by saying, "We're that glad of Willie as head gardener, my lady."

Another chorus of assent.

Setting her embroidery in her lap, J'non said, "I know he will breathe life into these old gardens." Absently, she added, "If only I could find someone as trustworthy and skilled as him to help with the roof." With a knowing look to each in the circle, she quipped, "It leaks like a church roof, if you must know."

Her guests laughed, the draper's wife snorting.

It might not be impolite to ask her guests if they knew of friends or family who could assist in the rebuild, but she did not want them to feel obligated or as though she had tricked them to the estate to beg for laborers. Instead, she hoped to earn their trust and provide opportunities for them to become involved in the rebuild as a community, an investment of wills, with everyone working together for a shared cause, all seeing to the needs of the village, estate, and environs. Her vision was to build a family amongst those in the march, a place where she could thrive as she had done long ago, and where they would know the local aristocracy looked after their needs, no one left to live under leaky roofs or otherwise.

"I daren't be presumptuous," Mrs. Gwen Harvey, the vicar's wife, said, "but Galfrid Thompson is a fine carpenter, best you'll find. Course you'll be wanting someone with characters, my lady, and Galfrid has none."

"Your word is good enough a reference for me, Gwen, and it would make me so much happier to have a *friend* help instead of a stranger who wouldn't care a snap about our march. You think Mr. Thompson would be interested in lending a hand?"

"He'd be honored." Gwen eyed one of their youngest members, a girl not yet twenty. "How did Gerard's interview go with the Welfords?"

Without looking up, the girl said, "They sent him home since he'd never been a footman before."

"Oh, that's too bad." Gwen winked at J'non. "Gerard will find a position, I'm sure. Keep your chin up. With the nipper on the way, he won't be disheartened."

J'non returned the wink with a conspiratorial smile. "I'm delighted you've mentioned footmen, Gwen, because Mr. Hawkins is looking for new staff. Do you think Mr. Gerard Sullivan would consider interviewing for a position here?"

The girl, Mrs. Sullivan that was, dropped her threaded needle, wide eyes fixed on J'non. "Would you give him a chance? Truly, milady?"

For the next half hour, the group shared thoughts, whinged, and sewed, only J'non embroidering while the others darned various items of clothing. She would have felt more comfortable mending, but that was now Edith's task, and it would be more expected for a marchioness to embroider. Keeping up pretenses on the outside, J'non simmered with delight inside that her communal restoration plan was underway.

Any other marchioness would have paid dearly to have the highest recommended architects, interior decorators, carpenters, landscapers, and so forth revive the estate, accepting only those with the most impressive references, but to what end? The estate would be repaired at considerable cost and without any personal investment, widening the gap between the villagers and their overlords, leaving the village and farms in disrepair. Enough money had been sunk into the estate without forethought, care, or budgeting. Her plan would work. It must work. The villagers and she must work together to restore the entire march, from estate to village and beyond, taking pride and ownership in their work.

Sooner than J'non expected, their time together drew to a close. At least they would meet once a week. Something to look forward to.

As the women packed up their sewing, the drawing room door opened. Lord Pickering stepped in and bowed. In return, they scrambled to their feet to curtsy.

"Are gentlemen permitted?" he asked, surveying the guests with a sweep of his gaze.

J'non waved a hand to an empty chair. "We would not be so coarse as to deny the lord of the manor. Join us."

No one mentioned they were readying to leave. Attention riveted on him, the women sat, wide-eyed and silent.

Did he not realize the guests were villagers, wives of tradesmen, farmers, laborers? Surely a man as high in the instep as Lord Pickering would recoil at this scene and follow with a reprimand about fraternizing with villagers in the drawing room. It was one thing to visit them in their own homes or invite them through the servant's entrance into the kitchen, but quite another to entertain them as guests, complete with a spread of sweets, savories, and tea. Her aunt would have suffered apoplexy.

Without a fraction of a smile, Lord Pickering looked at J'non with raised eyebrows to mirror her own. He then leveled his gaze at the women, turning from one to the next.

"Should I have brought something to sew?" he asked.

The women giggled.

"How do, m'lord?" inquired the innkeeper's wife, a woman with a freckled face and a wide smile.

"All the better for being invited into a room of sirens." Pickering's serious expression contrasted the flirtation. "How fairs Mr. Kingsley's knee?"

J'non observed, speechless, as the two carried on a conversation about the innkeeper's health and the prospects of Mrs. Kingsley's daughter who had, it would seem, recently been courted by three different lads. While the conversation itself was unremarkable, that it should happen between the innkeeper's wife and Lord Pickering astonished her.

Despite his stony stare, his replies showed rapt attention, and his knowledge of the local inhabitants displayed a compassion she would not have expected, not when she had yet to receive half this attention during their five and eight o'clock appointments. Not that she was jealous, mind, simply surprised to see a side of him she did not know existed.

"We're that glad you're here, m'lord," admitted Mrs. Robinson, one of the five newest members of the sewing circle. "With so many parishioners moved away after his late lordship left for the City, we were in some trouble."

Pickering inclined his head. "Instinctively, I knew a sewing group awaited my company if only I could move to Sladesbridge Court with haste and take up the mantle as marquess."

J'non stifled a laugh.

"Are the rumors true?" Mrs. Sullivan asked, then darted a glance about her and whispered, "About how he died?"

"My lips are sealed on the subject of the ninth marquess' demise. Rumors of *that* nature are not for the delicate ears of ladies." Pickering raised a haughty eyebrow and crossed one leg over the other.

J'non could not discern if his answer was a tease. Judging by the titters of the company, she thought he teased, but how could they tell?

"We all heard the rumors," said the haberdasher. "That rogue left us without a by-your-leave for his gambling and whoring."

Pickering tutted. "Now, now, Mrs. Robinson, I'll not abide by foul words in the presence of tender sensibilities."

"By gum, you know we're not ladies as like to swoon," one woman said with a laugh. "Go on. Tell us how he died."

Pickering leaned forward. *Sotto voce*, he said, "He met his end at the tip of a blade."

A collective gasp.

"Now," he continued, "don't play coy in pretending you aren't all perfectly aware his death represents the pinnacle of a gentleman's life. Nothing is more honorable than dying in a duel. We must assume he died a proud man for his achievement." His words were met with mixed laughs and tuts.

The meeting soon ended, as the women needed to return to their shops, their husbands, or their households. Lord Pickering escorted everyone to the door before bowing to J'non and excusing himself.

Was she disappointed or relieved he made no attempt at a personal exchange? Both, she supposed. She was not certain what she had witnessed. The nobleman she married spoke with ease and deference to the village women, egalitarian behavior she would not have associated with an aristocrat, much less Lord Pickering.

She wondered if he ever smiled.

Chapter 8

The breeze cooled his neck in the absence of his starched shirt points and linen neckerchief. Lord Pickering pulled back his arm and flung the stick with a *swoosh*. Gunner lurched into action, chasing the wood.

Despite September being three days away, the sun continued to scorch the land, unrelenting, the only saving grace a blustering wind. At Tidwell Hall, he could set the time by the afternoon rain. Here at Sladesbridge Court? It had yet to rain. His move-in date had been late July. He could not recall when, if ever, Tidwell had experienced a drought. How different everything was, even the land, especially the land. The land stretched as far as he could see, sloping down steep banks, nestling in house-bedecked vales, and rising again, undulating towards the horizon, in contrast to Tidwell with its marshy fens, flat lowlands, and pastoral farms.

Gunner lumbered to him, stick in mouth, tongue lolling. Pickering retrieved the drool coated branch and sent it flying again.

Checking the sheep's progress on the western slope had become an obsession, as though he expected to notice a difference from one day to the next in their eating and stamping of the noisome brush. Ever since having them moved uphill, he had grown anxious to see the fields cleared and ready for sowing. Poor Richard was onto something when he observed that a watched pot never boiled.

Today, though, it was not the sheep that caught his attention. It was his wife.

Lady Pickering perched on a flat stone, hugging her knees to her chest. Caught unawares, she made a stunning image. Wisps of her hair teased from under a bonnet. Her face, upturned to the sun, wore the brightness of the day, as if nature's bounty shone from inside her rather than onto her. He only ever saw her inside the house where she too easily disappeared into shadows, the quiet mouse with lowered eyes. Why did she suppress this beauty? At least there were no shadows here to hide her.

For the briefest of moments, he observed her unseen. For the briefest of moments, he considered turning and leaving before she sensed his presence. He hesitated too long. Gunner bounded to Lady Pickering, tail wagging, stick in mouth. She turned and laughed when she spotted the Lurcher.

By heavens, she could charm the very birds from the trees with that laugh. Astonished, he realized he had never heard her laugh. An embarrassed titter, yes, but never a genuine laugh.

Gunner promptly dropped his stick and held out a paw to shake.

She stood in greeting. Even her figure showed to advantage in the sunlight. Against the backdrop of gorse and heather, her slender frame was less coltish and more fae-like, a fairy queen in muslin.

"Good morning, my lady," he called out to her, advancing.

"Good morning," she replied with a curtsy.

"As the villagers oft say, how do?" He stopped a few feet away.

Before she could reply, Gunner circled her, tangling himself and his long tail with her legs and nuzzling her until she struggled for balance. She laughed again, her face pink from sun and happiness, and focused her attention on the dog. The pair danced a lighthearted game of chase. This was not at all how he expected to find his wife. He delighted in seeing her thusly. Who was this enchanting nymph? Why did she not act this carefree with him? How different life would be if their daily interactions were this uninhibited.

But then, he would not know how to behave in response. Had it not been her timidity during their first meeting that reassured him of the match's potential success? He did not want a boisterous wife. His life had always been regulated with precision, every decision calibrated and deliberate, every moment scheduled, every hour gauged against duty.

Unsure what to do, he stood, awkward, mulling over if he should break the magic by clearing his throat or romp in gaiety with the two of them. His head wanted the former, his heart the latter.

She looked at him and tilted her head, her smile waning. "Do you ever smile?"

His frown deepened. What an obtuse question. "I beg your pardon," he barked.

"It's only, I've never seen you smile. It's a beautiful day, and you're playing a game of fetch, yet no smile. Are you unhappy?" She petted Gunner, then walked towards Pickering, wrapping her arms about herself as though chilled.

What the devil was this woman's intention asking impertinent questions? Of course he was not unhappy. Of course he smiled.

"I'm perfectly content, Lady Pickering. There is not much in life to induce the outpouring of emotion, but yes, I smile, and no, I'm not unhappy."

He strode to the stone overlooking the western slope. What a tedious conversation. He came to check the sheep not to talk about happiness and smiles with an enigmatic woman. With a grunt, he motioned for her to resume her seat. Once she returned to the stone, fanning the hem of her dress around her half-boots, he settled next to her, propping a hand behind him and resting a forearm on his knee.

Gunner nudged his head between them.

"You told me about your father at breakfast the other day," she said, scratching behind Gunner's ears. "Was your childhood unhappy? Was he domineering?"

Did a man need to wear a smile when assessing sheep? Did he need to maintain affability to be labeled *happy*?

"My father was not domineering," he defended. "I apologize if I gave that impression. My father was the most honorable man I have had the pleasure of knowing."

"But you said he would be disappointed in you. You made it sound as though—"

He held up a hand. "As he should be, for I have done nothing to prove my worth. My father had expectations for both his life and mine that were not met, and that brought him unhappiness. That does not mean he was domineering. On the contrary, he encouraged me just as he did those under his command. I was rewarded when I did well. I was taught the cost of my mistake and how to rectify it when I did wrong. I wasn't raised with hugs and sweets, if that's your definition of a happy childhood, but I was raised with the affection an admiral shows the heir of his barony. I cared deeply for my father. He..."

Unsure how to explain his father or if he should, he stopped. This was not the conversation he wanted to have with his bride. Leaving the topic unfinished, he hoped she would not press the issue.

They shared silence, the bleating of sheep filling the air.

Lady Pickering spoke first. "If your father wasn't the ninth marquess, may I ask how you inherited? You spoke so comfortably with the village women, I would have thought you had lived here for years."

Ah, yes, the sewing group. He had not known she hosted a committee, not that her daily life was his concern. Had he known, he may not have intruded in the drawing room. Or maybe he would have. It chafed him not knowing her activities and interests, not knowing her. Yet again his head warred with his heart. His head said as long as she was a dutiful wife, their lives need not intertwine, but his heart wanted to know her. Just now, he had spoken about his father; what of her childhood? Best not to inquire. To what end would their acquaintance lead? He did not need her as his friend nor as his lover or mistress. She was his wife, nothing more. She would one day bear his heir. She would fulfill her duty as he fulfilled his, and neither friendship nor romance need enter the equation.

The problem was he could not convince himself he was not lonely or that he was not attracted to her. Would establishing a friendship not violate the peace of a convenient marriage? Yes. He could become too attached and end up like his father, dead from heartbreak and a bottle of laudanum.

Shaking off the melancholy, he explained in answer to her question, "This summer, I was informed that I am the only remaining male in the Gaines line. When the ninth marquess passed without an heir, they had to trace back several generations to find another son in the line. All the way to my great-great grandfather who was the youngest son of the fifth marquess."

With a tut, he added, "It would seem the eldest sons in the Gaines line are prone to producing girls, heaven sent given their heirs have turned out, one after the other, to be wastrels who flitter away money. Is it not ironic that a youngest son's progeny has turned out to be the one who upheld the male line? I can't say what that means for our future children. One boy, an only child? Or all girls, do you suppose?"

She looked up at him, a shy smile teasing her lips. Although she suppressed the hidden nymph he had witnessed, her eyes still twinkled. Then, her eyes had captivated him from the first day. Disarming eyes, he recalled thinking. It was their depth and wisdom he had revered, now their joy, bright from simple pleasures.

He studied her, admiring her flushed cheeks, her flawless complexion, a chin that narrowed almost to a point, and kissable lips he had yet to taste despite visiting her bedchamber every evening since the wedding — a task of duty, nothing more. She smelled of violets, a scent that seduced his nostrils. Driven by impulse, he reached over and tucked a finger under her chin, desperate to caress her lips. Would she be embarrassed if he kissed her? Would intimacy be unwanted?

Good heavens! The heat of the never-ending summer was melting his sanity. He dropped his hand and stroked his dog's head instead, as nonchalant as he could be.

"Not until I spoke with the trustees," he continued as though nothing happened, "did I learn the ninth marquess had spent the family fortune on first extravagant renovations to Sladesbridge and second a lavish lifestyle, and by spent, I mean he bankrupted the estate, plunging the whole of the march deep in debt and leaving nothing to see to the march's needs or to support the estate."

"Oh," she mouthed.

He did not see the benefit of reminding her the purpose of her dowry.

"I'm not resentful, my lady. Sladesbridge is etching a place in my heart even while being a thorn in my side. Once I make it mine, once I make my mark, it will feel like home. With this estate, I will be able to prove my worth. You've wasted no time in making *your* mark," he teased. "Don't think I haven't noticed the changes to the house."

The bustle around the court had taken him by surprise, young lads polishing and resetting the courtyard stones, the smell of turpentine in the vestibule replacing that of mold and decay. The drawing room, even as they spoke, was receiving new plaster where one of the myriad roof leaks had damaged the ceiling. A steady increase in staff over the past week was not beyond his notice, either. Only two weeks since the wedding, and she had already rallied the local parishioners to turn the rebuild into a communal effort, with villagers and their relations vying for employment or, in some cases, volunteering their time, all spreading word that this march would soon prosper. Quiet though she may appear, he suspected she was as capable of serving as an admiral as his father. Who was this woman?

Ah, yes, she was the daughter of a businessman. Was this the difference between marrying a woman of industry instead of a gentlewoman?

He had no time or patience for insipid women who knew nothing aside from playing a pianoforte, painting watercolor, sleeping all hours of the day, and gossiping during what hours they did not sleep. His wife was proving not to be this type of woman. Without trying, Lady Pickering was earning his respect.

Nudging Gunner, Pickering closed the gap between him and his wife and wrapped an arm around her shoulders. His movements were not abrupt or lascivious, but her squeak made him worry he had overstepped his bounds.

She tensed against his side and said in a higher pitch, "The villagers are the ones who deserve the accolades. They do all this for you to show how glad they are to have you in residence."

Gunner, dejected, hopped onto the stone at Pickering's other side and rested his head on his paws.

"They depend on me," he said. "Not only the local parishioners but all the residents of the march, including those in villages you've not yet seen. They depend on the estate's prosperity to employ them, maintain the upkeep of their homes, attract visitors to buy their wares and support their trade, and so forth. The estate, in turn, depends on tenants and tenant farmers, the agriculture produced, the newcomers who wish to let property, and so on. It's a symbiotic relationship that must be maintained. These people are my responsibility now, and I take that task seriously."

"I can see you take it to heart. Is that how you devote your time each day, tending to your responsibilities?"

"If you've read the motto on the stained glass of the great hall, you'll understand. *Ex pietas honore.* Out of duty, honor. Only by fulfilling my obligations am I honorable. I have duties to all my holdings, to the House of Lords, to this title and the continuation of the lineage, to my wife, and to the people dependent on me. Yes, I take my responsibilities to heart, especially the people. My father served alongside farmers and tradesmen and knew better than most that we must work together to survive. I will not abandon these people as my predecessor did."

She nodded, saying nothing. His arm, still draped over her shoulder, hugged her against his side. Was it his imagination or did she stiffen with his every movement? A reminder of how little he knew about her.

They sat in rigid silence, listening to the sounds of nature and the disgruntled huffs of Gunner. She clenched her hands in her lap. Pickering had felt a sentimental urge to display affection, a desire to be close to her and in some way signal his respect and appreciation for her work, and perhaps in a small way his attraction to her beyond duty, but her behavior made him realize the error of his decision.

How dashed humiliating. He shrugged his arm from her shoulders and rose to his feet, motioning to Gunner to stay.

"Walk with me?" he asked, holding out a hand to help her stand.

Tentatively, she placed her hand in his, her eyes wary, her expression unreadable.

"Come," he said, setting off along the ridge and cursing himself for causing her discomfort by pressing his unwelcome attention. "I want to show you my plan for the fields." He swept a hand before him as they walked. "What do you make of the sheep?"

"They look healthy, I suppose. I'm not too familiar with livestock," she said, quickening her steps to keep up with his long strides.

"Ah, it was a thoughtless question. This is, after all, my domain, while the house is yours."

He slowed his pace as they reached a path meandering down the slope. Offering his arm to help her balance, he escorted her into the midst of the sheep.

"I have a scheme, you see. At one time, this march was profitable from agriculture alone. I intend to make it that way again. This is only one of the many fields that needs to be prepared for sowing, but that can't be done with overgrown brush in the way. My plan is for the sheep to eat and hoof the brush until the field is clear. And then, I'll order the farm laborers to plough and sow, although I'm unsure how easy that will be given this drought. I remain optimistic. Do you wager I've had a stroke of genius to use the sheep?"

Looking about her, she shook her head with vigor. "No, you must remove the sheep before they damage the field. Your plan will never work."

Damage the field? He scoffed. She was a woman. What would a woman know of livestock and farming, least of all a woman from London? Aggravated, he crossed his arms over his chest and waited for her to explain herself.

When she did not continue, he commanded, "Speak. I'll not be contradicted without an explanation. Why will my plan not work?"

She dropped her gaze and worried her lips.

"Yes?" he prompted.

"It's too soon for grazing. They'll eat the brush but then have nothing to eat over winter, leaving the fields barren for the frost. Without a cover crop, the frost will damage the soil. Don't you see? This means starved sheep and infertile soil before the spring. No, you must remove the sheep back to the dale or you'll set back the farming by another year."

What the devil?

He gaped.

Who had he married?

This was not the knowledge of a merchant's daughter. This was not the knowledge of a woman from London.

"Who the devil *are* you?" he demanded to know.

J'non covered her mouth with a hand. How could she have been so careless? A merchant's daughter would not know about farming. After all, the idea of Miss

Whittington knowing owt about farming was laughable. But what was J'non to do? Allow a mistake to ruin the fields? Stay silent while the estate fell further into debt? The dowry was substantial, but not enough to support an entire march for a year, only enough, perhaps, to keep debt collectors at bay, purchase supplies for necessary renovations, and purchase equipment for the fields. The estate had to support itself or perish. This was now her home, and she would protect it as best she could, or rather it *could* be her home if she remained careful, if he never discovered the truth. Harrowed by the conflict, tears wet her cheeks and salted her lips. Protect the home farm by revealing too much or remain silent and risk the home farm.

He awaited her answer. She had already said too much. Careless, careless, careless.

Lord Pickering stepped forward, his face marble, his eyes penetrating. "Come here," he commanded.

So afraid this was the end, she closed the distance between them, wrapping her arms around his waist and clinging to him as a lifeline. To her shock, he enfolded her in a protective embrace, his mouth against her forehead, her bonnet pushed askew. Embarrassed by her behavior, she buried her face against his waistcoat, breathing in the scent of him, sweaty and masculine, the smell of security.

"I've upset you," he murmured into her hairline. "I should not have used vulgar language. I apologize."

The ribbons tugged at her neck as the bonnet slipped down her back. The tears of fear and shame dried, leaving her self-conscious.

His voice soothing, he said, "I had assumed you lived in London with your father, but I realize now that can't be true. I'm ashamed of my own ignorance. I meant no insult, my lady."

Releasing her hold on him, she stepped back far enough to tuck stray strands of her hair behind her ears. In response, he loosened his embrace to cup her elbows.

With trembling fingers, she reached up, hesitated, then touched one of his waistcoat buttons. He did not move, his hands steady on her arms. Emboldened, or perhaps merely biding time, she stroked the embroidery. One button after the other, she felt the soft ridges of the thread under her thumb and forefinger, in no hurry to speak. When she ran out of buttons, she fanned her fingers across his chest and staid her hand, gaze fixed on her wedding ring.

"I only lived with Mr. Whittington for one month," she confessed.

"Before that, you lived in Surrey," he said.

She tensed. "How did you know?"

"Your accent. It gives you away, I'm afraid." His fingers tightened around her elbows. "I should have suspected the truth sooner. I've seen enough signs, enough idiosyncrasies in your behavior, but I had not realized fully until now."

Ah. So, he knew.

She felt curiously more resigned than panicked.

They had been married for a little over two weeks, long enough for him to pen a letter to Mr. Whittington and receive a reply, long enough for his solicitor to investigate why the rumored-to-be-beautiful Phoebe Whittington looked disappointingly like a maid. Why had he not yet dismissed her from the house, instructed footmen to escort her from the property, petitioned for an annulment on the grounds of fraud? Instead of feeling the gripping fear she had expected, she felt only the chill of resolve. Now that he had pieced together the clues, she would be out of the house before sunset, if not sooner.

She shivered.

Rubbing warmth into her gooseflesh covered arms, he continued, "Naturally, Mr. Whittington would be so bent on making his fortune and building his reputation he would not want his daughter around to muck it up, not until he could use that daughter to his advantage to advance his social prospects. Forgive me, my lady, when I say your father is reprehensible. I implore you to trust me, to have faith in me when I promise you're safe now. No one will use or abuse you for their own gain again. You are no longer under his protection. You are now the wife of a nobleman. I will safeguard you in all ways."

J'non's vision blurred.

He tucked a finger under her chin and raised her face to look up into his. "Please know, I'm not angry you spoke your mind. You've already earned my respect in the handling of the renovations and the parishioners. What I wish is for you to tell me more. I want to know *you*. I want to know who you are."

Swallowing, she looked into his eyes, feeling no bigger than a worm for all her lies. This compassionate man, until now hidden behind a stone façade, wanted to know her. But she was a lie. She did not deserve his compassion.

Her throat tight and her words constricted, she said the only honest thing she could about herself. "I'm nobody."

His eyes darkened. "You're not nobody. You're Lady Pickering."

Pushing against him, she tried to escape his grip, his gaze, his concern, but she found herself trapped, unable to put space between them. He pinned her against him.

"I'm *not*," she protested. "I'm not Lady Pickering. I'm not a merchant's daughter. I belong to no one. I'm nobody. Nobody. Don't you see that? I'm an unwanted nobody."

He kissed her then.

Her first kiss. No, that was not true. *Their* first kiss, and her first willing kiss, however unexpected.

His lips met hers with a tenderness she had never known and did not deserve. Taut arms held her to him, but soft and yielding lips seduced her. Her body melded against his in submission. He parted her lips with subtle persuasion. When she complied, he tangled his tongue with hers.

To be kissed by him like this every day — how different life would be.

As abruptly as the kiss began, it ended. He stepped away but kept both hands on her waist to hold her steady.

His breathing labored, his expression ferocious, he asked, "Can you forgive me?"

"Forgive you? For what?" She blinked in confusion.

"Even as I tell you I respect you, I disrespect you with ungentlemanly behavior. It is unforgivable."

"No, please. Don't regret the kiss. If you do, you confirm I'm nobody, that I mean nothing to you." In desperation, she clutched his coat, frantic to be held, to be loved, to be known. Standing on her tiptoes, she invited him to resume the kiss.

His words of apology suspended, he accepted the invitation. She wrapped her arms around his neck as he tightened his hold to lift her off the ground. Her tongue traced the crooked line of his bottom teeth and along the back of his upper teeth, wanting to memorize every aspect of the kiss, afraid this would be her last.

When their lips parted, he lowered her until her boots met earth, then released his hold so he could cup her face. His hazel eyes studied her, her own gaze feasting on him. How could this moment feel like a homecoming, the welcoming embrace of safety and love for which she had yearned? In this moment, she knew only blissful awareness that she was home. *He* was home. This embrace. This place. This man was her *locus amoenus*. With him, she was somebody.

He ran his thumbs along her jawline before encircling her shoulders to hug her. Secure and protected, she nestled her cheek against the hollow of his neck.

Time passed before they untangled themselves. They had stood, locked in embrace, holding each other as though they might drift out to sea if they let go.

What had he done? What had *they* done?

She nuzzled against him, looking up at him with soulful eyes, her skin flushed, her lips reddened. It was then he became aware of their surroundings and his actions.

The sun shone, hot and relentless, the wind bless-edly cool. He wrinkled his nose at the sharp smell of pasture. Sheep milled about, while his dog watched from the stone on the ridge.

Deuce take it. He had kissed his wife with fervor while standing in a filthy field in broad daylight where any laborer could have seen them. She deserved more respect than this.

Later reflection would shed no further light as to why he acted with reckless, schoolboy passion, and the most rational explanation was anything but ratio-nal. When caught in the moment, he had sensed her need, her desperation to be known, and his response had been purely emotional, a new experience for him. She had needed *him*. He could not have turned his back on her, not when no one had ever needed him before. Yes, the march residents needed him, but they needed someone as the marquess, not *him*.

The moment now over, he was caught between gentlemanly honor and his own desires. Gentle-men did not lust after their wives, yet he had, and it had been the most fulfilling moment of his life, a moment when he felt whole. He could not regret their kiss and would do it again if she continued to look up at him.

Putting reasonable distance between them, he knew he had this moment to set the direction of their future. He hesitated, his thoughts oscillating. While he could not turn back the clock and choose to walk away instead of approach her, he could walk away now, resetting their marriage as it had been. All he had to do was offer to escort her back to the house and wish her a good day so he could return to his schedule. A gentleman would. A gentleman would show his wife this courtesy and save them from the embarrassment of their lasciviousness.

But he did not want to.

Even if he did make that choice, his life could not return to normal. He could not forget at will her desperate need to be known by him, nor could he forget the sensation of being known in return. Memories were not so easily manipulated. Dare he take the risk of deepening their relationship? His thoughts turned unbidden to the heartache his father had suffered and to the niceties of a successful marriage. *Passion* did not a successful marriage make. Devil take him for wanting what could ruin them.

This moment would decide their future.

This moment would determine everything.

What kind of marriage did he want? What kind of relationship did he want with his wife?

He had this moment to choose.

Leaning forward, he cupped her cheek in his palm and touched his lips to hers, infusing in that kiss all he did not know how to say. It was a chaste kiss, but with it, he willed her to understand that he wanted this again, often. He wanted her to know that he had not been Lord Pickering marking his wife as territory, rather he was Trevor making love to *her*.

He caressed her cheek with the back of his fingers. "Phoebe," he said, speaking her given name for the first time in their marriage.

She jerked from his touch, turning her head away from him.

"My name is J'non," she rasped, her voice hoarse but forceful.

He stepped back, running a hand through his hair. "J'non?" he echoed.

"Yes, J'non. My mother named me J'non." She, too, stepped back, a gap widening between them.

At first all he knew was confusion. Then it struck him.

It made sense, really, although he could not say it did not take him by surprise. She rejected the name her father had given her as a way to reject the man as a parental figure. No doubt she had lived with her mother, tucked away in the country, far from the business-minded father who had been emotionally abusive if not physically. If her father named her Phoebe, it would make sense she would prefer a pet name instead, shying from anything associated with Mr. Whittington.

So help him, Pickering would keep her as far from that man as possible. He knew little about the man and even less about her, but what he did know from the brief acquaintance they shared was that she had been poorly treated and lacked esteem. To her father, she was a possession, a daughter whose purpose served to gain him notoriety through marriage. Pickering felt sick to his stomach at the realization that until this moment, she had been little more than a possession to him, as well, a wife whose purpose was to beget an heir and pay the estate debts through the dowry. He could never see her this way again. *Trevor* could never see her this way. He was disgusted at himself for viewing his wife as a possession. Squeezing his eyes closed, he took a steadying breath. How long had it been since he had thought of himself by his given name? He had become a possession.

Opening his eyes, he focused on his wife—no, on J'non. She was a person. By not seeing her as such, he had done her a disservice and treated her no better than her father had. His duty was not only to whomever held the title of Lady Pickering, but to the person, to the person standing in front of him.

"J'non," he said, his voice tender, a smile tugging at his lips.

Eyes widening as if startled, she looked up from staring at her clenched hands.

The corners of his lips lifted higher. Then he proposed something rash, something wildly out of character, something that would set their life down a new path.

"What would you say to a day together, the two of us? We could go for a ride in the Pickering curricle to see the countryside, or swim in the lake, or set out for a picnic. Anything you would like to do. I will shock the household by canceling the day and spending it in your company."

She stared at him, her expression alarmed. Her lips parted, then closed, then parted again, finally pursing.

"Will you have me disgrace my nobility by begging?" Reaching across the space that divided them, he tidied her hair, strands escaping the simple knot without the bonnet to shield them from the wind. His daft smile would not abate despite her silence. At length, he added, "I prefer J'non to Phoebe, by the by. It fits you better, somehow. I feel discourteous using your given name, but I will accustom myself to it in time. No one, not even my father, has ever used my given name. I grew up as Gaines, the family surname, and then Tidwell after my father's death when I inherited the barony, and now Pickering. I think of myself in these ways, as the embodiment of duties entailed. I may not recognize my given name if you say it, but I would feel less intrusive calling you J'non if you called me Trevor. Will you?"

"Trevor," she said, the word spoken with uncertainty.

"Ah, I like it." The pesky smile broadened. "I'll have to live up to my new identity."

J'non shook her head. With more confidence than he had seen her display, she reached for his hand, then laced their fingers. "You don't have to live up to anything, Trevor. You need only be yourself."

He raised their twined hands to his lips and kissed her knuckles. "I promise."

A promise he was not sure how to keep. It went against his nature not to live up to something. Being himself would be challenging—who was he outside of being the bearer of responsibility? His goal in life had always been to be worthy of his entailed title, to make his father proud by proving himself honorable, a goal made infinitely more difficult with the addition of the marquessate.

But dash it all, he made the decision not to walk away. He made the decision to show her he recognized her as a person, not only as a wife. If she wanted them to be themselves, he would not deny her. They could find each other together. What a ridiculously romantic notion. He laughed out loud. The mere thought of him as romantic bowled him over in laughter, startling both J'non and Gunner, the latter leaping off the stone and dashing towards them, barking at the sound of Trevor's laughter.

Chapter 9

An hour later, they sat at a table in the knot garden. Trevor had offered the new gardener and his lads the opportunity to head home early but the crew instead chose to divert their attention to the walled garden. Meanwhile Hawkins setup tea al fresco so the marquess and marchioness could enjoy good weather and company with a backdrop of partially weeded parterres.

Trevor would have found any setting bewitching with J'non seated across from him. It did not escape his notice that he was acting like an infatuated schoolboy. His grin proved he did not care.

After a sip of tea, sweet in contrast to his black-as-night morning coffee, he resumed the conversation they had begun, reveling in every candid answer she shared, her honesty as in contrast with her meekness as his tea to his coffee. "You're not unhappy here?"

"Oh, no, not in the least," she insisted, adding sugar to her tea. "This is a new life for me. One to which I'm unaccustomed. However, this is the most content I've been in many years."

The lingering discomfort between them, founded only in unfamiliarity with each other, and in his case with himself, would pass in time. He was certain. With each question he posed, her words were less guarded, her smile brighter. As to himself, he wore a new face, the face of a man with a promising future, a man at liberty to express himself and act on emotional impulse. In some ways, he experienced the unhinging sensation of being too exposed, too vulnerable, but he fought against that, pushing deep down the voice of Pickering and Tidwell and even Gaines, listening only to the voice of Trevor, a romantic he had never met until now but liked exceedingly well. He was, at this table, not the bearer of responsibility, rather a man admiring a woman over tea and cake.

Trevor leaned back in his chair and crossed one leg over the other. Was it gauche to admire his wife over the rim of his teacup? More than once he caught her blushing at his lingering looks. Was she, too, recalling their kisses? If he were not mindful, he would blush, as well, for he had never shared intimacy of this kind with another woman. It was an experience he looked forward to repeating. The more she disclosed, the more he understood her, all clues of how to romance her and deepen that intimacy beyond the physical. From what she had divulged about herself so far, he ascertained she was an intelligent woman but humble. He thirsted to know more.

"You lived with your mother until this year?" he asked.

"Not exactly," she said with a slight stammer. She took her time before explaining, her attention on the sugar, then on the cake, then on her teacup. "Only until I was fifteen," she answered at last, her eyes still trained on the teacup. "I lived with my... my

mother on a farm in Surrey. The farm belonged to…"
She swallowed visibly and struggled to say the last.
"A baronet."

Ah, so that was it.

There could have been any myriad of conclusions
to draw, the most obvious being that her father let a
cottage for Mrs. Whittington and daughter on the baronet's property. That was not the conclusion Trevor
drew. J'non's hesitation, her rift with her father, the
way she explained, as if with nostalgic tenderness,
a touch of reverence, and perhaps notes of melancholy, all pointed to another conclusion. Not too
broad a leap in logic, he drew the conclusion that
her mother must have lived with her cicisbeo. The
baronet could, of course, be a relation if not a landlord,
but he doubted that, not with J'non's averted eyes and
stumbled words, not based on his own observations
and experiences. No, the baronet was her mother's
paramour. How interesting that Mrs. Whittington
would be married to a merchant while living with
an aristocrat who should have had his own family.
Perhaps he did.

On second thought… yes… that made more sense.
The mother had been the baronet's mistress, tucked
away in a cottage on the property while the man lived
in the manor with his family. The surprising aspect
was that Mr. Whittington allowed it. Unless he did not
know. Or did he encourage the affair, somehow using
the connection to his advantage? That seemed most
likely based on what Trevor knew of Mr. Whittington. He believed he understood Mrs. Whittington's
situation perfectly. Would J'non recognize how similar their childhoods had been if he divulged his own

tale? However much his mind wished to skirt the memory, he could not forget his father's choice to turn a blind eye.

"Tell me more," he prompted with an encouraging smile rather than vocalizing any of his theories. "You lived with your mother until you were fifteen, and then your father brought you to London?"

No, she had told him earlier she only lived with Whittington for one month, leaving five or six years unaccounted for. He raised his teacup to his lips.

"I lived with my mother until the pox." Eyes averted still, she fidgeted with her cup handle.

His own hand stilled, cup suspended halfway between his lips and the saucer. "Your mother died of smallpox?" He was shaken by the cold reality that aside from him, she had no family, no family worth mentioning anyway.

"Yes. But I don't know how long she was sick before passing. I wasn't told about their — that is, my mother's death until much later. You see, it all began when a few of the neighboring children fell ill. Mama and — that is, Mama and the baronet nursed those who had taken ill. He was the local magistrate, and from his perspective, responsible for helping. Try as they might, the sickness spread until it wasn't safe anymore. They — that is, Mama sent me to live with my aunt until we could be reunited."

Trevor reached across the table to cover her trembling hand. A twinge of guilt tugged at his heart for judging her mother's decision to live with her lover when she had died nobly nursing those less fortunate, a far cry from his mother who had thought of no one except herself.

"Only…" she continued, "we were never reunited. I lived with my aunt until —"

"Until your father sent for you," he finished for her, seeing the chain of events clearly, "so he could advance his career."

This explained everything. He surmised she had been foisted on the aunt, an unwelcome houseguest, dependent and resented. At their first meeting, he had mistaken her for someone's poor relation. Given the size of the dowry and the wealth of the father, he could not have foreseen being so right, but that was what she had been since she was fifteen — a penniless and unwanted relation. He would wager the clothes she wore to Sladesbridge Court were the same clothes in which her aunt had dressed her and thus the same clothes she took to London when her father summoned her. Since the man could not be bothered to dress her in new clothing knowing he would be hoisting her on someone else soon enough, those rags were her fortune.

"May I be so bold as to assume your new life here is not so terrible?" He meant the question to lighten the mood, but she turned to him with a frown.

"Oh, please don't think I'm anything but grateful. You've given me a chance I never dreamt possible."

He squeezed her hand. "Would it shock you if I returned the sentiment? You are far and away everything I never dreamt possible."

Her cheeks reddened, and he caught the hint of a smile.

He had not fostered close relationships since his youth, especially not with women, but everything about this time with J'non felt right. Even Gunner was taken with her, for the dog lay under the table, his head resting on her foot rather than his master's boot.

From the glimpses of her life, he inferred she needed friends and family. Passed from one person to the next, unwanted, she must need a place of her own, a place to belong. What had life been like with her mother? As lonely as with the aunt, he would wager, if her mother was more interested in the lover than the daughter, the product of a failed marriage. Now he was fictionalizing her life. Best stick to the facts, old boy. Fact or fiction, she was here now, and he would see to her happiness.

However unwise it had been to confess as much as she had, J'non justified her admissions. She knew nothing of Phoebe Whittington's childhood aside from Mr. Whittington being a widower, so she had no way to use Phoebe's version of the truth, and besides, this was J'non's life now; she could only use what she knew to build a relationship with her husband. Reservations or not, she *wanted* to know him better. As long as she was careful how she represented the truth, all should be well.

Truths or half-truths aside, her heart ached to have reduced her loving family to her mother living on a farm. Trevor most likely had assumed her father to be negligent of his family. While she did not have kind words about Mr. Whittington on the best of days, she hated that anyone might think ill of her real father. Her family had been the happiest, her father the best of men. Sir Julian Butler had been a father who was not opposed to his daughter riding on his shoulders as he toured their home farm, his devoted wife Non at his side, her lyrical Welsh serenading the dullest of topics.

It had been her aunt who served as villain in J'non's tale, but that was difficult to express to Trevor without revisiting events she had no wish to recall much less share: the scandal, the darkness, the cottage, and then London. What she referred to as *the bleak period*. On these events, she would remain mum lest he learn of her fall from grace, from happy home to servitude. A fraudulent marriage would be easier to accept.

No, she scolded herself, *you are being unchristian to think of Auntie as a villain and to blame for all that came to pass.* J'non had been her own undoing after her aunt's kindness in taking her in. Believing that in one's mind and feeling it in one's heart were different, for in her heart—treacherous organ—she thought unkindly of her aunt even while telling herself she ought not.

That was neither here nor there. Now, she was in Yorkshire at Sladesbridge Court, married to the Marquess of Pickering, regardless how that fact occurred or whose name appeared in the register.

Their conversation in the knot garden had progressed into his invitation for her to join him in the mornings for a swim and ride. In return, she shared her vision for the renovations to the home. She hoped she had not overstepped, but he had questioned her experience with farming, her having lived on the baronet's farm and having offered insight about the sheep. With caution, she had shared the rotation method her father had used, including arable crops.

She recommended, based on her limited observations from so long ago, that Trevor use cover crops to protect the soil from frost and to replenish nutrients, and to overwinter turnips and clovers, which could be used to feed the livestock during the winter months, followed then by rotating crops and livestock each season. In this way, she had explained, no field would be left fallow, and each field would serve to grow several types of crops throughout the year. The use of livestock to fertilize the fields was one of the key elements. If he could implement a viable plan this year, the profits would enable him to hire a qualified steward and a foreman to oversee the home farm, not to mention aid in finding new tenant farmers once those properties had been repaired and made livable again.

What J'non did not know was if he would follow through with any of her recommendations. While curious, he did not appear convinced. Truthfully, what man would take advice from his wife, least of all about farming? If he chose not to, then that would be that. At least she had said what was needed and done her part to save the home farm from ruin and thus the estate from debt. All was in his hands now.

Assured she had made the right choices, she pulled back her shoulders and lifted her chin with confidence before walking into the dining room to join him for supper that same evening.

That Trevor awaited J'non in the dining room rather than the other way around was only because he had arrived earlier than usual. A good thing he did. He would not have wanted to miss her entrance. She bore a confidence he had not seen her wear, a poise for which he wished he could take credit. Was it arrogant to think his kiss could affect her thusly?

Once seated with the first course served, he broached a subject neither of them favored. "The task is long overdue," he reminded her. "It'll take the better part of the day, but we cannot further delay meeting our neighbors. To remedy your frown, I will posit the task like this: we will be spending the day in each other's company and touring a fair length of North Yorkshire together, particularly the moors. If we're fortunate, the coachman will lose his way. Now, does that make our errand more appealing?"

"Indeed, it does," J'non said with a grin that invited him to return the smile. "Touring God's own country with a gentleman never sounded so promising."

Had his solicitor predicted that Trevor would be eager for a carriage drive with his bride, he would not have believed the man. His smile broadened as his attention focused on J'non, a woman—no, *the* woman—he heartily wanted to be trapped in a carriage with for the better part of a day.

After sampling the soup, he said, "We'll want to call on all tenants in the march before the year ends, what few remain, that is. Lucky for our schedule, there is more rural land than villages, hamlets, farms, or otherwise. Our two most important calls, however, will be not to tenants, rather to Sir Roland and Lady Osborne at Dunlin Meadow Abbey, and then to Lord and Lady Roddam at Creighton Hall. Our land borders one of Lord Roddam's earldoms."

"*One* of his earldoms?"

"As I understand, he has five. A man I do not envy, but a man important for us to befriend." Given Trevor had been a baron for nearly a decade, he should be better acquainted with his peers. Instead, he had kept to himself and paid little attention to politics outside taking his seat.

"Is he so unenviable?" J'non asked, the voice of innocence.

"Would you want to be responsible for five earldoms? Here I am struggling with a marquessate, singular."

"Perhaps he has employed trustworthy stewards."

Trevor harrumphed. The voice of innocence? No, behind the angelic tone, she was wise. Her simple statement expressed a world of meaning. If he were not so proud and so distrusting, he would already have enticed a steward using a portion of the dowry. Hiring a steward was a necessity, and yet which should come first? Use the money to hire a steward to restore the estate to sustainability, or use the money to restore the estate to sustainability so the profits could lure a steward? He trusted himself more than a stranger. Entrusting someone to save one's own property was a risk he was not willing to take.

However non-sequitur, Trevor proposed, "What are your thoughts on foxhunting?" At J'non's questioning look, he said, "It's an annual Tidwell tradition, one I'll miss this year. I'm uncertain if we should uphold the tradition by going to Tidwell Hall every October, or if we should host here. As the hunt is exclusive to gentlemen, you would be responsible for entertaining wives and daughters. I beg for your perspective."

"Are you asking for my preferences on location or date? Surely you don't mean to host it here in one month."

He waved a dismissive hand. "Preposterous, I know. Let me reapproach. Would this be something of interest to you, or should we replace it with a new tradition?"

He had always envisioned autumn with a wife who would arrange a weeklong house party, beginning with the hunt and ending with a ball. Granted, that vision had been at Tidwell Hall rather than here, before his inheritance, and long before he accepted he must marry a merchant's daughter rather than a gentleman's daughter, but what the devil was he about asking for a *new* tradition? In a single afternoon he had transformed from a traditionalist to a radical. At the thought, he chuckled to himself.

"I don't know. I've not thought of any of this before." J'non set down her cutlery with an expression conflicted by both anxiety and wonder. "If the hunt is a family tradition, there's no need to change it, not on my behalf, not if it is important to you." Under her breath, as though speaking to herself rather than to him, she asked, "What do I know of parties? I couldn't possibly arrange a foxhunt."

Addressing her mutterings only, he said, "After seeing your recruitment of the villagers, I would not doubt you could do anything you set your mind to do."

She bit her knuckle. He could not tell from the tremble of her chin if she were fighting a smile, eager to put herself to the task, or if she were fighting despair, fearful of failing. Her background, after all, did not recommend her to know how to plan for or entertain the sort of guests they would invite.

Both to encourage her excitement and allay her fears, whichever was needed in this situation, he said, "You are the Marchioness of Pickering. Any and all guests at Sladesbridge Court, be it for a fox-hunt, ball, or otherwise, will vie for your attention. Those who would question your ties to industry are not guests we would invite, or at least not invite twice." Invigorated by his own words, he added, "It's time we put to rest old traditions and begin anew with our own. I want you to plan our first October party, thus beginning a new tradition we can look forward to every year. What would you like to plan? Don't fret about whom to invite, as I will make a list appropriate for the event, and don't fret about the state of the house, for everyone will know it's under renovation. As I see it, this will be your informal introduction into society. Now, what would you like to plan? A dinner party? Something grander, say a ball?"

So enthused by his plan to imbue her with confidence and incite their collaboration, he had forgotten to eat. The second course now awaited his attention. It could wait a little longer.

"A *ball*?" Her eyes widened.

A ball would be a daunting undertaking with a rewarding outcome. Nevertheless, he had said it only as an example. Neither the house nor he was ready for a ball. Still, if that was what she wanted to plan, he would support her.

"I've never hosted a ball before," he confessed, "but women have an innate ability to plan parties, especially when dancing is involved."

Did he really want to host a ball? It would be Lord and Lady Pickering's first event not only as the tenth marquess and his marchioness but as a newly wedded couple. It would likewise be Trevor and J'non's first opportunity to coordinate. A dinner party would be easier to plan and less expensive. Could they afford to host a ball when he had qualms about hiring a steward, however different the two expenses? One ball could exceed a steward's annual salary. A quick reminder set him straight: hiring a steward was about trust more than money.

"Oh, Trevor, I have the perfect idea. Rather than a ball, let us plan a village fête. Would that not be splendid?"

His shoulders rounded. She had missed the point.

Shaking his head, he said, "I'm afraid you've misunderstood. While there's nothing undesirable about a village fête, the point is to host an annual something for our peers, that being the peers of the realm, not the villagers."

She pursed her lips and stared at her plate. "But they deserve a celebration. Who's to say a fête couldn't be our tradition instead? We could still invite your friends."

No doubt this was the difference between marrying a merchant's daughter and a gentlewoman. His attention now also on his plate, he took several bites before speaking.

"I suggest you remember who you are, Lady Pickering, and what your role is in society and in this marriage."

With eyes lowered, she said, "A fête would build morale."

"Yes, but we are not talking about a fête. In November, perhaps. Now, we are talking about starting a Pickering tradition with an exclusive guest list. I understand you must accustom yourself to your new position, but that task will be easier if you listen and obey me. I know what is best, as your husband and as lord of the manor. Following my orders will help you acquaint yourself with your station. We will work together to plan the event, but you must trust my judgment and obey my command."

"Yes, my lord," she yielded.

Finishing the course, he signaled for the next to be served. If he hoped she would engage in lively conversation about the event, whatever it would be, ball or otherwise, he was mistaken. She stared at an unfinished dish, her expression that of a biddable and submissive wife, her posture slumped, as if she hoped to disappear into her chair.

Clearing his throat, he asked, "Is this to be your reaction every time I disapprove?"

"No, my lord."

A gloom settled over the table. He watched as the plates were exchanged.

"I've upset you," he said at length.

"No, my lord."

"I have, *my lady*, or you wouldn't be *my lord*ing me. In one course, I've mangled our newfound friendship. How can I set this right?"

She tugged her bottom lip between her teeth.

"J'non. Look at me. Tell me how I can set this right."

Sparing him a quick glance out of the corners of her eyes, she said to her plate, "I'm not certain I like you as Lord Pickering. You're overbearing."

He scratched his chin. "You don't like me?"

"That's not what I said, not exactly. I *like* Trevor, the man with whom I thought I was conversing, but I find Lord Pickering to be overbearing." Her head bowed as she trained her attention on her hands. "I apologize if I've caused offense."

Trevor closed his eyes. He pinched the bridge of his nose between his thumb and forefinger. "It is not you who should be apologizing, J'non. Responsibility is a heavy burden. I'm thinking like a marquess, knowing I must befriend and entertain my peers. How should I be thinking instead? Speak truthfully."

She fidgeted with her napkin. After unfolding it, refolding it, then repeating the action twice more, she took a deep breath, sat straighter, and met his eyes. "Our attention must first be on what's most important. We can court your peers, or rather our peers, later. What's most important right now is life in the march, including the people in our care. We need to recognize them and show prosperity, even if prosperity is optimism rather than fact. Pardon me for saying, the guests you intend for a ball do not help rebuild estates. I believe if we are to set a new tradition, it should be one that celebrates our life here rather than pander to vanity."

Daft fool. Not her. Him. He was a daft fool. Undeniably, she was right. There he was proposing new traditions while remaining buried under the old.

"You're right," he admitted, mulling over what to say next.

"Am I?" Her brows rose.

"If you'll forgive my toploftiness, we can change the tone of our meal to planning a fête." He offered a smile and waited until she had returned it before he said more. "Pickering is correct, as well, that stuffed shirt of an alter ego of mine. It would behoove us at least to host a dinner party. That does not have to be soon, nor should it be our tradition. I—that is, *Trevor*— wished to know what *our* new tradition should be, and you answered brilliantly. There is nothing more appropriate than an annual autumn fête. You'll forgive me if my shirt points are too starched?"

Her smile brightened to its earlier radiance. "Shall we invite the Osbornes and the Roddams to the fête?"

"We should plan it first," he said with a wink.

That they made it through dessert in amicable conversation set Trevor's nerves at ease, although his hands trembled to think how close they had come to ending the meal as strangers, cold and indifferent. It did not take much imagination to envision how it would have ended: her *lord*ing him thrice more while his irritation mounted, his retreating with Gunner to the study after a brisk *lady*ing, their devotion of the evening expended with a heaviness of heart. Too close. Had they done so, which of them would have extended the olive branch first? May he never need an answer. As it was, supper ended with a blush and a curtsy from J'non and a smile and a bow from Trevor, both once again looking forward to the promise of losing their way in the moors.

Before bowing out of the dining room, he considered inviting her to take tea in the drawing room. Old habits tugged him to the study instead. One change at a time, old boy. One change at a time.

Chapter 10

J'non's tea brightened her morning, readying her for the day, a day with Trevor. Today was the first day of a new week and the last day of August, a day full of the promise of new friends, new sights, and a lost carriage roaming the moors. There was little doubt the coachman knew the routes and thus little chance of getting lost, but a girl could dream, could she not?

Across the table, Trevor enjoyed his breakfast.

Setting her teacup in its saucer, she said, "I shall enjoy sharing your company today without food between us."

He looked up from his plate. "Pardon?"

"Aside from one or two occasions, all of our conversations have been at table."

Trevor arched a brow. "We attended church together yesterday."

"Yes, but we did not converse, did we? This is becoming a habit, our only seeing each other at meals and—" She blushed and turned her attention to her tea.

"Are you accusing me of being inattentive?"

"Oh no, nothing of the sort!" She hastened to add, "I was teasing you."

His expression morose, eyebrow still raised, he said, "As was I."

It took three breaths for his words to dawn. His question had been in jest. Oh! She renewed her blush just as the corners of his lips lifted into a grin.

As she parted her lips to reply, she felt something touch her ankle. Eyes widening, she studied Trevor. Yet again, his expression gave nothing away. The *something* inched up her shin with a nudge. J'non swallowed, mortified. Never had he made advances of this nature. To do it now with Mr. Hawkins mere feet away? Unconscionable! Distressed, she moved her leg, hoping he would not take this as a rejection or insult, only admission of her discomfort. Now was not the time and this not the place. Would this kind of intimacy, this sort of flirting be welcomed in private? She would not admit it even to herself, but, well, maybe a little.

His touch found her shin with the cold press of shoe tip to stocking. A nudge, a caress, a tickle.

No longer grinning, Trevor asked, "Have I displeased you?"

Moving her leg again, she tucked her ankles beneath her chair beyond his reach. "There is teasing, my lord, and then there's... well... there's..." Her words sounding breathless, she cleared her throat. "I should like to concentrate on breaking my fast."

Brows furrowed, he said, "You're *my lord*ing me again, a sure sign I've wronged. Was jesting about my attentions as a husband in poor taste? My apologies if so, however well intentioned."

"Jesting about being attentive is one thing, being *over*attentive another," she scolded.

His reply was to tap his foot against her leg. Tap, tap, tap. So much for being safely tucked under her chair.

"Trevor, I—" Her words halted as she heard a peculiar snuffling sound from under the table.

A snuffle followed by a huff, then a noisy lapping. J'non pushed her chair back. Underneath the table, noshing on bacon, lay Gunner with one ear flapping as he ate and the other folded against his head, his tail thumping against her leg. She gasped, her eyes meeting Trevor's.

Bringing her hands to cover her hot cheeks, she said, "I thought... that is... I..."

His expression clouded. Without a word, he raised the table linen to investigate. Tilting his head in thought, he looked from Gunner to J'non, then laughed. He had the audacity to bark in laughter!

Making no attempts to stifle his mirth, he said, "No more needs to be said." Trevor raised his coffee in salute, then brought the rim to his lips, promptly snorting into the cup.

Whatever relief she felt that it had been the dog rather than her husband familiarizing himself with her lower leg was replaced by self-consciousness that he knew what she mistakenly suspected him of doing. At least he was humored. She tugged her bottom lip between her teeth, trying not to laugh at herself.

After his second attempt to drink his coffee, he said, "I've requested a horse be warmed and saddled for you. You still plan to join me for my morning ride?"

J'non let her cheeks cool before replying. Cradling her hands around her teacup, she hoped her voice did not shake. "Yes, but I've not ridden in a long time, not since before my aunt took me in."

"I believe you'll find it's *secundum naturam*, or second nature. Once you learn to ride, you never forget. Before setting off, we'll devote a few minutes for you to accustom yourself to the horse. Speaking of, I've chosen a docile mare. You'll want to tour the stables, I presume, to choose your preferred horse for subsequent outings. We've not many, I'm afraid, only the few I brought from Tidwell."

"I trust your choice, Trevor. Where will we ride?" J'non hoped she did not disappoint him or slow his ride, for she had not ridden since she was about thirteen, perhaps younger. Even then, she had never been a skilled horsewoman.

"Gunner and I ride to the lake, so I thought it best to keep to habit. Should I assume swimming is a pastime best saved until we're better acquainted? There is no bathing box to don your bathing gown, I must warn."

"I see. Yes, we had better wait. Or at least I had. I don't wish to keep you from what you enjoy, so what if I sit on the shore while you swim?"

"Hardly fair."

J'non turned her teacup one way then the other. "Fair enough." She darted a look his direction. "You ought to know I can't swim."

With no outward display of shock, he said, "I'm not daunted if you aren't. A welcome challenge, in fact, assuming you're amenable to resolving that inconvenience, or do you have an abhorrence for water?"

"I've always wanted to learn. I never had the chance."

His smile reflected hers. "It's settled. I'll teach you. I anticipate you'll be outswimming me before the weather turns cold. But not today. Today, we're on a tight schedule. We'll have only an hour for our ride before we'll need to return to refresh for the grand adventure three hours hence. The drive to Dunlin Meadow Abbey is not short, or so the coachman informed me. We'll call on the Osbornes first, and then carry on to the Roddams farther north." He glanced at the mail next to his plate. "You haven't any mail I'm disheartened to report. Do ladies not cherish writing letters to each other?"

A curious question. She had never corresponded with anyone before. Was it something women cherished? The idea seemed one she might enjoy, but to whom would she write?

Before she could answer, he folded his napkin next to his plate and reached for the stack. "I'll read aloud what I think will be of interest, then it will be as though we've both received correspondences. Yes?"

Nodding more enthusiastically than she ought for him to read mail aloud, she poured fresh tea in preparation.

"The first is Sir Roland's calling card." Trevor flipped the card front to back. "Ah. He's written on the back that he looks forward to making our acquaintance."

"Is he a baronet?" Under the table, she slid her foot out of her slipper and stretched her toes until she felt Gunner.

"Knighted, as I understand." Trevor set aside the card and reached for the next item in the mail. "According to the notes from my solicitor about our neighbors, he was knighted for service to the Crown, official business abroad, unknown as to what."

"Is he a *spy*?"

What she did not expect when she began rubbing Gunner with her stockinged foot was for him to roll over atop her other foot so she could better pat his stomach.

Trevor slanted her a glance. "If he were a spy, do you think he would add it to his calling card?"

"Oh. I suppose not. How thrilling to imagine him as a spy, though."

Trevor's lips quirked into a smirk. "I had not taken you for the fanciful sort, my dear J'non. In all likelihood he was, or still is, a diplomat or dignitary, or nothing more than a dependable clerk. No need to look crestfallen. You may imagine him as a spy if you wish."

"Is he one of your tenants?"

"On the contrary. He owns Dunlin Meadow Abbey and thus is responsible for the condition of its roof — one less I must worry about. Please laugh, or I shall think you do not find my humor amusing." He eyed her before continuing. "There are several landowners within the march, but Sir Roland happens to be the wealthiest. Hmm. On second thought, I surmise he's not a clerk then." Flipping over the next letter, he set it aside. The next received the same treatment. The third, he slipped a finger beneath the wax and unfolded the sheet. "Ah, from the curate of Hutton. Let us see what he has to say."

With each line Trevor read, his voice deepened and slowed. The curate wrote on behalf of the parishioners to request the marquess' attention on the deplorable condition of the roads.

He stopped reading halfway through. "Right. I'll save this for later, shall I? To what roads he refers, I can only guess. As far as I'm aware, there are only well-trodden paths through the moors. But never mind that now."

J'non relished in this moment, no matter how ordinary: two people in the morning room, sifting through missives. It was domestic. It was heavenly. She had not been allowed in a morning room since her parents lived. As Miss Whittington's lady's maid, she had downed toast in the kitchen—chased only on rare occasions with tea that tasted faintly of dishwater, steeped from overused and past their prime leaves—before preparing her mistress' morning attire, bath, and breakfast tray. Life with her aunt was similar, only it was her cousins she served rather than a merchant's daughter, cousins who were not the daughters of a gentleman but were nonetheless J'non's superiors given her dependence on her aunt's kindness. Toast in the Whittington kitchen surpassed the empty stomach suffered in her aunt's home. None of that mattered now. In this moment, with Trevor, she savored tea with freshly steeped leaves, at leisure to eat what she wanted and enjoy his company, a stranger who was becoming increasingly familiar.

"Disappointing," he said, scanning the next letter. Clearing his throat, he read aloud from it, as well, before setting it down with a sigh. "Considerate of Lord Roddam to write. I'm thankful he received my calling card courtesy of the Creighton Hall steward. A shame the letter is one of regret rather than welcome."

"It's not all disappointing," J'non offered. "While he regrets not being at the hall since he only visits once a year, he does express pleasure of there being a new marquess in residence, and he promises to bring his family in a month to meet us. An introduction for us to anticipate."

"I've married an eternal optimist. What if you were to write to the countess in the interim? Gain her acquaintance? You'd have someone with whom to correspond after all."

J'non smiled noncommittally. She would hardly know what to say to a stranger, never mind a countess. As courteous as Lord Roddam's letter was, how high in the instep were the earl and countess to be titled with no less than five earldoms? She set higher hopes on befriending Lady Osborne.

"We'll need to amend our agenda," Trevor said, pushing the remaining mail aside. "We'll call on the Osbornes, then we'll tour the hamlets along the return route. Without the drive north, we've gained at least three hours."

How pleasant it would be if the carriage wheel faulted on one of those well-trodden paths across the moors so they could have even more time. That she *wanted* to spend time alone with him surprised her. Had her plan not originally been to avoid him so she would not make an unfortunate slip in her identity? In addition, what she had said to him the day before yesterday had been true: Lord Pickering was overbearing. He intimidated her. The gentleman across from her, however, was *Trevor*, and she *liked* Trevor.

Exceedingly. More so with each conversation, however limited in number those were thus far. Did she not deserve companionship?

He interrupted to ask, "You would rather see the countryside than sit in a drawing room, correct?"

"I've been on tenterhooks since you first invited me."

"Perfect. Now, ready for a ride to the lake on the most docile mare our stables have to offer?" He stood and offered his hand.

Under the table, Gunner shuffled off J'non's feet and made his presence known, ready at the word *ride*. Slipping on her shoes, J'non accepted Trevor's hand, eager to begin their adventure. That the day had transitioned from calling on neighbors to touring the countryside together was enough to brighten even the cloudiest of skies, not that there was a cloud in sight.

Lady Siobhan Osborne handed Trevor a cup of tea. "We knew to expect you but never thought you would bring a friend for Caoimhín."

All eyes turned to look out the parlor window where a tongue lolling Lurcher was entertaining the Osbornes' son. The boy's nanny reined in the chaos.

"Lady Pickering insisted." Trevor grimaced his apology. "I'm too well bred to bring my dog, which leads us to only one conclusion. My wife is a heathen."

J'non was the first to laugh. "Only a cold-hearted villain would have left him behind, what with his long looks when he was not invited. In my defense, I intended him to stay with the coachman."

"We are to blame," said Lady Osborne as she handed J'non her tea. "Had we not been outside with Caoimhín, he would not have seen the dog." She looked outside again onto the merry scene of the giggling babe antagonizing the great menace that was Gunner. "Look how happy he is."

Sir Roland, who stood by the window, joined them, taking the seat next to his wife as she handed him his teacup and saucer. "You've set a precedent," he said. "The next time you call on us, we shall expect the doggo to accompany you, or you'll be turned away."

Trevor and J'non had been in the parlor for less than ten minutes, but Trevor already knew he liked the Osbornes. Judging from J'non's smile, she felt the same. Lady Osborne and J'non appeared to be of similar ages. Their hostess was confident and friendly, attractive with olive green eyes and dark brown hair, and unabashed by her slips into Gaelic. From County Wicklow, Ireland, she had told them in greeting, first setting foot on English soil only after her marriage to Sir Roland. From Trevor's assessment, the gentleman was what the poet Cowper might refer to as a lady's man. He was genial, handsome in a roguish way, and quick to laugh. Had J'non decided he was not unassuming enough to be a spy, or did his charisma brand his guilt? Trevor looked forward to asking her on the way home.

His attention on Sir Roland, he said, "I promise never to disappoint. Far too arduous of a drive to be turned away on ceremony."

"How your coachman traversed the moors is anyone's guess. The paths are only good for packhorses, you know."

"Yet I never doubted the skill of my driver." Trevor nodded to J'non, who seconded this.

In truth, had he known the road — and he used that word euphemistically — was so little traveled, he might have thought twice about taking the carriage. It was the sensible choice, he had originally calculated. When the ninth marquess moved to London to pursue his vices, he left behind an expensive and well-sprung carriage, complete with Pickering coat of arms, alongside a much cared for curricle. The only other conveyance in the coach house was a derelict gig. A gig would have been more practical and less gauche, but not in its present condition, assuming it could be resurrected. As if to confirm the carriage was the best choice, despite the complications with the route, dark clouds had threatened rain for the entirety of the drive, low hanging and heavy, although not a single raindrop fell.

J'non said, "I had hoped to invite you to my sewing circle, Lady Osborne, but after seeing the drive, I'm not certain that would be wise to undertake weekly. We've not set an official day, but perhaps you could join occasionally."

"I'm not discouraged by distance or drive," said Lady Osborne. "Sladesbridge Court is not far as the crow flies, a handful of miles, like, only made difficult by the terrain requiring a circuitous journey. With the nanny here, and my own horse as chaperone, I would be delighted to join, say once or twice a month. Send word when the day is decided."

"I should tell you," J'non added with hushed tones, "those in attendance are village women."

"And what do you think I am, Lady Pickering?" Lady Osborne laughed. "I'll not bleed a word of my humble origins in hopes you'll remain impressed by my fancy honorific."

Trevor listened as the conversation continued, his attention fixed on J'non rather than following the thread of words.

She was a woman of two identities, three if he had not known about her upbringing with her mother. With him, at least until the past two days, she behaved almost akin to a servant, her eyes lowered, her presence invisible, her responses monosyllabic, her will subservient. With company, she acted with the grace and poise of a gentlewoman, her words gentle but commanding, her conversation natural with smooth transitions between topics, and a humor that lightened the mood. She listened with rapt interest as though she would rather be nowhere else than by the side of her companion. Every movement, every look, every word took him by surprise.

Admittedly, between signing the settlement and meeting her, he had envisioned a vulgar woman, someone boisterous, loud, and inappropriate, someone who would embarrass him. Given the wealth of the father, overindulged had crossed his mind, as well. In preparation, knowing needs must, he had budgeted from the contracted dowry for tutors, namely for voice coaching and training in etiquette and manners. After all, why would a cit's daughter know owt about this life? What he never expected was a wife who acted like a maid in private and a lady in public, unstained by industry.

With a shake of his head, he turned to his host. "How old is your son?" Trevor asked.

Sir Roland answered, "Not yet two but thinks he knows it all."

"Like father, like son." Lady Osborne pinned her husband with a knowing look and added, "*Cad é a dhéanfadh mac an chait ach luch a mharú?*"

The meaning was lost on Trevor, as well as J'non, who cast him a questioning glance, but Sir Roland understood, for he replied by puckering his lips and blowing his wife a kiss. Trevor pretended not to notice. Except for raised eyebrows, he hoped he appeared nonchalant and only interested in his tea.

Yes, he believed he liked the Osbornes, however unconventional, and perhaps because of their unconventionality.

Turning to J'non, Lady Osborne asked, "How have you found the townlands? To your liking?"

"Today, Lord Pickering and I will see more of the area, but so far, I've seen the little village nearest the house," J'non said. "The only way I can describe it is picturesque. I can see the church spire from the drawing room window, and the hills... oh, the hills! I will never tire of the view. The village itself is no less beautiful, but it's a worn beauty. I hope that does not sound uncharitable. The village needs as much love as our home, if I may speak candidly."

Crossing one leg over the other and leaning against the arm of his chair, Sir Roland inquired, "You know the house is cause for curiosity? Rumors abound about the lavish renovations undertaken by the previous marquess and the..." He waggled his eyebrows. "...parties. Yet no one around has seen inside. Siobhan and I have been married — what? Four years? Four going on twenty?" A wave of his hand staved off his wife's anticipated interjection. "Never seen inside. Granted, the marquess had already moved to London by the time we took possession of Dunlin Meadow, but... one does wonder." He eyed Trevor with the expectation of a fan-waving matron at a London ball.

"Consider yourself invited." Leaning forward, elbow to thigh, Trevor asked, "Now, is it the renovations you're curious about, the dilapidation, or the—" he paused for effect then mouthed, "*duel?*"

Lady Osborne, so riveted, forgot to chew the biscuit she had bitten into. Sir Roland circled his hand for more but said nothing.

Continuing, Trevor said, "He died an honorable death, if you take my meaning. As for the dilapidation, he dismissed the entirety of the staff upon his move to London except for a lone caretaker who was instructed to keep the state apartments ready and the carriages clean, of all the preposterous requests."

Lady Osborne added, "Why the state apartments?"

Trevor shrugged one shoulder. "The renovations were nothing short of outrageous. He turned a house mentioned in the Domesday Book into an indoor pleasure garden. Allow me to paint the picture. The king's dressing room is now a Roman bath. Marble tub, Pompeian mural, Byzantine floorcloth painting, and don't allow me to forget the Herculaneum statues. The rooms are each exotically themed. The Japanese room features an authentic Samurai *hatomune dou*, and the Chinese room has a wall screen that must have cost the equivalent of my baronial annual income."

Before the Osbornes could reply, J'non said, "When you come to the house, we'll show you the state apartments. They cover an entire wing of the house and are a sight to behold. What I don't understand, and what you voiced, Lady Osborne, is why keep them in tip-top shape while the rest of the house decays? Houses do not do well abandoned. Did his lordship think the Royal Family would want to stay in an untended house with only a caretaker present or that they would not notice the condition of the house if their suites were clean to the point of divinity?"

Sir Roland shook his head. "It is a good thing to be a lowly knight, my lady, for I need never worry about a king or queen knocking on my door to beg for room at the inn."

Lady Osborne swatted at him then asked, "How are the two of you living there if it's in poor condition?"

Trevor said, "It's not unlivable. Had it sat longer, perhaps. The worst damage has been caused by a leaky roof."

Sir Roland studied his tea before asking, "So, he spent a fortune renovating the estate only to abandon it?"

"I suspect my predecessor miscalculated the contents of his purse, unwisely gave carte blanche to his decorator, or gambled what he needed to maintain the estate. I do not believe he intended to abandon the house until he realized it necessary to win back enough money to return. Speculation, of course."

"What a lark!" said Sir Roland. "If you'll pardon my saying, we didn't think you would sate our curiosity. What a delight this chinwag is turning out to be."

Trevor's gaze met J'non's. Her eyes twinkled with merriment, her lips curved. Conversation with the Osbornes flowed effortlessly, as though the four had known each other for years rather than a handful of minutes.

"Tell us more," their host insisted. "We know the marriage is recent, for *everyone* has been talking about it, but what we don't know is…" His eyes shifted, looking from J'non to Trevor to Lady Osborne, then back to J'non. "…if it was love at first sight."

Rather than be embarrassed, as Trevor expected J'non to be, or even subdued with downcast eyes, she laughed and said, "Lord Pickering, at first sight, was all frowns and gruffness. While Gunner offered his paw in greeting, Lord Pickering barked—orders that is."

Trevor arched a brow.

Sir Roland clapped his hands. "By Jove," he said. "This gets better by the minute. I'm positively giddy. More tea, *acushla*."

Lady Osborne prepared more tea while saying, "I was certain when I saw the two of you that your marriage had been as clandestine as ours."

J'non gasped. "Did you elope?"

Host and hostess eyed each other, exchanging unspoken words before Lady Osborne said, "Now that we've piqued your interest, you'll have no choice but to call on us again."

"No, no, no," Sir Roland argued. "They must receive us so we can see for ourselves the Chinese wall screen."

With a nod, Trevor said, "You're both welcome any time."

J'non added, "But only on the condition you bring Caoimhín so Gunner has a playmate."

The conversation turned to more sedate topics, much to Trevor's amusement. In any other drawing room, they would have talked about weather and fashion first rather than last. Lady Osborne recommended a local modiste for J'non when prompted, and all four commiserated about the absence of rain. Sixty-three days and counting, Sir Roland pointed out, with wells and lakes drying up. The extensive shore around the lake had caught J'non's notice during the morning ride, which Trevor explained was exposed lakebed where the water had receded.

Although the conversation continued, Trevor's attention returned to J'non. Since their meeting on estate grounds two days prior, he enjoyed her company more with each encounter. Teasing her, especially, was increasing its appeal. He could not say which thrilled him more, her reactions when she realized he was jesting or her reciprocal teasing. Both brought uncountable pleasure. The plan for his marriage had not been this. He married for money. She married because she had to obey her father. Never had he intended to inconvenience either of them, wanting to avoid her so she could live her life and he his, paths crossing only as duty dictated. Yet in a single unexpected encounter, all plans unraveled. She had accompanied him on his morning ride for pity's sake — and they had both enjoyed it!

Who was this siren?

As she carried on with the Osbornes, the trio cheerfully diverted, Trevor reflected on his thoughts from earlier, on his observations of her. How shortsighted for him to think of her as being of two minds, one part maid and one part lady, when he himself had a public face and a private face. Was that not a sign of good breeding? A public face of gentility and grace with a private face that could be whatever it wanted? Aside from his father, and aside from royalty, both of whom lived with their public face, even in private, living with two sides was the way of the aristocratic family. The trouble was, J'non was neither of good breeding nor of an aristocratic family.

Not for the first time he questioned: who the devil had he married?

Before the hearth, Gunner lay on a bespoke dog pallet. He huffed. He snorted. He growled. His front paws twitched. His back feet peddled.

What must he be dreaming?

"I'd wager he's chasing a rabbit." Trevor took her by surprise, his words in answer to her unspoken thought.

J'non sat in a chair opposite her husband. Her hands, idle, folded one over the other in her lap. Had she known he was going to invite her to the drawing room for tea after supper, she would have left her worsted-work ready by the chair. Not that she would have been able to concentrate on it—his invitation sent her thoughts spinning—but at least she could have busied her hands rather than sit prim and listless. What could his invitation mean? Their routine after supper was for him to return to his study and her to the lady's chamber. What could this change mean?

Her voice steady, in contrast to the quickening of her pulse that he had extended their time together, she said, "I was disappointed the storm clouds did not bring rain. In fact, the air was warmer after they passed, albeit windier." For the walk from the carriage into the house, she had had to hold down her bonnet to keep it from flying, knotted ribbons notwithstanding.

"This time last year, winter arrived early at Tidwell Hall, biting frost and all." Trevor shifted in his chair to cross his stockinged ankles. "It looks as though we'll skip autumn again, only with a never-ending summer rather than an early winter."

"At least it's not oppressively hot. Dry and warm, but not hot." She doubted he planned for them to talk of the weather, but as he had not broached another subject, she thought it best to fill the silence.

"The ground is cracking," he said. "Never thought I'd see a rainless England. Do you suppose it's only here or elsewhere, as well? No, don't answer. Speculation is pointless."

A low fire flickered in the hearth, enough to provide a welcoming glow without the added heat. The light set one side of Trevor's face in shadow. His hawkish nose appeared elongated, his eyes narrowed. At best, glowering. At worst, malevolent.

J'non smiled to herself. The lighting unfairly disfavored him. In truth, he was far from sinister. All afternoon she had regarded him with tenderness and affection. When leaving the Abbey, she had openly laughed at her former accusation that he never smiled, for how absurd it seemed now when he had not wanted for smiles today. Neither had she. For the drive home, there had been more laughter than she had thought possible for her life, much less her marriage. The best part, in her estimation, had been when they fantasized how the Osbornes had met, Sir Roland on a spy mission to Ireland, Lady Osborne on a spy mission for Ireland, both falling in love during counterspy assignations. The memory had her wanting to renew their laughter.

"The Osbornes were not what I expected," she said. "I liked them all the more for it. How did you find their company?"

"Enjoyable," he said without hesitation. "Although they're landowners, I gathered they're not of gentry, not from birth that is. I could be mistaken. Merely an impression. On second thought, I sound snobbish. Allow me to clarify my point: they were refreshing."

For her part, she could not wait for them to return the call or for Lady Osborne to attend the sewing circle. Her personality would suit the group. If she rode horseback to Sladesbridge Court, her travel time would undoubtedly be shortened. The distance was perhaps seven to eight miles, no more than ten. Via carriage, however, it had taken J'non and Trevor well over two hours to reach the Abbey since they had to travel the most meandering path known to man. Surely horseback would be more direct for someone who knew the moors well.

Interrupting her thoughts, Trevor said, "I plan to call on our other neighbors within the coming weeks, landowners and tenants. A few called here when I first took residence. The house was in no fit state to receive callers. Neither was I. I hope you'll join me?" When she nodded, he continued, "Most of our genteel tenants are gentlemen farmers, each overseeing farm laboring crews numbering in the thirties. I say that only because I'm responsible for many of the laborer cottages. After calling on the farmers, I want to see the cottages. I'll leave it to your discretion if you wish to join on those calls. While it will take several weeks, it is important I see the condition of the properties I'm letting, as well as the farms, both inhabited and vacant. Once a steward is hired, he'll take on this task."

J'non nodded again. "Your visit will be a good show of faith that you won't neglect them as your predecessor did."

"I'd like to think of it as 'building morale.'" He winked. "Ah, J'non, I'm pleased you'll be joining me. You're more apt to glean the state of the farmlands than I am."

"No need to mock me," J'non said with a play-ful tone.

"On my honor, I'm serious. No condescension. I've requested the sheep be moved from the estate fields, have I not?"

It would seem he had listened to her on more than one occasion. "Would the gentlemen farmers not be able to advise on the home farm? I wonder that you've not consulted them yet."

He shook his head. "According to my solicitor, they've not yielded impressive profits. Better than the home farm, certainly, but none are farming hillside. No, in times like these, a fresh perspective is needed."

That he trusted her caused a tightening in her chest. She was unsure she would be of much help, though, as her knowledge was rudimentary, only based on observing and listening to her father. The man had been passionate about farming. The trouble was what little knowledge she possessed about the subject was buried beneath everything that had happened since living with her parents.

Trevor pinched his bottom lip between his thumb and forefinger, lost in thought. J'non mulled over what to say to break the silence.

She could comment on the loveliness of the Osborne's parlor. Cozy and lived in had been her impression. The Abbey itself had taken her by surprise. She supposed she could comment on that and see if he felt the same. The expectation had been to see an Abbey, not a modern country home. All that remained of the original Abbey were the ruins in the garden and environs. If she were to guess, J'non would say the house was made from the Abbey's stone — had the Abbey been so ruined that was all they could do to make use of the stone, or had the remains been dismantled to build the house? She should ask Trevor his thoughts.

As she parted her lips to remark on Dunlin Meadow Abbey, Trevor asked, "Did your father hire a governess?"

J'non flinched. "I — I don't understand the question." Taken off guard, she had to gather her thoughts.

He reached for his teacup and saucer for the first time since she had poured the tea. "A governess. Did you have a governess when you lived with your mother?"

"No. A nanny for a time, but never a governess."

"Hmm. I see. May I inquire about your mother's lineage?" His tone was light and conversational, his attention on his tea as he sipped and savored.

Unsettled, nonetheless, J'non hedged her words. "She was Welsh. From a mining family."

"Now that's interesting."

He did not elaborate. J'non swallowed her nerves. Staring at her hands, she hoped he would not pursue the topic. While all she had said of her family had been true, it was difficult to frame everything from the perspective that Mr. Whittington had been her father rather than Sir Julian Butler. She dreaded slipping on one of the partial truths.

With a lilt to his lips, as though they were having the friendliest of conversations, Trevor held out his teacup for another serving.

As she poured, Trevor said, "What I cannot sort out is your education. Consider this a compliment, my dear J'non, when I say I observed a gentlewoman today calling on the Osbornes. Not just a gentlewoman. A *lady*. Obviously, you're Lady Pickering, but I'm curious how you came to be so natural at the role. I expected, if I'm honest, for you either to stare at your hands through the whole of the visit, as you're wont to do, or to be—how shall I phrase this politely—your father's daughter. I'm sounding snobbish again, I fear. I don't mean any insult, only voicing my observations and my curiosity to better know my wife."

Glancing up at him through lowered eyelashes, she set down the teapot and averted her gaze back to her hands. Her mouth was dry. She could not swallow. While far from flattering, his words did not sound accusatory, and yet…

"I was as surprised as you," she admitted. "Today was, as you called it, *secundum naturam*, like riding a horse. I thought I would be nervous or fumble or embarrass myself."

Trevor leaned back, his teacup and saucer balanced on the arm of his chair. "Second nature, eh? If your mother was from a mining family and your father a merchant, and if you had no governess, where did you learn it all? There is an art to being a gentlewoman, you see, and you painted a captivating portrait."

J'non bit her bottom lip.

"Was your aunt a gentlewoman?" he asked. "You stayed with her for, what was it, five years or thereabouts?"

"No. My aunt was not a gentlewoman, although she liked to put on airs." She hoped that did not sound too harsh. "There was no money settled on my aunt for my care, at least not that I'm aware. She saw me as nothing more than a burden. I… I earned my room and board as a maid and companion to my cousins."

Squeezing her eyes closed, she felt the shame he could not see. The years of servitude under that roof. At least she would never have to admit to him what came after. The scandal. The darkness. The cottage. Then London. *The bleak period.*

Before he could probe more, she offered, "The baronet was abundant in his kindness. For all intents and purposes, I was raised as a gentleman's daughter."

Trevor remained silent for an uncomfortable stretch of time, the only sounds a shifting log in the fireplace, the huff of a still sleeping Gunner, and the clink of a teacup against a saucer.

"I can see the past pains you," he said at length. "I don't want you to feel you're being interrogated or that I'm prying. I respect your privacy, and I would never want to hurt you by pressing subjects that upset you. I am only curious to know you better. You surprise me at every turn, J'non, and that is one of the greatest compliments I can bestow. My hope is that in time you'll trust me enough to confide in me. We are, after all, still strangers, are we not?"

Of all the silliness, she could feel the sting of tears prick her eyes.

Hoping he would not notice, she raised her gaze to meet his. "You're not a stranger, Trevor. You're fast becoming the closest friend I've ever had."

The truth of her words struck him. Despite her having a living father, aunt, cousins, and presumably an uncle, she was alone in the world save Trevor. This was not a novel realization, as he had already been made aware of this after her earlier confessions, but to see how deeply it affected her, how isolated she felt, was emotionally moving.

Which was worse, having no one or having family who rejected rather than accepted? While he did not know what happened under her aunt's roof, he would wager with confidence it had not been pleasant. Given she had only been with her father for one month, Trevor wanted to place the blame of her subservient esteem on the aunt rather than Mr. Whittington, who was not blameless, either, but the more hints he heard of the aunt, the more apt he was to believe her the villain of J'non's tale, likely using whatever money Mr. Whittington offered for J'non's keeping to her own advantage while exploiting her niece. *A maid and companion.* He would not press. There was nothing to be gained by paining her with the past. She was safe now. She had him as family now. That was what mattered.

Setting his saucer on the table, he said, "The contractors should arrive any day to repair the casement window in your bedchamber. I apologize for the delay."

"With the weather warm and without the dampness of the rain, there's no harm. The roof took priority, after all."

"Right. What's a crack in the window casement compared to it raining in the dining room, the parlor, the — well, the list does go on, does it not?" Trevor chuckled.

"We're fortunate not to have been rained upon while supping, then." She smiled, a faint ghost of a smile.

Dash it all, he should not have brought up the past. He had lowered her spirits unnecessarily. All day, though, her behavior had been on his mind, one thousand nagging questions waiting to be asked. Even now, he had more, but he would not bring it up again. *A gentleman's daughter.* Curious turn of phrase. He already suspected Mrs. Whittington to be the baronet's lover. What if…

"Do you have any aunts or uncles?" J'non asked.

Her question startled him from the direction of his thoughts. It took him a moment to reorient himself. Ah, the cheeky monkey was turning the tables on him.

"Two aunts," he said. "We correspond. They are older than my father was and find traveling difficult. Neither live in England anymore and haven't for some time. One is in France, the other in Scotland. My Aunt Constance, the one in Scotland, did make it to my father's funeral. Good to see her again. I hadn't since I was a boy."

"Cousins?"

"Yes, but none with whom I'm well acquainted. My aunts are *considerably* older, I might add."

All his curiosity to know J'non better, and he found himself offering lackluster answers in response to her own attempt to know him. But what else could he say? It had always been his father and himself. No aunts present. No cousins. Just the two gentlemen. He would be hard pressed to recall his cousins' names, especially those living on the continent since he had never met them, all the age his father would have been had he still lived.

J'non poured herself a fresh cup. "Did your father fight in many battles?"

"Indeed, he did. I could not tell you half of them. He spoke most often of his first and last, both in the British Americas. His first was roundabout 1744, King George's War. As fate would have it, his final battle, the one that would lame him and force him to leave the Navy, was some thirty years later, also in the British Americas. He was caught in a colonist skirmish, something to do with supply negotiations, and something with which he had no business involving himself personally."

"How lonely you must have been with him away at sea," she said.

"On the contrary. I had my mother and the nanny."

She tilted her head in thought. "Your mother? Oh. I don't know why I thought she died in childbed.

I'm relieved to hear she did not. But then, when did she pass?"

"She didn't."

J'non's teacup rattled on the saucer.

Trevor exhaled deeply. As with her reluctance to talk about her aunt, he would rather not share his family drama. Hypocritical of him. Had he not just voiced his hope she would one day trust him enough to confide in him?

With another deep breath, he said, "My father married during a time of peace, 1766 to be exact. His bride was young, in her early twenties, but from what I understand quite smitten with my father despite a notable age difference. A whirl-wind romance, the servants used to whisper when they thought I was not listening. I was born on their one-year anniversary, January of '67. He stayed with us until '69, then returned to sea. My mother was —"

His words halted. J'non waited, saying nothing, her keen gaze studying him. It was not lost on him he was recounting events as though reading from a ledger, each moment cataloged in chronological order. There was no other way to present the facts than just that, as facts. Dispassionate. Disconnected. Despondent.

"My mother was," he continued on a sigh, "rest-less. However doting she was when she visited the nursery, those visits were few and far between, fewer and farther each month and each year until I can recall not seeing her for a consecutive four month stretch. My father returned January of 1776, on my birthday. My mother left three weeks later."

J'non's mouth was agape, her teacup suspended halfway between her lips and the saucer. "What do you mean she *left*?"

"Exactly that. She left. No words of farewell for Trevor Gaines, the son she bore, or for Admiral the Lord Tidwell, the husband she pledged to love and cherish for all her days." Trevor grunted, his attention caught by Gunner rolling over with a contented yawn. "I was just a boy and understood little, but I overheard a great deal, things I was able to make sense of as I matured. Rumor had it she wanted freedom more than love, money, or family. Mixed rumors. Some say she fancied someone else. Some say she longed for lost youth. I know she had a lover, but I don't know if she left with him."

"Oh, Trevor."

Before she could say more, extend sympathy, ask his feelings on the matter, or whatever sentimental notion she wished to express, he said, "I don't dwell on it. I wasn't close to her. I preferred the nanny's companionship to be honest. Besides, I was too young to remember much. I know the facts from what I've been told by others, but I remember little."

A partial truth. Not quite a lie. He recalled her sweeping into the nursery after her lengthy absences, greeting him with hugs and kisses and whiffs of floral perfume. As ethereal as she would appear, she would disappear, leaving him watching out his window for her return. He spent a lifetime at that window. The view was imprinted. The view of an empty drive.

J'non asked, "Do you know where she is now?"

"I don't, nor do I want to know."

He had accustomed himself to her absences. She always returned. He had been so caught up in the anticipation of her return, he never had the opportunity to hate her for leaving or even mourn her departure. Anticipation was all he felt. He *knew* she would return. Not for years did that turn into self-blame, thinking he had not been good enough as a son. At some point, although he could not pinpoint when or why, he forgave her for leaving. His father used to say a wild bird should not be caged, which was a peculiar idiom since the nanny used to mutter a feral cat could not be tamed. The differences in meaning were not lost on Trevor. Which had his mother believed herself to be?

It did not matter. He did not resent her. Even if he could not forget and had no wish to see her again, he still forgave her.

Hoping J'non would not take this the wrong way, Trevor risked saying, "Promise me you'll never leave. A strange request given we've been married only two weeks, but it is only a request, not a command, not even a plea. A request of compassion. Whatever problems lie ahead, whatever conflicts and disagreements, we can reconcile. Just please don't leave."

The low flames of the fire cast shadows across her face. Her eyes lowered as she whispered her promise.

Trevor asked, "Do you think me foolish for not wanting to find her?"

Shaking her head, J'non said, "Not foolish, no. Although our circumstances are different, I understand not wanting to rekindle a wounded relationship. No matter what happens in my life, I will never reach out to my aunt, nor would I accept her hand if she

reached out to me. That does not mean I've not forgiven all that passed between us. Not to forgive would
mean allowing the wound to fester. I see no point.
What's done is done. It's best to forgive even if we
can't forget. Is that how you feel with your mother?"

He answered with a curt nod.

However different this was from his envisioned
conversation, he would not change it. She knew him
better and he her. Their marriage may not be the
whirlwind romance of his parents, but it would be
stronger for it. There was, after all, more to a successful marriage than love. Love was not enough.

Chapter 11

Afternoon sunlight streamed through the parlor window of the vicarage. Another warm summer day, never mind it was halfway through the first week of September.

Mrs. Gwen Harvey, the vicar's wife, said, "I've always been fond of the three-legged race. It's a must to include. Had it not been for the drought, we could have included a vegetable contest. As I said to Mrs. Oliver, even the flower committee will have their work cut out for them if it doesn't rain soon."

"Fortunately," J'non said, "we'll have a little over a month until the festival. Plenty of time for rain. What about Mrs. Sullivan's suggestion yesterday of a sewing contest?"

"Yes, let's." Gwen trilled her excitement. "I believe this will be a fête to remember."

J'non nibbled at her pastry while Gwen refilled their teacups.

The past three days had been productive. The carpenters, led by Mr. Galfrid Thompson, had arrived early Tuesday morning to set right the window casement. The sewing circle met Wednesday and decided that day should be their weekly do, prompting J'non to write a missive to Lady Osborne in hopes of enticing a new member to the group. Now, today, she and Gwen aimed to set in stone the plans for the village fête.

"Do you suppose," J'non inquired, "the ladies would want to sew anything to sell? Embroidered handkerchiefs or the like?"

"I wouldn't expect embroidery, but cake stalls would be popular." Gwen glanced out the parlor window, something having caught her attention. "I can see one of the dogs bounding along the drive. Obadiah won't be far behind. As I said to Mrs. Carmichael on Monday, the benefit of no rain is the dogs don't track mud into the house." With a rueful look, she added, "Neither does Obadiah for that matter."

It would be nice to see the vicar before returning home. He had been out for a ramble when J'non arrived, he and his two greyhounds. According to Gwen, the vicar was fond of hare coursing and had founded the local club. J'non did not admit she had never heard of hare coursing until now.

She peered out the parlor window. The view looked clear until, yes, there was one of the dogs darting across the lawn, then back down the drive out of sight only to reappear seconds later. The view was worth a contented sigh. The view of the moors, that was, not the bounding greyhound.

The vicarage could not have been better situated: perched atop a plateau, panoramic vistas of the moors, the church positioned next door, picturesque footpaths threading through the vale and into the village, and a favorable prospect of Sladesbridge Court on its own hilltop beyond the valley. A one-carriage drive wound up the bank, meandering so that a visitor would believe himself approaching the vicarage only to find he was looped back around, no closer than when he began the journey.

The home itself was quaint. A three bay, two-story, grey stone cottage with a single tree standing sentry. It would appear drab were it not for a cheery front door painted red. Inside could be described as either pokey or cozy, depending on perspective. J'non opted for cozy. The parlor overlooked the grounds by way of a lone, square window. To one side, the barn could be seen with its cows, poultry, and crop allotment, and straight ahead the wandering driveway. The fireplace was like everything in the vicarage, small and without adornment. A modest country home, befitting a humble vicar. The Harveys only kept one manservant who tended to the animals more than themselves and a housekeeper who arrived from the village in the mornings to cook and tidy, leaving by midday, unless guests were expected, then she stayed later but never past dusk.

In a way J'non could not explain, the cottage and Gwen's company felt like home away from home. Turning from the window, she realized with a start that Gwen had been talking.

"If it weren't for Mrs. Green, I don't know how I would keep the house clean," Gwen was saying. "I think at times—but not often, mind, as some things are best left in the past—what my mother would say to see Obadiah and the pups march down the hallway, mud prints and a halo of dust in their wake. When I *do* think of what she would say, I tell Mrs. Green to leave the mess a little longer." Gwen laughed.

"Oh dear. Am I to understand your mother wouldn't favor muddy prints?"

"My lady, J'non that is, my mother came from impeccable lineage, not a mar in the line. With her nose held aloft, she viewed the world below her. 'Tis no wonder she sniffed so often, what with the altitude of her nostrils. When she saw the new curate had caught my eye, she refused to let me leave the house for a month, not even for Sunday service, because, mind, who do you think was preaching the sermon? 'Twas my father who accepted the suit when he saw it a losing battle, but my mother never approved. She had in mind someone altogether different for me. You'll pardon my saying, I wouldn't trade Obadiah even for a blond-haired and blue-eyed prince."

As if on cue, the vicar opened the parlor door, rambunctious dogs pushing past him to snuffle out the guest, who they were certain had a hidden treat for them. J'non rubbed behind their ears and cooed in greeting.

Gwen exhaled from puffed cheeks. "Out! Out I said! No one is permitted entry without first changing shoes."

The Reverend Harvey bowed to J'non, patted his leg for the dogs to heel, then said as he turned to leave, "We have to change your paws, boys. Mummy's orders."

Tossing her gaze to the ceiling, Gwen said, "Should we be blessed with children, it'll be my luck to have all boys."

In less than five minutes, the vicar and dogs returned sans boots, the former clad in low-heeled shoes, the latter with lolling tongues and wagging tails, all paws intact and clean.

Mr. Harvey took his seat in a chair by the window, the dogs flopping at his feet, panting. "I have no doubt, my lady, my high-in-the-instep wife has been praising the housekeeper in my absence." After J'non's laugh confirmed his assumption, he continued, "Who she needs to be praising is the bishop. Had I not received the vicar living so soon after our marriage, I would not have hired a housekeeper."

"Nonsense," Gwen said. "You didn't have a house-keeper because you were a bachelor."

"Ah, yes, that must have been the reason, my toff-ish wife, nothing at all to do with my curate's income."

"Obadiah!" Gwen shrieked before turning to J'non. "You see with what I must contend? I should have married the gentleman Mother had chosen for me."

The vicar waggled his eyebrows at J'non. "You realize she's held that over my head these past six years." In a nasal imitation of Gwen, he said, "Shoulda' married that nice octogenarian with his fondness for asking 'wha' wha' wha''after my every word. That ear trumpet, my lady, *yoohoo!*" Mr. Harvey batted his eyelashes and fluttered his fingers in a flirty wave.

Gwen hid her face behind her hands.

J'non laughed until she had to dab her eyes with her handkerchief.

"I suppose," Mr. Harvey teased, "the two of you have been whinging all afternoon?"

Gwen scoffed. "Nothing of the sort. We're plan-ning the October fête. Important business, this."

"You'll have plenty more time to plan. Looks as though Lady Pickering may well be staying for dinner."

J'non sobered. "Thank you for the invitation, Mr. Harvey, but I'll be leaving as soon as I finish my tea."

"Afraid not." The vicar nodded to the window. "Storm clouds are on the move. Assuming they don't roll past again. You'd never make it to the Court in time, not on foot."

A glance out the window showed only sunshine, though the solitary tree swayed ominously.

Seeing her look past him out the window, he said, "They're coming from the other direction, my lady, heading towards Sladesbridge now. Fast approaching. Better stay here until they pass."

"Take her in the gig, Obadiah," Gwen offered. "You can make quick time that way."

"So I'm stuck in the rain on my return? No, thank you. Besides, I already sent Markle home for the day. No one here to hitch the horse. By the time I did, we could be halfway into our second course. No, 'fraid she's here until the sky clears. I'll hook up the gig after the clouds pass. Personally, I'm hoping for a biblical rain. Lord knows we need it."

As he talked, the room darkened, the sun presumably dipping behind a cloud. She hated to delay her return home, but the vicar was right. Best to wait out the storm.

Trevor's horse snorted as he trotted across the field, the marquess surveying the damage caused by the sheep. Only a week ago, he would have considered it progress. In the short time the sheep had grazed, they had trampled and eaten a hefty amount of brush, leaving bare swaths of land.

At the time, using sheep had sounded rational. Burning the brush would have caused more harm than good during a drought. Ploughing would have been impossible with the brush so overgrown, the ground hardpacked and rocky. Use the sheep, he had thought. A grand plan. *Ha.* He cursed his ignorance.

Why had he *not* consulted the gentlemen farmers as J'non pointed out? Although he had justified to her that their fields were not hillside, as his were, the truth was pride. He had been too proud to admit to his tenants he knew nothing about farming. Sheer arrogance. His father would not have sought aid. His father would have done as he had done—taken charge of the situation based on his own assessment.

Another lie he had told himself. Admiral the Lord Tidwell had put faith in his steward, Mr. Lloyd Barmby, Sr. The steward had served as his batman for years, loyal and trusted. No, the admiral would have delegated the task to those who knew better. Trevor cursed aloud, causing Gunner to bark and the horse to shimmy. Mr. Barmby, Sr. would not know anything about hillside or Yorkshire farming either, but he had the means to find out, likely sending recommendations within a fortnight. Had he not proven himself the most reliable of stewards with Tidwell Hall?

Pride. Dashed pride. Trevor clicked to guide the horse forward, Gunner pacing alongside.

Dark clouds loomed on the horizon. Would they pass by as they had the other day? He hoped not. Never had the need for rain been so great. As the thought occurred, a stiff wind blustered past, sharp and chilling, sending a shiver down his spine, in juxtaposition to the heat of the sun overhead. The closer he drew to the house, the windier and cooler the air, and the darker the sky beyond the Court. The distant moors were blackened by the rolling clouds. He flinched as a flash of lightning rent the sky, echoed by a crack and rumble of thunder.

By the time he arrived home, the wind howled.

The horse safe at the stable, Trevor strode into the house, Gunner on his heels. The butler stepped into the vestibule from the Great Hall and bowed in greeting.

"Hawkins," he ordered without breaking stride, "have Lady Pickering meet me in the study."

"Lady Pickering is from home, my lord."

Trevor pivoted mid-step to face the butler. "From home? Where?"

"She set out for the vicarage an hour ago, my lord."

"I hope Jimmy has enough sense to bring her home before the storm, or he'll have a devil of a time traversing the drive."

Hawkins bowed his head. "She walked, my lord, rather than take the carriage."

Trevor cursed again. More to himself than to the butler, he said, "If she tries walking home, she'll be caught in the storm. Have her horse readied—no, never mind, there won't be time."

Without another word to Hawkins, he signaled for Gunner to stay inside, then headed back to the stables, hoping his horse was still saddled. Had the clouds not looked so ominous, he would not have given rain a second thought, letting her wait out the weather at the vicarage. He could not take that risk.

If the sky were as angry as it looked, she could be stranded for hours. He did not think the Harveys had a closed carriage, only the gig, leaving her no safe way to return home.

He made it to the stables as they were leading his horse into the loose box. A nod and grunt had him back on the horse and headed in the direction of the vicarage. Behind him, darkness rolled. A reconnaissance cloud blotted out the sun, a forbidding chill in the air. Their prayers for rain would soon be answered, and he feared they would be answered in spades.

A persistent rumble spurred his mount towards the valley.

Throughout the village, parishioners were battening down the hatches, as his father used to say. Trevor did not spare anyone a second glance. His destination was beyond the vale. With each clap of thunder, he winced, knowing the sky behind him was black as night, strobed with the zigzag of lightning.

The drive. At last. He wound his way up the bank, pushing his horse as though the hounds of hell were behind him. Who could be afraid of a little English rainstorm? He chided. His answer was a demonic roar, a cacophonous symphony of wind and thunder. It was too late to question if they could make it back to the Court in time. Grab J'non and go, he told himself. Fling her onto the saddle like a damsel in distress and set off at a gallop. Harrowing romance was better left in Gothic novels.

Steadying his horse by the front door, ready to ride, he pounded a fist to the red oak. He waited. He grunted. He cursed. From inside, he could hear dogs barking. He pounded again.

The Reverend Harvey flung open the door, his expression changing from one of pique to perplexity. "Lord Pickering—"

"No time. Where's Lady Pickering?"

"In the parlor, my lord. We're—"

As Trevor dodged the overexcited pups and stepped past the vicar into the narrow, wood-paneled hallway, a gust of wind pushed its way through the door, growled, then retreated, pulling the door behind it with a hearty *bang*.

The vicar had the audacity to laugh. "The Lord knows how to answer a prayer. Storm's a-coming right enough."

With a grunt, Trevor led the way to the parlor at the far end of the pokey hall. He stepped into a peaceful scene of J'non and Mrs. Harvey tittering over tea, as though the apocalypse were not at the doorstep.

Mrs. Harvey rose with a curtsy. "Lord Pickering, what a pleasant surprise."

Trevor bowed, then turned to J'non. "I hate to interrupt or appear ill-mannered, but I've come to bring you home before the storm arrives. We should make it if we leave now."

Mr. Harvey came up behind him. "No need to hurry, my lord. Stay. We can celebrate the rain together."

J'non stood, smoothed her hands over her dress, and began to thank the vicar's wife just as the house groaned and the front door rattled. Before she could finish her sentence, a sheet of rain slapped the parlor window, startling all and sundry. The room dipped into darkness.

Mr. Harvey said, "That settles that."

"My horse," was all Trevor said before darting past the vicar and back down the hall.

The greyhounds waited by Mr. Harvey's chair, whining. Gwen set about retrieving and lighting candles. Mrs. Green, the housekeeper, had not yet departed for the day, and was now as stranded as J'non, but took it in stride with a smile, peeking into the parlor to inquire if she should bring a fresh tray.

J'non stood at the window, arms crossed to hug her torso, watching Trevor and Mr. Harvey secure the thoroughbred into the barn. The rain rolled in waves, silent and clear, then torrential on a billow of wind, then once more silent and clear. He had come for her, she marveled. He cared about her safety. It might not strike some as unusual for a husband to care for the safety of his wife, but it struck her. Save her parents, no one had cared if she lived or died. Her death, to be honest, would have been more convenient for some. A burden relieved. *He had come for her*.

"They'll be wet through," Gwen said, accepting a handful of linen from Mrs. Green.

Her eyes roving from window to parlor door, J'non awaited his return, her heart in her throat.

His unexpected entry had not taken her by surprise as it had the Harveys. The two had been playfully quarreling when J'non had seen him approach on horseback. Rather than question his arrival to the vicarage or fear something was wrong, she had been starry-eyed by the dashing figure he had cut atop his steed. Powerful and commanding with a determined and noble brow. His thighs had shown to advantage, the musculature evident beneath the buckskin, flexing as he nearly leapt off the horse to dismount before stopping, all in his single-minded urgency to reach her, the damsel in distress.

It did not matter that she was not in distress. Had he not thought of the likelihood of Mr. Harvey taking her home in the gig? Or of her setting out at first sign of the storm? She could have, at that very moment, been arriving home. But then, he might have thought to overtake her in either circumstance.

When he had stormed into the room, his tall, lean frame filling the doorway, J'non had flushed. His usual stodgy demeanor had been windswept, replaced with a passionate exigency. From across the room, she had felt his desire to rescue her, the masculine protector ready to save the damsel. Again, it did not matter that she was not in distress.

The dogs, Sammy and Simon, scrambled to their feet with yips and yawns seconds before the parlor door opened. Mr. Harvey and Trevor shouldered their way into the room with a shower of droplets and shared laughter. J'non raised her hand to her heart. With his hair matted to his face and his coat clinging to his shoulders, Trevor was a sight fit for a storybook hero.

Gwen made short work of doling out the linen.

Hushing her flustered nerves, J'non approached Trevor. "Allow me to take your coat. We can let it dry by the fire."

He regarded her with a half-smile then relaxed his arms so she could tug off the coat. Underneath, his shirt and waistcoat were remarkably dry. Turning to face her, he bent low enough for her to unknot his cravat, which was as damp as his coat and clearly chafing his neck. Although she moved with methodical efficiency, she could feel her cheeks warm beneath his steady gaze. The dripping of his hair onto his waistcoat sobered her thoughts. She bowed away with a shy smile so he could dry his hair with the linen.

Mr. Harvey was explaining to Gwen, "This is why a gentleman ought to wear proper shoes at all times, ready at a moment's notice."

As J'non returned to her chair after draping the coat and cravat over a stand Gwen had readied, she saw Gwen swat at her husband's arm, both chortling. The couple could not be more obviously fond of each other. In a way, they reminded her of her parents with their verbal sparring and life-loving nature. Their ages were even in keeping with J'non's fondest childhood memories. The Harveys were, if J'non hazarded a guess, in their early thirties at a stretch. She wondered if they would fare well with the Osbornes. Gwen and Lady Osborne might favor each other, but she was not sure about Sir Roland and the vicar. Sir Roland bordered on being dandified, while Mr. Harvey was more of a sporting man, a jolly chap one might invite to the public house.

Trevor, as dry as he could be without a change of attire, accepted the seat next to her. Between dandified and sporting, what sort of gentleman was Trevor? Stealing a glance, she blushed to see him looking at her.

He leaned in to say, "Seems we'll be trespassing on their kindness until the storm passes. Will you mind riding back with me, or should I send for the carriage?"

"I would find no greater pleasure than to ride with you," she said.

His eyebrows raised, and his lips curled into a smirk.

She could feel herself flush from neck to hairline. Her words had sounded far saucier than she intended. She had only meant, well, that was to say, oh, fiddle-sticks. This was *Lord Pickering* for pity's sake. Her attention on her folded hands, she ignored his pene-trating gaze, hoping her cheeks would cool before the Harveys stopped bickering long enough to engage with their guests.

In the time it took Mrs. Green to bring a fresh tray, the parlor had darkened into what could have been mistaken for the black of night, the only light that of candles and hearth fire. Outside, the storm raged, beating against the walls as though it meant to come inside. The bellow of the wind was so fierce at times, it silenced conversation.

By the second cup of tea, they had relaxed into the humor of Mr. Harvey's narratives, the storm nothing more than a backdrop.

"They were in their eighties, I tell you," he said, regaling them with a couple he had wedded during his first year as a curate. "A widower and a widow, more deeply in love than any couple I had seen. Which brings me to the disagreeable couple who wed only so the bridegroom could avoid jail. Forced to marry the girl after she found herself in an *interesting* condition. The father threatened the law. Being but an inexperienced curate, I had the luck of officiating in place of the rector. Never have you seen a gent kick up the dust in a church quite like this beau. I tell you, he was protesting through the whole ceremony, claiming—and I shouldn't say this in front of the ladies, but I will because if there's one thing I've never been accused of it's being a decorous gentleman—that he couldn't be certain he was the father."

J'non gasped. Trevor clucked his tongue.

Gwen said, "Obadiah paints himself as a blackguard, but don't believe a word of it. He rises at two in the morning some days to prepare his sermons. Not once has he accepted payment from the laborers for christenings or burials. What tithes he earns, he gives back to the parish by way of dinners, charity baskets, and the like."

"She would turn me into a saint if you let her," said the vicar with a chuckle. "It's for her own sanity, I tell you. To convince herself she married a good man." He leaned in conspiratorially and said, "What she won't tell you is I brew my own ale." He winked.

Gwen waved him to hush. "Ignore him. He comes from a long line of clergymen, all educated at Oxford."

"She sings my praises, my lord and lady, because she fears the marquess will be wanting to assign the church living himself."

Although he said it in good humor, the room fell silent, all eyes avoiding Trevor's.

The marquess cleared his throat and said, "I have it on good authority the church living is already well assigned, and I don't just say that because I'm being held hostage until the storm abates."

J'non did not think herself mistaken in seeing Gwen's shoulders relax.

Before the vicar could respond, Gwen said, "It was glad tidings when the bishop paid us a call to bring the news of the vicar living. Obadiah had moved from one parish to the next, called to serve as curate for a vicar on holiday or a vicar who had taken ill or... well, I don't mean to sound ungrateful, as he must go where he's called, but he needn't have bothered to unpack. He won't admit this, but he worried he had upset the bishop to be moved so often. I believe it was because the bishop had faith in him that he sent him."

"It was the hand of the Lord himself," the vicar said, "who brought me to Gwen's parish. Not long after we married, I received the vicarship. As John Heywood said, we can't always see the wood for the trees. In time, His plan becomes clear."

J'non held her tongue. While she understood the Reverend Harvey's point, she could not say her experiences proved that to be true. She was not in jeopardy of losing her faith, but she could not bring herself to believe all that happened was preordained as God's plan. To think so *would* shake her faith. There were too many grievances, too many tragedies. The hand of God? She hoped not.

No one noticed her silence. There was no opportunity to notice it, as the dogs leapt onto their feet in a barking frenzy. Startled, everyone looked at everyone else. The rain pounded. The wind whipped. The thunder hammered. Over the din, they could hardly hear the banging against the vicarage door or the cries for help.

Chapter 12

A t the racket of raised voices in the hall, Trevor bade J'non and Mrs. Harvey to stay in the parlor. The Reverend Harvey, along with the greyhounds, had left to answer the front door, but as the shouting increased, so did Trevor's concern. He presumed the callers wished to be heard over the storm. The ruckus from the dogs, however, drowned out the exchange between the vicar and whomever had knocked, leaving Trevor at a loss as to if an argument ensued or otherwise.

Closing the parlor door behind him, Trevor walked towards the entry. Ahead, Mr. Harvey held the dogs at bay. Past the vicar, Trevor could see not one man but several.

Patting a hand on the vicar's shoulder, Trevor asked, "May I be of service?"

The men at the door began shouting all at once, their voices overlapping incoherently.

Mr. Harvey angled to say, "The valley is flooding."

"Flooding?" Trevor eyed the men in alarm. "It hasn't been raining longer than half an hour."

"Flooding, your lordship!" One of the men cried above the storm in a broad Yorkshire accent. "Into the houses an aal."

The marquess nodded curtly. Leaving the vicar to reassure the men of their aid, he returned to the parlor in brisk strides. The ladies wore their concern in their expressions. J'non was pale, worry lines framing a frown.

"Men from the village are here. There's flooding in the valley. Don't know the extent," Trevor said, brief but pointed, not wanting to dally. "Mr. Harvey and I will offer what assistance we can. Stay here. Both of you. Aside from the Court, the vicarage has the highest ground. You'll be safe here."

Mrs. Harvey stood, hand to heart. "The church. Take as many as you can to the church."

A quick nod, then he turned his attention to J'non, who had also risen from her chair. "I'll return as soon as I can. I must make haste. Stay with Mrs. Harvey."

"But—" she began to protest.

He held a staying hand, offered a cursory bow to take his leave, then rejoined Mr. Harvey. The housekeeper and vicar were trying to entice the dogs into the kitchen with treats.

Mr. Harvey said over his shoulder, "It'll be too short for you, but I've an extra greatcoat in the cupboard." Muttering as he nudged the dogs, "Not that coats will do any good against this deluge."

Trevor flung open the door to the garderobe where the Harveys kept hats, umbrellas, and sundries. He grabbed two greatcoats. Both were on the shabby side, but they would serve, never mind his tailored coat and cravat were still drying in the parlor. Passing one to the vicar, he shrugged into the other greatcoat.

Trevor said, "Mrs. Harvey recommends we direct them to the church."

"Sensible." The vicar reached past Trevor to swap his shoes for boots.

They were taking an eternity. Wasting time. Coats. Boots. Dogs. Wives. Plans. All the while the villagers needed help and leadership.

Ill equipped with little more than his riding boots, good intentions, and a calf-length greatcoat that had seen too many winters and rainy days, he jogged alongside the vicar down the driveway towards the valley. They nearly lost footing several times. The lawn around them was slick, the drive a muddy stream. The rain pounded overhead, limiting visibility. By the time they reached the rough and uneven road to the village, water lapped at their ankles.

Although they were a quarter of a mile from the village's edge, they had an uninterrupted view. Ahead was chaos. Goats and sheep were led out of paddocks and onto the road. Children screeched. More than one family had settled atop their roof holding aloft blankets in a failed attempt to stave off rain. One woman tried to sweep the water out and over her threshold. A couple barricaded their front door. A few men tried to repair a leaking roof in the downpour. Families retrieved valuables from their homes. Shopkeepers loaded supplies into carts. Animals wandered loose. Dogs barked.

"What awaits beyond the main road?" Trevor questioned aloud, more to himself than to Mr. Harvey. "Where are we supposed to begin? How are we to help?"

His companion pointed to the men who had sought their aid at the vicarage, the group waving them over to help move a cart and donkey, the wheels stuck, the cart laden with children, poultry, and goods. He had to rein in Mr. Harvey from running to assist, for just past them were several more families shouting for help.

A crack of thunder shook the earth.

Above the rain, Trevor cried, "We need to slow the water."

The vicar shouted in reply, "A fruitless effort, I fear, when the water is coming from the sky."

Everywhere Trevor looked, water flowed. Yes, it was rushing down the road towards the hill on which stood the vicarage and church, but it did not seem to be coming from a single source rather streaming in between buildings and showering off rooftops.

As Trevor splashed down the road, the vicar with him, they ordered everyone in sight to head for the church. The farther they slogged, the stronger the current.

The Reverend Harvey pointed ahead. "The worst is coming from Sladesbridge."

Of course. Water flowed downstream. The estate was the highest point. Water sought the lowest level. An obvious assessment, but the harder it rained and the higher the water rose around his boots, the less clearly he was able to think.

Trevor slowed his pace. "Too late to block the flow, but we could divert it."

Rain streamed down the vicar's face. He blinked rapidly. "The beck. Northwest of the village."

Trevor nodded. "Last I saw, the streambed was dry. I'd wager it isn't now," he said, shielding his eyes from the rain with a hand over his brow. "Even if it's overflowing it'll be better for the floodwaters to follow the beck than through the village."

"And into homes, paddocks, and farmlands."

Plan formulated, however tenuous, they signaled to every man they passed.

"Women and children to the church!" The vicar cried.

"All men follow us!" Trevor shouted in command. "We must redirect the flow of water to the beck!"

She could not swim.

Trevor recalled this fact with clarity, thankful J'non was safe at the vicarage. She and Mrs. Harvey were probably polishing off another round of tea and cutting up gaily.

Mmm. Tea. He was parched.

At least J'non was safe.

While the worst of the waterflow had been diverted to the beck and away from the village, several smallholders' farms suffered. Around the outlying homes, he had needed to tread water to reach stranded families and animals. The undercurrent in the deeper waters was surprisingly strong.

It could have been worse, he knew. Much worse.

The rain had abated, only an intermittent drizzle now. The sky had lightened, hinting to a late afternoon sun. He had lost track of time. Surveying the extent of the damage would be tasked for later, as well as an investigation of what caused the flooding, at least to this severity. He must prevent this from happening again. For now, he had done all he could.

Trevor, alongside a bedraggled Mr. Harvey and several other men, trudged uphill to the church. His stockings squelched in scuffed boots. His clothes were soaked and torn. The greatcoat lent by the vicar was in tatters. It was time Mr. Harvey had a new greatcoat anyway, Trevor reasoned. If his valet did not resign after seeing the condition of his attire, Trevor would task him with reimbursing the vicar for his kindness by way of a new greatcoat, nothing ostentatious or with too many capes, but something new and fine in quality, nonetheless.

As ardently as the marquess longed for the comfort of his bed, it would be endless hours before he could retire. Provisions would need to be made for the parishioners temporarily housed in the church, a task he could delegate, but he needed to ensure all had arrived first, no missing families, at least of those who had not stubbornly refused to leave their homes despite the rising waters. His attention misbehaved. He wanted his wife. One boot in front of the other to the church, his eyes darted to the vicarage instead. He wanted his wife. He wanted to rest his cheek against her temple and feel her embrace, reassuring and safe.

The church doors stood open. A few people looked out to the valley. Worry? Curiosity? Fear? Trevor did not turn around to survey the village scene. His shoulders rounded, encumbered by the burden of responsibility.

Inside, everything was far more organized than he had expected. Families grouped together with clean linens and blankets. A few noshed on food. Some of the children played, laughter rather than tears filling the nave. Halting, he looked around, confused. He expected huddled disarray, sounds of sobbing, bouts of hysteria, hungry children, chaos, all needing more than he could provide, more than he knew how to provide. Near the pulpit, he spied Mrs. Harvey tending to a gentleman's leg wound. Her housekeeper carried a basket from family to family, doling out what looked to be an assortment of fruit and mince pies.

A hand on his shoulder shook him.

The Reverend Harvey said, "Our better halves have been busy."

Whatever Mr. Harvey said after that, Trevor did not hear. His eyes swept the room until he spotted her. J'non, disheveled and muddy, mirrored the vicar's wife on the opposite side of the room, kneeling in attendance to an elderly man, this one with a nasty cut on his arm from what Trevor could see at a distance.

Relief mingled with anger. Her hair clumped in wet tangles. Her mud splattered dress clung to her figure. Her half-boots—no, she was barefoot in only stockings that were torn along one side and black on the soles. Ignoring the tightness in his chest, the marquess curled his fingers into his palm and marched across the room. When he reached her, she looked up in surprise. The man mumbled gratitude and platitudes aplenty, none of which Pickering heard. J'non stood on trembling legs, looking him up and down before clasping his hand in hers with a featherlight touch.

She turned his hand over and said, "Bruises and cuts, nothing terrible. I'll be careful not to rub the blisters." Reaching into a basket at her feet, she retrieved what looked like a small container of tallow. "At least you needn't secure new riding gloves." She chided, "Yours are still at the vicarage, being of no help to your hands." With a whisper of a touch, she rubbed his palm with the tallow, a balm to the chafed skin.

Resisting the urge to enfold her in his arms, he growled. "You disobeyed me."

She ignored him, turning her attention to his other hand, unfurling his fingers and soothing with a thin layer of the whipped tallow.

"I ordered you to stay at the vicarage," he said, his voice low, his words shaking with anger. "As my wife, you swore to obey my command."

It was not about her being his legal property, about his being her master. It was about his being responsible for her safety, about her putting herself into harm's way. His orders were for her own good. Could she not see that?

When she said nothing in her defense or even in submission, he continued, his tone as hushed as he could manage. "You've endangered yourself by going against my orders." He exhaled through clenched teeth. "Did you not understand the danger? The storm, the high waters, the debris — did you not understand why I bade you to stay?"

Rather than appear chagrined or chastised, her cheeks pinkened, and her lips curved into a smile. "Because you care?"

He seethed. "Of course, I care. You're my wife. I'm duty bound to protect you."

Her smile broadened as if he had spoken words of flattery.

"Damn it, woman." Trevor gave into the urge and pulled her to his chest, wrapping his arms around her. Resting his cheek against her damp hair, he muttered,

"If I ever thought you delicate or afflicted by tender sensibilities, I know better now."

All his words of compassion stuck in his throat. Had she gone into the village to help guide people to the church? Had she merely walked back and forth between vicarage and church to bring supplies? He could not bring himself to ask. Of all the things he could say to express his anger, to reassure himself of her well-being, to convey his relief and happiness, to share his affection, he stood in silence, hugging her to him.

From beneath lowered eyelashes, J'non eyed her husband. She pretended to embroider to busy her hands and appear occupied. Trevor, meanwhile, was preoccupied by his thoughts. Although a book lay in his lap, he had not turned a page in half an hour. The only one in the room genuinely engaged in activity was Gunner, who chewed a bone before the hearth, none the wiser that anything unusual had happened over the course of the day.

After spending over an hour at the church, they had retrieved his horse and coat from the vicarage and headed home via a lengthy, circuitous route to avoid high water. The storm had passed. The sun shone for the ride to Sladesbridge. However warm the rays, the air had turned frosty following the rain. A biting wind had chilled her through the damp dress. Upon their return, Trevor had requested hot baths for them both and ordered all staff to meet in the Great Hall an hour later.

He had apprised everyone of the situation in the village, offering the evening and morrow for anyone needing to visit family at the church or elsewhere. No one knew the condition of the surrounding lands — how extensive was the flooding? — only that of the village in the vale. The route Trevor had found for their trek home had been unaffected by floodwaters, so was the damage only along the valley? J'non resolved to write to the Osbornes.

Supper had been a quiet affair, yet Trevor had invited her to the drawing room for tea afterwards. The quietness resumed. As unsettling as the silence might have been, she found it comforting. It conveyed unexpressed emotions, much of which felt like solace.

When Trevor had walked into the church, J'non's heart seized. Or perhaps, conversely, it had resumed beating at seeing him safe. She and Gwen had not remained in the parlor longer than a quarter of an hour, too worried about their husbands to sit still, and then fretting about the villagers making it to the church. They had set in motion the gathering of food, linen, and supplies before braving the storm. It had been a long afternoon. As focused as she had been on her work, her attention had turned to the church doors every time they opened, hoping the newcomer would be Trevor, worrying when it was not. Every manner of possible tragedy had haunted her. Until he arrived at last.

All she saw as he approached was a man on the brink of exhaustion who nevertheless put the care of others ahead of himself. His words had been harsh, his tone angry, but he had not been the autocratic tyrant he tried to portray, only a husband scared for the safety of his wife. No, make that Trevor scared for J'non's safety. For *her*.

The *thud* of his book closing drew her attention from the forgotten embroidery.

"I'll not come to you tonight," he said. "I'll spend the evening in my study. I need to plan my approach for repairs, damage assessment…" He waved a hand rather than finish the sentence, as though words took too much effort.

Ignoring the flush of what he implied, she studied him. His forehead creased with worry lines. His eyelids drooped. His shoulders slumped. Although he studied her in return, his eyes did not focus.

"No," she said firmly. "You need sleep. I'll see you to your bedchamber myself if I must. You're in no condition to make plans."

He quirked a brow but said nothing.

"Don't think of disobeying me," she said. "You'd be foolish to disobey an order from the Marchioness of Pickering."

She held his gaze, fighting the impulse to bite her lip or avert her gaze.

"As you wish, my lady," he said, his reply subservient, his expression in recognition of her tease. "Shall we rise at the usual time? Break our fast, then make plans in the study?"

Setting her work aside, she clarified, "Meet in the morning room, then go our separate ways rather than the ride to the lake?"

He shook his head. "Unless you're opposed, I mean *we* shall make plans. Together."

Oh. This time she did bite her lip and avert her gaze. She hardly knew what to think. It had been a gamble to poke fun. Perhaps she should give him orders more often.

Emboldened, she raised her chin and met his eyes. "Yes. We'll strategize. Together. Until then… is it too early for us to retire?"

However exhausted he was, the corners of his lips inched into a slow smile.

Chapter 13

Head in his hands, Trevor fisted tufts of his hair, his gaze on the smooth finish of his desk.

"You can't shoulder the blame, Trevor," J'non said from an adjacent chair, extending a tentative hand to pat his arm, then rub his shoulder, as if to massage away the burden.

"Your reassurance is a kindness I don't deserve." He heaved a sigh.

With a squeeze to his shoulder, she said, "I'll give you this. Your decision did not help matters. In fact, yes, I agree it exacerbated the situation."

Tilting his head, he studied her askance.

"No, don't look at me like that. You are *not* to blame. I'm merely acquiescing that your actions didn't help, but I don't see how an overstocked field and a few days of hoofing and grazing could cause an entire village to flood."

He returned his attention to the desk. "If not for your advice to move the sheep, it would have been worse."

"You've spent only one day assessing the damage. Most of the village isn't even accessible yet, not until the waters recede more, so you can't possibly know all of the contributing causes."

"The ground was too hard to retain water." He groaned. "Had the sheep not eaten and hoofed the heather, gorse, and moss, the undergrowth could have helped soak up the water. My choice diverted the waterflow *into* the village."

"But you then diverted it *out* and saved lives," she reasoned.

Trevor dropped his hands to the desk and fanned his fingers, the cold wood soothing to his blistered palms. "All I can do is make it right somehow. I've waited too long to address the home farm. At one time, you claimed knowledge of hill farming. Will you help me make this right?"

"You know I will. As best I can. For now, our attention needs to be on the people, at least until the waters recede."

"But we can plan. I should have already recruited farm laborers. I'll do that while we plan."

Why did it feel as though days had been wasted? It was illogical, as he could not move any faster. The day following the flood had seen J'non helping at the church while he walked the home farm and what parts of the village he could access, not only assessing the damage to prepare for repairs but to understand what caused the severity of the flood. Mr. Willie Hawkins, the head gardener, had accompanied, along with a few men from his landscaping crew, as well as Mr. Galfrid Thompson, the construction overseer.

The realization of the destruction caused by Trevor's simple sheep grazing plan had resulted in a quiet evening at home and a sleepless night. Only today, the day after his survey, did he feel brave enough to confess to J'non his sins. Married only three weeks, yet he curiously anticipated her reaction, craved it even, never mind he fought against her reassurances with his insistence of being the villain.

Reaching out to her, he clasped her hand in his and laced their fingers, letting their entwined hands rest on the arm of her chair. He needed this. He needed her. Did she realize how much?

"I'm going to make this right, J'non. I'll not disappoint our neighbors and tenants again."

She started to speak but changed her mind, allowing silence to fill the space. They shared the silence, comfortable, content in each other's company. He rubbed his thumb over hers.

With a deep breath, he said, "I never learned how to run an estate."

It was not an excuse or a defense of poor decisions, merely part of his self-blame, one of the realities that kept him tossing in his sleep last night. As a baron's heir, he should have been groomed from birth onward, taught estate management by dedicated tutors. Instead, his mother had been the primary caretaker through his formative years, leaving him overlong in the nursery with a nanny, not a tutor in sight. Once that part of his life passed, his father had relied heavily on the steward rather than lead by example. In his authoritative way, the admiral had guided only by rules.

"My father," he continued, "was not neglectful of my education, merely too distracted to take part personally. He mourned my mother's departure and suffered from his injury. Don't think I'm blaming him for my ignorance."

Trevor had been too busy idolizing his father to think there may be a time when the admiral would not be present. His father had seemed immortal. Even after Father's passing, Trevor left everything to the steward, who ran the estate singlehandedly.

"I never prepared for life after Father's death. I wasn't equipped to oversee a barony, much less a marquessate. The barony is little more than a collection of tenancies. Now I have land to oversee, farms, farm laborers, tenant farmers, legalities…" He let his words trail off before scoffing. "I even have the power to replace the vicar with someone of my choosing. One ought not inherit without the proper education, the training to know how to make good, altruistic decisions. There are ways this is done, J'non. There is training, tradition, education. An aristocrat is not someone like your father. Not a wealthy business-man with a year or ten of trial-and-error experience. Rather we are trained from birth for a lifelong role, the security and efficiency of Crown and Country in our hands. Yet how was I prepared? Endless games of spillikins with my nanny followed by unquestioning obedience to my father."

Laughing humorlessly, he squeezed her fingers.

"Did your father not arrange for your education?" J'non asked.

"My father was a military man. His values were not in the estate. To him, the barony was nothing more than another war medal. He arranged for my education after he returned home, but his instructions for my lessons were military history, battle strategies, and the like. While he never mentioned my future in the Royal Navy, instilling instead the importance of my continuing the family line, I suspect he hoped the lessons would impassion me to follow in his footsteps.

I know he wanted more sons, two at least, one to be heir and one to follow his path, but he was stuck with only me — the embodiment of both and neither. As such, he prepared me for both yet neither."

"And then he died." She lowered her eyes and added, "I didn't mean that to sound unfeeling. I only meant — "

"I understand you," he reassured. "I was a month from my majority when he passed, already a man. My only goal was to ensure his baronial legacy continued, easy enough when the steward did all the work — and still does, I might add."

"Was it his age?"

"You mean, how did he die? In his sleep. From too much laudanum."

"Oh."

"Let me rephrase. It wasn't how that sounded." Trevor's conscience begged to differ. "He had sustained an injury, one that pained him. Every year was worse until, that final year, the pain was so debilitating, he could no longer walk. He had the ability but not the will. The nights were the worst. He suffered from night terrors. The laudanum helped ease his pain. The pain must have been unbearable that night, for he took more than the physician recommended." An understatement. The bottle had been empty.

"At least he passed peacefully," she consoled.

"Yes. There's that."

What Trevor did not add was that he had attended his father's bedside that evening, as with many evenings before, and knew neither injury nor nightmare pained the admiral that night. It was not Trevor that his father had wanted at his bedside. It was for Lady

Tidwell he yearned, for his wife. Always his wife. There was no reason for Trevor to blame himself for leaving his father unattended during those crucial moments—had it not been that night, it would have been the next.

The study door creaked open. They both looked up, but no one stepped into the room.

J'non, who sat closer to the edge of the desk, exclaimed first, her tone from somber to charmed. "You've found us at last. Are you terribly bored?"

Panting his way to the desk was Gunner. The traitor went straight to J'non rather than to Trevor and rested his snout in her lap. Wide, expectant eyes looked from her to Trevor.

"I do believe," J'non said, "someone wants to play fetch outside."

With a laugh, Trevor said, "That's the best idea I've heard all day."

The queue to exchange words with the vicar was short given so many of the parishioners attending the Sunday service were residing in the church until further notice. J'non had wondered if Mr. Harvey would even hold service under the circumstances. She had considered offering the use of the chapel on Sladesbridge Court grounds, the same chapel where she and Trevor had wed, but not only was it far too small, it would be an arduous trek for those staying in the church. However soft the ground, the floodwaters had not yet receded. The light rain of the evening before did not help. Good intentions proved unnecessary, for after conversing with those in the church, Mr. Harvey decided it would be business as usual.

Those not residing in the church were forgiving of the makeshift housing around the perimeter of the nave, and doubly forgiving of the nose-tickling odor of unwashed bodies and clothes.

J'non stood next to Trevor in the queue, awaiting their turn to thank the vicar for his sermon. Traditionally, they would have been first to speak with the vicar, but today they had lingered at their pew, welcoming the opportunity to share words with several of the families before making their way to the doors. Once they reached the queue, they declined the offer to move ahead so they could talk with those already in line. Nothing brought J'non greater joy.

Trevor's mood had brightened since their talk in his study the day before. Determined to right the wrong he charged himself of committing, he had spoken of little else than the logistics of village repairs. His resolve proved contagious, filling J'non with anticipation for all the ways they could help turn a dismal situation into one of promise.

Mr. Harvey greeted them with a warm smile and nod as they stepped forward.

After a brief exchange of pleasantries about the sermon, Trevor said, "We'll return in two hours with additional supplies. Cook is working the kitchen staff into a frenzy. We'll have ample food."

"Assuming no one overindulges," Mr. Harvey jested.

J'non touched the vicar's hand when she leaned forward to say tacitly, "I've spoken with the staff, and they're in agreement of *the plan*. If you could prepare what's needed when we return, we'll make the arrangements."

"Gwen will vouch for your sainthood," the vicar said. "Speaking of my better half, you'll notice her absence at my side." He lengthened a wave to the emptiness next to him. "She's gathering, discreetly and in her delicate way, the particulars."

If the villagers had to stay at the church for too long, alternative arrangements would need to be made to set up washing basins and hanging lines in the churchyard, but until necessary, the laundry-maids at the Court had agreed to take on the extra loads. It was one of many such arrangements.

Before leaving, Trevor said to the Reverend Harvey, "If I may, I wish to request a private consultation this afternoon."

"I'll excuse myself the moment you arrive. A clerical matter or a matter of faith?"

"No need to interrupt your work. Whenever is convenient. I merely wish for your opinion, and in small part to recruit your help. I've been sorting the plans for the village repairs and need your advice. Once I resolve the hillside farming complications, we shouldn't see flooding again, but I want to ensure my immediate ideas prepare us for any heavy rains to come."

"Oh, yes, I see." Mr. Harvey puffed out his chest. "You wish for my opinion. Yes, I see." He grinned at them both before saying, "I can't think there's anything we can do to prevent the next flood, though. Inevitable, is it not?"

Trevor furrowed his brows. "Not if I correct my mistake. I caused the flood, however inadvertently.

That is, my decisions with the home farm caused the problem, although I'd rather that fact be kept between us."

"You'll have to tell me what you did or did not do, or *think* you did or did not do, when we talk this afternoon. I can say now, Lord Pickering, you are not to blame. To say so would be akin to blaming Moses. How do you like that, my lord? I've now equated your heroism to Moses's own. You'll be toasting at dinner to my charity with similes."

J'non laid a hand to Trevor's sleeve.

Trevor rested his hand atop hers. "We'll speak on this later," he said to Mr. Harvey. "Suffice it to say, I'm to blame."

As they stepped away, the vicar asked, "You know the valley floods every five years?"

Trevor stopped and turned around. "I beg your pardon."

"I thought you knew. You do know, yes? Every five years. Well, not so predictable. Sometimes not for seven years, but never longer than ten. Or so the villagers told me when I took the living. It flooded our first year. Not as bad as this year. But flood it did. A river right down the main. Nothing you could have done to cause it, my lord, but I'll hear your thoughts on how to prevent it."

As though shocked into silence, Trevor said nothing for the journey home, not until they were in the vestibule and a footman was helping to remove their coats, and even then, not until J'non prompted.

"Are his words a relief or more of a burden?" she asked, her tone light and conversational despite the quickening of her pulse. To have this burden lifted from his shoulders would be a blessing. How could one man carry so much responsibility, most of which he need not carry?

Trevor looked at her, his expression blank.

She clarified, "Relief you're not at fault after all? Or concerned your plans to prevent future floods will not work if the reason for the flood is not the reason after all?"

He was slow to respond, either distracted or trying to unravel her question. She had worded her inquiry carefully, so carefully it sounded convoluted. J'non laced her fingers at her waist, mulling over how to rephrase. It was not that this was a sensitive subject so much as she knew his feelings were tender from the guilt over those silly sheep. Really, his idea had been good. Not well timed during a lengthy drought, but good, nonetheless.

"Both." He rubbed his chin in thought. "When the gardener and carpenter accompanied me, they mentioned their astonishment at having discovered, after all this time, the cause. I hadn't understood their phraseology at the time. Now I do. They implied as much, never said directly. I suppose they, too, thought I knew of the frequency of flooding."

"I wish they had been more direct." She did not want to speak ill of Willie or Galfrid, for they would never have allowed Trevor to blame himself had they known the direction of his thoughts, but she did wish they had spoken about previous floods.

"I feel I've taken two steps backwards," he said. "If I don't know the cause, how can I prevent this? Ah, I'm thinking aloud. We have the villagers to consider today."

As Trevor bent to greet Gunner, Mr. Hawkins stepped forward with a bow and presented a letter for J'non. Flipping it over, she recognized the Osborne insignia stamped in the sealing wax. Not waiting until she returned to her suite, she broke the seal, unfolded the paper, and scanned the letter.

J'non said, "No flooding near the Abbey."

"So, it's only our valley?" Trevor grunted before leading Gunner to his study.

Chapter 14

One week had not been long enough for significant drainage, but it had been long enough to recruit several farmhands and to meet with a few of the surrounding farmers, from tenants to landowners. Or more to the point, for Trevor to meet with them. J'non was satisfied with the vicarious appraisal of the meeting after the fact. "Meeting" sounded impersonal and formal. Casual gathering of likeminded gentlemen over a carnivorous fare wherein the host collaborated with the guests about flood prevention tactics and interrogated them about local farming practices? Much better. Together, J'non and Trevor had decided an invitation to dinner would serve best, with J'non playing the role of quintessential hostess, excusing herself so the men could enjoy their port and conversation.

Now, seated in the study and warmed by the hearth fire with Gunner napping on her feet — a paw draped around her ankles to ensure she could not escape — J'non admired Trevor's profile, one of conviction and purpose. He alternated between pacing from chair to mantel, jotting notes at his desk, and sitting in the chair across from her either pensive with elbow propped on the arm of the chair and chin in palm or leaning forward with arms on his thighs, hands animated as he spoke. J'non enjoyed the spectacle. A man in action. A man turning responsibilities into possibilities.

Currently, he paced, one hand circling the air, the other on his hip. "The more they advised me to lease the farm, the more adamant I became to do the opposite. The farmlands not immediately surrounding the Court are already leased. I'll not lease the home farm. With an estate of nearly sixteen thousand acres, you would think I could handle a fifteen-hundred-acre farm. I wonder that the former marquess had not leased it, honestly. If he had separated the farm into one hundred or even two-hundred-acre leaseholds, he could have turned a tidy profit rather than leaving it to fall to ruin. He could have leased it in its entirety, really."

"You won't consider that option?"

He punched his palm. "Not for a second. Their persuasion has made me my own champion."

J'non smiled to herself. A man of action.

"I've been reading the book my solicitor sent, or books rather. Bloody five volume set on *Practical Husbandry*. I'll say this much for what I've learned: once a foreman is hired, I don't want to lord over him, pretending to know aught about farming and undermining his expertise in the process. What we'll do instead is have the framework decided in advance. I'll hire the man who supports the method of our choosing, and from there, will rely on his expertise. Do you think that's reasonable? Am I being short-sighted?"

"No, that's perfect, Trevor. What did the gentlemen say about the book Mr. Barmby sent?"

"They'd never heard of it and scoffed at learning farming from a book. They'd likewise never heard of this… this… rotation method you describe," he said, stopping at the fireplace to rest his arm on the mantel. "Their recommendations for approaching upland farming consisted of a strip method — we plant in rows around the hill to improve water retention and drainage by slowing the flow at each tier. Several voiced that nothing could be farmed on this land, only good for grazing. When I mentioned your rotation plan, it was met with unanimous nays, with those in favor of trying to farm the land suggesting a four-field rotation instead, the rest returning to the tired point of leasing or putting the sheep to pasture permanently."

J'non shook her head, annoyed the experts were recommending the very methods that had left the farm in this condition. "Field rotation is what I believe was already being used. That, coupled with the poor sowing method, is why the fields have been left too long either fallow or overgrown."

Perhaps the four-field method had worked at one time but became problematic with the former marquess' neglect. Or perhaps the method had not worked, frustrating the marquess into neglecting the fields. There was no way to know. She felt ever so foolish thinking her suggestions superior to those who knew their trade, knew the land, and likely had been passing the knowledge for generations, but the method they advised was, to her mind, outmoded. Why not try something new? There was logic and safety in tried-and-true, but that had obviously not worked on this home farm. It was a gamble.

Trevor perched on the edge of his chair, then stood again, pacing before the hearth. Gunner raised his head to watch the back-and-forth movement before stretching himself back into slumber.

"We don't want to repeat the same mistakes," Trevor said. "I want to try this rotation method you've suggested, rotational grazing and crops. You've told me twice now, and I explained it at the meeting, but I've not made good enough notes for either laborers or foreman. I need this mapped out." He returned to his chair, forearms resting on thighs this time.

Her smile deepened. Encouraging. Confident. Not at all what she felt inside.

Inside, she bumbled and tumbled. What did she know of farming? Her knowledge was based on the observations of a young girl. Her father had taken her with him for his walks about the home farm, explaining his strategies with pride. His meetings were open to her, as well, from sitting on his knee as a youngster while he gave instructions and listened to the foreman's reports, on through to her early adolescence when she would accompany him as his jokingly dubbed "lady squire."

All she knew of farming came from the memories of youth. What if she misremembered? However many times she had cautioned Trevor, he had insisted he trusted her, no matter how old the memories. That should have inspired confidence. Instead, she struggled with his pronouncements of *trust*. He was trusting in the knowledge of a man he believed to be her mother's landlord rather than husband, and he trusted *her*, the interloper. But she ought not think of that now.

Smiling, again, deeper, more confidently, J'non said, "The Surrey farm was notorious for infertile soil. The goal was to increase fertility by way of rotating arable crops, as well as livestock."

"Right. Yes. That. Keep talking." He removed to the desk to ink a quill.

She waited while he scribbled, dipped into the inkwell again, swiped the excess ink, scribbled more, then repeated three times.

"Yes?" he prompted without looking up.

Shaking her thoughts of the light stubble on his cheeks, a sign of how eager he had been to meet her in the study, she said, "Turnips and clovers were used to restore fertility. That and they provided food for livestock over winter."

"You had said. Yes, I see I've already made those notes. More." Scribble, scribble.

"Summer and winter are the grazing periods. Autumn and spring are the planting periods, autumn for planting the cover crops, and spring for planting the primary crops. In the summer, the sheep and cattle can graze on the hilltop — make a note that we should designate the rockiest areas for sheepwalks. In the winter, they graze in the valley in preparation for overwintering and for the spring's lambing season — soggy winter moors would not make for pleasant grazing either. The crops should be arable. Our primary crops were barley, potatoes, wheat, and beets. Please confer with the gentlemen as to the best crops, Trevor, or to the foreman when he's hired. My childhood farm was in Surrey, not

Yorkshire. I haven't the first idea what will or will not grow here."

"Mmm hmm." Scribble.

"Oats might work best for the weather. I don't know for certain. For autumn, we should sow legumes. Turnips are best grown in winter and have deep enough roots to reach the minerals regardless of the field's condition. Clovers will help fertilize the soil initially, but livestock rotation is critical. Once livestock is rotated for grazing, the soil will be fertilized for the future."

"From their manure, yes?" he mumbled as he scratched the quill across the parchment.

J'non grimaced, but confirmed, "Yes, manure. There are two rotations: one between livestock and crops, the other with crops themselves. In this way, we have the nutrient replenishing crops of autumn that also serve as overwintering cover crops to prevent erosion and frost damage, and the grazing crops. This will clear the field for spring planting of our primary crops, which, too, will be rotated."

"But first, turnips?"

"They're fast growing, and if planted in intervals, will continue to grow in stages, providing new grazing. They grow in the cold and heat, love full sun, are edible through the roots, and are high yielding."

Propping the quill in its stand, Trevor eyed her with a bemused expression, his lips curved into a half-smile. "Now that you've campaigned, I'm ready to cast my vote for Mr. Turnip as Lord Mayor of London."

She blushed, embarrassed.

Trevor laughed. "You're fetching when you're campaigning for legumes. Did you know?"

Her heart skipped a beat.

"By fetching," he added, "I mean beautiful."

Fixing her gaze on her hands, she remained silent until the fire in her cheeks simmered. She would never grow tired of his compliments. They were few and far between and by that nature all the more precious. As plain as she was, if not downright unattractive, as her aunt had oft reminded her, he made her feel like a rare pearl.

"Thank you, J'non," he said. "Thank you for your patience and wisdom. You had explained all of this to me before when I was foolish enough to move the sheep to the hill in the first place, but I hadn't understood. I believe we have a real chance here, not only for the future of our farm but also the issue of drainage. I know this doesn't resolve the valley's drainage problem, but it will help prevent our fields from — as you so eloquently said last week — exacerbating the situation."

"It is I who should be thanking you for listening to my foolishness. I do hope you'll consult with the gentlemen again and the foreman. My memories are — "

"From your youth. I know. I trust you. Have faith in yourself."

Trevor took a moment to sand the ink of his notes before returning to the chair by the hearth. Gunner raised his head with a yawn, stretched his paws, then shuffled a turn so he could lie on Trevor's feet. J'non flexed her toes. Sensation tingled back into her feet from where Gunner had lain.

"Do you think," Trevor asked, "the advertisement will be necessary? I would prefer he hire the remaining hands based on his needs. If we wait for word to spread, we could have someone local step forward for the position, a relation or acquaintance of a neighbor maybe." He propped an elbow on the manchette. "But the question is, to advertise or not to advertise? What say you, my lady?"

"I think it would be wise to post the ad for the foreman." J'non hesitated before saying, "Generally speaking, I've had good luck with the hires recommended from my sewing circle, or so Mr. Hawkins tells me. I'm saddened to admit not all have worked as I hoped."

Trevor arched a brow. "Oh? You hadn't mentioned this."

"I didn't wish to speak ill of anyone."

"Or admit you're too soft-hearted?"

"And that," J'non said. "One poor man, a cousin of Mrs. Bramble, arrived to his interview smelling so soused of stale ale, Mr. Hawkins had to feign a chill to excuse his holding a kerchief to his nose. An in-law of Mrs. Stalingworth had an exceptional interview but never showed up to work. Then there was the fellow who fell asleep during the roof repairs—on the roof, hammer in hand. Oh, I could go on." She stifled a giggle. There she was not wanting to speak ill of anyone, yet she could not forget Mr. Hawkins's expression when he told her about Dozing Dan. "I won't admit that more than not have been sent home without a position, not when so many have worked out better than we could have expected, such as Willie with his team of young apprentices."

"As I thought. You're too soft-hearted. In time, you'll see it pays to harden your heart until it's cold and shriveled." Trevor smirked. "Speaking of your gardener, when you told me he was employed at the estate before the war in the British Americas, I had imagined an older man. He can't be a day over forty, thirty-five if I were feeling generous. Forgive me. I'm gossiping like an old tabby." He reached down to rub behind Gunner's ear until a back leg thumped against the floor. "He tells me your ideas for a community kitchen garden have proven popular."

"Not that we'll see the fruits of labor for another few weeks, but yes. Is it because the villagers are bored at the church, do you think, that they want to fiddle with this idea of mine? Without the direct route through the village, they're traveling quite far to play in the garden. It must be boredom."

"No, I think they're invested. Time will tell. Once the waters recede and the repairs are underway. Once everyone returns to life. If my guess counts for anything, I'd say they'll be making good use of the garden, at least those who do not have the means for one of their own." Just as J'non was feeling pleased with herself, Trevor added, "Unless they're using it as an excuse to eye the estate, all vying to see inside."

"Don't crush my hopes," she chided. "But now that you've said it, why did no one accept the offer to stay at the estate?"

As silly as it sounded to lose sleep over this, it had concerned her for days. Not but a day after Sunday service, after much deliberation with Trevor, she had approached the vicar offering the guestrooms at the Court for villagers. What was there to decline? A warm bed, feather-down, clean linen, privacy, wash-basins, and more. If nothing else, would they not value a private chamber pot? The vicar had been as enthused as she, but when he put the offer to his temporary guests, no one stepped forward to accept.

Trevor tossed off one of his shoes and stroked Gunner's back with his stockinged foot. Gunner sighed in his sleep.

"Discomfort I suspect," Trevor said. "It's one thing to want to spy inside, quite another to stay as a guest. Embarrassment may factor in."

"Embarrassment? What could possibly cause embarrassment? They're sleeping on straw over cold stone for pity's sake."

He shrugged a shoulder. "If Queen Charlotte invited you to stay at Buckingham House, what would you say?"

"The Queen's House?" J'non gasped. "I could never!"

Chuckling, Trevor said, "Yet you very likely will be invited. But back to your point. Put that into perspective of the villagers. You're hesitant even though your circumstances are far more improved from theirs."

"There's no comparison. I'm not a queen! They're our neighbors, the same people who attend my sewing circle, who helped repair the leaky roof, who have been working in the garden, who accept us into their homes and offer baked apples. We're all acquainted. There's no comparison."

"Obviously they would beg to differ."

J'non huffed. She wanted a different answer. She did not like the thought of her neighbors, her *friends* seeing her or her residence as intimidating. The ivies were still working their way into the mortar. The smell of mold and decay still lingered in some rooms, although the fresh paint had improved the air in the vestibule at least. While the plaster had been repaired where the roof had leaked, the floor was so badly warped, a rug and strategically placed table — one that wobbled and sat askew — had to cover the boards. So many repairs had been made, but the house still showed its wear. Hardly intimidating.

With a sigh, J'non said, "I hope life returns to normal soon. Gwen and I were planning the fête. And what of the sewing circle? Lady Osborne hopes to join, but will it ever meet again?"

Trevor grinned cheekily. "Settling into domesticity well, I see."

"It's my soft heart. Us soft-hearted folk long for domesticity. As we are now. Is this not bliss? Seated before a crackling fire, our faithful hound at our feet. Perfection."

"Not even a crackling fire can thaw my cold, dead heart. All I see is a dusty room full of unread and moth-eaten books, money burning in the grate in place of each log, and my foot caught in parson's mousetrap."

So fixed was his expression, vacant and inscrutable, J'non sat straighter. Until he laughed.

Trevor slapped his thigh, waking Gunner, and laughed heartily. "Am I pleased you almost believed me or insulted?" He waved a hand. "Don't answer. In all seriousness, this *is* bliss. I never thought to live so comfortably."

Although he gazed at her with a smile in his eyes and a lingering chuckle on his lips, he did not explain his meaning further. She wanted to know more but did not dare ask.

Instead, she asked, "What were your original plans for matrimony, before the inheritance?"

"Before I realized I must marry for money?"

She flinched at the honesty. Why should she be bothered? It was not her money after all.

He continued, "Late I know, but I had set thirty as my marriage age. What any normal man would have done is marry as soon as he inherited, in my case the barony. I couldn't bring myself to do it. I knew I should. For so many years it had been only my father and me. My example of matrimony and motherhood had come from my mother, and that was not a fate I wished, to be so deceived and then abandoned. After my father passed, rather than become lonely, I relished the solitude. It gave me the opportunity to pursue my own interests. When I wished for companionship, I spent time with friends, who one day soon I hope you'll have the opportunity to meet. I traveled with my solicitor, with whom I spent my youth, by the way, he being the son of the Tidwell Hall steward. I lived life. The thought of marriage never entered my mind. I set it for the future, and that's where it remained. I had hoped, when the time came, to find someone with whom I could live comfortably."

That phrase again. What did it mean?

Enraptured, J'non had not realized she had leaned forward in the chair, her hands tucked unladylike between her knees.

Before she could inquire further, he asked, "And you? Prior to your father arranging a marriage with a stranger, what was your vision of marital life? Hopes and dreams? Tell me. I'll only be insulted if you say you had hoped for someone blond and blue-eyed."

She laughed, the tension eased, but only for a moment. His question was impossible. Her vision had changed with each stage of her life. In the beginning, before the smallpox, she had a fairytale vision, dreams of a marriage like her parents had, of a man not unlike her papa. She was a different person then. With different opportunities. Hope of marriage had died with her parents. Her aunt had seen to that. Circumstances saw to that. Without dowry, without appeal, without introductions, who was there to marry? No one wanted to marry a dowdy maid. Then the scandal. Then... *the bleak period.* Who cared about marriage when survival was priority? After that, she knew there would be no marriage. Ever.

Until you.

J'non closed her eyes, searching for strength.

When she opened her eyes, it was to find Trevor studying her intently, as if trying to read her mind. "I was too busy frolicking in crop fields to think about marriage," she said. "I supposed it was inevitable, but not for many years to come. If I thought of it at all, I assumed I would marry someone local or someone Papa introduced to me."

She sucked in a breath at her use of *papa*. Trevor's expression gave away no notice of the slip. She exhaled. A reference to Mr. Whittington, he must assume, not to Sir Julian.

Trevor folded his hands over his middle, lacing his fingers, and leaning back in his chair, the image of comfort. "Did you never dream of love? I hear some women do."

With a soft laugh, J'non said, "Many girls do, young girls, before reason and practicality. What is love, though? Passion? Lust? Companionship? Adoration? Friendship? I've seen love destroy people, or what they thought was love, whereas I've seen companionable marriages form the deepest affections over time. I don't think I ever hoped for love as some women do, only a happy marriage."

"With a local boy who picked his nose in church. I can see the attraction."

"Trevor!" she exclaimed before laughing. "We're being serious, are we not? Oh, I never know what to expect from you. You're all serious expressions and scowls one minute then joking vulgarities the next. Now, I put to you a question you once asked me. Who on earth did I marry?"

She asked with laughter, not at all serious, yet once more he surprised her with a serious answer.

"A lost boy trapped in a man's body, still looking out the window for his mother's return." His voice was low, his eyes on his laced fingers rather than her. "I never sought love. I saw what it did to my father. *They* were passionate, I was told. Besotted with each other. Did she ever really love him? I don't know. There can be no doubt my father loved her, but as you pointed out, there are different kinds of love. He was obsessed with her, never could let her go. Don't think he ever let me witness that. No, he never talked about her once she left, but I knew. Evenings wasted gazing at her portrait. Periodic breakdowns. Calling for her at night. He was a proud man, a strong man, a leader of men, never one to show weakness. What I witnessed were private moments, but they were enough to strike a fear of love into my heart. Is that a terrible admission to make to one's wife?"

J'non shared a tender smile. "Your wife is the best choice for so terrible a confession. If she can't understand you, who will?"

"I'm glad it was you who stepped out of the carriage," he said.

She stared, wide eyed, confused. Then his meaning dawned. Happiness warmed her from head to toe.

J'non left the study and headed for her bedchamber. When she reached the staircase, a hidden gem tucked in the back of the house with promises of escape to private quarters, she paused. Beneath her hand, the railing spoke of the house's strength and grandeur, supported by acanthus scroll carvings. Looking up, she admired the ascending square as the stairs marched up, turned on a landing, marched again, then another landing.

The words of Samuel Johnson came to mind. "The world is a grand staircase, some are going up and some are going down."

Only a month had passed since her arrival. How did this already feel like *home*? She knew which steps would creak. She knew the sound of the creak. She felt each creak in her soul as though the house spoke to her. It, like her, was undergoing a transformation.

For the first time in years, she felt safe, free to be herself. Each day increased her confidence. This house was *hers*. Trevor was *her* husband. This was *her* life. Everything would work. One day, they would have children together and raise them in this house, the long gallery filled with laughter, running feet, and the echoes of Gunner's barks.

The difficulty was not only in accepting this but relaxing into living it. What if, when she least suspected it, when she grew complacent, disaster struck? A single tear in the fabric of lies and she would be living in servant's quarters or without a home. She knew what it was to be so hungry the stomach no longer rumbled or felt the pain of emptiness, to pass the point of hunger altogether. This time, having discovered what it was to live and to love would make the emptiness unbearable. She could not so easily forget the circumstances which brought her to the estate, but spending her days braced for tragedy, hiding pin money in case she would need it for survival, was no way to enjoy life. There had been little time to worry about Miss Phoebe Whittington; nevertheless, the fear of her appearance on the doorstep, or worse, Mr. Whittington arriving unannounced, haunted her unguarded moments.

J'non stroked the banister, relishing the feel of the cold wood, admiring its strength.

Had Miss Whittington found the happiness she sought with Mr. Wilkins? J'non hoped so. However bossy of a mistress she had been, spoiled by her father, she had a kind heart. Did not everyone deserve love? That was all Miss Whittington had wanted, so much so she sacrificed everything to follow her heart. Had she been scared by the arrangement her father made, afraid of being trapped in a marriage with a domineering man not unlike her father? Mr. Whittington had doted and lavished and bestowed, but his kindness came at the cost of his tempers and machinations.

J'non hoped Miss Whittington had found the love she sought and was at that moment making a happy home for herself and Mr. Wilkins in the wilds of Scotland.

Feeling confident, J'non decided it was time to focus on happiness, to trust in the life she was building and release her fears.

With a foot on the third step, her heart pounded faster at the familiar creak underfoot. Each step brought her closer to her chamber. Trevor had promised to come to her after washing and shaving. Was it wicked to look so forward to his arrival? Biting her bottom lip, she hoisted the hem of her dress and raced up the stairs.

Chapter 15

L ess than a week later, the village brimmed with activity. Trevor walked along the main with Mr. Tillson the mason and his sons, as well as Mr. Pritchard and sons, the latter all farmers.

Mr. Tillson said to the group, "My boys and I will tackle digging the swales and building the bunds on the morrow. You have the buffers and hedges, Tom?" he asked Mr. Pritchard.

"Aye. Along the beck and around the smallhold-ers. Gideon and his neighbors ought to help, seeing as it'll encircle their pastures. If not, Gideon can drink alone at The Valiant Stallion."

"Off to see the missus you trot," Mr. Tillson joked to Trevor as they approached the terraced house in which J'non was rumored to have been last seen.

Trevor shook hands with his companions, an equal this week, a marquess next week.

The waters had receded enough for most to return home and all to launch into repairs. Under Trevor's and the Reverend Harvey's direction, all able-bodied men were tasked with either repairs to the village or flood prevention. They had strategized methods to help slow and redirect waterflow, and detain flood waters. Would any of their plans work? They would only know when it next flooded, but their efforts had to make an impact, no matter how minor.

One team decreased the chance of water runoff by adding manure and compost to the fields most apt to soil compaction, the first step of what would be an ongoing, annual process. Another team aimed to slow water by increasing resistance with grass buffers around the riverbank, hedgerows around the smallholders where the flooding was the worst, and woodland planting to reduce riverbank erosion. Yet another team built earth bunds in addition to digging detention areas and swales to retain water. The most significant task, which was paid with a combination of tithes and Trevor's modest income from Tidwell Hall, was the connectivity of waterways. Using cross drains, woody debris and fenced dams, raised embankments, and meanders in the beck, they created a guided path for water that connected to the river and to designated floodplain wetlands.

All in all, it was a laborious endeavor that would not only take many weeks to complete but had already taken the agreement and coordination of all smallholder farmers, landowners, and tenants whose properties would be affected. Trevor wondered more than once why none of these preventative measures had been attempted before, but then, they might have, only to result in lack of maintenance, lack of funds, lack of manpower, and even lack of cooperation by those who did not wish their lands or enclosures to be disrupted. It was fortunate the flood was fresh in mind, as the sense of urgency drove their will to prevent future damage.

Trevor raised a hand to rap knuckles against the front door only to find the door already ajar. The occupant, he knew, was the mother of one of his footmen. With a hearty knock, he peeked inside. The mistress of the house, Mrs. Sullivan, was kneeling on the floor before a young man with a scraped knee.

When she saw Trevor peering around the door, she scrambled to stand. "Ey up!"

He waved for her to remain as she was. "No need to stand upon ceremony. I come as a humble husband in search of his wife."

The house had only one room. With a sweep of his gaze, he could see all in its entirety, a bed in the corner, four other children cleaning the debris from the floodwaters, and the kitchen where a maid stood with her back to the room, her hands busy kneading dough.

When the maid turned, a sunny smile brightening her features, Trevor took a step back, arrested. It was not a maid. It was J'non. He shook his head to dismiss the apron and cap and the frizzed strands of hair escaping said cap in order to register her as his marchioness. Reconciling the image had a curious effect, a tug in his chest cavity, a stir of desire to stride across the room and kiss her. Inexplicable. He had never desired a maid or servant of any sort, so why seeing his wife in a mobcap, flour dusting her cheek, and looking for all intents and purposes like a scullery maid caused his heart to pound faster, he could not guess.

"Lord Pickering," J'non said in greeting. "One moment, please, and I'll be all yours." She stopped kneading to reach for a bowl.

As she added flour to the bottom of the bowl and tucked the dough inside, a curly haired child peeked from around the skirt of J'non's dress to eye him. Trevor winked at the cherubin face. The little boy ducked back out of sight behind J'non.

Trevor turned his attention to Mrs. Sullivan. "I see I can't leave Lady Pickering alone with you. You've trained her as a cook. What will the Sladesbridge Court cook say when I announce Lady Pickering is taking over her post?"

"Her Ladyship's a reet saint, your lordship," said Mrs. Sullivan.

"You needn't persuade me. I'm already convinced," he said, leaning against the doorframe. A chilly breeze swept in through the open doorway. The daily afternoon drizzle would be upon them before they knew it. "Will you be attending the sewing circle tomorrow? I assume it's still planned. It's all Lady Pickering could talk about during supper."

Mrs. Sullivan stood, swooping the boy in the chair into her arms to take his spot, then settling him onto her lap when she sat. "Wouldn't miss it. Nowt t'do here but t'work. If t'weren't for her ladyship's sew and brew, we'd go balmy."

"Am I to assume the main topic of conversation at said sew and brew will be the October fête?"

The children squealed.

"It can't happen soon enough, my lord. I'll be selling my famous pies."

"Will your new cook be baking those famous pies?"

Mrs. Sullivan cocked her head to the side, then glanced at J'non and laughed. "Reet. My new cook." Peals of laughter followed.

Trevor waited a hair's breadth longer as J'non bade farewell to the children and exchanged good-byes with Mrs. Sullivan. He donned his tricorn to free his hands so he could help tie her bonnet ribbons and secure her traveling cloak. It would be a cold walk back to Sladesbridge. With luck, though, they would make it before the rain.

As they began their trek home, J'non said, "They're all beyond excited about the festival. The plan is to raise money for further repairs."

"What I wish to hear more about is you baking in the kitchen."

She bowed her head and laughed softly. "All our talk about them being embarrassed to stay at the Court and my worrying they're intimidated by me somehow has come to naught. No one tugs at their forelock or scrapes their knees curtsying. Don't think them disrespectful. It's only, they seem to have accepted me as a friend. Is it too much to hope? I know I should befriend our peers, but none of them live as close as these women, and I *like* the village women."

"You'll hear no chastisement from me. Befriend whomever you wish."

"Thank you, Trevor." She leaned against him for a second, her cheek nudging his shoulder, before saying, "I've delivered baskets, entertained children, bandaged scrapes, advised on furniture arrangement, and baked bread. A productive day, would you not agree?"

"More productive than mine. All I did was stand around barking orders while the Tillsons and Pritchards repaired a barn. Can't be bothered to roll up these aristocratic sleeves. I might dirty the white linen."

She scoffed. "The filthy state of your breeches tells an altogether different tale, Marquess Pickering."

"Why, pray, have you been eyeing my breeches?"

Her *meep* made him chuckle.

"If I have to herd another goat, sheep, or cow into a paddock, it'll be too soon," he said. "I was not bred for this. My lot in life is to roast my toes next to a warm fire recently stoked by an invisible but no less appreciated parlor maid."

"Toff."

"Cit."

"Stuffed shirt."

"Blowsabella."

Giggling, J'non tucked her hand into the crook of his elbow.

They strode in silence until terraced houses turned to cottages then to open fields dotted with sheep or standing water. The early winter wind brought on by the storm whipped about them, flapping the capes of his greatcoat and fluttering the hem of her cloak. He could not see her face beyond the edge of her bonnet, but he knew her cheeks would be rosy from the chill air. Her lips would be curved in the smile of blissful contentment. Her hair would be disheveled from that hideous mobcap she had worn while baking, likely straying loose about her face. She fascinated him more with each passing day. Resilient and intelligent with an understated beauty that enchanted him. How could he have ever mistaken her for a quiet church mouse or a submissive lamb? She was all that was strong and compassionate, a lady who knew her own mind and knew when best to voice it or keep mum.

"I've been thinking," he said without preamble, "of selling the former marquess' curricle. Ridiculous contraption to own where there are no roads. Besides, no self-respecting gentleman over thirty ought to own a curricle."

"But you're only eight and twenty."

"Pfft. That's neither here nor there. The only people to own curricles are the rogues and Corinthians on the fast track. It's a town vehicle, not made for the mule-paths of the moors, and only intended for winning races, frightening young ladies, impressing fellow rogues, and generally being seen as one careens around a corner in London to overturn a blameless applecart. We should have something more sensible. A barouche?"

J'non looked up at him long enough for him to confirm that yes, her cheeks were becomingly rosy, as rosy as the apples in the tumbled applecart.

"A barouche?" she echoed. "You want to purchase a barouche?"

"Cavorting about in the Pickering carriage is beyond ridiculous, as we've discovered. We need something smaller and more sensible, something that allows us to enjoy the beauty of our surrounds while transporting us to our neighbors without smelling like a horse at the end of the journey. The height of insult to arrive on horseback for dinner parties. We can't very well change out of our riding boots and habits and all that as a guest, can we? No, we need something sensible."

She made a noncommittal *hmm*. That did not bode well.

"Or a donkey and cart?" he offered.

After another *hmm*, she said, "I'd rather a new sidesaddle, one of my choosing."

"A new saddle, eh? So you can ride to that dinner party looking the first stare of riding fashion, never mind the aromatic horse perfume?"

"Yes." She skipped in her step. "Yes. The more I think about it, the more I like the idea. A new sidesaddle. We *will* be resuming our morning rides soon, yes?"

"I had hoped to, although it's too cold now to teach you to swim." He leaned down to whisper, "I can't wait for spring so I can dip you into the lake."

She swatted at his arm before resuming her skip. Each skip tugged his arm and drew a laugh from his lips.

"Think how silly it would be," she continued, "to purchase a new carriage. We would have to travel all the way to London. Or does York have a carriage builder?"

"It does not. I took the liberty of making inquiries in hopes of a Pickering Day Out—a proper noun, that, complete with capital lettering. Alas, while there is much to do in York, perusing a carriage builder's catalogue and stock is not one of them."

"Pity," she said, her tone anything but disappointed.

In fact, *pity* had never sounded more cheerful.

Heaving a dramatic and most-put-out sigh, he said, "I knew at first glance you would be a demanding wife, spoiled and needy, unreasonable and vaporish. I suppose if I don't agree to the sidesaddle, opting instead for the barouche, you'll have a fainting fit? Develop a migraine? Fall into apoplexy?"

"Nothing of the sort. I will merely retreat to my suite where I may cry in privacy. You will not see me for the whole of the evening since my eyes and nose will be too red and puffy to bear witness."

With a tut, he said, "Our laundry-maid will quit when she sees the amount of extra laundering to wash your pillows free of so many tears. Spoiled *and* dispassionate, you are, not to think of the woes of the laundry-maid. I hear wife selling is still popular. Think I could earn enough from your sale to buy a matching pair for my new barouche?"

"Not so much as a ha'penny because I will escape on horseback, with or without the new sidesaddle, before you can collar me."

"Clever wench." He covered her hand with his and leaned over to smack a kiss to her bonnet. "Lest I disappoint my bride, a new sidesaddle it'll be, just no escaping on horseback unless you invite me. Pickering Day Out, eh?"

Her *hmm* turned to a happy *mmm* before she changed subject. "Tomorrow evening will be fun, will it not? With the Harveys dining with us?"

"Hawkins will arrange for the game table after dinner. Have you heard from Lady Osborne? If she'll be attending the sewing circle, she could stay for dinner. I would enjoy Sir Roland's company in the interim, while you all poke fabric with needles."

"She *is* coming," J'non said, "but I've not ascertained Sir Roland's plans. Is it too late to send a missive to them, do you think? I'm ashamed I'd not thought of their joining for dinner. I hope they don't mind that Gunner has a playdate with Sammy and Simon. Mr. Harvey will bring the greyhounds, of course."

As conversation transitioned from one point to the next, Trevor inhaled the fresh, crisp air as though breathing the elixir of life. There could not be a man more contented than he.

So dark, so cold, J'non fumbled to find her footing. However warm the night, her body trembled with chills. The candlelight had flickered bright, deceptive in proximity. Just down the hill, she had told herself. Just through the woods. The canopy of trees blocked the moon. Disoriented, she stumbled, shuffled, her feet aching, her hands throbbing from cuts. Had her throat not been dry, her tongue not heavy, her body not empty, she would have cried with frustration. The candlelight had not been her imagination. She had seen it. She knew she had.

Forward was the only direction.

A creak.

A snort.

Yes, she heard noise ahead. A flicker beyond the forest? She quickened her pace, a branch catching her cheek and tugging her hair, another stumble.

A smell.

A scent.

Yes, she caught a whiff ahead. Had her throat not been dry, her tongue not heavy, her body not empty, she would have salivated. How long since her last bite? Hours? Days? She had lost count. Time merged.

A creak.

A sign creaking on a breeze, a carriage creaking as a horse tugged, a door creaking on hinges. *An inn.* The flicker of candlelight shone through the edge of the forest. She quickened her pace, a stump catching on her sole-torn shoe, another stumble.

The trees parted. It *was* an inn! On the outskirts of a town? A posting inn? No, it was too quiet. Lanterns swayed, the innyard well lit, not a soul in sight, only horses. She could not have asked for better. Prayers answered.

Crossing into the innyard, she kept to the shadows, eyes darting, heart pounding. She licked cracked lips.

A snort. Not from a horse. Oh, blessed be! Prayers answered indeed! She had learned what to listen for, what to avoid, what to hope for, and yes, those were pig grunts. Head bowed, body hunched, she crept towards the pigsty. Eyes darted. Heart pounded. Creeping shadow. Her body trembled with chills. She licked cracked lips.

Laughter from the inn. She paused, still as a rabbit, still as a fawn.

All clear. She reached the pigsty. Ginger coated darlings noshed from a trough. Oh, blessed be. Unable to restrain herself, she rushed to join them, kneeling in the slop, nudging one of the gingers aside. With an ache behind her eyes from the desire to weep, she cupped her hands into the trough and brought the scraps to her mouth. Prayers answered. Long minutes she relished the sustenance. At first a gag, a cough, fear she would not be able to swallow, but then, all was well. Food. Food. Food.

Whistling from behind her. She froze.

Boots against gravel.

Silence.

A snort.

A grunt.

A trickle.

Whistling resumed. Ah. The privy connected to the pigsty. A drunkard from the inn relieving himself. Still as a rabbit, still as a fawn, she chewed, wiping her mouth with the back of her hand.

Boots against gravel.

Silence.

"What's that? Who goes there?"

Eyes darted. Heart pounded. *Be still. Do not move. Be a shadow.*

"I said, who goes there?" Boots on gravel. "Bloody hell. Taylor! Taylor! Quick as you can! Blasted beggar or gypsy or summit!"

A creak.

A thud.

Boots on gravel.

Eyes darted. Heart pounded.

"Taylor, quick, 'fore it runs!"

"Away from my hogs, banshee." The whistle and crack of a whip.

Gagging, J'non flung herself from the pigsty towards the forest.

Boots on gravel.

Strong hands gripped her arm and wrenched her backwards. Her scream rent the air.

Turning to face him, J'non looked up into Trevor's eyes. He gave her a gentle shake. She blinked. Looked around. It took long minutes to settle her breathing, to gain her bearings. She lay in a bed, in her bed, in her house. She blinked again, steadying her breath.

"J'non?" Trevor asked, his voice scratchy from sleep.

The room was chilly, the fire having long since died, but the bed curtains were drawn closed to capture the warmth like a cocoon. The feather-down was soft, the bedlinen clean. An edge of the bed hangings was pulled open, allowing a ribbon of cold air and the faint flicker of a candle Trevor must have lit.

"J'non?" he repeated, stroking her cheek with the back of his fingers.

Nodding, she said, "I'm so sorry to wake you. It was only a silly nightmare." She laughed hollowly. "I can't recall anymore what was frightening."

"Would you like me to return to my room?"

"No!" she shrieked, panicked, grasping his upper arm. With another deep breath, she said, "I would feel better if you stayed. If you don't mind, that is."

The thought of falling asleep without him sent chills down her spine. His arms offered more than warmth. They offered security, reassurance, compassion. Afraid to close her eyes, she rested her cheek against his shoulder.

"Maybe a glass of water?" he asked. "You must be parched."

She licked cracked lips.

Chapter 16

T here were few sounds happier to J'non than that of children's laughter. The cool weather daunted no one. Children frolicked, gay and carefree, chasing each other across the green and dirtying their festival clothes. Parents were not immune to the call of freedom, for they too laughed, frolicked, and dirtied their clothes, quite a few forego-ing customary attire altogether in favor of fancy dress. Today, there were no rules. Even Gunner romped and rolled with Sammy and Simon, darting between fair-goers and raising a ruckus with leaps, bounds, and barks. Reminiscent of her childhood but not wanting to dwell in the past, J'non treasured every moment of the October fête, here at last.

Tables of goods and food lined the perimeter of the green, the long stretch in between reserved for games and contests, ranging from three-legged races to strongmen competitions. At the farthest end, the assembly would be held to conclude the festival, com-plete with country dances. At the opposite side of the green to where J'non stood with Gwen, Trevor worked with the Reverend Harvey and Mr. Tillson to repair the makeshift pen for the sheep herding contest—the mischievous sons of the haberdasher thought it endlessly amusing to wrestle on the beams, testing each other's mettle and to see who would fall off first. Trevor bore a smile, not the least bothered by the youngsters' antics.

Only two months of marriage. J'non could not believe she had once thought Trevor stiff, cold, and humorless. Was it that he had changed, learning to loosen his cravat on occasion, or was this the Trevor as he had always been, perceived as stiff only because of the awkwardness of their first meeting and marital arrangement? Not that it mattered. All that mattered now was she was enamored by her husband.

"The bright of day yet I can see stars reflected in your eyes," Gwen said from behind her.

J'non turned with what she thought might have been a sappy smile. "If one cannot be dazzled by their spouse, there's no hope for the marriage."

"Oh, I wouldn't say that. You're still enjoying your honeymoon." Gwen rearranged embroidered hand-kerchiefs on the table, each for sale, all proceeds for the village repair and recovery fund.

"Are you implying the dazzle fades?" J'non did not believe that for a moment. Her parents had always looked at each other with affection. "If you're planning to convince me, you must first deny your own starry-eyed looks at Mr. Harvey."

Gwen laughed but could not hide the tell-tale blush. "You wouldn't know it to look at him, but he's quite the charmer." She watched the three men reassembling the pen. "The first time I laid eyes on him was at Sunday service. We arrived to find him at the door rather than our good Mr. Swensen. While my mother fussed not to be informed of Mr. Swensen's absence, all I could think at first sight was, 'a new Heaven is begun.'"

The haberdasher, who had set up her table next to Gwen's in hopes the handkerchiefs would inspire buyers to consider her goods, said, "When you've been married as long as I have, you've no need of stars."

Gwen dismissed her reply with a wave of a hand, a laugh, and a comment about her never seeing a happier marriage. The two dipped into conversation, leaving J'non to wander the festival grounds.

Pennant strings swayed in festive heraldry. The aroma of food scented the air, mince pie mingling with baked apples. In a sniff, one could smell bread, pork, cinnamon, and rosemary. Her first stop was to one of the confectionery tables. She eyed the sweet-meats. Plates of marzipan, biscuits, barley sugar candy, Turkish delight, and *oh*, was that—

"Lady Pickering!" exclaimed the girl behind the table as she dipped into a curtsy. "The syllabub is the best." Without waiting for a reply, she handed J'non a glass of froth.

A nod of gratitude, J'non tipped back the glass. A zest of sweet lemon, fluffy and rich, tantalized and overwhelmed her pallet.

Returning the glass to the girl's outstretched hand, she said, "Delicious. Did you make this your-self?" The table attendant could not be more than ten years old.

With a giggle, the girl nodded, placing the empty glass on a tray behind her, alongside other empty glasses and plates. When the girl turned around and continued to giggle, J'non touched a finger to her lips. Sure enough, she could feel a frothy mustache on her upper lip. With a grin to the little confectioner, J'non licked away the mustache.

She turned her attention to the game stalls. Where to begin? There were raffles, bat and ball, hoopla, guess-the-number-of-lemon-drops, archery, miniature painting, axe-throwing, arm wrestling — and to think, those were just the ones in her immediate vicinity. The blacksmith's stall was tempting. His game was for contestants to try their hand at flattening a heated iron rod with his hammer and anvil — flatten it in three hits to win. Was the hammer so heavy? She aimed to find out.

Before she could approach the blacksmith, however, the millwright and his wife caught her attention. "Try your hand at the axe toss, my lady," he coaxed.

How different could it be from wielding a blacksmith's hammer? Goodness. She did not like the look of the sharp end of the axe. That edge meant business. Her expression must have voiced her thoughts as she approached.

"No need to fear, my lady," the millwright assured. "Allow me to show you."

He waved for her to stand next to him. Gripping the axe handle, he demonstrated the necessary hand positions.

J'non asked, "Will I be able to grip the handle with my gloves, or should I remove them?"

"Best to wear them, my lady. Now, grip like I showed you." He waited for her to tighten her hands around the end. "It's not a cricket bat," he said with a chuckle. "Loosen your grip and move your hands down. May I?" When she nodded, he reached over to tap her hands until they were at the base of the handle. "Line your thumbs along the edge. Ever played the Scottish game of golf, my lady? No? Well, if you had, I would advise to grip it like a golf club rather than a cricket bat. No matter. Now, look at your target."

Across what seemed to her to be the distance of the entire green itself was a plank of wood. She was supposed to hit that? From this distance? She scoffed. Could she not try splitting a piece of wood on a stump? That should be manageable. Who thought *throwing* an axe was a good idea?

"Lighten your grip, my lady. You're not chopping wood."

She wished she were. Loosening as instructed, she eyed the plank, giving it her fiercest steely look.

Mr. Farley continued to guide her. "Arms back overhead. Keep it light. You'll release when the axe is right in front of your line of sight."

Mrs. Farley shared words of encouragement, words echoed by an unexpected crowd gathering behind J'non.

Eyeing the target, J'non focused, the axe light in her hand. Overhead. Pull back. Light as a feather. *Swish*. The axe spun towards the wood. Head first, the axe bounced off the plank into the meadow grass.

A collective sigh behind her intermingled with comments of "lovely try" and "nicely done," along with a few, "I want a turn."

Mr. Farley said, "A strong throw, my lady. Your wrist flicked, causing more spin than needed. Care to try it again?"

J'non laughed and shook her head. "I think my calling is not as a lumberjack."

"Allow me?" A man asked behind her, his words deep and sonorous.

J'non's heart fluttered at the sound of his voice. The crowd's muttering increased as they moved aside to allow the marquess to step forward.

He made a show of retrieving loose coins from his greatcoat pocket and clinking them into the pay-to-play bowl next to Mrs. Farley. Trevor then turned his back to the millwright, and without a word between the two, Mr. Farley reached up to remove first Trevor's greatcoat and then his frock coat to allow for more flexibility of movement. Mrs. Farley took them both in hand as her husband retrieved the fallen axe.

"What's the prize?" Trevor asked.

Mr. Farley said, "A slice of currant cake or two ginger biscuits."

"Mmm. The stakes are high." Trevor winked at J'non, lifted his arms overhead, and swung the axe, sending it flying forward.

It rotated two revolutions before sticking sharp side first into the plank of wood. The crowd applauded with *oohs* and *aahs*.

J'non batted her eyelashes. "Was that win on my behalf? Do I now choose a treat?"

"Nonsense," Trevor said straight-faced. "Win your own biscuits."

He waited until Mr. Farley helped him don the frock coat and greatcoat and after Mrs. Farley had selected the biscuits for him before he offered an arm to J'non. After a smirk, he handed her one of the two biscuits. The crowd parted for them to pass, some dispersing to explore other games but most queuing for their turn with the axe.

A hand on his sleeve, J'non said, "You're not allowed to win me more prizes. I've already enjoyed syllabub, and now a biscuit. If you ply me with sweets all day, I'll not be able to eat supper."

"I promise only to win you prizes from the stalls giving away ribbons and baubles."

"Yes, that's better." She tapped her lips with the tip of a finger in hopes no errant crumbs remained to form a ginger mustache. "Do you think Mrs. Farley baked these herself?"

"I have it on good authority they were donated from Mrs. Sullivan's table, as were the prizes at both the skittle and apple shy stalls. Care to try your hand at knocking apples from wooden sticks?" Trevor nodded in that direction.

"Count me out of any game involving tossing objects. Now, guessing the weight of Mrs. Warriner's pig is another matter."

They ambled, in no hurry to reach a destination. Gunner raced past them twice, in one direction with him in the lead and the greyhounds following, and the other direction with the greyhounds in the lead. The fair was bustling with pets, children, and people. There were hayrides and donkey rides, and craft shows with artisans, handicraftsmen, and tradesmen demonstrating their skills, such as wood and leather working. Trestle tables were piled with jams, pies, and cakes. Ongoing contests from log rolling to the best garden vegetable entertained guests, although there would be a few center-stage contests to come, including tug-of-war.

The whole village had rallied to make this fête a success, bringing family and neighbors from the far reaches of the march and beyond in celebration of life after the flood. Even the staff at the estate were offered a half day to enjoy the festivities, with those hosting a stall receiving the full day. With so many guests, including several wealthy landowners, there should be ample coin raised for the flood recovery fund. Evidence of the flood's destruction remained, but the repairs had come a long way in restoration, many of the houses and shops in far better condition than before the storm.

Everyone J'non and Trevor passed smiled, nodded, curtsied, bowed, or caught their attention for brief conversation. There were a few strangers who ogled or tugged their forelocks, but most of the fairgoers were people they knew well. Not a word or greeting did she take for granted. Every acknowledgement and every friendly exchange were treasured. She marveled at the novelty of being part of this.

A home of her own. A place of belonging. A village of supporters. It was not self-deception to believe any of them would help her if she knocked on their door in need. They had not known her for long, but she believed their friendship was genuine.

And there was Trevor.

Beneath her hand, she could feel his warmth and strength, a firm and powerful arm, a protector's arm. However much her attention turned to the fair, she was cognizant of his every move. He epitomized masculinity today. Boots rather than heeled shoes. Breeches of white leather, more fitting for riding than dancing. An unadorned blue frockcoat. A complementary waistcoat beneath. She knew he wore a white linen shirt but could not see it now. All tailored to show his figure to advantage, and all topped with a simply knotted cravat, a tricorn, and a caped greatcoat, not with too many capes, mind, just enough to mark him as a gentleman of distinction.

Was it the divinity of his musky cologne, scented with spices today, or the cleanly shaven cheeks that had her wanting to blush with his every look? And look he did. As they walked the fair, he glanced at her every few steps, almost as if he were asking himself the same question. Or maybe she still bore evidence of the froth mustache.

Gunner raced by again, but this time he stopped, galloped over to them, and panted at their feet.

J'non scratched behind his ears.

Trevor said, "You speak loudly, sir, although you say not a word. 'Did you see me?' you repeat ad nauseum. Yes, sir, we saw you. We are as proud as any parents can be."

"Prouder," J'non added with a pat to Gunner's head.

Satisfied with the praise, Gunner dashed off in chase of the greyhounds, who now took the lead. Rather than make it to wherever the imaginary finish line was, Gunner nipped at Sammy's shoulder, tripping Simon in the process. Sammy gnawed in the general direction of one of Gunner's ears as the three tumbled to the lawn, rolling with playful snarls and growls before leaping up and giving chase again.

Elbowing J'non, Trevor said, "Not in a million years had you thought you'd become mother to a Lurcher."

"I admit, the thought never crossed my mind." They resumed their walk. "How long have you had him?"

"Three years. I lied when I said I was not lonely after my father's death. No, not exactly. I did enjoy the solitude, but it was not long before I filled it with traveling. The hall didn't feel like home without him. Once I finally settled into life at Tidwell Hall, I kept to a rigorous schedule, one long set by my father. It provided familiarity, contentment in stability. Yet after a time, I had to admit I was lonely. Not lonely for a person, but alone. I'm not certain how to explain that."

"I understand. There's peace in one's own company, but it's frightening being completely alone in the world."

"I wouldn't say I was frightened, but yes. When I learned my coachman's cousin was breeding Lurchers for hare coursing, I couldn't resist taking one of the pups for my own. A noble hound. Sleeps more than he hunts, naturally."

They watched Gunner stop again, mid chase, and elegantly and decorously lick his nether region. J'non covered her eyes with a hand and laughed.

"He would have enjoyed the fête," Trevor said.

J'non raised her eyebrows. "He appears to be enjoying it well enough."

"I apologize. My thoughts had wandered elsewhere. I was thinking of my father."

"The admiral? I had the impression he was autocratic."

"He was, but don't imagine him as an authoritarian. He was a leader, not a ruler, and yes, there is a difference. When he returned home, I was only a young boy. Pardon me if I gave the impression he set rules then ignored me. I had been ignored by my mother as she favored her friends and society over me. My father, in comparison, doted on me, at least in those early years. We did everything together. He taught me to ride, to hunt, to swim. We never missed a fair. You should have seen his throwing arm. He would have won you the entire currant cake if challenged."

They had slowed their pace until they stood before the archery stall, two young men currently in competition with bows.

J'non looked up at Trevor. "This paints a completely different portrait of him."

Her thoughts strayed to Trevor's words of being unworthy of his father's memory, of disappointing his father. She struggled to reconcile the man those sentiments implied the admiral to be with this man Trevor now described.

"When I say I idolized him," Trevor continued, "it was not because he ruled with an iron fist. I idolized him because he succeeded at all and seemed to know everything. There was not a question I could ask that he did not know the answer. It seemed to me he knew all and could accomplish anything. His later years are freshest in my mind, unfortunately, rather than all the good years when he first returned. His later years were…" He hesitated, as if searching for a descriptor. He finally settled on, "*difficult*. Those early years, though…." With a deep breath, he looked around, his gaze not so much on the surroundings but in the past. His expression was dazed, dreamy, and strangely happy. "This festival brings back the best of the memories, long forgotten. Can you guess which contest was our favorite?"

She shook her head.

"Tug-of-war. We never missed a match." Punching his palm, he said. "I'm going to compete today. Do you approve? Will you cheer me on?"

J'non eyed the mud pit near where the sheep herding pen was assembled. Oh dear. A long length of rope lay next to an ominous pit filled with sludge.

Smiling brightly, as though flinging oneself in mud of questionable origin was the grandest of ideas, J'non said, "We had better sign your name on the roster, then, before the slots fill."

He waggled his eyebrows. "Kiss me if my team wins?"

Moments later, they stood at the registration table, Trevor signing his name to the roster.

A voice behind them said, "Well, well, well, if it isn't Lord and Lady Pickering."

They turned to find an immaculately dressed Sir Roland eyeing them from behind a quizzing glass. With his free hand, he twirled a decorative walking cane.

Looking them up and down from behind the lens, Sir Roland asked, "Are you *really* going to chafe kid gloves on coarse fiber before slipping into a ditch of dung? Should you lose, take no offense if I pretend not to know you." Having secured their attention, he dipped into a courtly bow.

J'non extended her hand for him to take. "Happy tidings. I'm pleased you could come after all."

"Try as I might to convince the wife of the rustic nature of village fairs, she insisted we attend." Sir Roland favored J'non with a roguish smile before releasing her fingers and drawing her attention to Gwen's handkerchief table. "You'll find my heart there."

Across the green, J'non saw Lady Osborne talking with Gwen. Turning to Trevor, she opened her mouth to excuse herself, but he beat her to it.

"Go on, then," Trevor said. "Roland will distract me from my broken heart to be so easily replaced."

With a rueful look, J'non took her leave of the gentlemen.

Gwen and Lady Osborne were already deep in conversation when J'non approached, or more to the point, Lady Osborne was deep in conversation while Gwen listened. Without missing a syllable, she smiled at J'non and kept talking.

"And I asked him, 'Why must we go to York *now*? Could we not wait until next week, like?' But he insisted we must go now, now, now. *Men*! At least I was able to convince him to attend the festival. I said to him, 'If you don't stop the carriage, I'll be forced to jump out while it's in motion and attend alone.' I won't admit I might have included a wink-wink and a nudge-nudge about finding a rustic but charming laborer eager to steal my heart. So, you see, he could not leave me unattended." She tittered, then reached a hand to J'non. "I'm so happy to see you. Will you come to York with us?"

"York?" J'non looked from her to Gwen, flustered. "When? Why?"

"We're leaving as soon as the festivities conclude."

"No, you're not!" J'non protested. "You'll be supping with us this evening and leaving tomorrow. The fête won't conclude until late afternoon. It'll be far too late to continue on to York."

Lady Osborne flicked a gaze towards her husband. "You're right, of course. He'll have no say in the matter, not when I insist. After all, who wears the stays in the family? Now, will you be joining us for supper, Mrs. Harvey?"

"Oh no, not this evening," Gwen said. "Obadiah and I will help the cleaning committee tidy after the dancing. He wouldn't blink an eye for me to join you both, but I would feel guilty about abandoning him. And please, you must call me Gwen. How long have we known each other? Please."

Lady Osborne looked from Gwen to J'non. "Now I look the hoity toity lofty for not offering first. Siobhan. I insist."

"Where's Caoimhín staying while you're in York?" J'non asked.

"He's over there, like." Siobhan nodded towards Mrs. Sullivan's table. "With his nanny. Looks as though he wasted no time in finding his dearest friend." The trio laughed to see him hugging Gunner's neck. "Did you get two more dogs?"

Gwen chimed in, "Those two are mine. I'm only thankful they've not spied the mud pit yet. Mark my words, they'll be in it before the fair ends."

With little persuading, J'non returned the conversation to the York trip.

"You must allow me to take you one day," Siobhan said. "Both of you. A ladies' trip. You can't mistake it for London, to be certain. In fact, it's grander in uncountable ways. For this trip, we're to see the traveling showmen. They're rumored to have a menagerie of exotic animals — do they mean husbands, do you think? — along with rope dancers and other entertainment. Usually, we attend the assembly rooms, pretend not to wager at the horse races, spend at the shops all the winnings we pretend we didn't earn, and, let's see, what else? Well, never mind what we usually do. The important point is what would happen on the ladies' trip. There's the theater, the bowling green, countless shops. If the husbands insisted on joining, there are dozens upon dozens of coffeehouses to amuse — and by that, I mean distract — the gentlemen while we shop. Oh! The most divine confectionery in England — a pox to any in London once you've been to York! There are no less than three asylums one can tour — if you go in for that sort of entertainment, which I do not, to be certain."

She carried on, exciting both J'non and Gwen with the possibilities of a ladies' trip. Not long into the conversation did a commotion at the opposite end of the green catch their attention. They craned their necks to see, but it was too far, and there were too many people in the way.

Gwen asked, "Is it time for the tug-of-war competition?"

"I thought it was after the assembly," J'non said. "Otherwise, how will those who lose be able to dance? They'll be covered in mud."

"All the more fun," said the vicar's wife with a twinkle in her eyes.

Setting out a "closed for now" sign, Gwen ushered them to the site where a crowd had gathered. The men who had signed up to participate were lining up. J'non looked around for Trevor but did not see him. This was where she had left him not but half an hour before. Then a hand touched the small of her back, sending warm tingles down her spine. She turned.

Trevor leaned down and whispered, "Don't forget my kiss when I win."

With that tease, he joined the others.

The teams looked evenly matched, as far as J'non could tell. They huddled on either side of the rope, conferring with each other on whatever plan was needed to win a tug-of-war competition. Sir Roland, she noted, had not signed up, rather sidled next to his wife to watch the show. Mr. Harvey, however, had signed up, and was huddled with Trevor's team. The other team consisted of a few familiar faces and a few strangers. The ones she knew were two gentlemen farmers and a couple of their fieldhands. The ones she did not know looked like burly lumberjacks who would have made an easy win of the axe toss game. One in particular could have passed for a pirate with his swarthy complexion from too much sun and his broad-shouldered physique from climbing topsails with a cutlass at his side.

She turned her attention back to Trevor, who looked positively aristocratic in comparison to the pirate. Despite him being *Trevor* to her now, she could see, in comparison to the other man, the same Lord Pickering she had met when she first descended from the carriage.

Her thoughts drifted to the myriad *what ifs*. What if she and Trevor had met under different circumstances? Had her parents lived and had they known him, would they have arranged an introduction?

The Reverend Harvey's words about predestination came to mind. It troubled her to think anything in her life could be of God's will, but without the sequence of events, she never would have met Trevor. Surely, though, there could have been a better way, a less destructive way involving the survival of her parents and Trevor's meeting her as she was, a baronet's daughter, not as a broken and fraudulent woman, a penniless nobody. As enamored with him as she was, she could not say if her feelings would be different if he did not represent safety. She would like to believe it was the man himself she cared for, but how could she be sure?

What of his affection for her? Would there come a time in life when his love and trust was so unconditional, she could confess everything to him? She did not think so. Confessions would be better sooner rather than later so as not to live a lie too long, but the sooner, the riskier, since it would take time to earn the requisite unconditional love and trust. Then, did it matter when, if by admitting their marriage was fraudulent, she would undermine his trust? It would be impossible to explain that she was herself despite the fraud, that her affection was real, that *she* was real, only the name being false.

There was more to her confession. Admitting the lie would require recalling the events that led her down this path. After hearing all she had done, all she had been, he could not possibly forgive and love her.

The crowd applauded as the teams lined alongside the rope, waiting for the referee to whistle for them to begin.

J'non pushed her doubts out of her mind. What silly thoughts to have at a fair! Worrying about *what ifs* did no one any good. For now, she was safe. Trevor looked over to her before picking up the rope. In that single look, he conveyed his desire for the prize should his team win. Her cheeks warmed.

The referee whistled. The tug began.

A hush fell over the crowd. At first, it did not appear anything was happening. Both sides leaned away from each other, rope in hand, all posed as if frozen in place.

One of the teammates grunted. Another dug in his heels. The rope edged in one direction, then the other. The opposing team took a hearty step backwards, pulling Trevor's team forward towards the pit of doom. She could see the strain on Trevor's face as he braced and heaved.

Siobhan tucked her arm through J'non's and said in a hush, "This would be a far better show if they had taken off more than their frock coats. Imagine if they had removed their waistcoats, as well, or…" She paused, then in the barest of whispers said, "their shirts."

J'non gasped and leaned away.

Siobhan tittered. "Don't tell me you don't wish to see the sinew of your husband's muscles as he flexes."

Had the sun brightened overhead? J'non could feel a trickle of sweat bead down her forehead. She could not think of anything so scandalous, much less say it. Siobhan, by contrast, was fearless, though J'non could not recall her saying anything so vulgar before. Vulgar yet… *tantalizing*.

J'non bit her bottom lip and admired Trevor's efforts anew.

Just when his team was a shoe's breadth from the mud, they surged backwards, three steps, then four, then —

Their opponents were dragged into the mud pit, some flying face first, others dragged in by their heels. They did not go silently. A few cried for mercy as they fell, while others laughed, and at least two whooped with inexplicable delight. The crowd applauded, a few jeering at the losers and some cheering on the winners. Rather than rush away from the rope, the teammates clapped shoulders and exchanged words, the winning team helping their opponents out of the mud, all laughing over the game.

"Are you disappointed not to see him covered in mud?" Siobhan asked.

Gwen, who J'non had not realized was standing behind them, said, "Shocked, more like. I swear Obadiah finds every excuse on earth to play in mud. Just you wait. Before we return home, he and the boys will be romping in the mud together, Obadiah under the pretense of retrieving the errant dogs — his usual Banbury tale for these occasions."

Trevor and Mr. Harvey joined them then, followed by Sir Roland and a mud-covered gentleman who — oh, it was the pirate. J'non quirked her head.

Smiling from ear to ear, Trevor came to J'non's side and said for her ears only in a sinfully husky voice, "I'll collect my winnings the moment I get you alone." He then turned to his companions and said, "May I introduce to you this charming fellow?"

The mud-covered pirate stepped forward with a bow.

"This," Trevor said, "is the Earl of Roddam. And this is my wife, Lady Pickering."

J'non hid her shock as they exchanged salutations. In short explanation, Trevor went on to say Sir Roland — now with wrinkled nose — had introduced the earl before the game began.

So, this was their mysterious neighbor in the north, the earl with five earldoms. Goodness. He was not at all what she expected. He was almost brutish. But then, now that he stood up close, if one could look past the sun-kissed complexion and intimidating physique, he was rather handsome, she supposed, in an unconventional way, assuming one also ignored the caked mud. Although, what was handsome about him, she could not pinpoint, for his eyes were black as coal, his nose too large for so a lean face, and his hair unfashionably long even if tied back with a large bow. To make matters worse, he spoke with a faint Scottish burr. No, she could not put a finger on what made him handsome, but the dangerous mystique about him held an appeal.

"Come," the earl said to Trevor, including the group with a sweep of his hand. "Meet my countess."

He nodded to where J'non saw Siobhan's nanny and son playing with Gunner, Sammy, and Simon. Petting the dogs were two other toddlers and behind them a lovely young woman. *That* could not be his wife, could it? Trevor offered his arm and led her towards Gunner's new friends, the Harveys and Osbornes following behind the sludge-soaked pirate.

Chapter 17

Morning rain delayed their guests' departure. When the drizzle passed, so did the eagerness for an early morning start, all parties enjoying camaraderie. What was an additional hour or three in good company?

Trevor walked with Sir Roland and Lord Roddam through the knot garden. A cold wind had him shrugging deeper into his greatcoat. The overcast sky, grey and gloomy, offered no warmth from the friendly sun. J'non trailed behind the gentlemen, deep in conversation with Lady Osborne and Lady Roddam, three children and one Lurcher gathered around their skirts.

The voice of petulance cried behind him, "I wanter. I wanter. I wanter."

The gentlemen turned to see Lady Roddam scooping her three-year-old son Cuthbert Lancaster, Baron Embleton into her arms and cooing gentle words. The baron's fists flailed at her shoulder as his face turned a remarkable shade of red. To add to the drama, tears flowed, followed by a wail to end all wails. Trevor's expression remained unchanged, but he could see J'non's smile tighten around the corners. Lady Roddam's four-year-old daughter left the safety of her mother's side to approach Lord Roddam.

Lady Freya eyed Trevor and Roland with bashful curiosity as she walked to her papa and said with such quiet politeness, Trevor had a curious longing for a daughter of his own. His gaze lingered on J'non, who had turned her attention to helping soothe the boy.

"Papa," Freya said. "Cuthbert wants to see the labyrinth. May we?"

Lord Roddam squatted on his haunches, eye level with his daughter. "What does Mummy say?"

Freya looked down at her hands and fidgeted with the ribbon at her waist. "Not without adult. She's with friends and promises later. But we'll leave and there willn't be later. Cuthbert wants to go. May I take him? I will adult."

He took her hands in his and raised them both to kiss the air above her knuckles. "You think only of your brother? You'll sacrifice your time with the ladies to chaperone him?" When she did not answer, he said, "I think you want to go too. Just a little."

She glanced at him through lowered lashes then turned her attention back to her hands, still held in her Papa's bearpaws. "A little."

"As I thought. Did you ask Lord or Lady Pickering if you, Cuthbert, and Caoimhín could see their labyrinth?"

She shook her head, eyeing first the ladies at a distance, then turning her attention to Trevor. Her face wrinkled in concentration. Just when Trevor expected her to ask him if she could take the boys for a tour of the labyrinth, she hid her face against her father's shoulder, too shy to ask.

Trevor said to Lord Roddam, "You're welcome if you're daring. I confess, I've not explored it so can't say with confidence it's fit for children. The gardener has accomplished feats these past two months, but if trimming the hedges in the maze is one of them, that remains to be seen."

Roddam nodded, stood with his hand holding Freya's, and turned to his wife.

Before he could walk over to them, Lady Osborne called out, "No need for gallantry, Lord Roddam. I wish to see this fabled beast's lair. Caoimhín, Gunner, and I are off for the hunt. Anyone wishing to accompany may do so."

Trevor arched a brow, curious what the ladies had told the obstinate baron, for this was the first he had heard of a beast hiding in his labyrinth. Freya, on the other hand, tugged at her papa's hand, undaunted by man or monster and eager to accept the invitation. Lady Roddam, still holding her son, began to follow Lady Osborne. Were they all to explore the labyrinth, then? Not that Trevor minded, necessarily, but he was not inclined to change the course of the morning because one little boy threw a tantrum. Perhaps after distracting the children for an hour, they could all agree to explore; in this way, the child would not think he had won the war with a few tears. Was this Trevor's approach or the internal voice of his father?

He had no time to wonder, for Lady Roddam stopped halfway across the garden to hand her son to J'non and grip the corner of one of the statues, looking for all the world as though she expected to faint.

Lord Roddam rushed to her side.

Trevor would have been concerned had J'non not appeared unworried. She set down little Lord Embleton at Freya's insistence. The children paid their mother no mind, Freya taking her brother's hand, and traipsing behind Lady Osborne, who also did not seem worried about Lady Roddam. J'non shared hushed words with both Lord and Lady Roddam, a smile on her lips, the only concern showing itself as a slender furrow between her brows.

Roland stepped forward at Trevor's side. "I hadn't thought her delicate, but then, so many women are. It's all the rage, is it not? To be of a delicate constitution, tender, fainting, prone to migraines. I'm fortunate to have a wife who could scale a mountainside if needed. Not that I mean any disrespect to Lady Roddam."

"No need for apologies, Roland. I understand. J'non may be softspoken, but she's as hardy as an ox, or so I'm discovering." He turned one of the garden chairs to face the walled garden as the troupe of children and dog, led by Lady Osborne, disappeared through the gate. Sitting, he crossed one leg over the other. "Will the York trip affect our Wednesday ride?"

Roland shrugged a shoulder. "I'll send word if it does. I've promised Siobhan at least one excursion to the traveling showmen's camp. Meanwhile, I've, er, business to attend to. I don't expect it to take more than a day, but one never knows."

He did not explain, nor did Trevor ask. After a month of growing friendship given Lady Osborne's attendance at the weekly sewing circle and never failing to bring Roland with her, Trevor had shared with the gentleman the ongoing joke of Roland being a government agent of some sort. To add to the fun, Roland never denied the fact and fed it as often as possible with hints about clandestine meetings. The truth, Trevor and J'non had decided, was far less exciting, so they continued with the fiction.

Lord Roddam rejoined them. Trevor could see J'non sitting on a bench with Lady Roddam, who, despite looking pale, appeared unfazed by the dizzy spell or whatever had ailed her.

Bluntly and without preamble, Roland said, "I never knew her ladyship was the fainting sort."

The earl took a seat, crossing his ankles beneath him. "You'd feel faint, too, if you were carrying my third child."

Raising his quizzing glass, Roland looked Roddam up and down. "Is that an invitation or a threat?"

Roddam scowled for half a minute before bellowing a laugh. Roland reached a hand to shake Roddam's with words of congratulations. Trevor did the same.

"When's the happy arrival?" Roland asked.

"By my sister's guess, April or thereabouts."

"Your *sister's* guess?" Roland questioned. "Am I to assume, then, your sister is prophetic?"

"Wouldn't be surprised." The earl grunted. "She's a midwife. Or rather she was."

As Roland and Roddam talked about the earl's sister, Trevor's attention drifted to J'non and Lady Roddam. J'non's face was brightened by a laugh at something her companion said. She was at ease and happy. How dreary life had been without her. Had someone said that a few months ago, he would have disagreed, but seeing life on the other side of loneliness, he could realize his old life for what it had been. Without trying, she had given his life new meaning, a reason outside the memory of his father to prove his worth and find honor in duty.

He drifted back to his mates, the earl in the middle of an explanation of his sister's midwifery skills. Trevor was unsure if he liked the man or not. What he was sure of was the relief of J'non's having invited the Osbornes to join for the evening and now through the morning. Without conferring with her, he had invited Lord Roddam to sup with them after the festival, and although he had extended the invitation to Roland, the latter had declined with the intention to make for York before evening. That J'non had convinced Lady Osborne to stay made everything far more congenial than Trevor and J'non dining with strangers and having them as overnight guests. Roland did not know the earl or countess well, but he was, at least, acquainted from their previous visits to their Yorkshire estate. An opposing pair those two gentlemen made, Roland being a dandified rogue with mischievous smiles and flirty winks, and lest anyone forget, a generous amount of flair and good fashion, while Roddam was as gruff and hard around the edges as the local blacksmith. Lady Roddam, for that matter, appeared her husband's foil. All gentleness and tenderness, grace personified.

Trevor asked Roddam, "For how long will you stay in residence at Creighton Hall?"

"Can't say." Roddam laced his fingers behind his head. "We only came for the fête. Lizbeth's excuse to meet you and Lady Pickering. Mine too, 'spose. Typically, we spend a month at Creighton en route to London."

"I'm honored to be the reason for an impromptu visit," Trevor said. "If you're not rushing back to Northumberland, join us Wednesday? My wife hosts a weekly sewing circle, and Roland and I use the excuse to stretch our legs."

Roland said, "What he means is we ride hell for leather across the barren wasteland that is North Yorkshire. If our horses aren't frothing at the mouth by the end, we've wasted the day."

"He's jesting, of course," Trevor said, "about the horses."

Roddam merely arched a brow.

Trevor's attention wandered back to J'non, lingering for a moment on the swanlike slope of her neck. He turned back to the gentlemen in time to see them exchange a glance. Good grief — they knew him to be lovesick. He could see it in their expressions, never mind their faces were meant to be inscrutable. Was it so wrong to be enamored with one's wife? Even now, when surrounded by companions, all he wanted was to tease her into a ride to the lake. They had to break in her new saddle, after all. He cleared his throat in nonchalance and shifted in his chair.

"I hear you've had trouble with flooding," Roddam said.

Trevor thanked him silently for broaching a new subject rather than pointing out the looks of longing. "The fête was intended to raise money for recovery. We've been working this past month on repairing damage and adjusting the terrain to better divert floodwaters. Prevention is the key, I believe."

"A shame my canals aren't routed closer to your moors," Roddam said. "Alas, we're planned for the west to meet up with the Ripon Canal."

Roland swung his quizzing lens on its ribbon and yawned. "I should have known you'd find an excuse to mention mining. Can you not see we're in polite company? Let us gossip instead about the speed of Mr. White's thoroughbreds — anyone in the market for a new horse? I might be in love."

Ignoring Roland, Trevor said, "I can't say I've oft heard mining introduced in conversation."

Roddam unlaced his fingers to rub the arms of his chair, then prop himself with his elbow. "Entrepreneurial project. Not much to tell. Bootstrapping in the coal mine industry. Began construction in '91, turned a tidy profit, gathered a stakeholder or two, now solving the problem of coal transport by way of southbound canals. Next will be using the shareholdings to purchase a new steam-driven piston engine."

"Don't encourage him," Roland warned Trevor.

A bell clanging drew everyone's attention to the labyrinth. It clanged once. Paused. Clanged again with fervor. Paused. A tiny half-hearted clang. Then following a *whoop* of delight that sounded unmistakably like Lady Osborne, another clang. They must have found the center of the labyrinth.

Amidst the chuckles in the knot garden, Trevor lost himself in thought. Coal mining? Trevor could see Roddam involved in mining, but more as a miner than an owner. What was an earl doing with a mining company? He did not ask. Instead, he inquired more about the canal, curious if he could use the insight for any sort of flood prevention. Could this be the answer to their problem? Not that he did not have faith in the preventative measures they were undertaking, but canals held promise above and beyond the extension of embankments and the like.

Roddam replied, "Since canals aren't in your future, you could dig ditches, man-made streams and rivers."

"We've been working to add meanders in the beck to connect to the river," Trevor said with a touch of pride.

"There you go. Problem solved. If you're concerned, make more of them."

As much as Trevor tried to pull the conversation back to the canals, curious to explore that possibility in more depth, Roland was yawning again, and Roddam was not offering unsolicited information.

Aiming for a different approach, Trevor asked, "What interested you in coal mining?"

"The way of the future," Roddam said. Rather than explain his meaning, he continued with, "My family has been bitten by the entrepreneur bug. Even my sister started her own business."

Roland's attention piqued. "The midwife turned baroness?"

"Aye," Roddam said with a laugh. "She's a force to be reckoned with, our Lilith. Purchased a healthy portion of Hampshire and built her own village. Foundling hospital, orphanage, schoolhouse, workhouse, women's home…" He circled a hand as though it continued his list for him. "Noach Cottage, she calls it. A pity the fête was not a couple of weeks ago. She, along with her family and resident physician Dr. Knowlton, was staying with me to help our cousin's neighbor with a war injury of some nature. Had the timing been better, she and her family could have attended. I should have mentioned it to her. She loves charity cases." He winked at Trevor. "They left not but two weeks ago. Ah well, my nephew is only eight months, so he may be too young for the frivolity of a fair."

Roland leaned forward in his chair. "A women's home? What sort of women's home?"

Roddam quirked the single eyebrow again. "For women who have fallen on troubled times."

"By fallen, you mean *fallen*?" Roland asked.

"I mean, troubled times. Any woman seeking refuge, be it from a heavy-handed husband she cannot divorce or otherwise. Lilith offers them shelter and safety, training, even relocation. It was an undertaking of an idea, and she's succeeded with zeal."

Roland slumped back into his chair before muttering almost to himself, "Siobhan will find this interesting. Had there been a Noach Cottage in Ireland before we met—" He stopped midsentence, looked from Roddam to Trevor, then said, "She would have wanted to tour the facility." His laugh sounded forced.

Neither Trevor nor Roddam commented, but Trevor found Roland's interest in Baroness Collingwood's project to be curious. How he and his wife met remained a mystery, although they teased about elopements and secret nuptials. Why the fixation on a women's home? Polite conversation? Or was this part of the spy craft fiction? At this moment of natural transition into a new topic, Roland returned Roddam's attention back to the cottage, asking how the baroness relocated the young ladies. Roddam offered what he could but admitted he knew little about the endeavor.

As interesting as the cottage sounded and as curious as Roland's interest in it, Trevor's thoughts flitted back to the canals. He eyed J'non again as she talked animatedly with Lady Roddam. What would she think of the possibility?

After a time in the chill air, Trevor had begun feeling peckish and had ceased feeling his toes. As he was wishing J'non would lead them inside for tea, Lady Osborne emerged from the walled garden with three sleepy children who denied they needed a nap and a dog who expressed much the same sentiment. As soon as Gunner set paws in the knot garden, he flopped at J'non's feet.

Lady Roddam said, "Sebastian, love. What do you think of getting a dog? How cozy the castle would be with a Lurcher of our own."

That awakened the children, both Freya and Cuthbert clamoring at the idea of a puppy.

Lord Roddam grunted before nudging Roland and nodding towards the snoozing dog. "Didn't you say you were in the market for a horse?"

Later that afternoon, after the guests had departed, Trevor sat at his desk in the study, mulling over Roddam's coal mine. He was not interested in entrepreneurship, and investing sounded a risky gamble, but he could not stop thinking about the coal canals — could he mimic something similar on his own? He did not have the coin for any such endeavor. Could Roddam's canals be rerouted through the moors?

Undecided about his intention or how to phrase his thoughts, he readied his quill and inkpot and began a letter to his solicitor. Lloyd would interpret Trevor's fumbling and put intention to action, answering all the questions Trevor had not known to ask. Lloyd would also offer an objective perspective.

J'non tightened the shawl around her shoulders before resuming her sewing. There was a draft in the drawing room. A hearty fire crackled in the fireplace, yet she could discern an unmistakable draft from one of the windows. Pulling the thread through the fabric with a gentle tug, she looked across to Trevor, who wore a banyan over his shirt and breeches and evening slippers over stockings, the image of comfort after their meaty supper. Whatever she intended to say about the draft was brushed aside at seeing him so positioned. Trevor had slipped halfway into the chair, ankles crossed, his attention on the hearth. He was distracted. He had been distracted all afternoon following the departure of their guests and again through the evening. Was the canal possibility so exciting? Must be. A letter to Mr. Barmby, Jr. had already been dispatched, and he could talk of little else at the dining table.

Turning back to her work, she allowed Trevor to mull over plans. Best not interrupt.

If only both families had been able to stay longer. The company had been delightful. Lord Roddam perplexed her, but Lady Roddam was kind and gentlehearted. Having now met her, J'non wished she had taken Trevor's original suggestion of writing to the countess to form an early acquaintance. Their daughter was a gem and tugged at J'non's heartstrings with every spoken word and bashful expression. More than once, J'non's gaze had lingered on Trevor, thoughts of children on her mind. As for little Baron Embleton… *well*. He was a darling when not in the thralls of a tantrum. Four tantrums in one morning. How many he might have thrown while they supped the evening before, she could not say, because he was safely tucked in for the night with his nanny, but *four* that morning. The tantrums, in truth, were not what had her enthralled, rather speculation as to what sort of father Trevor would be when the time came, if the time came.

She stole a glance at him, still deep in thought. Rain tapped at the windowpane. The weather had more than made up for the drought. Thankfully, only one biblical flood.

She sat back and admired her work. There. Complete. At least for now. Earlier, the tear had littered the drawing room floor with cotton and straw. All better now.

A hand shielded her work from view. Palm up, fingers curling in invitation, Trevor's hand waved her attention.

J'non looked up with a bat of her eyelashes. "Does his lordship wish to inspect my sewing skills?"

"Nothing of the sort. I want to dance."

She blinked, her smile faltering. "Dance?"

"We never had an opportunity at the fair. Come. Dance with me now."

Leery, she set aside her project and took his hand. "How are we to dance alone?"

Rather than replying, he hooked an arm about her waist and pulled her against him. Her eyes widened and her body stiffened. This was not at all proper, even in their own drawing room. Her cheeks flared with embarrassment.

"Relax," he coaxed. "Follow my lead."

She would never call his movements *dancing*, but once he set a rhythm, it was easier for her to relax against him, soon allowing him to persuade her arms around his neck. He did little more than sway to an unheard beat and move them at snail speed across the drawing room.

"Is this something you learned during your travels?" she asked, admiring the softness of his features as he gazed back at her, their faces so close she could smell his shaving soap.

"Nothing of the sort. I made it up. Just now." He grinned and twirled her once, then twice, then thrice until she squealed for him to stop.

However unusual was this dance, she preferred it to the country dancing at the fair. It had been splendid fun, but she had not danced since before her parents died. Not only had the steps and music changed since then, but she had forgotten what few steps she had once known. It had been a godsend that the country dances were lively and forgiving with many of the villagers not having any idea how to properly dance either. The lead couple in each dance had demonstrated the steps, but most of the villagers made up their own versions anyway, causing much laughter and confusion. There she had been saved. Trevor may not be so forgiving. Then, could she get away with not knowing how to dance since her background was supposed to be of industry? Another saving grace.

Trevor rested his cheek against her temple as they continued their so-called dance. "What did you think of the earl and countess?" he asked.

Rather than stare at his cravat, she closed her eyes and relished in the scent of his spicy cologne mixed with soap. "I have every intention of corresponding with Lady Roddam. She invited us to spend a week or two in Northumberland next summer." J'non knew an earlier invitation had not been offered since Lady Roddam was with child, but until that fact became obvious for all to see, it would not be polite to mention the condition to Trevor. Before he could say more, she said, "Lord Roddam must have made an impression on you. You've been distracted about canals all evening. Do you think they could truly prevent future flooding?"

"It's possible. We'll see what Lloyd thinks. I'll be impatient until I hear from him." He twirled her one last time before disentangling their arms and leading her to his chair. Perching on the arm of the chair, he kept her standing before him, her hands clasped in his. "This could be the key, J'non. This could be how I prove my worth." His smile broadened, the fire in the hearth reflecting in his eyes and making them appear to twinkle. "I keep thinking what he would say. My father, that is. I believe he would be proud of this idea. This is me earning honor through duty. *Ex pietas honore.*"

"*I'm* proud of you already. You've accomplished so much, Trevor, more than most would accomplish in years. All the repairs to the estate, to the village, to the surrounding lands. The preventative measures you've already enacted. The foreman you've hired for the home farm. The fête. Only look how successful the fête was with stalls and vendors from well beyond the march, all wanting to help support our neighboring little village."

His smile slipped at the corners as he shrugged off her words. Looking down at her hands, still held in his, he said, "I can't take responsibility for most of that. The people helped. Mr. Harvey helped. Many of the ideas were not even my own. *You* can take responsibility for a great deal of it, right down to the home farm. I admire you. I wish I could take command like you do. Recognize the problem and charge in to resolve it."

She laughed. "I've done nothing of the sort. I've never done anything of the sort. I'm a shriveled leaf, at mercy to the wind, taken wherever I'm led."

He shook his head and brought her hands to his lips. "No, you're the driving force. I'm the leaf."

Tugging her hands free, she cupped his face in her palms and angled him to look at her. "*I* am proud of you, Trevor. That's all that matters."

Unexpected hands wrapped around her waist and pulled her between his knees. "I've yet to collect my winnings." He waggled his eyebrows.

His fingers massaged her lower back, inching her closer. His eyes met hers, this time a fire of their own burning in his gaze. Nervous, excited, shy, J'non giggled as she leaned towards him. Before their lips could meet, something bumped against their legs. Something pushy and insistent. J'non drew back to find Gunner nosing between them. Once he realized he had their attention, he sat on his haunches, looking from one to the other of them.

"He wants a kiss too," Trevor said. "You, sir, can wait your turn. I'm first."

Trevor pulled her back to him and puckered for the kiss, ignoring the whining of the Lurcher.

"Oh!" J'non gasped, leaning away again. "Mr. Macaroni!"

Wriggling out of Trevor's grasp, she returned to her chair to fetch the toy she had repaired. Behind her, Gunner's tail thumped in rhythm with the rain. Nothing but a child's fabric doll stuffed with cotton and straw, button eyes replaced by embroidery in case Gunner thought them edible, yet the little toy was his most treasured possession.

"There you are. Stuffing replaced and hole mended." She handed it to the patiently waiting dog.

Gunner took it with care from her outstretched hand, then shook it vigorously between his teeth with a growl. Just when she thought he would burst the new seams, he trotted back to his place at the hearth, licked the doll, then rested it between his paws where he turned it into a pillow.

"A happy customer." She smiled after him. "Goodness. What time is it?"

Trevor, still seated on the arm of his chair, said, "No idea. Now, come here."

"*You* don't know what time it is? Impossible."

"I'm far more interested in collecting my winnings than keeping time. Now, *come here*." He flexed his forefinger and pointed between his knees where she had last stood.

Blushing anew, she took a step closer. Then another step. He growled. One more step. He pushed off from the chair just far enough to grab her hand. Ignoring her squeak, he tugged her to him and resumed his seat.

Her pulse racing and her skin afire, she swept a hand through his hair. Tucking a finger beneath his chin, she raised his face to look up at her. Inch by inch, she drew closer. He growled again. She shushed him before brushing her lips against his. Emboldened by the pride she felt for him and hoping he would sense it, she deepened the kiss, his prize not for the tug-o-war win but for being, by her estimation, all that was worthy and honorable.

Chapter 18

A glance down, palms up. Empty but clean. A green door. J'non raised a hand to the knocker. Lift. Drop. *Tap.* Lift. Drop. *Tap.* She looked to either side. *Tap. Tap.* Silence.

A glance down. Empty, dirt beneath nails. A yellow door. J'non raised a hand to the knocker. Lift. Drop. *Tap.* Lift. Drop. *Tap.* To either side, she peered, trembling. *Tap. Tap.* Silence.

A glance down, palms sweaty, dusty. A blue door. She raised a hand to the knocker. Lift. Drop. *Tap.* Left and right, she looked, pulse quickening. *Tap. Tap.* Noise within. Hope without. Air *whooshed* as the door opened. Straw *whizzed* as a broom hit her shins. A shout. A cry. A slammed door.

A glance. Dirty palms. A brown door. She lifted and dropped the knocker. *Tap. Tap.* She eyed around her. *Tap. Tap.* A shout within. A sob without.

A glance. Cracked, caked, blistered. A black door. She raised the knocker. *Tap.* Over hunched shoulders, she searched. A lean. A daze. A doze. A kick to the leg. Another kick. Numb to pain.

A glance. Raw and itchy. A grey door. *Tap. Tap.* Askance, she peered. Snarls within. Emptiness without.

A red door. *Tap. Tap.* Peering, shuffling, shaking. Air *whooshed* as the door opened.

The footman opened the front door, permitting the stocky figure of Mr. Lloyd Barmby, Jr. While Hawkins stood at the ready to greet the guest, Trevor stepped past the butler to clasp his solicitor's extended hand.

"Had I not seen for myself the approaching coach, I never would have believed it," Trevor said in greeting. "A letter would have sufficed. What the devil are you doing here?"

It had only been a week since he had written about the canal idea.

Lloyd looked him up and down. "I should ask you the same thing. Where's Lord Pickering? All I see before me is my old friend, Trevor Gaines. What the devil are *you* doing here?"

Only for a moment did Trevor furrow his brows in confusion. In the next moment, he closed the space between them and embraced his friend. His laugh grew heartier at Lloyd's perplexed expression.

Stepping aside, Trevor waited while one of the footmen took Lloyd's cold weather garments. "I wish J'non were here to greet you and show you to your room—I assume you're staying? But of course you're staying. I'll brook no argument to the contrary. Mr. Hawkins will see you to a room." With a nod to the butler, he said, "The blue room, I should think."

Hawkins cleared his throat and said, "Very good, my lord, the yellow room. Excellent choice."

Yes, that was right. The blue guest suite still had a dampness that the carpenter's team needed to see to. How did anyone survive without a butler? He winked at Hawkins, who remained impassive.

"Speaking of devils," Lloyd hedged, "who is J'non?"

"Ah. We have catching up to do, I see. My wife, Lady Pickering."

"You mean *Phoebe*?" Lloyd's voice was timbered in the sort of way one might expect a best mate's to be when reminding a friend that he had mistaken his mistress' name with his wife's name.

"We'll talk more in my study. Meet in, say, half an hour? Will you need longer?"

"You take me for a popinjay, my lord. I've come to talk investments and canals. I'm ready now." After whatever he saw in Trevor's expression, he added, "But I will not insult my host, who has forgotten himself and is treating me like a guest rather than his man of business. Far be it for me not to take advantage of hospitality." He smirked and followed the butler through the vestibule.

Arms laced, J'non walked down the village main with Gwen, a laugh on her lips.

Gwen said, "Obadiah will think us mad to be planning next year's fête already."

"But as you said, best to plan while this one is still fresh in mind." J'non nodded to Mrs. Millgrove and her daughter as they passed, then soon after Mr. and Mrs. Tuttle.

All around, people bustled, today being a market day. While J'non had arrived too late to see the cattle parade — as Gwen called it — down the main, she had been able to enjoy the end of the auction. The aroma of freshly baked bread lingered, thankfully overpowering the residual scents from the parade. She had never attended a market day before. As such, not only had the morning been as exhilarating as the fair, but she could not say if it was common for aristocrats to attend. Was she making a spectacle of herself by ogling like a child in a confectionary shop? Then, who cared what was common or traditional or expected?

Gwen slowed her pace as they approached the last terraced houses in the village. "We must host a dog contest. It was a pity our boys attended the whole of the festival without winning a single prize. Next year, let us remedy that."

"A prize for the waggiest tail?" J'non asked, stopping before the last house.

"And the pup most like their owner."

"A prize for the best trick?"

Gwen released J'non's arm and clasped her hands below her chin. "Oh, what about a prize for the most loyal to a child of or below the age of ten?"

"Yes to all. I'm certain when we propose the idea to the sewing circle, they'll have more prize suggestions. You can never have too many prizes when it comes to a dog contest."

"Right, well, this is where I must leave you," Gwen said. "You'll be fine for the remaining walk? Not too lonely?"

J'non laughed. "I'll have you know, I find myself to be good company."

They parted ways, Gwen to call on a parishioner, J'non to continue her trek home. It was not a far walk to Sladesbridge and one she knew well, one she loved. Familiar sights, sounds, and smells. Even the sheep she passed were familiar, each with a name, each looking up to watch her, as if recognizing her as an old friend.

She glanced down, palms up. Empty but clean. Palms down, pristine with trimmed nails and clean cuticles. The hands of a lady. A lady's hands. Lady Pickering's hands. *Her* hands. The chill in the air tingled her skin, and she was tempted to slip on the gloves she had tucked in the pocket of her cloak. But no, she might want to glance down again, remind herself of the smooth skin and clean nails. J'non shuddered at the memory of her most recent dream. Could it be considered a nightmare? There was nothing horrifying about it, nothing that would warrant it a nightmare, but calling it a dream did not encapsulate the fright it caused. Fright was not the correct word. Hopelessness? *Helplessness.* Yes, that was the correct word. There was nothing more frightening in this world than to feel *helpless*, a leaf in the wind.

She shuddered again, this time from an ambitious breeze fluttering the hem of her cloak, or so she told herself.

The front door of Sladesbridge opened before she had reached the steps, a warm welcome home. Before the footman could close the door behind her, Mr. Hawkins greeted her with a bow.

"My lady," he began, "his lordship is in the study with Mr. Barmby."

"Mr. Barmby?" she echoed. "Mr. *Barmby*? Wait, the steward or the solicitor?"

"The solicitor. Mr. Barmby, Jr."

"Oh. *Oh*! Oh, yes, he must have come as soon as he received the letter. This must be good news, then, yes?"

"As you say, my lady."

Should she go straight to the study, or should she refresh and change first? Had it been anyone else, she would not have hesitated to return to her room, but it was Mr. Barmby about the canal. Eager to hear what tidings he brought, she made straight for the study. Hopefully she did not smell like sweat or livestock. Maybe freshly baked bread?

A glance down, palms up. Empty but clean. A beige door. J'non raised a hand to knock. *Tap. Tap.* A mumble within. Anticipation without.

Too eager to wait, she opened the door and stepped inside. Trevor was seated behind his desk, studying parchments of some nature. Across from him sat the person she assumed to be Mr. Barmby — a man of square physique with a shock of blond hair, spectacles perched on his nose, and a quizzical expression raising his brows.

Both Trevor and Mr. Barmby rose when they saw her.

Trevor came around the desk and arrived at her side in a few strides. "I can see from your expression Hawkins has spoiled the surprise. No matter. May I introduce my childhood friend turned solicitor? Mr. Lloyd Barmby."

J'non inclined her head, unable to keep the smile from her lips. The solicitor had rushed to Yorkshire upon receiving Trevor's letter. This *must* be good news. "Welcome to our home, Mr. Barmby. I hope you'll be staying for dinner."

Trevor said, "This, dear friend, is my wife."

Mr. Barmby's quizzical expression transformed to one of what J'non could only describe as dissatisfaction tinged with anger. Her smile faltered.

Rather than bowing, nodding, extending a hand, or otherwise, Mr. Barmby pulled his shoulders back and said, "*You* are not Phoebe Whittington."

Chapter 19

He stared at Lloyd from the other side of the desk. J'non had already excused herself. His elbow against the desk, his forefinger to his temple, he scowled.

"My humblest apologies," Lloyd mumbled for the fifth time, his neck flushed.

Trevor opened his mouth to reply but thought better of it. His mood had shifted in a dangerous direction, one that did not inspire trust in polite replies.

"As you explained, my lord, she is not Phoebe Whittington but J'non Gaines, Lady Pickering, a distinction I have noted and will not mistake again. I am mortified to have caused offense. At the first opportunity, I will apologize to her ladyship."

Taking a deep breath, Trevor calmed his nerves. Lloyd's rudeness was not the only point that angered him, more so was Mr. Whittington's deception to have caused Lloyd's reaction in the first place.

In a controlled tone, not wanting to reprimand his solicitor any more than the man was already berating himself, Trevor said, "As you've explained, Mr. Whittington is a blackguard. Is it any wonder she prefers to use the name her mother called her?"

"Indeed." Lloyd fidgeted with the corner of one of the maps. "Do you think she can forgive me?"

"She has a heart of gold," was all he said.

"I'm ashamed to have spoken out of defense. I took one look at her and knew Mr. Whittington had deceived me. He had described his daughter as a remarkable beauty with a vivacious personality, a buxom beauty at that. I never saw her personally. Should have done. Took his word, the scoundrel. I falsely represented your betrothed, unwittingly duping you. What must you have thought of me to realize my description deceptive?"

Dropping his hand to the desk, Trevor drummed his fingers. "On this point, let us be clear. Not another word of insult to the lady. She is my *wife*, and she is the most remarkable beauty I know, ever have known, and ever will know. As a balm to your conscience, I never thought myself deceived. When she first stepped down from the carriage, you should know, I was relieved."

He did not elaborate. Discussing his thoughts about his wife was not something he intended to do, not with anyone except the lady in question.

Lloyd nodded and mumbled additional apologies.

"Put it out of your mind for now," Trevor said. "We understand each other, and soon, so shall she, although you needn't explain your confusion to her. A simple apology will suffice. Knowing her, she's already forgotten the slight." Turning his attention back to the maps, he said, "Let's focus on this for now, then we'll retire to the drawing room, where I hope you'll take tea with us."

"Of course, my lord."

"Can I convince you to call me Trevor?" He attempted a grin, however strained, trying to lighten the mood.

That he still felt rankled to have seen J'non's smiling visage stricken pale should not interfere with business matters. Despite Lloyd's rudeness, she had been as stoic as ever in the face of disaster, begging their pardon as if it had been she who had wronged rather than their guest, then inviting them to take tea when they had finished their discussion.

The conversation soon turned back to the maps scattered across the desk. The most notable ones included a detailed map of the north moors from cartographer Robert Wilkinson, the *British Itinerary* depicting all turnpikes in England from Daniel Paterson, and the road maps from John Owen and Emanuel Bowen. While none showed the topography of the area, namely the rivers and dales, several came with notes on the important geographical features. He wished there were more on the moors, specifically, but the area was still mostly uncharted, even by the best cartographers.

Lloyd drew his finger along a section of the Paterson map. "This is the path of River Derwent. We want the canal to lead here. With minimal effort, we should convince the Earl of Roddam this is a superior route. His plan of going west and meeting the Ure or the Ouse would require more locks, thus more expense. I assure you, the route to the Derwent is superior."

"Good. I don't want to propose to him a new route because I'm being selfish. 'Dear Lord Roddam, would you please pay from your own company's stock to put a waterway through my lands so I can avoid future flooding? Thank you for footing the bill for me.'"

"Rest assured," Lloyd said. "This *is* superior. We should ride the route before proposing this to him. Soon. Before dinner? Tomorrow? I suggest before dinner. We'll need to note conflicts and barriers. I have in mind terrain and any landowners along the way. As many as we can circumvent, the better."

"Do you think landowners could be a problem?"

Lloyd shrugged a shoulder. "Given the uprising in Yorkshire over the Great North Road, I would err on the side of caution. Crossing a landowner's property will require their signature on the petition. They may be hesitant. Wouldn't you? Thinking they'll lose land, be forced to help build and maintain the canal, even fear being taxed for it. We'll need to confer with the Earl of Roddam about hiring contractors to build and maintain. A proposal of my own: what if landowners could use the canal for their own goods? Quite the enticement. If his lordship were amenable. For the right coin, they could use the canal to ship and receive goods. Must it only be for transporting coal from Lord Roddam's mine?"

"What about the market towns?" Trevor eyed the map. "Could those not also be used to convince both the earl and landowners? The coal, or whatever goods, would not only be destined for York but the towns along the way. This could increase clientele for anything being transported down the canal. It's one thing to make a purchase knowing you'll have to travel to York to retrieve it—think of the time and expense of pack-mules and the like—and another to learn you can have it delivered at the nearest market town."

Lloyd nodded, rubbing his chin in thought. "We'll need to confer with the earl. Next task will be to solicit signatures from landowners. All we need is a majority. Then the petition can be presented to Parliament. I anticipate no more than two months for the authorization by Act of Parliament to begin building the canal."

"And the investment in his mine you mentioned from the outset?" Trevor set aside the maps and steepled his fingers, feeling confident and hopeful.

"Yes, yes, as I said, it would behoove you to invest. I know your concerns, but I've spoken with Father, that is, Mr. Barmby, Sr. He is confident you can pull from the Tidwell Hall accounts to invest as a stakeholder. A gamble worth making."

"How is it I'm able to pull from the Tidwell accounts to invest but was given the runaround about using any Tidwell money for Sladesbridge?"

"That's between you and your steward," Lloyd said. "Knowing Father—er, Mr. Barmby—he would say the investment is worth the gamble while renovating a 'money pit' is not, but don't tell him I said that. Oh, and before I forget, I'm under strict orders to tell you from him, if you don't hire a steward for Sladesbridge before the year ends, he'll send a new candidate every week until you do."

"I believe he would." Trevor chuckled. "With the home farm planned, I have high hopes Sladesbridge will be generating a sustainable income by this time next year."

"So you said. You wrote that the method to be used came from Lady Pickering?" Lloyd shook his head. "Astonishing. Under normal circumstances, I would advise against listening to a woman, but as she is the daughter of Mr. Whittington, it might be the wisest decision. The man is as rich as Croesus. I mean, they don't call him the Textile King of London for nothing! The man is brilliant when it comes to matters of money and progress. It's in her blood."

Rather than accompanying Trevor to the drawing room for tea, Lloyd begged for a moment's reprieve in his suite, promising to join them in half an hour. Trevor made his way to the drawing room alone.

He entered to find J'non standing at one of the windows, hands wrapped about her upper arms as if chilled. "I'll have Mr. Thompson see to the draft," he said. "Until then, come by the fire and warm yourself."

She flinched at the sound of his voice, as though she had not heard him enter. Her eyes were wide and her face still pale.

He could throttle Lloyd anew. No, he reminded himself, it had been Mr. Whittington's deception to cause Lloyd's rudeness. He could throttle them both to have caused her any discomfort.

With tenderness in his tone, Trevor said, "I apologize if my solicitor startled you. Although he's never met you, he was led to believe you were… different… in appearance." He hesitated, wondering if it would make matters worse or better to explain just how different. He settled on it making matters worse for her to know her father had described her as being voluptuous of figure in order to snare a husband. "Lloyd is both mortified and humbled," he said instead. "While I hope you can accept his apology when he joins for tea, I'll understand if his introduction was not just beyond the pale but offensive."

Rather than reply, J'non closed her eyes.

When she opened them, she dropped her arms to her side, then looked down at her hands, flexing her fingers.

At length, she turned to face him, smile renewed. "I'm so happy he'll be joining us for tea. And dinner?"

"If you wish?" He waited for her nod. "Cook will have my head on a platter for dessert. I want to take Lloyd for a ride, which will delay dinner."

Her eyebrows raised. "Good news, then? About the canal?"

"Come and sit by the fire." Trevor rubbed his hands together. "I've much to tell you."

Chapter 20

H e lifted the cup to his lips and savored a sip. *Mmm.* Lord Roddam had not exaggerated. The best coffee Trevor had ever tasted. Closing his eyes, he enjoyed another taste. Without a doubt, he would frequent this establishment again. The inn in question, The Black Anvil, was closer to him than to Roddam, but the earl had insisted they meet there for the divine cuisine. Trevor had assumed the man jesting. If this coffee, which the earl had written to order first, was an accurate gauge of the food to come, then Trevor would be hard pressed not to eat here once a week.

The door to the private dining room swung open. The Earl of Roddam stepped in, handing his riding adornments to an awaiting footman.

With a nod, Roddam accepted the seat across from Trevor. "Pickering." Glancing at the coffee cup, he said, "I see you took my suggestion. And?"

"Finest I've had, although you'll not hear me confess it to my kitchen staff."

The earl grunted a laugh. After settling himself at the table and indicating he was ready for refreshment, he said, "You're fortunate, Pickering. I've not yet petitioned Parliament. Any changes to the route can still be made."

"Fortunate for us both, as I see it. Initial thoughts on the notes I sent?"

"You've no need to convince me. I know the route is superior." Roddam's attention turned to the arrival of his coffee before continuing. "I chose west because your predecessor was unresponsive to my correspondences. I could not very well plough through another man's land without his approval, however much I might have wished to, and so I opted for the more costly and roundabout route. West proved less obtrusive, ultimately meeting with the Ripon Canal."

Trevor leaned back in his chair, nodding to the footman to bring the meal. "You didn't think to proposition me after I inherited?"

"It crossed my mind. Briefly. I had already settled on the route west and considered it inappropriate timing to approach you. Had you been in residence longer, had we already met, perhaps, but my plan was to submit the petition this November. Poor timing."

Would he have considered such a proposition had Roddam approached him? He rather thought not, at least not before the flood. The idea of building an extensive canal across his land and that of the landowners within the march, all so a stranger could have the convenience of transporting his coal south would have made Trevor uncomfortable. Now it seemed a godsend. That Roddam had not approached him increased Trevor's respect for the earl.

Trevor said, "I've spent the past three days studying and riding the route with my solicitor, but I've not spoken to any of the landowners or tenants who would be affected, nor do I have any formal paper-work to share outside of the notes I sent you. I'm afraid we wouldn't be ready by November."

With a wave of his hand, Roddam said, "I'm confident. The session opens October 29th, this Thursday. We need only around a week to collect the signatures—assuming you're persuasive, Pickering—then add those to my existing documentation, which is ready to submit. Petitioning in November offers the advantage of this passing before spring. I promise we will be home before Christmas and bypass winter weather. Then, lucky us, ready to make the trip all over again in spring, but at that point with our families—nothing is more heartwarming than a snail-speed carriage ride with cranky and bored children. Just you wait," he said with a laugh. "You're not opposed to a quick London trip, are you, Pickering? Without families and carriages and all that, we could make it in a day if we wanted."

Trevor nearly choked on his coffee. "A day? I think not."

Roddam grinned. "You've no sense of adventure."

"Let us table this for a moment to talk investments. I have another proposal for you that could affect our departure."

The earl arched a single brow as the plates arrived.

They took a moment to dig into the fare before Trevor added, "Typical, is it not, that we must petition the House of Commons to build a canal across our own lands before then presenting to the House of Lords. Ridiculous, if you ask me. This is our business, so why can we not simply tell our peers our plans? Why involve MPs? Why require votes? It's *our own lands*." Trevor chuckled, not expecting Roddam to answer since his questions were rhetorical, absurdities emphasized between two likeminded peers.

Roddam, however, swallowed his first bite of venison, and set down his cutlery. "I'm afraid we've reached an impasse."

Trevor tilted his head in confusion. "I don't follow."

"Our business dealings are about to end with a theatrical, Shakespearean death."

Stunned, he set down his own cutlery and studied the earl across the table. What had he said to offend the man?

Realization was slow to dawn.

With a scoff, Trevor said, "By Jove. You're a *Whig*."

Roddam awarded the accusation a curt nod. "So, you see, Pickering, we cannot be friends or business partners, for you are obviously a devout Tory."

He was unsure if he should laugh or scoff again. How absurd for a peer to be a Whig. Did that not undermine all one stood for as a peer of the realm? Uncertainty of how to respond stretched into silence. Regardless of Roddam's political views, Trevor believed the deal a good one, both the investment in the coal mine and the canal route, but if the earl was offended by Trevor's staunch support of the Crown, there was little more to be said.

Roddam surprised Trevor anew by slapping an open palm to the table and howling with laughter. "Almost had you." Still laughing, he winked before adding, "Not about the politics, but about the business deal. I won't hold your ideals against you, even if they are rubbish."

The shock took slow minutes to fade before Trevor was sharing the laugh, more relieved than offended.

"Your proposal?" Roddam prodded, resuming his meal.

"Ah, yes, as to that, I'd like to host a dinner at Sladesbridge Court, one in which I invite a few friends who may be interested in investing in your mining company or at the least in being involved in the canal."

The earl grunted, then mulled over the proposal with three consecutive bites before saying, "I'm not accustomed to soliciting investments. I'm likewise hesitant to increase stakeholders, least of all people I do not know."

"It's unlikely the individuals I have in mind would be interested in becoming stakeholders, merely interested in helping fund the canal build or other minor enterprise with the company. Return would interest them, be it in coin or benefit, but I doubt any would want a say in the company's decisions. To the first, you wouldn't be soliciting investors. I would."

"And you want to plan this dinner before London? Hmm. We'll miss the King's opening if we delay." Four bites of mulling, then Roddam said, "I'll have my man of business draw up investment options I'd be willing to offer. You arrange the dinner, and I'll be there, along with my man of business."

"Wives and family invited, of course," Trevor said. "Lady Pickering will enjoy planning a dinner party. A social occasion amongst friends. We can talk business after dinner."

"I like the way you think, Pickering. By this time next year, you'll be a self-proclaimed Tory with your investments in industry."

"Not a chance." Trevor smirked. "I will, however, have a roof that does not leak, financial security beyond my dismal attempts at farming, and a legacy to leave the generations to come. I believe this endeavor will make my father proud."

Roddam quirked that solitary eyebrow again. "Not to sound insensitive, but... I suspect your father will never know nor care."

"That depends on your views of the afterlife, but I take your point. It's not a matter of what my father would think so much as how I feel about my accomplishments. I want to do all that would have made him proud. By doing so, I make myself proud. I earn self-worth and honor, you see?"

Brows furrowed, Roddam said, "Not particularly. Self-worth isn't *earned*. You make decisions and act because you have worth, because your life has worth, not in order to earn some philosophical sense of chivalric honor. One does not live to find meaning, rather one lives because there is meaning. Life has meaning; therefore, we live. Yes?"

Trevor studied the table. He wanted to defend himself, to explain the family motto, yet the earl's words made strange sense. To earn honor through duty or to be dutiful because one is honorable?

Before he could respond, the earl rerouted them to their former topic by saying, "I'll understand if you'd prefer to remain a silent partner."

"I have a stronger backbone than you give me credit for, Lord Roddam." With a wink of his own, he added, "Even for a Tory."

Chapter 21

Crossing the room from one of the drafty windows to join the ladies near the fireplace, Mrs. Coombe perched on the edge of her chair. "Rumor has that it was an angry mob marching on Whitehall, intent to kill."

"Will this turn into a revolution?" Gwen twisted her handkerchief in her lap. "Will they storm the palace as they did in France? What will become of us?"

Siobhan waved away the worries. "Roland doesn't believe it was an assassination attempt. While an anti-war group is believed to have instigated the mob, the plan wasn't to murder, only rile. As Roland explained to me, the crowd pelted rocks at the carriage, and one punctured the carriage window. Horrifying, to be sure, but purely accidental."

"I heard otherwise," Mrs. Coombe insisted. "Rumor has that the attack was planned for weeks by this group, the goal a royal massacre." Leaning in conspiratorially, she said, "The mob was stirred to increase the instigators' chances of escaping after they shot through the window with an airgun, not a rock. If this had been an accident, they *only* would have attacked when the King was on his way to open

Parliament, but they didn't. They attacked *again* as his carriage departed, and *then again* the next day when the family tried to leave the palace."

Gwen dabbed her cheeks with her handkerchief, overcome with emotion. "I refuse to think anyone would wish ill of our beloved King. It must have been an out-of-control mob, no intention of harming anyone."

After casting Mrs. Coombe an exasperated look, Siobhan turned to Gwen. "As Roland has explained to me, people are upset the Crown is spending so much money and resources for this war with France, a war no one wants. Enter the anti-war group pressing people to protest — *only* to protest."

J'non stood next to Gwen's chair, a hand on her friend's shoulder. This evening was the investment dinner party, although J'non could not have predicted conversation in the drawing room would turn to so heated a topic. The assassination attempt, or whatever it had been, had occurred nearly a week ago. As distressing as it was, her tears were not for the King alone but from relief Trevor had not been in London at the time. Had it not been for this dinner party, Trevor and Lord Roddam would have departed in time to arrive for the opening of the Parliamentary Season, caught in the middle of the mob. The close call sent J'non's emotions reeling. Never had she been so happy to host a dinner party, it now being a symbol of survival.

The guests for the evening included Mr. Barmby, as well as three other men of business, Sir Roland and Siobhan, Gwen and Mr. Harvey, Lord and Lady Roddam, and two of Trevor's old friends. One of the friends, Sir Ralph Whitfield, was unmarried, but the other, Mr. Teddy Coombe, son of Viscount Bartley, had brought his wife Mrs. Coombe. The gentlemen remained in the dining room, talking business, while J'non played hostess with the wives in the drawing room.

"I can't imagine the gentlemen going into London now," J'non said. "Not after this. It couldn't possibly be safe, not when we don't know if it was an organized attack intending to kill or a desperate protest resulting in an accident."

"If they went to London," Gwen said, "they would be in the heart of the madness. They can't go, and that's that."

"Oh, but arrests have already been made." Siobhan looked from face to face, her tone reassuring, as if to prove London was now safe. "An investigation is underway to determine if the group intended to kill, maim, or frighten, but the rock throwers — who happen to be part of the political group — were caught on scene and arrested. Roland thinks the people in the crowd were innocent, wanting to be heard, and the group used that to show their might without meaning real harm."

"It's high treason," Gwen said. "Regardless of their reasoning, and regardless if they intended to kill, maim, or frighten, their actions were treasonous. We do not live under greedy rulers or tyrants. The voices of the Members of Parliament, all speaking on behalf of the people who voted for them, combined with the voices of the Lords, make the decisions, all for the health and betterment of our country. To act against the King as these people did shows their ignorance and the need for punishment."

Lady Roddam, who had initiated the conversation but had said little about it, offered, "I don't think it matters if the people arrested intended to kill or frighten. The point is they weaponized the starving and desperate. If the group had acted in favor of the people, I could understand, but to use people's desperation to force action? It's unconscionable."

J'non returned to her chair, her legs wobbly from the emotional tension. "Can we be certain it was a group of political insurgents and not simply a hungry crowd? Desperation can drive people to do the unthinkable."

Siobhan said, "No matter how desperate or dire circumstances seem, there is always a way without resorting to violence."

"Tell that to the starving people in London who surrounded the King's carriage begging for help," Lady Roddam said.

J'non agreed but did not speak. Was it paranoia to think everyone could see through her, see her own desperation from once upon a time?

Mrs. Coombe said, "If I were starving in the streets of London, I don't believe first on my mind would be to stalk the King's carriage on its way to Parliament, then pelt it with rocks. Ridiculous! What would that achieve? A waste of time, I say, not to mention more likely to work against rather than in favor. Personally, I would be out in search of work so I could no longer starve, not harassing the King."

"There are different kinds of starvation," Lady Roddam said. "Those in the crowd in all probability *do* have jobs, but it doesn't pay enough to survive, not with heavy taxes. Whatever they earn goes right back into the hands of the King to fund the war with France, not leaving anything for food or rent."

Mrs. Coombe replied, "It's easy to theorize when we're sitting pretty in a parlor. All our talk about the people, but what do we know about their plight? Have any of us ever been homeless or starving?" Her tone was playful, her words tinged with mirth, as though sharing a joke with present company.

J'non, however, felt the sting of the words in a way no one else in the room would understand. Looking down at her hands, palms up, a lady's hands, she could not meet anyone's eyes.

"I have," said a soft voice from near the hearth.

All heads turned, eyes widening.

J'non jerked her gaze away from her lap to see the somber expression of her dear friend. While J'non had thought the words, it had been Siobhan who said them. Shock tremored down J'non's spine. Siobhan?

No one spoke.

"Your lesson for the day, ladies." A flicker of a smile ghosted Lady Siobhan Osborne's lips. "Never assume you know someone or their past."

Everyone waited for Siobhan to explain. She did not.

J'non's throat ached, and her eyes burned. Looking only at Siobhan and no one else, J'non said, "As have I."

This time, Siobhan's head jerked to face J'non. Their eyes met, and in a way they never had before, they opened wide, unshielded, revealing to each other a shared kinship they had not known nor could have guessed, although neither knew the other's story. Before anyone could ask for details, question their meaning, soften the tone with a joke, or otherwise, the door to the dining room opened, and the gentlemen joined the ladies in the drawing room.

Sir Roland looked around the long faces. "I hear no pianoforte, no laughter, and no cards slapping tabletops. What, pray tell, are you ladies discussing?"

J'non swallowed against the lump in her throat, her attention turning to Trevor as he walked towards her. She could hear the rush of her pulse and the beat of her heart. One part elation to see him striding across the room—he was here, not in London, safe, unharmed—and one part fear—someone could say something to him of what had just passed, specifically her confession.

"Thursday's mob." Lady Roddam was the one to answer. "Is that not the current topic in every drawing room across the country? Or is my big mouth to blame? If anyone has any doubt about my ability to initiate inappropriate conversation, ask my aunt," she said with a laugh. "She discovered during my first Season she couldn't take me anywhere in polite society without my political gossip embarrassing her somehow."

Lord Roddam asked, "I take it this is a bad time to announce we're going to London next week?"

By "we," Lord Roddam meant the gentlemen, as they explained to their wives after a clamor of protests. Not that the explanation stopped the protests, for the concern was not about the wives joining, rather the safety of the gentlemen attending Parliament so soon after the mob attack.

Trevor sat in the chair next to J'non, surprised the ladies had discussed so gruesome a topic. Only after the women had withdrawn to the drawing room did the events of the 29th enter the gentlemen's conversation, and even then, only as it related to the canal petition and the London trip. It did make sense, however, that the women would be concerned. While voices overlapped, Trevor's attention turned to J'non's profile, feeling fortunate to have her concern, feeling the affection she projected to be worried about his safety.

Rather than talk about safety, the gentlemen's conversation over port had been if the timing was right to present the petition. An important point Mr. Teddy Coombe had ventured was how interested would either House be in this petition when they had more important matters to contend with regarding the riots, but as Sir Roland responded, what better time to petition — a quick vote of yay and move it out of the way.

As to the riots, as disturbing as they were, especially the attack on opening day, the situation was under control. Trevor trusted Roland's account, which made it clear a political group had meticulously planned the attack, both riling a crowd into protesting and using the crowd as cover, so that on the surface this would appear a food shortage protest, disguising the true intentions of the group. Those involved had attempted to flee the scene but were apprehended and soon would be tried for high treason. Not all at the dining table had agreed with Roland's account, and Trevor admitted to himself there was no way to know for certain which account was correct, but he trusted Roland enough to feel secure about the

London trip. With the instigators off the streets, the gentlemen should not run afoul of additional riots or attacks.

Reassurances made matters no less frightening. He would be traveling to the location of the attack. As a member of the House of Lords, he would be one of the men the protestors detested. Instigated by a politically motivated group or not, that did not change the fact that food shortages were real, and people were angry. Desperate people took desperate measures.

Trevor convinced himself that nothing served by living in fear. He reached for J'non's hand and squeezed it. It was fortunate he had already decided she would not accompany him, even if she asked, for he would not risk her safety. He did not suspect she would want to accompany him—was there anything for her in London? Yes, her father was there, but a reunion with him would be of little interest to her, he suspected.

Roddam stood at the hearth, his forearm resting along the mantel. "This goes to show the importance of self-reliance," he was in the process of saying.

"Do you refer to yourself, the people, or the King?" questioned Sir Ralph Whitfield.

"All of them. Everyone. All of us. No one can depend on anyone else for their safety, their health, their well-being, so on and so forth. Carriages can't rely on outriders for safety. The King can't rely on his guards for security. Are you going to put your faith in a handful of Bow Street Runners to save you when pulled into a dark alley of London, or for a magistrate to be in the right place at the right time when highwaymen attack?"

Mrs. Harvey said, "You are *not* going to London, Obadiah. Highwaymen? Dark alleys? *Riots*? I'm putting my foot down."

Roddam waved a hand. "You mistake me, Mrs. Harvey. What I'm saying is to be confident, not fearful. Fear comes when you've put your well-being in someone else's hands only to realize they're not there to save you, be that saving physical, mental, metaphysical, etcetera. If you're reliant on yourself, on your own abilities and knowledge, however, there is nothing to fear."

In Trevor's periphery, he saw J'non nodding. In agreement or acknowledgement?

The vicar, who had taken the chair next to his wife, said, "You, my lord, may rely on yourself, but I will put my faith in God."

"Do you believe God was in the carriage with the King the day of the riot?" Roddam asked.

"Obviously. He came to no harm and escaped unscathed, or as much as he could."

"Yet God allowed him to be there at that place and that time where harm could have befallen him," Roddam argued. "What would you say if harm *had* come to him? That God abandoned him? What of *his* faith in God in that moment of abandonment?"

Trevor's attention on J'non, he observed her eyes widen as they met those of Lady Osborne, the two seeming to share a silent conversation in response to Roddam's rhetorical questions.

"Hardly the time for a theological discussion," Mr. Harvey said. "I should like to continue this, however, but not here. I'll say this much, Lord Roddam. We cannot always understand His intention or His plan.

Does that plan include death? Yes. I believe if the King had come to harm that God would have been with him at every moment, making clear the plan, showing the purpose of death, showing the grand scheme of what that death would mean. Our beloved King's death was not to be, praise the Lord, but had it been, it would have been part of a greater plan."

Roddam nodded, respectful, even as he said, "Whatever gives you confidence, Mr. Harvey, embrace it. We are both, in our own way, dependent on our faith."

Unaware Trevor had been watching her rather than their guests, J'non leaned over the arm of her chair and whispered, "You can't really be thinking of going to London, not after what happened."

"I am, and I will. I won't be away long, two weeks at most."

She made to respond, but Roddam's mention of Trevor's name caught both their attention.

"It's like something Lord Pickering and I were discussing last week," Roddam said. "You're responsible for yourself, be it your health, your wealth, your happiness, your success. No one can keep you fit and healthy, only you. No one can bring you happiness, only yourself. No one can define your purpose in this world, only you."

Lady Osborne said, "Hear, hear, Lord Roddam. Well said. If we don't look after ourselves, who will?"

Sir Roland, looking positively bemused, blew a kiss to his wife from where he stood next to Teddy, the two in a conversation of their own.

"So true, Siobhan. I concur," J'non said before leaning in again to whisper to Trevor, "I don't think it's safe for you to go to London. What if they didn't arrest the right men? I'll worry about you the whole time. The petition for the canal can wait, can't it?"

Arrested by her response to Lady Osborne, he ignored her concern and asked instead, "Wait, you agree with Lady Osborne and Lord Roddam? About self-reliance?"

J'non's neck flushed as she looked away, nodding. Was it that she believed this *now*, that he would not look after her or her best interests, or that she once experienced having to look after herself?

His thoughts circled back to the few points she had hinted about her aunt and living as a maid to her cousins. Her father had allowed it. Her aunt had forced it in exchange for her care. With an experience like that, why should she believe anyone outside of herself would look after her? He hoped her sentiments had changed, that she felt safe with him. Trevor would move heaven and earth to protect her. She knew this, did she not? He felt a strange surge to prove it to her somehow, to confront those who had harmed her, even if that harm was to her esteem rather than her person.

"This is why he now prefers your company to mine," Trevor said, nodding to the feather-stuffed pillow J'non was sewing for Gunner.

"Don't be silly. He still prefers you."

She tied off the thread, then turned the monstrosity of a pillow-bed-throne-thing to face Trevor. Across the front, or inside, or outside, or whatever part he was looking at, it read *Gunner* in fine, calligraphed embroidery.

Trevor harrumphed. "You realize he can't read."

"You're a spoiled sport. He doesn't need to read to know it's his." She looked down at his royal dogness, who was curled around her ankles, his tail thumping in anticipation. "Isn't that right, Gunner?"

The traitor looked up at her with worshipful eyes, and with all the grace his long limbs could afford, trundled up to sniff the thing in her hands. J'non underscored the embroidery with her finger. Gunner licked his name.

"See?"

Trevor rolled his eyes.

"Shall I make you one? To match his? I'll even embroider your name."

Her smirk was so slow in showing, he at first thought her serious. What made him laugh was not her jest but that he had been tempted to accept before he realized she was teasing. A pillow-bed-throne-thing to take to London sounded not half bad, complete with his name embroidered. He would be the envy of his friends.

As she situated Gunner's doll-toy with the pillow, Trevor said, "I'll be home before December. At the latest, I'll be home before Christmas."

Ever since their dinner guests left earlier that evening, they had been on-and-off arguing about the London trip. He hated to bring it up again. Worse, he hated to leave it as a point of contention.

She *hmm*ed, the sound expressing her disapproval.

"I know you think this is about me making my father proud, about proving myself worthy of this title," he said, "but it's about more than that. It's about our home, the village, our neighbors, our future — so much more. If I delay the petition's presentation, I delay the decision. I can't risk another flood. Building the canal will take months, potentially a year. What if the delay doesn't have them making a decision until next autumn?"

She gave another *hmm* as her answer.

He waited, giving her a chance to argue, but when she said nothing more, he decided to lighten the mood. "It'll be our first Christmas together. How do you typically celebrate? A large party with guests stretching the twelve days, family only until Twelfth Night, or…?"

After settling Gunner, she said, "I've not celebrated one way or another since I was a child, since living with my mother." Her gaze drifted into the distance, as if remembering the past. "Mama loved the whole season, always beginning festivities on St. Nicholas Day. We hosted dinners, attended dinners, made gifts, gathered greenery, crafted décor — oh, everything. We *always* had a Yule Log, and we never missed the wassailing." She sighed, a dreamy smile on her lips. "Mama used to tell me about the childhood in Wales she left behind. Think me silly if you will, but I used to imagine we would one day spend the season in Wales so I could experience plygain, the Mari Lwyd, and all the traditions she told me about. I don't know why I imagined that when she had not been back since her marriage."

"Did they not approve of the marriage?" Trevor asked, crossing his ankles and settling deeper into his chair.

She did not rush to answer, rather furrowed her brow in thought. "I don't know. She never spoke of her family. I know they were a mining family, but that's all I know. I'm ashamed to admit I never knew her maiden name. Even if I wanted to find my kin on her side, I wouldn't know where to look."

Trevor had more questions than there were minutes in the day. How had her mother met Mr. Whittington? How long were they married before Mr. Whittington left her with child in a rented home owned by a baronet? Did Mr. Whittington ever visit during J'non's childhood? Was the aunt she stayed with before moving to London Mr. Whittington's sister? Each question led to more questions, an endless queue of unanswered curiosities. He asked none of them, however. The past pained her, he knew, and he suspected she did not know the answer to many of the questions, just as she did not know anything about her mother's side of the family. Were these points her mother had planned to share when J'non was older, or secrets she intended never to tell her daughter? Blast, more questions.

Rather than asking anything personal, he opted instead for, "We can now begin whatever traditions you would like, our own annual traditions. How would you like to celebrate the season?"

Her eyebrows rose in surprise. "Oh, goodness. It's *my* decision?" She reached for her embroidery basket to tuck away her thread. "I suppose, had I thought about it, I would have assumed we would do whatever you wanted, but then, I don't believe I've thought about it. The holiday season always seemed so far away." While she fiddled with the basket, she *hmm*ed a few more times, glancing between him and the basket. "I don't know, Trevor. What do I want?"

He chuckled. "That, my dear, is for you to decide."

She set her embroidery supplies next to the chair. "*Must* you go to London?"

Ah, back to this.

He groaned. "I've agreed to go, so I shall."

"How are we to plan Christmas with you away?" she reasoned. "Now you see that you must stay."

"Alright, I admit it. My presence there is superfluous, for the canal petition will be presented only to the House of Commons. With luck, it'll be approved either while we're in London or at least before the spring when I warm my seat in the House of Lords. At that point, Lord Roddam and I will present it to our peers for their votes. For now, there's nothing we can do other than sit in on the presentation and subsequent discussion. We cannot participate, not in the House of Commons. We'll be onlookers only."

"Your evidence about timing is overruled. Try again with a better defense. *Why* must you go? By your own admission, the Member of Parliament who will present the petition can write to tell you the result. For all you know, the petition could be set aside for the spring and not even debated now, especially when they have more pressing matters to attend to. If that happens, your trip will be for naught."

"That's a possibility, but I'm not going solely to eavesdrop on the House of Commons. We'll be meeting with Roddam's legal team to sort the details of the investments, see to the purchase of the piston engine, and other related errands. There are a few personal tasks I want to accomplish, as well. For instance, I want to see the condition of the previous marquess' London residence. He had a terraced property that's now ours, one I've never seen. I still have my own London residence. Lloyd and I plan to make a keen assessment of both to determine which we should sell and which we should keep. Neither are entailed, so we may do with them as we wish. I'd like to settle that, among other tasks, before we go in the spring."

"It seems to me we could accomplish most of your tasks in the spring or via correspondence. But for that matter, if Parliament is in session *now*, why are we not there? I'm thankful we're not given the mob attacks, but…."

Trevor steepled his fingers. "Technically, I should be there, at the very least in my capacity as Baron Tidwell, but more poignantly, taking my seat as Marquess of Pickering. I have no intention of doing more during this trip than answering the summons and shaking the Lord Chancellor's hand. I'll attend regularly when we go in the spring. Although Parliament is technically in session, the House of Commons is more active now, while most peers will remain at their country estates until after the last frost before venturing to London. There *are* those who remain in London or live near enough to be active now, but not many. I suspect, but don't quote me on this, that one day, they'll see reason and schedule the Parliamentary Season to begin in the spring and continue into summer rather than this silliness of winter weather interruptions. It does give time for those in the House of Commons to debate and vote, then send things our way for our arrival in the spring, but… well, no one asked me, did they?"

J'non shook her head. "I'm glad to be a woman. That all sounds terribly complicated."

"Oh, but you *will* need to be presented at court." Trevor grinned. "You'll need to take your curtsy before the Queen. Not something we need to think about until then, although we will want to decide sooner rather than later who will sponsor you for the presentation. I was thinking, maybe, Lady Roddam?"

"I shall write to her and ask." J'non returned his grin with one of her own, looking for all the world as though this were the best idea she had heard all day. "Since you and Lord Roddam will be in London, I wonder if she and the children would consider staying at Sladesbridge for a few days. I don't think she's planning to return to Northumberland until Lord Roddam returns, but I don't know for certain."

"Write. Ask. I like the idea of you having company in my absence." If he were honest, he hated the thought of being absent at all. This would be their first time apart since marriage. Good heavens—she would have at least two weeks to further steal Gunner's affection.

"I can't say curtsying to the Queen is on my list of dreams to come true," she said, "but I shall accustom myself to the idea. I'll be more nervous about tripping over my train than meeting her."

"Now it is *I* who does not envy *you*. I'll attend Parliament twice over to avoid curtsying in a court dress."

J'non laughed.

All evening, he had been eager to ask for her thoughts on Lord Roddam's unusual philosophies, and even planned to tell her what the earl had said at The Black Anvil, the point about duty from honor rather than honor from duty. Yet now that he had her alone, all he wanted was to make her laugh again.

Even his discussion about Christmas fell to the wayside in his desire to see her smile.

His original reason for asking her about Christmas traditions had been in hope of questioning if she would consider inviting her father. As much as he disliked the man based on everything he knew of him, it was a season for forgiving. Did she wish to be reunited with him? Did she wish for a chance to forgive him? Did she want a connection with her mother that only he could provide through anecdotes about her family? Trevor would be in London, a perfect opportunity to meet Mr. Whittington at last and invite him to return to Sladesbridge for at least a week in December, then back to London the man could go before the first frost. He would be hard pressed not to confront Mr. Whittington on his poor treatment of J'non, especially with the aunt situation, but that did not mean he could not also make amends and invite him for the season. He would have the entire trip to London to mull over his approach.

For now, he chose against mentioning the plan to J'non. He could not bring himself to watch her smile wane. All he wanted was for her to laugh.

He nodded to Gunner. "If I leave you and your woman's work unsupervised, I'll enter the drawing room one evening to find you fitting him with a matching court dress."

She hid her face behind her hands, peeking at him between her fingers. "Then you had better hurry back from London. Take too long, and I'll have one ready for you too."

Chapter 22

His footsteps away from Mr. Whittington's London home beat the rhythm of a requiem, a requiem in d minor with variations on a theme. What should have been a prelude had proven otherwise.

Who had he married?

Half an hour earlier, Trevor discovered the walk from the Tidwell London residence to Mr. Whittington's home was a remarkably short distance. It confirmed for Trevor he had made the right decision in choosing to sell the Tidwell terrace rather than the Pickering residence. He had spent little time at the old London house since inheriting it from his father, and so it held few memories and was in need of upkeep. The Pickering house, in contrast, was in tip-top shape, having been the ninth marquess' primary residence. That it was a fair distance from Mr. Whittington's home proved an added benefit.

Visiting Mr. Whittington was to be the final task of his London errands, so it being one of his first actions surprised him. The need to meet his father-in-law bedeviled him.

The driving force behind the visit was his growing affection for J'non. Did he dare call it love? With a glance to either side of him in assurance no one would witness his smitten expression, *yes*, he dared call it love. He was a man in love with his wife. Visiting her father was Trevor's way to prove he cared for her, prove he could protect her, prove he could make her happy.

The J'non he had come to love was the same J'non who had stepped off the carriage that first day of her arrival to Sladesbridge Court, and yet she was a different person entirely. Rather than the staid little mouse, who wore like a shroud the evidence of her life as her cousins' maid, she now laughed freely, chin held high, wearing like a mantle the evidence of her life as a marchioness and loved wife. There remained, however, *something* that kept her at arm's length. In moments of shared humor, even in moments of intimacy, they relished in each other's honesty and vulnerability, nothing keeping them apart, no secrets withheld, but in other moments, she was guarded.

Trevor blamed his mother. Had his formative example of a married woman not been one living a dual life with lovers and secrets, he would not notice guarded behavior. *What* guarded behavior he noticed, he could not describe. J'non's expressions, her words, her actions—nothing demonstrated guarded behavior. It was a feeling, nothing more. An inexplicable intuition.

Her past was her own, and he did not wish to pry nor know all her secrets, but he knew *something* in her past pained her, enough to frequent her nights, turning dreams to nightmares, enough to strike her pale and silent when the subject of either her aunt or her father arose. He was not concerned with her keeping secrets from him, for they were hers to keep, but he was concerned about the pain she endured, a pain he wanted to salve. If she could trust him to know the past would never hurt her again, that Trevor would protect her, come what may, he was sure she would be able to release whatever haunted her. He was in search of answers, not *about* her past but how to free her *from* her past.

This was the driving force that brought him to Mr. Whittington's doorstep. But there was more. So many layers of *more*. His desire to confront Whittington charged his steps. The tone of that confrontation depended on the man's responses. Would Trevor blot Mr. Whittington from J'non's life, or would he invite him for Christmas? Trevor could not say if remedying J'non's secret melancholy meant forgiveness and peacemaking, a rectifying of wrongs by way of apologies and reunions, or if it meant the opposite, severing all contact. It depended on the man himself. Would the revelation be a cruel tormentor or a remorseful father?

Trevor had sent his calling card in advance with a hand jotted note that he would call the next day. Lloyd was to join, but at the last minute, Trevor changed his mind and rescinded the invitation. He could not hide behind his solicitor on this occasion, nor did he want anything about J'non or her life to be revealed for anyone's ears but his own. Lloyd understood. They planned to take tea afterwards, if for no other reason than to help Trevor unwind.

From the street outside, Trevor looked up at the terraced house. *Deep breath, old boy. In, then out.* His fingers unfurled from tightened fists. His shoulders relaxed away from his ears. He was the Marquess of Pickering.

With a nod to his accompanying footman, he waited. The footman made use of the door knocker, then stepped aside. *Remember to breathe.*

In a heart pounding motion, the front door swung open. A footman answered, took the card from Trevor's man, bowed, then opened the door wide. *Here we go*, Trevor thought with another deep breath.

His first impressions of the house had him raising his eyebrows. He followed Whittington's footman down a hallway to what he assumed would be a parlor overlooking a private, walled garden. He assumed because the other houses in this square were of similar floorplans, most owned by aristocrats, a few Trevor knew, many he did not, but to own a house in this square meant not only that one had a considerable amount of ready coin in the purse but that one wanted everyone else to know there was ready coin in said purse.

Opulent was the first word to come to mind, replaced in four steps by *gauche*. What had been the term Lloyd had used? *Nouveau-riche*? Yes, Trevor believed that was it. Not a word to be found in a lexicon, to be certain, and with any luck a word never to pass the lips of polite society, but it somehow encapsulated, even in its simplicity of syllables, the sort of gaucheness Trevor witnessed with each step down the hallway. The décor bordered on vulgar. Every nook and cranny held a treasure, be it paintings, statues, furnishings, or urns, and every treasure within those nooks and crannies displayed wealth and world travels, an eclectic combination of cultures and eras from gilded Rococo consoles to chinoiserie art.

There was grace in simplicity. No one must have informed Whittington of that. Reconciling J'non's understated grace and suppressed beauty with this bold display of wealth proved challenging. She was the antithesis of this house.

Simultaneously, two footmen opened the double doors. The footman ahead announced the marquess as he entered the room. Trevor had not been mistaken. It was a parlor overlooking a private garden. The parlor, wallpapered in rich reds and golds, was as cluttered and garish as the hallway. As to the garden, he could not judge, for standing before the garden doors was Mr. Whittington, the Textile King of London and Trevor's father-in-law.

Rather than bow, nod, or any other variation of acceptable greeting, Mr. Whittington flung his arms wide and descended on Trevor with a toothy smile and aromatic plume of mead.

"Welcome, my boy! Come here and greet your father properly." With those opening words, Whittington embraced Trevor in a hug that squeezed him of breath.

Petrified, Trevor stood motionless, his body tense, his frown frozen in place. This was, he decided, the single most awkward moment of his life. No one had ever *hugged* him in greeting, least of all his actual father. Whittington clasped Trevor's hand and pumped it in a hearty handshake, his other arm still wrapped about Trevor's shoulders.

Gregarious, beaming, red-nosed, round-bellied, and uncouth, Mr. Whittington laughed mead vapors into Trevor's face as he continued to stand too close, his sausage-fingered hand tightening its grip. Trevor closed his eyes, fighting a wave of nausea. Musky cologne mingled with alcohol and cigar smoke. Gold rings clinked. The laugh reverberated, too loud, too close.

Fleetingly, as Trevor extricated himself as politely as he could and took several steps away, he recalled *this* being his fear when the carriage had arrived with his bride. To think, *this* could have stepped out of the carriage that day. *This* in female form. He shuddered. Thank the Lord J'non had taken after her mother. There were reasons aristocrats did not consort with cits. There were reasons the dowry, despite being obscene in amount, had not snared an aristocrat before Trevor. This man embodied all the reasons. Lloyd had warned him when presenting the list of potential brides, but the dowry had been all that mattered. Had Trevor met Whittington himself, life would have proceeded differently.

Mr. Whittington, without giving Trevor a chance to offer a good morning or otherwise, walked to his sideboard, still laughing as though the two had shared a joke. What the devil was so funny?

"Your timing is impeccable, my boy," Whittington said.

Trevor swallowed his temptation to tell him it was *my lord*, not *my boy*.

He took another deep breath, curling his toes in his shoes rather than his fingers into a fist, schooling himself to relax and focus. This was about aiding

J'non, nothing more. It remained to be seen if that aid would be offering the opportunity for father and daughter to reconcile their grievances or choosing to cut all ties. At this point, he wanted nothing more than to cut ties, but he must give the man a chance.

"I was thinking to myself only yesterday," Whittington continued as he poured two glasses of wine, unsolicited, "that I needed my son-in-law to invite me to White's. It's time I make use of my alliances and form new friendships. I'm aiming for Lord Mayor of London by next Michaelmas, you ought to know. With the right influences, the right buzzing bees in the ears of the voters, my newfound friendships and alliances should serve in my favor. *You* can secure my membership to White's."

He carried the wine glasses across the room, sloshed them onto a low table, then plopped—quite literally—into a chair that groaned under his weight. Waving a hand to the vacant chair across from him, he topped his feet on an embroidered ottoman, or as Trevor's father would have called it, a tumpty. Whatever one might call the footstool, Trevor was offended by the whole encounter. His view, after all, was of the soles of the man's shoes.

Not wanting to be rude, he offered Whittington a curt nod, then accepted the seat. Back straight, body rigid, he eyed his father-in-law. The man, in contrast, leaned back in his chair, elbows propped, wine glass cradled.

"To be honest, I hadn't thought to meet you," Mr. Whittington said. "My lovey isn't the sentimental sort when it comes to family. Whatever benefits her is the direction she blows. Thought she'd either be too mad at me for forcing the marriage or too bitter not to be in my pockets anymore. Both, more like. Yet here you are. You're not wanting to give her back, are you?" Mr. Whittington squinted at Trevor, sober and frowning.

Before Trevor could respond, the man laughed again with a spray of spital.

Trevor's first words, softly spoken but firm, were, "Are you not concerned if she is well cared for and happy?"

"That depends. Is she misbehaving?" Mr. Whittington asked before a two-gulp imbibing of his wine. Hardly words of affection.

Trevor laced his fingers. "I fail to understand your meaning."

"After—what's it been, three months?—yes, three months or thereabouts of wedded bliss with my Phoebe, you must know her tendencies. Sharp tongue, will of iron, flirtatious wiles. You know how she is. If she's disobedient, a firm hand will right her quick enough. Take my word for it."

Clenching his fingers to control his anger, Trevor parted his lips to express that Lady Pickering was, in fact, well cared for and happy, but before he could affirm what had not been asked, his host spoke again.

Whittington raised his glass. "Took her in hand, did you? Well done, son. 'Twas all she needed to learn who wears the breeches in the marriage. I won't lie when I say I was worried. She had a line of beaux before you, and not all were the marrying kind, if you take my meaning. With one in particular she had formed an attachment. Half expected her to run off with the bloke. All worked out in the end." With a glance at his fingers, Mr. Whittington grunted and began biting at the edge of one of his nails. He spat at the floor before saying, "Now, to more pressing matters. I'm not one to mince words. Didn't get where I am today with prevarications. Tell me: when are you taking me to White's? I'm a busy man but will set aside the necessary time. Tomorrow? What do you say?"

Trevor blinked once. Twice. Thrice. "Are you not curious how your daughter fares?"

The gold rings clinked as Whittington waved a hand, his other perching his glass on his lips as he nursed the drink. "She's yours now. I paid you enough to take her off my hands. As gratitude, you can introduce me to the right people."

"Do you not wish to inquire how she's adapting? New home, stranger of a husband, new role. As a devoted father, should you not be asking after her?"

"I'm not sure I like your tone, boy." Whittington's eyes narrowed. "She's a strong wench, adapts easily enough. I'll have you know I lavished her with gifts and riches and all she could want. How's that for devotion? Now tell me; what's she claiming?"

Trevor took his time in answering, wanting to word his reply carefully. "I've been made aware of your lengthy absences but would like to believe your concern for her well-being has superseded past oversights." He stopped before accusing the man of outright neglect. Memories flickered of J'non's threadbare clothing when she arrived, of her traveling across the countryside without a maid or chaperone, of working as a maid under her aunt's roof.

Snorting, his host said, "I'm a merchant. The finest merchant. Been building an empire. They call me a *king*, but *emperor* is more apt. Do you think I made my wealth sitting on my backside, entertaining a girl with pigtails? Of course there were lengthy absences. I've traveled the world to make my money, money *you* desperately wanted, if I need remind you. Like a panting dog was your solicitor, practically humped my leg. Greedy for *my* riches, the wealth I made from *working*, not babysitting a brat. She wanted for nothing, son, nothing. If she says otherwise, she's lying, painting me in a bad light out of spite. Can't win with women. Give 'em sapphires, and they want emeralds. Give 'em emeralds, and they want sapphires. My wife was the same. Greedy wench."

Flinching, Trevor looked away. As far as he was concerned, he had the answers he sought without needing to ask more pointed questions. Now more than ever, he felt he understood J'non and what she must have suffered, what her mother must have suffered. He would not, after all, be inviting Mr. Whittington to join them for Christmas. More importantly, he would not be pressing for a reconciliation between father and daughter. When he looked back to his host it was to find the man engrossed in scratching the inside of his nostrils.

Trevor closed his eyes and swallowed against the rising bile.

Whittington chuckled. "Bring her 'round. She'll be wanting to see her Papa. She talks a good tale, but it's all part of her game. A game I taught her, I'm not ashamed to admit." He looked Trevor up and down. "As stiff as the rest of them nobs. Watch out, son, or she'll run circles around you." Nodding to the wine glass on the table, he added, "You going to drink that?" When Trevor did not immediately respond, Whittington swapped his empty glass for Trevor's untouched glass.

Why was your daughter dressed in rags? Why was she sent across the countryside unchaperoned? Why was her aunt not paid for her care? Why did you allow her to work as a maid? How could you marry her to a stranger you had never met? How could you not care enough to ask after her?

The questions Trevor wanted to ask circled his mind. The answers did not matter, not really. They all questioned rational motive from a man who was self-absorbed, self-serving, and a drunkard, lacking both reason and intention. The questions also accused and pried, neither of which served his goal of bringing J'non peace about her past.

Alas, Trevor had failed J'non. His aim had been to help her, to understand what pained her. He would need to find another way to encourage her to let down her guard and trust him.

While he could only guess from whence her nightmares came, he knew with certainty her father did not know her, the merchant's only knowledge from the unreliable aunt who wanted to blacken her niece's name in hopes of removing J'non from her care. Flirtatious wiles? A line of beaux? Sharp tongued? None of these descriptors matched J'non.

Trevor came away from the meeting with several suppositions: Whittington did not know his daughter. The aunt had likely received ample coin to care for her niece but kept it for herself, along with any gifts

Whittington might have sent. Something changed to cause the aunt to feed lies to Whittington in hopes of marrying J'non out from under her care.

The walk from the Whittington house to the Tidwell residence was of short distance but long torment, the whole of the visit replaying in Trevor's mind. He had been trapped in a satirical caricature, his host mocking him. All he wanted was to pull J'non into his arms. Never had he felt so protective. That Whittington had spoken in the same context of both spoiling his daughter with riches and using physical violence gave Trevor chills. He could not regret the visit, however unpleasant. Even had J'non warned him away, Trevor still needed to experience the man for himself. As far as he was concerned, they need never interact with him again. Thankfully, Whittington did not expect future interactions. While the merchant did expect to bandy about the Pickering title to his advantage as proof of being well connected, he did not express interest in seeing his daughter, only that his daughter would wish to see him — who would not want to kiss the ringed fingers of Emperor Whittington?

Trevor's thoughts drifted to a question he had asked before. *Who had he married?*

By his estimation, he had not married a cit's daughter. Rather, he had married the daughter of a Welsh woman from a mining family, a woman who married, presumably, against her family's wishes, and lived out her motherhood under the watchful eye of a baronet. Not for the first time did Trevor question if Mr. Whittington was even the father. If the woman lived with the baronet as a tenant or otherwise while

Whittington traveled, who was to say J'non was not the baronet's natural daughter? Whittington could have been oblivious or simply not have cared. As Trevor saw it, J'non was, for all intents and purposes, a gentleman's daughter. There was not a vulgar bone in her body. She was the quintessential English gentlewoman.

God help him, he loved her for it.

Correction. He loved her. Full stop.

The murmur of voices and aroma of freshly brewed coffee and steeped tea leaves enveloped the two men. The marquess sat across from Lloyd. The coffeehouse had been recommended by Lord Roddam, a location Trevor never would have tried otherwise, but after the exquisite fare at The Black Anvil, he would not doubt any recommendation offered by the earl.

"I warned you," Lloyd said.

"A more appropriate use of 'I told you so' could not exist. Yet you still recommended Miss Whittington knowing her father was outrageous."

Rather than look sheepish, Lloyd shrugged a shoulder. "You wanted the wealthiest. She was, and remains, the wealthiest."

"My name will forever be tied with his. I shudder to think what my peers will make of that association. Fortunate I'm not particularly social."

"So you lose a few invitations. Would you have accepted them anyway? No? Thought not. Besides, I have it on good authority there could not be a better match for you than J'non Gaines, née Whittington."

"You think so? Here I was imagining you were disappointed she was not, what was it, sharp tongued with flirtatious wiles." Trevor sat back against the wooden bench, his forefinger circling the rim of his cup.

Lloyd had the decency to look abashed. "Let us not revisit that misunderstanding. I'm still ashamed of my first words to Lady Pickering. A kinder woman I've never met. A perfect hostess. From my perspective, the perfect wife, as well, at least for you." With a laugh and sweep of his arms, he said, "Look at us! We're enjoying a brew at a coffeehouse! That would not have happened before she came into your life."

Lloyd's words rang with truth. Trevor felt like a new man. Rather than wake each morning with the weight of responsibility, he awoke unburdened, anticipating what the day would bring, what new tidbit he would learn about her or about himself, what they would do together or talk about. While Teddy had teased him on the road to London about being in the honeymoon phase, Roddam had claimed that after five years, the bloom had not faded in his marriage and never would. Trevor liked the sound of that. The change in him was not solely his adoration for J'non, after all, but the eyes-open view of life he now had. In so many ways, he had catching up to do. For instance, how had he allowed his friendship with Lloyd to disintegrate to a business relationship?

Trevor chuckled. "I feel a changed man, for the better. There's something about her, something I can't explain."

"Could it be she brings out the best in you?" Lloyd asked rhetorically. "Before you become sentimental, let's return to the point at hand."

Trevor shook his head. "Before we talk about the investment meeting with Roddam's legal counsel, I have one more quick word, or request rather, regarding Lady Pickering. I've already instructed the staff to expect her in the spring and to see to all her needs. I anticipate we'll arrive together after spending at least a week in Lincolnshire at Tidwell Hall, but in the event I'm detained longer at the hall and she proceeds to London before me, I want all at the ready. Will you see to the shops? She'll need to be fitted for a court dress, of course, but I'd like for her to enjoy the shops at her leisure. Carte blanche. Ensure the credit is in order and the bills paid. I'll not have her walking about with a purse full of coins like some peasant or—"

"Cit?" Lloyd offered.

Trevor angled a nod.

"I'll see to it," Lloyd said. "There won't be a shop in London that isn't ready to see to her needs. In the event you're held captive by that stodgy Barmby, Sr. steward of yours at Tidwell Hall, and her ladyship arrives before you, would you like me to be present at the London house to greet her?"

"Appreciated, but no need. I'm anticipating Lady Roddam to be in town. The two can spend the few days to a week shopping together."

"Should you change your mind, just send word. I'll already be in London. Now, to the investment. Whitfield and Coombe, along with their men of business, will meet us at the law offices. As I understand, Sir Roland will not be attending, but has arranged the details with his secretary. Mr. Harvey?"

Trevor finished his beverage before saying, "Mr. Harvey will not be investing in the mine, but he is overseeing the current flood prevention plans with Mr. Tillson and Mr. Prichard, and he will oversee the canal work should things go favorably. I wish he were investing, though, because I believe, based on your numbers and research into the company, this could be a tremendously lucrative investment, but I understand his reasoning. Man of God and all that."

Conversation slipped into their investment strategy. While meeting with a legal counsel should not be exciting, Trevor was looking forward to it. This deal could be the making of them. If anything went awry with the estate, be it tenants or farm, this deal would secure their future. If all went well with the estate, this deal would double, if not triple, their fortune, securing their livelihood for this lifetime and future generations.

The thought of future generations had him almost grinning over his empty cup. Future generations meant children with J'non. After only three months of marriage, he was not exactly champing at the bit to begin their adventure in parenting, but he could not deny a certain elation at the thought of wee ones with J'non.

Refocusing, he turned his attention to what Lloyd was saying about the investment meeting.

There was still the petition to present to Parliament, which was scheduled for the end of the week. Following that, Trevor would head home. Was he a silly sap to miss J'non and Gunner already? He could not return home fast enough. His focus slipped again.

With any luck, the return trip would be as successful as the journey south. While it had been unpleasant to his backside given they traveled horseback rather than by carriage, the Earl of Roddam had arranged everything for the smoothest trip Trevor had ever experienced. Horses were arranged along the way, meals at the ready practically upon their arrival at each inn, and rooms booked in advance. Trevor could learn quite a lot from Roddam. As he understood it, the earl had spent the past decade bringing his properties back from ruin, a ruin that far surpassed Trevor's issues with leaky roofs, handfuls of empty tenancies, and overgrown fields. Yes, Trevor had a lot to learn from Roddam. On one point, at least, he and the man were equals: a blissful marriage.

Chapter 23

He urged his horse into a gallop, the wind stinging his cheeks. Gunner took the lead. Trevor's eyes were not on the Lurcher, though. Ahead, tossing a laugh over her shoulder, was J'non, besting the marquess and his thoroughbred. To say he let her win the race would only be to salve his ego, for she was a natural in the saddle. All her talk of forgotten riding lessons from her youth were not the least convincing when she rode as though the horse were an extension of herself.

As they approached the lake, he slowed his horse, allowing J'non and Gunner to arrive first. Was he trying to appear nonchalant about her beating him? Of course.

Gunner flopped under the willow, tongue lolling and tail wagging, awaiting whatever treat Cook slipped into the saddlebag for him. J'non patted her horse's neck and cooed words before flashing Trevor a grin.

"Pretending to have a leisure ride to disguise your loss?" she teased.

Trevor smirked, then dismounted to help her do the same. While a groom would have provided a step or cupped hands for her to use in descent, Trevor grasped J'non at the waist and caught her weight against him. She slid down his chest until her feet touched the ground. Trevor did not release her. He tightened his hold instead. When her arms wrapped around his shoulders, he dipped his head to kiss the tip of her nose.

How was he so fortunate?

Once horses and dog were settled with treats and attention, Trevor wrapped a warm blanket around J'non's shoulders before leaning his back against the tree trunk and nuzzling her against him, their view the lake. Early December, yet the weather remained relatively warm, at least in comparison to previous years. The air was cold, the wind colder, but it felt more like October than December. Still, he shivered beneath the blanket they shared and pulled her closer.

"Are you trying to steal my warmth?" she asked.

"I resent that accusation. I'm a consummate gentleman, after all, ensuring your comfort."

"As in, you're encouraging me to steal your warmth? I suspect your motives, but I'll accept the invitation." Draping an arm around his middle, she laid her head against his chest.

They remained thus for uncountable minutes, sharing warmth, listening to the gentle lap of the lake water in the breeze, the occasional huff of Gunner, and the snorts of the horses. Trevor would not trade this moment, or any moment with J'non, for the world. This was paradise.

At length, Trevor said, "I've invited a portrait painter from London. It was intended as a surprise, but the more I think about it, the less I like the idea of a stranger arriving at the house and startling you."

"He's to paint your portrait? How lovely. I presume it'll hang in the gallery alongside the portraits of the previous marquesses."

He stroked her upper arm over her blanket. "To paint *our* portrait, actually. I've commissioned three paintings, one of each of us, and then one of us together."

"A family portrait? Of us?"

"You sound more incredulous than excited. Did I choose unwisely?"

The decision had been made on a whim, one he thought would make for a spectacular surprise. He had envisioned her eyes brightening and her smile widening, seeing these portraits as he did — a way to move them from an arranged marriage for money into a love match between smitten parties eager to begin their family together. Now, he questioned his rashness.

"I've never had my portrait painted," was all she said, her tone wistful.

Heartened, he said, "The week after Twelfth Night is when he's supposed to arrive, although I can't say what day."

J'non sat up with a start, staring back at him in horror. "No! Oh no, he can't arrive then. Write to him. He mustn't. Everyone will be arriving!"

He quirked an eyebrow.

She bit her bottom lip and looked down, a faint blush across her cheeks. "It's a surprise."

"A surprise?" he repeated.

"Now you're the one who sounds incredulous." She tutted before returning to his side. "You must forget I said this the moment we leave for home. It'll ruin the surprise if you already know."

"Hmm. Yes. I see the logic. Funny thing about lakes. They're prone to cause selective amnesia."

"Perfect." She patted his waistcoat much like she patted Gunner's head when he accomplished a well-behaved feat—curiously, Trevor felt just as pleased as Gunner at the accolade. "Your birthday party. I'll say no more than a carefully selected group of friends have been invited, and there will be the world's largest cake, enough pennant flags to be seen from sea, and so much confetti we'll be picking candy and fruit from our hair for weeks. There, that's all you get. The rest is a *surprise*. So, you see, you must reschedule the painter. There won't be any time to pose during the party!"

Flattered, shocked, besotted. There was not a word to capture the buoyant sensation filling his chest cavity, one that might well lift him into flight if he allowed it. J'non had arranged a surprise party for him. He could not recall ever celebrating his birthday, much less being surprised by a party of friends. When had she arranged this? Did his London companions already know during the trip to the capitol, or did she write to them while he was away, using the opportunity to organize everything? A surprise party. Well!

He cleared his throat, which had inexplicably constricted, and said, "I can't seem to recall what we planned the week after Twelfth Night, but something tells me I should reschedule the painter's arrival. The week following, do you think?"

That would still be early January with less of a risk of snow. February tended to be the heaviest snowfall at the hall, but then, he was unsure what to expect from Yorkshire weather or that on the moors.

Rather than reply, she patted his waistcoat again. He smirked, feeling like a good boy.

"The more time I spend with Lord Roddam," Trevor began, changing the subject away from surprises, "the more I like the man, even if he's an odd duck."

"London went well, then? You've not said much other than the petition was delayed. Was it a wasted journey?"

"*Au contraire.* I accomplished a great deal, even put the Tidwell residence on the market. Lloyd expects a swift sale. The location is near the gentlemen clubs, prime real estate, and only needs minor renovations in terms of upkeep and modernizing. It's still stuck in my father's time, I'm afraid, not at all fashionable. But there's more. I sorted details with Lord Roddam's legal counsel — we're officially stakeholders in a mining company, my dear. What else? Answered my summons as marquess but thankfully avoided a ceremony since I had already suffered the pomp and circumstance when taking my seat as baron. Hmm. There's more. Something of interest to you. Now, what was it?" he teased, tapping a finger to his lips in exaggerated thought. "Ah, yes. Prepared the shops for your arrival in the great search for your court dress. An important shopping venture, that. To be spoken as a title, complete with capital lettering."

"Dress Shopping Extravaganza? The Marchioness Goes Shopping? The Great Pickering Fitting?"

"That's the spirit." He chuckled.

J'non followed with a story about Lady Roddam, who had been unable to stay at Sladesbridge Court while Trevor was in London but had exchanged letters, or perhaps simply letter, singular. Trevor could not be certain, as his attention was distracted while J'non talked about the countess. He loved hearing her stories, and he did not mean to be distracted, but his attention slipped. Should he mention his call to Mr. Whittington? This seemed the appropriate opportunity. It was not as though he had sneaked behind her back to meet the man. What did he have to hide? Something kept him from admitting his excursion. Was it the shame of having disliked the man? While he knew J'non did not have a close relationship with her father, it sounded traitorous to tell her the man disgusted him. Even thinking it made him feel guilty, dishonorable, downright unchristian. He would have to tell her at some point. Just… not now.

Instead, he let them slip into shared silence again following her tales of Lady Roddam's correspondence. Beneath the layer of blanket, he could feel her tremble. They should head back soon, warm their toes by the fire.

Before leaving, he did have one question to put to her, something he had been wanting to ask all morning but did not want to broach a tender subject amidst joviality.

With a deep breath to muster courage, he asked, "Will you tell me about last night's nightmare?"

"Oh." Her voice was soft, almost a whisper.

They had not spoken about her nightmares after the initial moment of waking. The frightful evenings were not frequent, but neither were they infrequent.

This was an area in which he was helpless, and he did not like that sensation one bit. If he could understand from whence her fear came, what caused her dreams, perhaps he could help her best them.

For ages after his mother left, he had suffered from nightmares. There was nothing *frightening* about them, no monsters or highwaymen, simply a feeling of utter helplessness, which was, perhaps, the most frightening sensation of all, not unlike how he felt about J'non's dreams. So long ago, he could hardly recall what all he had dreamed, variations of the same vision, he suspected. Him waiting at the window for her return, sometimes witnessing her departure. There was only one dream he could recollect with a fair bit of vividness, a reoccurring one.

A curiosity how terrifying a dream could be in the moment, when his waking memory saw nothing more than his mother entering the nursery to say goodbye. In the moment of the dream, he recalled being too paralyzed to speak, to stop her, to do anything other than watch her depart.

J'non sighed, the sound akin to resigning oneself to recall a bad experience, or so he attributed her exhale. "Coldness. Hunger. An endless walk. Nothing happened in the dream, nothing of note anyway. I was walking down a country lane, destination unknown. I kept walking. That was the whole of it, me walking down an empty road, cold and hungry."

He thought about it. An endless road. A destination never reached. The deepening chill, the worsening hunger.

He offered, "In the nightmares from my childhood, I often stared down a never-ending driveway.

Its sheer emptiness was what induced terror for me. The frustration that I couldn't bring her back, that I couldn't dream a version where she walked forward in return."

J'non nodded against his chest. After a moment's silence, she said, "The peculiar aspect of last night's dream was I didn't feel frustrated. I didn't feel anything. *That* was what made it frightening. I felt nothing. I was empty. My mind told me there was coldness and hunger, but my body didn't feel it. I felt… empty. There was no fear, no anger, no desperation, nothing. Even calling it resignation would invoke a feeling. Hopelessness would invoke a feeling. There was *nothing*."

He kissed the top of her head, the silky strands of her hair tickling his nose. What did it say about him that he felt closer to her with these dream confessions? They were *only* dreams, not reality, not real experiences, and he did not wish to cause her pain by remembering whatever emotion or lack thereof they evoked, but that she told him about them helped him feel closer, as if he were inching his way towards a deeper understanding of her. It was better to build new memories, supplant bad dreams with good, share stories of the now rather than the past, for they were not the same people they had once been, at least he was not. Yet he hungered to know everything about her and especially what fueled these dreams.

Startling him out of his thoughts, J'non stood up and flung the blanket from her shoulders. With a laugh tossed over her shoulder, she challenged, "Catch me if you can!"

The vixen lifted the hem of her riding habit and darted across the meadow where the horses were grazing. Gunner figured out what she was about before Trevor did. The dog lunged onto his feet and lurched forward, barking and bounding after her. Trevor sat dumbly for half a minute before it dawned that she was going to mount her horse on her own by some feat of gravity defiance, then leave him here, blanketed under the willow.

The devil she was! Trevor gathered the blankets with sloppy haste to pursue his wife, the chase afoot.

Trevor's escape for the day was to the long gallery, the only place in the house where he could not hear the clang of hammers. An entire wall in the west wing was being repaired, in-wall rotting having been uncovered. How it escaped everyone's notice for so long was anyone's guess, but Trevor assumed it was because there was much else to contend with, visible decay. Difficult to discern one smell of mildew from another when everything, it seemed, had gone to mold where the roof had leaked. While Trevor was away in London, J'non begged Mr. Thompson to investigate the draft around the drawing room window. There, he uncovered the problem.

As long as the repairs were finished before Christmas, Trevor would be content to sacrifice his peace of mind for a few weeks. They were fortunate to have Mr. Thompson and crew.

The pounding of hammers was not the only reason Trevor found himself in the long gallery today, although the relative quiet was welcoming. After surprising J'non with the news of the paintings, he had requested Mr. Hawkins see to light rearrangements, namely to make wall space for the new and future paintings.

The gallery extended the width of the Court, a stunning but unloved portion of the third story. In time, Trevor would see to its complete restoration, but it was low on the list. The paneling was original to the home's sixteenth century build, and was, unexpectedly, in good shape. What showed the most wear was the plaster ceiling, intricate in design but cracking. Thankfully, the stained-glass windows, with each pane depicting the coat of arms of influential families from the Court's build date, were intact and showed little signs of wear.

The space was versatile, perfect for exercise or a game of bowls on a rainy day, guest entertainment from conversation to dancing and promenading, displaying art collections, and any number of other purposes. Currently, it was the ignored location for portraits of long deceased marquesses. Trevor hoped to make better use of this in the future.

It did not take effort to discover the portrait rearrangements, as the first set of panels was now empty of paintings, room for the present and future. The paintings would be the first collection seen upon entering the gallery.

For at least half an hour, perhaps longer, Trevor stood before the empty panels, lost in thought. Here would hang the visual representation of his family, of the people in his life whom he loved and cherished. For now, once the artist came in January, there would be Trevor and J'non, captured for all time, forever to reside in memory within the Court even after their bodies and souls had passed. In the future, the portraits of their children would join them. He imagined how it all might look once the family was complete, imagined the portraits of their children. He could not predict how many children they might have, but the space for their portraits awaited their arrival.

That was not to say he was pressed to have children soon. Goodness, they had only been married a few months and were still discovering each other, but now more than any time in his life he felt the importance of creating a family, not just for himself but for her, especially for her. It was the meeting of Mr. Whittington that sealed Trevor's resolve and deepened his affection for J'non. In that single meeting, he realized he — Trevor — was her only family. He felt the weight of this on his shoulders, not as an added responsibility so much as a medal, an honor, the King's blade upon ceremony. *He*, and he alone, was her family. More than anything, he wanted to show her this was where she belonged.

Chapter 24

A nother week into the west wall repairs meant another week Trevor and J'non were unable to retire to the drawing room after dinner, thus another week they had to make use of the quaint sitting room between their chambers. The sitting room did not connect the lord's and lady's chambers directly, but it was accessible by both. So contemporary in design, Trevor suspected it was a newer renovation to the house, although he could not imagine one made by the ninth marquess since the man had no wife and doubtfully spent much time in his chamber when in residence.

"This is terrible, is it not?" Trevor asked. "To be sequestered to the lord's and lady's suites when there's a perfectly good drawing room to be enjoyed."

"Mmm. Yes. Terrible." J'non stretched her toes towards the fire before snuggling closer.

They both lounged in banyans this evening, scandalously barefooted. The settee on which they lay was too short and too narrow to fit them both, but they managed, Trevor lying on his side, J'non's legs draped over his, her back against the seat cushion, affording her a view of the elaborately plastered ceiling. He twirled a loose strand of her hair with his forefinger and admired her profile. How had he ever thought her plain?

"In case I've not told you, you're beautiful."

J'non sniggered. "Only fifteen times in the past five minutes. I didn't believe you the first time, and I believe you less now."

"Your protests beg for more compliments."

"My protests are as much because you're a fibber blinded by the binds of marriage as they are because I'm too modest to accept extravagant declarations of beauty."

"All I hear is, 'tell me again how beautiful I am, how smitten you are, how you're my slave.'"

Nudging his knee with her foot, she said, "You're impossible." However exasperated her voice, the blush pinkening her cheeks belied her true sentiments. "Very well. If it'll hush your flattery, I'll accept. You think me beautiful. There. Accepted."

"Mmm. I don't think you're beautiful." He pressed his finger to her lips when they parted in protest. "You *are* beautiful."

She harrumphed, but her blush deepened.

So lost in the moment, in his admiration of J'non, not only skin deep but the vibrancy of her soul, the selflessness of her day-to-day actions, her kindness, her everything, he almost missed the invisible veil.

He was uncertain how else to describe it. It was not a wall between them so much as a shield, a kind of protective shell. He did not sense she sought protection from him so much as from something… else. Her past? Her father? Herself? Here they were, the two of them, alone. What was there to protect against?

This was the feeling that had nagged him into wanting to confront Mr. Whittington. In this unguarded moment, she remained guarded. There was no other way to explain it. He could not be closer to her if he tried, and yet they were miles apart.

Trevor attempted a jovial tone, one that would tease an equally jovial answer, but what slipped through his lips echoed his thoughts instead, a tone mixed with confusion and desperation, preluded by a forced chuckle that made him cringe. "Is that so difficult to believe?"

J'non angled to face him, a crease between her eyebrows. "That you could think I'm beautiful, or that I could be beautiful?"

"There is no conditional 'could.' I know you're beautiful because you are beautiful. Before you protest again, tell me why you feel otherwise." He stopped before he asked who broke her spirit.

Turning back to face the ceiling, J'non slipped into silence. Trevor listened to the steady inhale and exhale of her breathing.

"My mirror does not agree with you," she said, in what he suspected was a deflection. With a giggle, she said, "As long as I keep my mirror away from you, all will be well. You'll continue to think me a ravishing beauty, none the wiser of what the mirror says."

So that was how it would be. She would tease him away from this line of questioning. The invisible veil fluttered, taunting him. Given his inexperience with women, he did not consider himself an expert in understanding the nuances of female behavior, but he would bet his horse she was hiding something from him, and he would bet his saddle that "something" had to do with her aunt. He cursed himself for not questioning Mr. Whittington about the aunt. There was a woman he heartily wished to confront—but about what exactly?

Kissing her cheek, he matched her giggle with a chuckle of his own, one he hoped sounded more convincing than her forced laugh. "I'll have words with that mirror when you're not looking, do my best to talk sense into it. Meanwhile, I'll continue knowing you're a ravishing beauty."

"Splendid. Tell me again how beautiful you think me?"

"Vain woman. Have I not said it enough? Let me rephrase to feed your ego. Your beauty outshines the sun, out twinkles the stars—"

"Don't forget about the moon."

"That envious moon."

Her laugh this time was genuine. "Envious moon? Am I the sun, now, killing the envious moon?"

"'That thou, her maid, art far more fair than she,'" he said, his tone seductive, his lips inches from her ear.

"You *are* impossible. Quoting the words of a rogue bent on seducing a maiden will not win my affection, Romeo."

"No? You're not taken with me?" He kissed the tip of her ear.

She shied away, tittering.

"Can you blame a man for being in love with his wife?"

With a playful batting of his arm, she said, "Now you're being silly. Am I going to have to question Gunner to find out what you've done wrong that requires my forgiveness?"

Propping himself onto his elbow, he looked down at her. "You don't believe me?"

"That you're in love with me? Pish."

He grinned rather than reply. She was teasing him, diverting again. Although he could not understand why she chose to dance her words rather than take him seriously, he did not think she was rejecting him or his confession of being in love. Lacing his fingers with hers, he extended his arm again to use as a pillow, returning to his former view of her profile.

"What if…" she began. "What if circumstances were different? What if, oh, I don't know… hmm. What if I were an impoverished cousin of Miss Whittington rather than Miss Whittington herself?"

He raised his eyebrows, never mind she was staring at the ceiling, not at him. "Do you mean, would I still be in love with you?"

"That too. Would you have married me?"

"The short answer is no. I married because I needed money, remember? It has merely been my good fortune to have married *you*. But I assume you are referring to a hypothetical situation wherein I did not need to marry for money. Would I have fallen for you at first sight? Not care that you were a poor relation? Is that what you're asking?"

"Yes. No. I don't know." Her pitch dropped, her words hushed. "What if Miss Whittington were your houseguest, for whatever reason, and I was her maid? What if we met by chance in the hallway of the estate or outside in the garden? Would you have noticed me? Would you have considered me?"

He thought about the scenario, assuming she meant if he had not needed the money, of course. He tried not to assume she meant would he have considered her even if he needed the money, for that was not a question he cared to entertain even to himself.

Chuckling, he said, "You're trying to catch me into confessing I'm in love with my wife rather than with you, never mind those two people happen to be one and the same."

"As in you would fall in love with anyone who happened to be your wife? Even a vulgar cit? No, I'm not trying to trick you."

"Good, because I couldn't fall for just anyone, you know."

Would he have fallen in love with his wife had she been someone else? What a question! He did not believe so, although that would do a disservice to the hypothetical wife, but the fact was *love* had never been part of his equation, not even before he realized he had to marry for money. Marriage was about duty. Love, if anything, was to be avoided. He saw how it had destroyed his father. He would never have set about putting himself in a similar situation, never would have married out of passion.

In that same hushed tone, J'non continued, "I'm not asking about love. Not exactly. I'm not sure what I'm asking, really. Consider the scenario, would you? If I were Miss Whittington's maid and we met by chance, would you have noticed me?"

Tricky question, even if she was not setting out to trick him.

He puffed an exhale from his cheeks. "Impossible scenario." He squeezed their laced fingers. "No, don't interrupt. Let me explain. It's an impossible scenario because there is a continental difference between *you* and a maid. Even if my eyes met with a maid, be it a lady's maid or otherwise, and we struck a congenial conversation, a relationship would be impossible. A maid with a servant's background? She would be unprepared for society."

"Gentlemen marry servants all the time."

"I wouldn't say all the time. Occasionally, yes, but that woman is typically his second or third wife, after he's already secured an heir from his first wife and retired into the country where he would do little mingling with society. You must understand a servant-turned-wife would be shunned from good society, as would the gentleman's family. It's an impossible situation. The woman would not have the first idea what to do, how to run a house, how to act, how to speak, how to *anything*. The house staff would never respect her. The marriage would be doomed from the start, she feeling the pressure of the position, and he feeling the pressure from society."

"So, you wouldn't have noticed me."

"I didn't say that." He laughed, more out of frustration at being presented with an impossible scenario—and for what purpose? To prove his sincerity? "I offer this scenario instead. Let us suppose you're not a maid I meet in the hallway. Let us suppose, instead, you are a cousin, a *guest* of the estate. We happen to walk down the same hallway at the same time. Our eyes meet. You cast me a shy smile. Yes, I would notice you. Yes, I would consider you."

"Because I'm ravishingly beautiful?" she jested.

"Because you carry yourself with the comportment of a lady. You epitomize Lady Pickering. How could I *not* consider you?"

J'non laughed as though he told a joke, but he could not help but notice her laugh did not reach her eyes or ring with her usual merriment.

Trevor propped himself on his elbow again. "Ah. I understand now."

Her eyes widened as she turned to face him.

"This is because your aunt forced you to act as a servant while she cared for you. Am I right?" When J'non did not respond, Trevor continued, "Let me make something clear. You are not a maid. You are someone who found herself in an unpleasant situation under the care of the careless. The situation is not altogether uncommon, especially when poor relations find themselves without a guardian. Such individuals are often forced to live with family who don't want them and require them to act as companions rather than whatever best suited them from birth. As far as I'm concerned, your father is a villain and your aunt his accomplice. To treat you as a servant is nothing short of abuse, least of all when your father was alive with all the wealth imaginable. You, J'non, are *not* a maid. You are a lady, and you belong here. I'm your family now. Understand?"

He flinched that his words sounded harsh and commanding, but he did not think the tears brimming in her eyes were caused by his tone. Or he hoped not. She lowered her eyes to stare at his chest.

Slipping her fingers from his, she began to fidget with her banyan. "There's something I want to tell you. Several somethings, actually. I'm not sure where to start, but my father would be a good place."

Trevor pressed his fingers to her lips again. "There's no need. I already know about him. You see,

I have a confession, as well, and I'm afraid you'll be beyond angry when I tell you."

She pursed her lips but said nothing.

"I met Mr. Whittington while I was in London." He clenched his jaw, ready for fire and brimstone for not telling her sooner, for waiting so long it might seem he had kept it a secret from her.

She moved away from him on the settee, sitting up to stare down at him, her expression of either shock or horror. What he had not expected to see was fear in her eyes. Anger, yes, but not fear. Just the mention of the man's name had caused this. Trevor regretted bringing up the visit. Cursed if he did and cursed if he did not. Guilty to keep it a secret and guilty to confess.

Trevor said, "I apologize profusely for not admitting sooner. You see, I'm ashamed of my own distaste of the man. He is, after all, your father." He took a deep breath. "I called on him on a whim, nothing I wanted to hide from you, but after meeting him, I could not bring myself to tell you. He was, and you may never pardon me for saying this, and I'll understand if you don't, *vile*. You are his antithesis, J'non. You must take after your mother in every possible way, for you are all that is gentle and graceful, while he is... not."

J'non had turned to face the fire, her back to Trevor. She remained silent for so long, he thought he was truly done for, to be banished to his own chamber from this moment until death did them part. That would teach him for deceiving his wife, for keeping secrets, for speaking ill of family.

When she spoke, her words were so quiet, he thought it was the wind. "He said nothing about... me?"

He mulled over her question, mostly in an attempt to understand what she had whispered, the words so softly spoken. "The villain never even asked how you fared. All he could talk about was gaining membership at White's or whatever club he had in mind."

Trevor shuddered to think of her living in that house with that man. Thank goodness she had only lived there one month. But then, which would have been worse, living with her aunt for several years, as she had done, or living with Mr. Whittington for those years instead?

In a swift motion, he moved to kneel behind J'non on the settee, then wrapped his arms around her, pulling her back against his chest.

Burying his face in the crook of her neck, he mumbled, "I don't care about your past. I'm in love with *you*."

The voice of the wind whispered again, so faint, he had to strain to hear. "I believe you."

Chapter 25

J'non looked out the carriage window, appreciating the passing landscape, the contour and greenery changing with each new town, hilly to flat, open fields to enclosed paddocks. She had never approached London from the north. How different would it look than from the south? Had the city changed since she left? A foolish question, that, when it had only been seven months. Seven months since she left London for Yorkshire. Seven months of marriage. She stole a glance to Trevor, who sat across from her, his back to the horses.

He raised his eyebrows. "How are you feeling?"

"Better." J'non tightened her grip on the leather strap to steady herself against the rocking. "No need to stop yet."

With a nod, Trevor said, "We're about half an hour from the next changing post. We'll take in the fresh air, admire the scenery, have a bite to eat, then be on the road again when you're ready."

Although she had warned him of her carriage sickness, her nausea had only been intermittent. In comparison to her trip north with Miss Phoebe Whittington, she was faring well. Trevor had arranged for the carriage to stop every hour. She also sat facing the horses rather than with her back to them as she had done with Miss Whittington. That they had not once ridden through the night helped, as did the overnight stays in style rather than at dodgy inns. The evenings were, frankly, wonderful in their restfulness and good company. They spent several days as guests of Mr. and Mrs. Teddy Coombe, a two-day stay at Sir Ralph Whitfield's home, and a week-long stay at Tidwell Hall. The least fun had been at Sir Ralph's home since he had not been in residence, having remained in London through winter. His invitation instructed they make themselves comfortable in his absence, which they did, but it was not the same without their host. The most fun was their stay at Tidwell Hall.

To say J'non loved Tidwell was an understatement. If she could have extended their time, she would have. The most captivating was not so much the house and grounds — stunning in their own right — but rather the knowledge it had been Trevor's home until eight months prior, his childhood home and then his home into adulthood. She walked every hallway, imagining him at play. Then, had he been a serious child, quiet and studious rather than the type to run through hallways? Regardless, she had imagined him in every room. Most of J'non's explorations were alone, as Trevor had spent hours each day sequestered in the study with the steward, a grandfatherly man who did not in any way match the militant authoritarian Lloyd had described. The only militant part was his brow line, a more orderly yet commanding pair of brows J'non had not met.

It was a pity she and Trevor could not have stayed longer in Lincolnshire, but as it was, they would be hard pressed to make the canal bill petition, already scheduled for debate. They would have more time on the way home. She would insist on staying another week at Tidwell.

Trevor had confessed he had anticipated remaining longer at Tidwell, potentially having J'non continue to London on her own so she could begin her shopping adventure. Thankfully, it had not worked out that way. Their extended stops along the journey had eaten into their travel time, and in truth, a longer stay had proven unnecessary, as Trevor and Mr. Barmby, Sr. had accomplished all they needed during the week.

A bump in the road sent her stomach reeling. J'non squeezed the leather strap, her free hand covering her mouth.

Leaning forward, Trevor asked, "Should we pull off the road?"

J'non shook her head with careful slowness. Only after a few gulps of air, did she say hoarsely, "I'll make it."

She was not so sure, but fresh air would right her good as new, and that kept her focused. Less than half an hour to go. How dreadfully embarrassing being sick in front of Trevor. With luck, it would go no further than her feeling nauseated.

Settling her head against the seatback, she relaxed into the sway of the carriage and drew encouragement from Trevor's expression.

"Distract me," she said.

Without missing a beat, Trevor prattled. "Christmas was good. My birthday better. Your lessons in how to curtsy in a court dress best."

She groaned. "Don't remind me of the lessons. At least the tutor had the patience of a saint."

"Personally, I looked forward to each lesson. Every one of them."

"Because you devoted every one of them to laughing at my expense!"

He shrugged with a devilish grin. A glance out the window then back to J'non, he offered, "I bet Gunner is having the time of his life."

"You don't think he's moping since we're not there to coddle him?"

"Nonsense. The Harveys will spoil him on our behalf. More to the point, he has his mates to chase. We'll have to promise puppy playdates to coax him home after all his time with Sammy and Simon."

"Because he doesn't have those enough as it is," J'non said with a laugh. "Nearly every meeting of the sewing circle, those two troublemakers accompany. Oh! Have I mentioned I offered the drawing room for them to use while we're away?"

"For the dogs to play?" Trevor arched a brow.

"Don't be silly. For the sewing circle. But now that you mention, I would wager they bring the pups with them if they accept my invitation. In all likelihood, they'll meet at the vicarage, but I saw no reason plans should change simply because we're away for a handful of months, and so I extended the offer."

Trevor's attempt at distraction proved successful. J'non had forgotten her nausea. Once she recalled it, she was not bothered, thinking only of home. However exciting to visit London under better circumstances than before, nothing compared to home. Hmm. London. So much uncertainty of what to expect. So much worry mingled with anticipation. Considering the conditions of her first trip to London, this time it would appear as a different city altogether, a city of glitz and glamour rather than grime and fear.

As though reading her thoughts, Trevor said, "I hope you're ready for a whirlwind. Shopping and meeting the Queen to start."

J'non mocked a laugh. "Talk of meeting the Queen will have me revisiting my queasiness faster than a bump in the road. Let's talk of Lord and Lady Roddam instead. I've not had a letter from Lady Roddam since before the frost, but did you not receive one from Lord Roddam while we were at Tidwell? I'm certain you did. Yes, I can see you now spying the seal and commenting on reading it later, as you were late to meet Mr. Barmby. I forgot all about it until now. Does that make me an inattentive wife?"

"Unforgivably inattentive." Trevor pushed off his side of the carriage to join her. Capturing her hand, he laced their fingers, then said, "I liked the idea more than the reality. Changing seats, that is, not reading the letter. I thought to myself, 'I could have an arm wrapped about her shoulders and her head against my chest. The image of love and romance.' That and I thought you could warm me. Chilly on my side. Now that I'm here, however, I see the reality doesn't match. Bench is too short, and I can't see your face to talk to you. I'm instead talking to the empty seat in front of me."

"Correction, you're now talking to a horse's arse."

Trevor stared forward, presumably at the tiny window that had been behind his head, one that looked out onto the horses. He howled with laughter before kissing her temple.

Sinking lower into the carriage seat, he propped his feet on the bench across, then laid his head against her shoulder.

"Not fair," said J'non. "I thought I was to lay my head against you."

"I'm looking out for your best interest. Staying upright is better for carriage sickness."

Fingers still laced with his, she pinched his thigh.

"Ouch! Wicked woman. Where was I?"

"Lord Roddam's letter."

"I'm positive we talked about it. Don't you recall? Investment stuffall, something about canals, even less about Lady Roddam's confinement. Yes? No?"

J'non thought for a moment. "No. I don't believe you did. Perhaps you discussed it with the steward."

"Ah. Yes. Probably."

"That's your cue to tell me about it." She nudged him with her elbow. "Start with Lady Roddam. Did she have a little boy or girl?"

"Neither. Not yet anyway. She'll be spending the next few weeks in confinement. They headed to London early so she could settle in, at least from what I understood from the letter. Did we really not talk about this?"

"She'll be in confinement for the next few *weeks*? But…" J'non sat up straighter and angled to look at Trevor. "But what about the dress and…"

"My apologies, love." Trevor grimaced. "I should have said all this before we left Tidwell. I had it in my head we talked about it, but you're right. I was so distracted with Mr. Barmby, I must have told him instead. Not that I've confused you for my steward, but you know what I mean."

"Yes, well, get to the point. She's sponsoring me for my presentation to the Queen. She can't do that if she's in confinement." J'non's thoughts were less about the curtsy and more about Lady Roddam's health. It was no wonder her ladyship had not written, not when her attention would be on the impending arrival of the baby.

"It's all taken care of," Trevor reassured. "Lady Roddam did not abandon you. According to Lord Roddam's letter, his sister has agreed to sponsor you. She'll also accompany you for shopping. It makes me happy to be the bearer of good news — yet another friend for you, Lady Socialite."

Settling back against the carriage seat, J'non sighed, not from relief so much as resignation. Snuffed was the fleeting flicker of hope not to be presented to the Queen after all. "You had me worried, Trevor. I thought all my lessons on how to curtsy would come to naught." She waited for him to chuckle at her sarcasm before saying, "I suppose this means I will not be able to call on Lady Roddam until I've heard word she's out of confinement."

"On the contrary. We're expressly invited to call on them. I think she wants to be the one to introduce you to her sister-in-law."

"I'm ashamed to admit I didn't know she had a sister-in-law. Do men really talk more about family than women? Most of my conversations with Lady Roddam, including our correspondences, have been about her children."

"I've gathered all the information you could possibly want to know about Lord Roddam's sister. The man talks about her at length. When Roland is around, that length stretches for miles. He, Roland that is, is fascinated by her ladyship's humanitarian efforts."

"Oh?" J'non shouldered Trevor to sit up so she could converse with him rather than the top of his head.

"Baroness Collingwood is a busy woman from Lord Roddam's tales. Entrepreneur of some sort."

J'non tensed, her heart skipping a beat. "I misheard you. Did you say Agnes Alligood?"

"Baroness Collingwood."

Her stomach churned, and her pulse pounded. She knew she was going to be sick before he said more, and it had nowt to do with the sway of the carriage.

"Lady Collingwood founded something called Noach Cottage. According to Lord Roddam —"

Wrenching herself free from Trevor, J'non swung open the carriage door to retch onto the road below.

J'non tossed, turned, and fretted. Trevor, bless the man, had insisted they stop for the remainder of the day and evening, not wanting to distress J'non further. He had comforted in every way he knew how, none the wiser that her distress was not to do with carriage sickness, but to do with Lady Collingwood.

Curious how fear of Mr. Whittington had not made her panic like this, yet fear of her past did.

At least once per day along the drive south, she had envisioned Mr. Whittington's face, bringing with it a fresh wave of nausea from the worry of him calling at their London house. On more than one occasion, she deliberated believable excuses to avoid a confrontation, excuses Whittington would believe had been said by his daughter while also being convincing for Trevor. This was precisely what J'non had not wanted, to live a lie. Easier to put fears aside.

It was not as though she worried they would meet anyone who knew Phoebe Whittington or Mr. Whittington. The Whittingtons' crowd was altogether different from Trevor's peers. The invitations Trevor planned to accept were to be private soirees, at least this year, with a crowd that would never mingle with the likes of the Whittingtons or their ilk. Next year, J'non could set about worrying all over again. But not this year.

Curious how her fear came from a different source, one that had nothing to do with the Whittingtons.

Try as she might to convince herself there was nothing to fear, for Lady Collingwood would never divulge the truth to Trevor, the sheer shame of all she had done, of the monumental lie of a life she was living, of all she hid from the one man she loved more than anything and anyone, it was too much. Facing Lady Collingwood was to face the shame, the lie, and the secrets. She could not do it. What excuse could she give? If the baroness was Lord Roddam's sister, there was no escaping the acquaintance even if the presentation to the Queen could be delayed.

Was it fear? Or was it shame? Was there a difference between the two?

J'non could see Baroness Collingwood's expression, could see first the confusion then the dawning of understanding. J'non could not face her.

What no one except Lady Collingwood knew was J'non owed her life to the baroness. Her ladyship *knew*. She knew everything. She had done all in her power to aid J'non and secure employment, saving J'non from what she called the bleak period.

To take all her ladyship had done and slap it back in her face with this lie was too shameful. *This* was how J'non thanked the baroness? By pretending to be someone else to trick a man into marriage? Oh, but it had not been J'non's plan, she could explain. Oh, but she had been tricked herself into following through, no recourse available, she could explain.

Lady Collingwood would say nothing. She would accept the situation with an understanding of unspoken motives, but J'non could not bear to see the disappointment in her eyes.

There was no choice. She had to stand before the gates and be judged. The more pressing question was if she should first tell Trevor how she came to know Lady Collingwood. The acquaintance was before London, before the Whittingtons, but it involved the period of darkness she never wanted to admit, never planned to share with anyone, least of all him. Then, it was the truest part of herself she could offer him.

Decided, but more frightened of his reaction to her past than to Lady Collingwood's judgement of her present, J'non tried her best to sleep. She would tell him tomorrow evening, their first evening together in London. Between now and then, she would steel herself against his disgust.

Chapter 26

The carriage stopped at a terraced house of dark terracotta brick accented by columns and stone. This was her city home, where she would live for several months every year, a home she was eager to love as much as Sladesbridge Court and Tidwell Hall, although the latter had been only a promise of the great times to come. However weak in the knees from traveling, J'non smiled at Trevor. She hoped he did not notice her weariness. There was too much to see to feel ill. The remaining drive from their overnight stop had been only a couple of hours, but it took minutes for carriage sickness to return, leaving J'non with a slight headache. She took deep breaths, determined to feel better. She wanted to meet the staff, then convince Trevor to tour her about the house.

Although she lost sleep from worry, she was now resolved in her decision to tell Trevor about the baroness and the bleak period. While not a confession of her marital deception, which she was far from ready to disclose, the sharing of that dreadful time in which the baroness had rescued her would be important to voice, necessary before they both met the baroness, and critical to any further admissions, especially if she hoped to tell him the truth one day about the real Phoebe. Knowing he would possess the knowledge of the most secret of times in her life should have filled her with fear. Instead, she was more confident than ever. Or so she tried to convince herself.

She smiled brighter to disguise fear.

Trevor guided her up the four steps to the open front door. He leaned in with a whisper, "I'll make the excuses so you may retire to your suite. All else can wait until after you've rested."

"I feel well enough for introductions and a tour," she assured. "Please? I can't bear to wait."

He chuckled. "I see through your too-broad smile. You're ready to faint. Even your hand on my sleeve is trembling."

"With excitement," she defended.

Whatever he might have said in response was stymied by their crossing the threshold. A chorus of bows greeted them from a tidy line of staff. J'non did not know where to look first. From the marbled floor, fireplace with columned mantel, and filigreed banister framing the stairs, to the liveried servants with staid expressions but expectant eyes, there was much to spy.

Trevor said low to the butler, "As eager as her ladyship is to meet everyone, could you see her to her chamber for a respite first?"

On her lips were the words to decline, but not only would it be in poor taste to argue with the marquess, she knew he was right. Her head was swimming, and her throat tight. She was on the verge of collapse. Yet there was no time for the silliness of a rest with so much to see and so much to do!

The butler flicked a gaze to J'non before requesting, "A word, my lord."

Trevor said, "Certainly, but it can wait until she's situated."

Another glance, and the butler said, "With all due respect, my lord, it cannot wait."

While Trevor's expression revealed nothing, J'non saw his jaw tick from irritation. A nod to the butler, he murmured for J'non's ears only, "A moment, my love, and I'll see to your comfort."

The butler stepped far enough away that J'non could not overhear their exchange, not that she would want to eavesdrop on a private conversation, but curiosity gave her yet another reason to delay her retirement to the lady's chamber. She looked about her while they spoke. In addition to the cantilevered stairs marching parallel to the entrance hall, there were two doors, excluding the double set behind her between the vestibule and entrance hall. She assumed one door led to the study, a sensible room for the ground floor. The other door must lead to a parlor or reception room. The drawing room would most certainly be on the floor above. Would it be so terrible of a transgression to request that tour first after all? The wobble of her knees answered for her.

Conversation concluded, Trevor said to J'non, "My humblest apologies. I would not ask this of you if it were not a matter of some urgency — no, nothing for you to worry about — but would you be willing to wait here for no more than five minutes? I must see to something in the parlor, and then I'll escort you myself to the lady's chamber." In an added whisper, he said, "I'll even tuck you in with a kiss."

Who could argue against those terms? With cheeks warm enough to be blushing, she nodded for him to carry on with whatever was so urgent. Trevor took his apologetic brow line to the end of the hall and entered the room beyond, door closing behind him.

There was nothing to do but wait. The line of staff did the same, the butler standing sentry at the parlor door.

Should she go about greeting the staff? Ridiculous, was it not, for everyone to stand about awaiting the marquess' return? It did not seem appropriate to introduce herself without him, though. And so, they all waited in silence.

The wait proved longer than five minutes. After at least ten, J'non was feeling the full effects of the carriage ride and wanting nothing more than to be horizontal. If she were home amongst her beloved staff, she would not deny the urge to lie on the cold marble floor and invite Gunner to join. As it was, she did not think the Pickering house staff would be impressed by her behavior. The visual brought a smile to her lips, but her queasiness dashed it quickly enough.

The parlor door angled open.

Mumbled words between an unseen figure and the butler were exchanged.

The butler nodded with a muffled response.

From the parlor beyond, came an audible shriek. "Your *wife*?" The shriek was distinctly female.

A chill ran down J'non's spine. Her limbs weighed heavily as the butler approached her with a bow.

"His lordship wishes you to join him," he said, then escorted her to the parlor.

J'non's heart pounded. It had to be Baroness Collingwood. But of course, Lady Roddam would have shared the given name of the Marchioness of Pickering, and since she was, in all likelihood, the only *J'non* in all of England, the baroness would have known who married the marquess. It would not have taken many questions to discover that the background of the marchioness did not match the background of the J'non whom the baroness had helped.

Fists clenched and shoulders squared, J'non tried to swallow against the rising bile. This was too soon. She had not had the opportunity to tell Trevor about her acquaintance with the baroness, about the bleak period.

The march to the gallows was both the longest and shortest walk in her memory. Her steps were slow and heavy, her limbs stiff, yet in mere seconds she had crossed the hall to the parlor. Was it too late to demand a respite?

When she entered the parlor, her line of vision was of Trevor standing before her, awaiting her. Only, it was not the Trevor she knew. It was a man she had long forgotten. It was Lord Pickering. The marquess stood as a wall, stiff and impenetrable, his expression granite and unreadable.

The door behind her closed to the sound of another shriek. "*You?*"

J'non pivoted to face the voice.

Where Baroness Collingwood ought to have been standing was not, in fact, occupied by Baroness Collingwood, rather Miss Phoebe Whittington.

So shocked to see her former mistress, J'non blanked. The woman's presence, Trevor's expression, J'non's fate, all lost to shock.

Miss Whittington was, if possible, more beautiful than J'non remembered, or perhaps that was accentuated by the familiarity of her own mirror's reflection, one which showed a plain, mousy maid in the guise of a lady, a nobody in fancy dress.

"You're married?" Miss Whittington asked Lord Pickering with a tone more accusatory than questioning. "You married *her*?" She waved a hand towards J'non, opened her mouth to speak, then shut it, waved more emphatically, then finally said, "But you couldn't have married her. She's my lady's maid, J'non Butler. *You married my maid?*"

J'non lowered her gaze to the rug. No matter how hard she tried, she could not lift her gaze to look at Trevor, could not meet Miss Whittington's eyes, could not even flee. Petrified, ashamed, confused.

What was her mistress doing here if she did not know Lord Pickering had married Miss J'non Butler? For that matter, *what was she doing here*? Where was Mr. Wilkins, the man with whom she had eloped? Was she Mrs. Wilkins now or still Miss Whittington? Why was she shocked to find J'non had gone forward with the scheme she had concocted? Why had she returned from Scotland, or from wherever she had gone with Mr. Wilkins?

J'non maintained her gaze on the rug, not daring to blink. If she did not move, perhaps they would forget her presence. A skill of a maid, she had learned, was to blend into one's surroundings, to disappear. That was what she would do now, invoke invisibility.

Miss Whittington breathed a single *ha*, then muttered under her breath, "You went through with it. You actually did it. I can't believe it. It was mad. I never dreamt… You said you wouldn't…. I never…" Her words trailed off.

From the flutter of fabric, J'non assumed Miss Whittington was gesturing or moving or motioning, but without looking up, there was no way to know. J'non refused to look up. Eyes fixed to the rug, she remained still and silent.

"How did she convince you?" Miss Whittington asked, presumably to Lord Pickering. "Did you know she was my maid, or did you think she was me? This is mad!" Miss Whittington's laugh was hollow. "Wait. Does this mean my father believes…?" More fluttering of fabric, this time with inaudible mumbling, then, "Good God." Her tone changed from incredulous to hushed horror. "I shouldn't be here. I've ruined everything. Oh, God in Heaven." A strangled cry muffled behind a hand.

For the first time since J'non stepped into the room, Lord Pickering spoke. His voice was flat, his pitch low. "Is it true? Are you Phoebe Whittington's lady's maid?"

There was no way for J'non to know what had been said before she entered the room, but after her mistress' declaration, there was no denying the truth.

Eyes on the gold and red weave, unable to face the man she betrayed, she confirmed, "Yes, my lord."

She waited for a response, a reprimand, a shout, a calling of the guards, something. Silence was her only response. Willing herself not to swoon, cry, or throw herself at his feet, she continued her longitudinal study of the rug's weave.

A shuffle, a click, then Lord Pickering's voice. "You may see her to her room now."

Only when the butler's shoes came into view did she stir. Rather than look up, she dipped a curtsy, then followed the shoes out of the parlor.

Chapter 27

The door closed with a soft *thud*, more of a feeling than a sound.

Lord Pickering shook his head, as though waking from a dream. Disorientated, he stood with his back to the parlor door, not seeing the hall before him.

He shrugged his shoulders. A curious heaviness weighed them, a tension that had not been there earlier. Responsibilities, duties, titles, holdings, employees, tenants, the family name. How had he lost focus?

"The front guest chamber on the third floor, my lord."

A voice. Disjointed. Disembodied.

"…the most appropriate location, given the misunderstanding and, er, complication."

Same voice. Funneled. Distorted.

"My lord?"

Pickering pinched the bridge of his nose between his thumb and forefinger and squeezed his eyes closed.

"Shall I have Matthew see to—"

"Stop talking," Pickering said to the back of his eyelids.

His temples pounded. Where was Gunner? He needed Gunner.

Scrubbing his lids with thumb and forefinger, he rubbed a sting, an irritation, grit in his eyes. He blinked once, twice. Focused on the blurred face before him. Blinked thrice. A butler. The butler. What was his name? Samwell was at Tidwell Hall. Hawkins was at Sladesbridge Court. Bainbridge? Yes, that was it. Mr. Bainbridge. A funny name. It was a Yorkshire name, North Yorkshire. Pickering shook his head again.

"My apologies, Bainbridge," Pickering said, pulling back his shoulders and standing straight. "You were saying?"

"Shall I have Matt—"

"From the beginning, please."

"Yes, my lord. I have situated her ladyship in the front chamber on the third floor. If you wish, I can send for her while Matthew sees to our parlor guest."

Steadying himself with a hand to the door frame, Pickering said, "Thank you, and no thank you. Third floor. Good choice. No need to send for her. I'll see to her myself. As to our guest, send a tray into the parlor for her refreshment, then move her belongings from the lady's suite to one of the guest rooms on the fourth floor."

"Yes, my lord."

That his "guest" had taken up residence in the lady's suite three days prior was not a point he wished to ponder beyond the fact, nor was the realization that he was legally married to that same "guest," as it was her name on the register, not that of J'non Butler, a truth he did not think either woman had realized and one he refused to consider further at the present time. Gathering his scattered wits, he strode through the entrance hall and up the stairs, only peripherally acknowledging the line of staff had long since dispersed. It had been nigh twenty minutes since the butler had escorted his counterfeit wife from the parlor to a room, after all, twenty minutes in which he had become as well acquainted with Miss Phoebe Whittington as he ever wished to be.

Up the stairs. A pivot on the landing. Up again. Another pivot. Five steps. The first floor, home to the reception room and drawing room. Crossing the reception room, he mounted the stairs again. Pivot on the landing. Up. Pivot. Five steps. The second floor, home to the lord and lady's suites. Crossing the hall, he mounted the stairs one last time. Pivot. Up. Pivot. Five steps. The third floor. Pickering stood on the hall landing, a door to his left, a door to his right. The right door, ironically coined.

The door was six paneled with an egg and dart motif above carved architraves and pediments. Twenty carved eggs above the door. He knew because he stood on the landing and counted each one. And then he counted the darts.

What the devil was he supposed to say to her?

All he knew was he deserved answers. She owed him that much.

Smoothing a hand over his frockcoat, he covered the distance, then rapped his knuckles against the door. A wave of nausea swept over him. Deceit. Betrayal. Lies. Manipulation. How was he to look into his wife's face and admit she wore the face of an imposter?

He would demand to know if she cared for him or if it was a farce from beginning to end. He should demand to know her motives, but that dimmed in importance. He needed to know if it was the marriage that was fraudulent or their relationship. Come to think of it, she had never reciprocated his words of affection. An admission by omission?

Again, he rapped. When no sounds stirred from within, he pushed against the door, expecting it to be locked. The door creaked ajar.

Pickering did not want to barge into the room. He trod unfamiliar ground in this state of limbo between married and unmarried. What was he to call her? J'non? Lady Pickering? Miss Butler?

With a nudge to widen the door a few more inches, he asked in a tone of its own state of limbo, somewhere between authoritative and servile, "May I enter to discuss the situation?" He winced at both the hitch in his voice and the awkwardness in wording.

Silence responded.

Right, then. Smoothing his hand over his frockcoat once again, he pushed the door fully open.

Empty.

He swallowed.

Empty?

Bainbridge must have mistaken the room. Pickering about-faced and crossed the hall to the mirroring guest room. A smart knock, a push, a blink. Empty, as well. Could she be in the dressing room? Neither room showed signs of occupancy, both beds neatly made, untouched, all items unmoved from original arrangement. He peeked into both dressing rooms. No signs of use.

Mounting the stairs once more, he took steps two at a time to the fourth floor. One room empty, one

in the process of being readied for Miss Whittington. Up again. The fifth floor featured only one room,
the door opposite leading to a terrace overlooking
the park. The one room was as the others had been:
empty of life.

He knew before he would admit it consciously.
He *knew*.

He charged down the stairs, back to the second
floor. Goaded by desperation, he flung open, without
knocking, the door to the lady's chamber. Empty. He
crossed the hall, pausing with a hand against the door
of the lord's chamber. Squeezing his eyes closed, he
steeled himself. This was it. This was the last door.
She had to be behind this door, waiting in his chamber
to confront him, to admit everything, to beg for forgiveness, to shower him with an outpouring of love.

Eyes wide, he stood tall and opened the door.

Empty.

Before him, stretched the empty drive of Tidwell
Hall, a familiar view from the nursery, one of which
a little boy watched for a mother who never returned,
a woman who did not love him enough. Pickering
hardened himself against the threatening flood of
emotions.

When one looked at the situation rationally, he
had not lost anything, not really, not if she never felt
affection for him, only used him for whatever means.
She being Miss J'non Butler, or whatever her real name
was, for there was no certainty she had shared her
real name with the Whittingtons. He had known she
left him before he checked the second room on the
third floor. He had known but could not bring himself
to admit it. Leaving meant only one thing: she had

lied. Beyond the obvious lie of identity, her fleeing the house confirmed *everything* had been a lie, every blush, every kiss, every story. *She* was a lie. Just as his father before him, he had been seduced by a deceptive woman, one who, in the end, had left.

Glancing down, he saw he still wore his traveling clothes. Best change out of these. His valet, along with the luggage carriage, had arrived well ahead of his own carriage. Good thing, too. He would wash away the grime and change attire. Then, to business. Of the utmost importance was to send for his solicitor. Yes, Mr. Barmby, Jr. would know the best course of action.

With one foot over the threshold of his room, he darted back across the hall to the staircase and bounded to the first landing. She could not have gone far. Bainbridge would know who to send. Parties could disperse in all directions to search the streets and park. She could not have gone far.

His hand gripping the cold banister, he stopped in flight. Senseless. Who was he chasing? Nothing more than a ghost, a shadow.

Shoulders rounded, he returned to his chamber. Best change out of his travel clothes. He would wash away the grime, change attire, then to business. Mr. Barmby would know what to do.

Chapter 28

She looked down at her hands. The hands of a nobody.

Would Baroness Collingwood take her in a second time? There was nowhere else to go.

Palms up. The palms of a coward.

If she was too afraid to face him, how could she face the baroness?

The butler had shown her to a guest room. But of course he had. She was not the marchioness. She was an imposter. An imposter, a coward, and a nobody.

What did she fear most? The street, the consequences, his reaction, her motives, the judgement, the loss…? Control slipped through her fingers. Powerless.

What did she *want*? To defend herself, to stand her ground. This was her home. He was her husband. Curling her fingers into her palms, she clenched them into fists.

Because she was powerless, did it follow she was also defenseless? It was futile to fight when defeat was inevitable. She must bow her head and accept the punishment.

J'non paced, her eyes trained on her fists.

Long ago, a lifetime ago, Mama had taught her that no matter the situation, a lady should behave as a lady. Come scandal or a guest's bad manners, be it in one's own drawing room or a host's, a lady should never turn her back or run away, rather defuse the situation with poise, grace, and humility. As a maid, however, she was taught to remain invisible while others decided her fate. If she was ever to face herself in the mirror again, it was time to make her own choices, to be the lady her mother raised rather than the maid she had become. Lord Pickering could toss her out without a coin, charge her with fraud, or do whatever he felt must be done, but she had the choice to face it as a lady with poise, grace, and humility. That was her only defense, her only way to fight a losing battle. In the end, she had no one to blame except herself, but at least she would not have allowed herself to be buffeted by the wind.

The door to the ground floor study opened. J'non spun around, her heart in her throat, her knees dipping in weakness. Steadying herself with a hand to the desk, she faced him.

Lord Pickering stopped midstride, one hand on the door, one on the frame. His features hardened, his body rigid. He neither moved nor spoke. As when she had descended from the carriage and glimpsed him for the first time, he was an austere aristocrat, carved from stone, an imposing stranger.

Quivering from a loss of fortitude, she lowered her eyes to the floor and bowed her head, a nobody who meant nothing to this man, nothing except a conniving maid who had outmaneuvered him to gain advantage.

One word grazed the silence, carried by little more than an exhale. "Why?"

J'non swallowed, her throat constricting. The rug in the study was less ornate than the one in the parlor but no less interesting with its floral motif and vibrant reds, yellows, and greens. Scrollwork braided with wreaths along the border, each corner featuring a golden leaf roundel.

"I never intended to deceive you, my lord. It spiraled out of my control before—"

"I meant, why did you stay. I—I thought you had left."

She looked up, meeting his gaze for the first time since their arrival to the London house. His eyes were shuttered of emotion but bore into her, unblinking.

Her words drifted when she began, "I wanted a chance…"

"To defend yourself?" he finished for her.

"No, I wanted a chance…" Her words drifted again.

How to finish the sentence? A chance for them to talk? A chance to defend why they should be together? A chance for them? There was no chance, not after her deception. She left the words lingering in the air.

Wait. Why did he think she had left? Had he gone to her room? To what… to talk? Her pulse quickened. Of course he would have gone to her room to talk, to demand an explanation, to demand she leave. She had only stayed in the room for five, perhaps ten minutes. It had not been her room. She was not a guest. She did not belong there. No one noticed her departure, her descent down the stairs, her slipping into his study. No one noticed a maid who did not wish to be seen. She had lingered at the door to the lord's chamber, curious if he would go there first after speaking with Miss Whittington, but she decided that was too intimate, too inappropriate given the circumstances, for she was not his wife. The study had been her next choice. No one noticed her slipping through the first door on the ground floor.

J'non studied his marble features, the expression that of Lord Pickering, masking the face of Trevor. Digging her fingers into her palms, she willed herself to speak. This was it. This was her chance, her only chance. There was no changing the course of events, and if he had already made his decision, so be it, but she could at least say her piece, no matter how humiliating to say to a man who had lost all respect and trust for her half an hour ago. *A lady never turns her back. A lady faces all situations with grace, poise, and humility.*

"I stayed," she began, "because I wanted a chance. Just that. I wanted a chance. However deceptive the original circumstances, I married you before the eyes of God. This is where I belong. With you. Reject me if you will. Disbelieve me if you will. There's no reason for you to trust anything I say. I do not fear being turned out into the streets, for at one time those streets were my home. The only fear I have remaining is losing you, but I suppose I lost you half an hour ago. So, fearlessly, I can admit I stayed because you are my husband, and my place is by your side. I wanted a chance… for us."

He stared, unresponsive.

She curled her toes in her shoes. So, this was the end. All her pretty words fell on stone ears. Looking back on this moment, she could at least say she spoke her mind and did not go lightly on command.

In the same low, controlled voice, he spoke at last. "You stayed because you made vows before God."

Uncertain what he wanted in response, she said nothing. Flexing her fingers, now aching from being curled in her palms so long, she tried to ignore the heat behind her eyes.

"You stayed because you feel obligated, because it is your duty as a wife, because losing me means failure of that duty in the eyes of God."

Tilting her head, she studied him anew, trying to read what he was thinking. Either he had not understood, or she had poorly articulated herself. It was not as though she had time to write a speech, to outline her thoughts and order them with precision, to word her thoughts for the greatest rhetorical impact. She was a woman at the end of her tether, facing the consequences of a single poor decision, a decision, in her defense, made under duress, but a poor decision, nonetheless. Then, if she had not made that decision…

"Have I ever been a dutiful wife?" she asked with a soft laugh. "No, Trevor, I stayed because regardless how much you must hate me, that does not change the fact that I love you. The words mean little in light of the situation. What do you care if a maid loves you, especially a deceitful maid who tricked you? Fearlessness does a funny thing to a person, though. It frees them. A nobody I may be, but I admit fearlessly and freely that I stayed because I love you and believe my place is as your wife."

"You're not my wife, J'non."

The words stole her breath. She knew they would be said, but in all her prosing, she had not expected to hear them so boldly stated.

After a deep breath, he added, "You're the love of my life."

"Oh," was all she managed before her chin trembled too violently to say more. The taste of salty tears on her lips confirmed it would be best not to try to speak.

If she thought he would rush into the room and embrace her, she was mistaken. He remained standing in the doorway, as rigid as before.

"I do not condone your decision to marry me under false pretenses or not to confess at any point during our marriage," he said, "but I can appreciate the delicacy of the situation. Whatever your reasons, whatever your past, they don't matter in so far as my feelings for you." He took one step forward, his first step since opening the door. "I'm not going to fight for someone who doesn't care a fig for me. I'm certainly not going to fight for something that isn't real."

J'non swiped at her cheeks and made to speak, but he held up a staying hand.

"If you mean what you say," he continued, "we'll find a way. However, if you're confessing affections from the very fear you deny, trust that you have my word I'll see you safely through this so that you may walk away into a new life without scandal, consequence, or an empty pocket."

"Oh, Trevor," she said on a sigh.

It took her seven steps to walk from the desk to the door and two heartbeats to embrace him. She encircled his waist with her arms and buried her face in the ruffle of his shirt. Inhaling the fresh scent of soap and starch—the sneaky man had changed out of his travel attire while she still wore the dust of the trip—she did not care that he stood rigid as a post and did not move in response to her hug. At last, she wept, spoiling his freshly laundered linen. She wept with happiness. *He loved her.* Not the doe-eyed love of the honeymoon stage or the passion between lovers but the love needed to trust beyond reason, to accept without prejudice, to fight hopeless battles, to release if unrequited, to aid without reciprocation. Maid or lady, he did not care. He loved her unconditionally.

"You've not rested since we arrived," he said, moving his lips against her temple and enfolding his arms around her until she nestled in the cocoon of his embrace.

"But we have so much to discuss," she protested.

"After you've rested. You were on the verge of collapse when we arrived. Shall I see you to your room? We can talk this evening."

"I should have stayed in my room after all. It was silly to leave."

Tightening his hold on her, he said, "You were right to leave. It wasn't your room."

Was he implying…? She smiled into the folds of his cravat, knowing he would be escorting her to the second floor.

Chapter 29

She spoke so animatedly, he could only chuckle and admire her further. Trevor thought he knew J'non, and yet this woman was someone different, not unlike the wife he had raced to the lake on multiple occasions or bantered with on the settee, but this woman was fearless and vibrant. Saying this evening was the happiest of his life would be misleading since there was a legal complication hanging overhead. The sentiment held true, nevertheless. Whatever residual sting remained that she had not told him herself, it was nothing in comparison to the unadulterated love he now experienced. There were no barriers, no walls, no guards. There was only unconditional love. For the first time, he was seeing *her*, a woman not needing to tip-toe or carefully word her answers, not needing to guard her feelings. She was free to love in the safety of his arms.

Well, not literally in his arms, although he wished it were so. J'non sat across from him on the terrace overlooking the garden. It was not as romantic as he had hoped since a fog overcast the twinkle of stars, and the pungent bouquet of horse perfumed the air. Despite it being late into the evening, there remained a hubbub of noise, if not below, then from somewhere, another street over, sounds that carried on a stale wind. And yet that they were together was romantic enough for him.

She loved him. She loved him enough to stay, to face whatever consequence, to fight for them to be together, to express her affection in the face of potential disdain and rejection. So happy, he pushed away all thoughts of legalities. There was no point in worrying, not until he spoke with Lloyd, no point in pondering the myriad of negative outcomes, including him returning to Sladesbridge Court with J'non as anyone other than his marchioness. For now, there was only this moment, and this moment was bliss.

She nudged his leg with her foot. "Are you listening? You're practically drooling on yourself from boredom."

"Merely admiring your beauty, my sweet." He leaned over to capture her foot and pull it into his lap. "You were telling me about your father."

With narrowed gaze, obviously not believing that he had been paying attention, she launched into another story from her childhood. Trevor had yet to learn the darkness in her past, but he knew more about her childhood than he could remember of his own. What he knew thus far was she was *not* a maid. She was, to his shock, a perfect candidate for marriage. Had life proceeded differently, they might have been introduced at a ball as potential mates. While he would not have considered marrying a maid he met in a hallway or garden, as she had once asked him, he would not have hesitated to consider marrying Miss

Butler. He suspected, however foolish it sounded, he would have fallen for her at first sight.

Miss J'non Butler. Daughter of Sir Julian, baronet, and Non Butler. She was a gentleman's daughter. Her memories from youth painted an idyllic life with flawless parents. Was it terrible he was not merely relieved but ecstatic to learn his father-in-law was Sir Julian rather than Mr. Whittington? Again, he pushed away the pesky legal concerns complicating matters such as in-laws. His only wish this evening was that life had allowed him to meet Sir Julian. Her confessions had yet to surprise him since he had sorted out for himself some time ago the baronet was her father, although he had thought the fathering had been by nefarious means, so learning of a happy family had him all smiles, in addition to being a boon to his inductive reasoning skills.

Her tales of childhood dipped in spirits as the chronology brought her to the smallpox that ravished her village.

He offered, "This is when you were sent to live with your aunt." A curiosity she had already told him so much about her real past, a curiosity and a blessing.

"Yes. It was meant to be temporary. A few weeks at most. I didn't know my aunt or either of my cousins well. You see, she is my father's sister-in-law. There had been a rift in the fam—"

"Ah, I see where this is going," Trevor interrupted, proud to make more connections between the stories she had already told and the new information. "They didn't approve your father's marrying a Welsh woman from a mining family. Am I right? Let me guess the next part, as well. They blamed you for the supposed sins of the father."

J'non scoffed. "Who is telling this story, you or I?"

"Here I thought you were raised as a gentleman's daughter. Did your mother not teach you that wives should obey their husbands?" Pinching her toes, he added, "I'll not tolerate this brazen insolence of yours."

With a smirk he could see even by candlelight, J'non asked rhetorically, "I'm not your wife, remember?"

Trevor laughed a single *ha*. "Touché."

"Now, as I was saying before I was so rudely interrupted."

"You know," he said, pointedly interrupting her again, "we shouldn't be here together if we're not married. Could cause a scandal."

"Hush. I'm telling a tale of woe."

She joked, making light of what was to come, but he sensed the next part was nothing to laugh about.

At first a guest of her aunt, albeit an unwanted guest, J'non's role shifted with gradual, slight changes, initially a guest who was not introduced to callers or invited to join family events, then a guest who was instructed to serve as chaperone and companion to her cousins, soon moved to a smaller room, and before long, moved downstairs with the staff, and eventually branded as her cousins' lady's maid and sometimes chaperone.

The further into the tale, the more somber her tone, her earlier teasing at an end. Trevor could do no more than listen and hug her foot between his hands.

"I never had the opportunity to mourn their passing," she said regarding the death of her parents. "I have no way of knowing when they passed. It was months before I learned the truth, but even then, I was never told directly. My aunt oft played the martyr, and this was one of her great sacrifices, tasked with caring for me, who was nothing more than a burden. She wailed at the expense of my care, but what I never could understand was *what expense*? Was nothing settled on me, even before their passing? I was not a costly ward regardless. I never required new clothes since I mended what I brought with me, eventually letting down the hem as I grew taller, adjusting as needed in other areas. I never required additional food other than what was already served downstairs, as I ate with the servants. My uncle was not a poor man, neither was my father. And from the sale of my father's estate after his passing—which I only overheard the servants discussing when they didn't know I was nearby—they made a pretty penny. *What expense*?"

Trevor suspected but did not voice that he had little doubt her parents paid her aunt well to look after J'non, and then after their passing, the uncle would have undoubtedly become guardian to whatever inheritance and dowry she might have had. Trevor had half a mind to put Lloyd on the case, ferret out these thieves, but he would do so only at J'non's request.

J'non's silence drew his attention.

He asked, "Did they arrange for your position with the Whittingtons, or did you apply to the position by post?"

He assumed that was the next stage in the story. From unpaid lady's maid to her cousins to paid lady's maid for the Whittingtons. Without characters, it would have been impossible to gain so prestigious a position as lady's maid, but it was possible her aunt or uncle was acquainted with the Whittingtons. He tallied the years. According to the story so far, she would have lived with her aunt for about five years. If what she had said before about only living with Mr. Whittington for one month was accurate, he was short at least a year. What had happened for the stretch of a year before working for the Whittingtons?

"Neither," she said in answer to his question, her gaze dropping to her hands.

He waited, not wanting to press. Whatever came next, she would tell in her own time. After each deep breath she took, he was certain she was about to begin, but still, she did not speak.

At length, he asked, "Is it difficult to tell me because it's unpleasant, or is it difficult to tell me because you fear my reaction?"

Studying him before replying, she said, "Both."

"Easy enough for me to say while in a position of ignorance, but could we eliminate the worry of my reaction? Then all you must contend with is the unpleasantness of the memory. You're fearless, remember?" When she offered only a humorless chuckle, he added, "If I've not run away after learning you married me as someone else, I think it's safe to assume whatever else you have hiding in your past will not send me running for the dales either."

"It could change your opinion of me."

"If anything that has happened to you or anything you have done might change my opinion of you, then it would say little about the unconditional love I profess and even less about my judge of character. Between the two of us, I pride myself on being a decent judge of character." He said the last light-heartedly, hoping to assuage whatever distressed her.

Her gaze dropped again, but she said, "Very well."

He braced himself for all darkness he could fathom, from her turning to a life of crime as a high-waywoman to being held hostage by a rogue. In truth, while he could not guarantee his opinion would not change, it did not say much about him if it did. What-ever she had been through, it had affected her, be the incident great or small. Whatever it was, she would remain the woman he saw before him. Knowledge on his part did not change the woman herself.

"One of my cousins expected a proposal any day from her most ardent suitor. So confident he would propose, they would often find excuses to leave her in the parlor alone with him, me serving as chaperone, the shadow in the corner. I was only the poor rela-tion of unknown position, never acknowledged by callers, unseen and ignored. I provided safety with-out intrusion. They would flirt, she teasing, he never declaring."

She paused in her story, leaving him to hazard a few guesses as to what happened next. He hated to consider the darker possibilities. A precarious posi-tion, a young lady's, especially one without security. He hugged her foot tighter, wishing it were her instead, if for no other reason than to provide his support.

After a deep inhale, J'non launched into the next part, talking so quickly her words jumbled together and tripped over themselves. "Over the next two or so weeks, he found ways to sneak attention my direc-tion, and while I made a point never to encourage him,

I must have done so inadvertently, for his attentions increased rather than decreased, all until one day we found ourselves quite alone in the parlor, and despite my insistence that I must leave to attend to other matters and did not find him as congenial as he thought himself, he accepted the invitation I did not believe I had offered and kissed me."

After a long enough silence to indicate to Trevor the transgression ended with the kiss, he cleared his throat. "What you mean to say is he forced his attentions."

"Not according to my aunt," she said, rubbing her palms against her dress, "who happened to open the parlor door at that same moment. No gentleman would press intimacy upon a woman without provocation."

"Correct. No *gentleman* would. I say now, J'non, that rake was no gentleman."

"Well, yes, he was, a much-respected gentleman, one for whom all the ladies were setting their caps, but I assure you I was not. He should never have noticed me. I made myself as invisible as I could and discouraged him at every turn." Adding in a hushed voice, she said, "But I must not have been insistent enough."

Trevor groaned. Nudging her foot off his lap, he reached across the space between their chairs and tugged her hands until she complied. He pulled her onto his lap and urged her head to nestle on his shoulder, settling in the crook of his neck.

"There. Better already," he said. "Now, listen to me. You did nothing to encourage his attention. Before you argue that I wasn't there to form a reliable opinion, I want you to consider this: I'm a man. I'm a man who knows other men. I know of men who are wolves in sheep's clothing. I say with confidence there are men who press their attentions where they're not wanted, most for sport, sometimes for more sinister purposes, but rarely ever because they misunderstood a *no* for a *yes*—I qualify that with 'rarely ever,' although I want to say 'never,' because I concede there are a few daft bulls out there. This so-called suitor, I wager, was not one of them. He knew he was not invited." Wrapping his arms around her loosely, he brushed her forearm with his fingers. "Is this what you were afraid to tell me?"

Her voice cracked when she said, "In part. It was the catalyst. I did not want you to think I was wanton."

"I don't."

She nodded against his neck. "My aunt accused me of tempting him in hopes of stealing him from my cousin. She threatened to tell everyone I was a… a… a woman of loose morals. I could no longer live under their roof given my 'disposition,' and if I dared show my face at a neighbor's, it would be to discover my name ruined, as everyone would know before nightfall what I had done and what sort of woman I was. No son, husband, brother, stablehand, or footman was safe from my diabolical ways. She assured me no respectable family would accept me over the threshold. I believed her. Looking back, I see how foolish it was, for she would never have subjected her daughters to scandal. At the time, it was enough to convince me I had no friendly face to turn to. My only hope was to seek aid in the next town."

"Wait," Trevor interrupted. "Wait. I've missed something. I understand your aunt threatened scandal and ruination, but what do you mean you sought aid in the next town?"

J'non tensed. "I was told to leave."

"Your aunt forced you out of the house?"

"Yes."

Trevor exhaled sharply through his teeth.

As much as J'non did not want to share the next part, *the bleak period*, she was encouraged by his reactions thus far. He had not thought her wanton, as her aunt had accused her of being, nor had he blamed her for something she had been led to believe was her fault. However brief the moment in her life, that kiss was enough to ruin her in the eyes of society. It alone was something she had feared to share with him.

What came after surpassed it by leaps and bounds. Could she form the words?

Her mouth moved, but she could not be sure of what she said versus what she thought, how much she shared versus how much she remembered, the whole of the memory visceral.

There was no chance to gather belongings, food, coin, no chance to change or swap shoes. I was escorted in a vice-grip about my upper arm through the front door and into the street, empty handed, empty hearted. The noon sun shone high. The air warm despite a cool breeze. A full day ahead to find a friendly face. Worn shoes on my feet, but sturdy enough, I followed the row to the next town. A young lady needing assistance, be it a room for the evening, a coin for a coach, a bowl of bits, a word of advice. I looked the part of a maid, but I was poised, gentle, uncalloused, nonthreatening, and clean-cheeked.

A knock at the first door followed with an apology and a shake of the head. A knock at the second followed with another apology, another shake of the head. Oh, but there are many doors in a town, you might be thinking, and at least one public house. The sun dipped by the time I ran out of doors. The evening chill brought gooseflesh to my arms. My soles ached. I am clean, friendly, polite, well-meaning, yet why does every door close? The innkeeper, with sympathy in his eyes, shook his head. No coin, no service. Run along home, little pup. The first night was the most difficult, for where is a young lady accustomed to the comforts of a bed to sleep in the cold dark of night? Every sound, every whisper of wind, every tickle of nature shuddered my breath. Did it bite? Would I ever be warm again? Was it hungry? Why did my heel throb?

Morning brought new promise. Another town down the row, more doors, a new inn.

The trouble with new mornings was each brought another layer of dirt, another new smell, another callous, another blister. What doors once would have apologized with a sympathetic eye, even passing a bit of bread if lucky or offering the hayloft for the night, soon turned hostile. Where had the gentle maid gone, the poised gentlewoman, the kindly meant but displaced soul? In no more than a week, she resembled a vagrant, a wretch, a thief. Who was she to argue when, in truth, that was who she was?

One never expects to reach a point when the sight of a warm stable means safety, the canopy of trees means shelter, the feel of insect-infested hay means comfort. One never expects to reach a point when stealing food is morally acceptable and in its own way God-sent.

What is normalcy? The definition changes. What is acceptable? The definition changes. The needs of survival change. Have you ever stolen food from a horse trough, eaten alongside sows, poached rabbit and eaten it raw? I have. Two words no lady in our modern society will ever say: I have. Imagine the beauty in her ball dress, dancing beneath the glittering candlelight with a trussed beau, her dreams of a village wedding, his dreams of a full brood, and then hear her say, I have.

Society moved forward, yet I remained still. Life moved forward, yet I remained still. I was trapped in a world I did not understand, with people who ought to have been kind but were sinister, with door after door of rock throwing, broom beating, word tossing, and spitting, a release of the hounds, a call of the magistrate. One day became a week. One week became two. Two weeks became a month. One month became two. No calendar to tick off time's passage. I lost myself in a desperation to survive.

Was there a friendly face or two along the way? Yes. For a single bowl behind the stables – don't be seen, would say the friendly face. I don't blame them. How is one to distinguish the evil of the world from a lost lady in need of aid? The longest help received was one full week in paradise thanks to a childless couple. My first bath in three months. My first full meal. My first pillow. A coin to help me on my way. But to where? They could offer no more aid than that, a temporary reprieve. How gaunt I looked in their little mirror. I hardly recognized myself. Stringy hair, dead eyes. Who is she?

From your position, you wonder why I did not seek employment, why I did not go to a church, why I did not return to my hometown where I would be known. You assume I did not do these. I did. And yet each evening I found myself sleeping on the dank ground once more.

At first, I knew hunger and desperation, a concern about my dress, my skin, my hair, for I must stay clean if someone is to help me, must look unmenacing. Then, I forgot to care.

Have you ever been so hungry you forget you're hungry? I have. There's a comfort in the numbness. No more pain. No gnawing in the belly. No awareness of emptiness. Merely numbness. It spreads through the limbs so that a blister no longer hurts. Does this insult your tender sensibilities? Do you wish to remain ignorant that gentlewomen can suffer this fate? Do you wish to deny a family could be so cruel or neighbors so heartless? Oh, there's always a relative or kind neighbor somewhere, you say. For your sake, I hope you're right.

J'non leaned away from Trevor, unable to look him in the eyes. She shivered. When had it become so cold on the terrace? How much she had shared compared to how much left to memory, she could not be certain. Her hope was she had sugar-coated the worst of it, kept the grappling hands of not-so-gentle-men who stumbled on her in the stables reserved only to memory. She was proud of her right hook, though. Still, some memories were better kept to oneself.

Rather than speak, Trevor rested his forehead against her shoulder and held her. She liked this better than words of sympathy or acknowledgement.

Bolstered by the shelter of his arms, she continued, "In the end, an innkeeper helped me. He found me." She omitted that he found her in one of the stalls after the first meal in days—a feast of horse mash—had disagreed with her. Such things were not for a gentleman's ears. "He offered me a room and had his wife pamper me like a princess. I worried at the cost, for they knew I had no coin. Instead of a charge, he told me about a place I could go, a safe haven for destitute women. I suspected there was no such place, but he offered to take me himself, promised if I did not like the look of it, I could stay and work at the inn as a maid."

The memory of the haven filled her vision. Picturesque. Stone and thatch. Flowers. Cobbled paths.

"It was its own village," she said. "Noach Cottage is what it's called, and although that implies a single home, it was an entire village, a working village. Northeast of Southampton. Not only for destitute women but foundlings and orphans, as well. It's a temporary home, never permanent, and one must earn their stay by working in some capacity, be it teaching, looking after the orphans, cleaning, or whatever is needed and whatever one can offer. While there, one can recuperate while learning a useful trade to prepare for a new life. Since I had already been a lady's maid, although untrained, I chose that as my trade, and I learned the skills well enough to convince a family like the Whittingtons even if not the highest sticklers of an aristocratic family."

Trevor leaned back to look up at her. "This is the same Noach Cottage patronized by Baroness Collingwood, yes?"

"Both Lady and Lord Collingwood."

"It was she who placed you with the Whittingtons?" he asked.

"Not exactly. She, or Noach Cottage rather, has agreements with several employment agencies to allow the women who have graduated, so to speak, to apply for employment without characters to said agencies. The agencies then try to find the best fit. Something to understand is this is not meant to be a return service, neither the cottage nor the agencies. This is an opportunity, singular, and nothing is guaranteed."

"I understand," was all he said.

"I—" she stuttered on her words. "I—I never intended to deceive you. I intended at every turn to tell you. I make no excuses and do not ask for sympathy when I admit I held my tongue because I feared the outcome of telling you, both before our marriage and after. Knowing you now, I *know* I could have told you the moment I stepped off the carriage, and you would have helped me, offered a position at your estate, introduced me to the Harveys, *something*, but I did not know you then, and I'm not accustomed to kindness."

Returning to lean against her shoulder, he closed his eyes and pressed his lips to her arm, although he did not pucker for a kiss. Instead, he said, "I must have made an intimidating figure."

J'non laughed softly. "Yes. You did."

"So intimidating that you thought I would make a better husband than helper."

She sucked in a breath.

Then he chuckled. Then laughed. A laugh so hearty he had tears in the corners of his eyes by the time she joined him in laughter. With tenderness and a gentle touch, he tucked her into his arms, stood, then set her in her own chair. When he returned to his chair, he leaned forward and clasped her hands in his.

"I want to see you when I say this, J'non." His eyes still shone with the tears of laughter, although his lips curved into a frown. "I see you now as I've always seen you, as a marchioness. You are the strongest and most confident woman I have ever known. Everything you've told me this evening deepens that perception. Although this next point doesn't matter to me since *marchioness* is how I see you, I feel it important to say for *you* to realize and believe. No matter what roles you've played or what you've suffered, you are a lady. Yes, you were born and raised as a gentlewoman, but there is more to being a lady than birthright. Your actions, your perspectives, your ideas, your behavior, everything defines you as a lady. You are a lady, not a maid. Do you understand?"

She nodded, although she could no longer see him through the blur in her vision.

"If it takes me a lifetime to convince you of that, I will make it my life's work. What I'm about to say next you already know, but I want to make it abundantly clear given how wrecked you must feel having just shared every dark corner of your life." He paused for her to blink away the fresh onslaught of tears. "I *want* to be married to you. No matter what it takes, I *will* have you as my wife. We have built a life together, J'non. You're not just a wife to me, not even just the woman I love. You're my partner. I can't *not* see you as these things. Whatever you've done, whatever has been done to you, whatever secrets you've withheld, none of it unmakes you as the person with whom I've partnered."

He stopped to tug a handkerchief from his pocket, first dabbing at his eyes, and then offering it to her to do the same.

Once he held her hands again in his, he laughed. "Think of all we've done in our short marriage. We've saved neighbors from a flood, invested in a coal mine, rebuilt a village, established a life, renovated a house, made friends. I want you to be the mother of my children and I the father of yours, the two of us raising a happy brood in remembrance of your own family, all at Sladesbridge Court. We have a problem to solve, but if you're still in agreement after my jumbled reply to your Tale of Woe, as you aptly titled it — in proper capital lettering, of course — then we will find a way to be married… again."

"You know I want it. I've already given my pretty speech, remember?" She squeezed his hands in hers. "But what of Phoebe? Her name is on the register. She'll surely use that to her advantage to claim you as her husband. I wouldn't put it past her to establish herself in London as your marchioness to prove it, if she's not done so already. Your hands will be tied."

He shook his head. "It's not that bad. Yes, it's bad, but not *that* bad. I don't have the answer, not until Lloyd arrives and walks me through the legal avenues. I assume an annulment will be required, but how to do that without scandal or claiming fraud, I don't know. I also don't know how to deal with Mr. Whittington and the dowry we have already spent, but again, I'll wait until Lloyd arrives to worry. As to Miss Whittington, it is *not that bad*. I know you have reason to distrust her, and I have no reason to trust her, but I have spent a collective half hour speaking with her today, and what I see is a broken woman."

"She's manipulative, Trevor. She cannot be trusted. Her skill, if it can be considered a skill, is in manipulating men, specifically."

"I understand," he assured. "I'll use caution in all conversations with her. If we set that aside for a moment, allow me to express who I met in the parlor: a broken woman in search of help. While incomparable, I would hedge to say at least similar to the situation in which you once found yourself. If she's to be believed, she came here expecting to find me still heartbroken from the jilt and hoping I would reconsider marrying her after all. She did not know I was married nor that you had followed through with her proposal."

"Whatever she may have thought upon arrival is nothing to what she must be thinking now," J'non argued. "She'll use this to her advantage, I tell you."

"Maybe so. I choose the benefit of doubt and will wait for Lloyd before thinking otherwise. What I witnessed was a desperate woman with nowhere to turn. Yes, I see you about to argue she could go to her father, but for whatever reason, she did not seem in agreement with that. She did not speak forthright to me, share her own tales of woe, rather focused her time on trying to convince me to reconsider her as a spouse, and following the revelation of you as my spouse, she was, how shall I describe, defeated? She's staying here for the evening, fourth floor, but with your permission, I'd like to invite her to stay at my father's former London house until we resolve this. It is on the market, but her brief occupancy should not affect purchase prospects."

J'non tugged at her bottom lip with her teeth. She did not trust Miss Phoebe Whittington. As her lady's maid, J'non had been privy to the machinations and inner workings of Phoebe's plots to get what she wanted. If, however, what Trevor witnessed was true, and Phoebe had found herself in a desperate situation, how wretched of a person was J'non not to offer help after all her espousing of no one helping her during her own time of need.

With a curt nod, J'non said, "Very well."

Chapter 30

"He's not due to arrive for another two weeks," Lloyd was saying. "A perfect buyer. Unlike the other prospects, he's not bothered by the antiquated décor and, according to his correspondences, prefers it."

Trevor nodded to a footman who replaced his empty coffee cup with a fresh one, steam roiling from the top. He and Lloyd convened in the morning room, which was inconveniently located on the lower ground floor and notably without windows. They could move into the study soon enough, but Trevor had priorities, namely devouring a plate or four of meat.

"Perfect," Trevor said. "Her presence won't interfere with showings, then. Aside from my preference of her not staying here as a guest, I would rather avoid the awkward dynamics between her and J'non. It's not every day a woman must contend with the fact her lady's maid is now a marchioness."

Lloyd grunted but said nothing.

"Spread word," Trevor continued, "that she's a friend of Lady Pickering, staying at her ladyship's request. If we don't start the rumors first, others will arise, and I suspect they will not be savory."

Lloyd mumbled under his breath about ladybirds. Trevor did not respond but had been thinking the same.

"I have the canal petition to contend with," Trevor rambled between bites of bacon, "which passed from the House of Commons into the House of Lords yesterday, scheduled to be debated in a few days. Happy news but dismal timing. I'll need to meet with Roddam tomorrow." He would make an excuse then as to why they had not called yet.

It had only been three days since their arrival. He struggled to keep track of time. Each day passed with the length of a week. On his task list was to secure J'non's court dress, accept a few invitations, and begin the introductions of his marchioness, but the snag was not knowing the outcome of this *inconvenience*. To his mind, all would conclude as he wished, but was it wise to proceed into society until that conclusion was fact? He thought not.

His solicitor rotated his own cup of coffee, disinterested in the morning feast. Lloyd had arrived early enough to catch Trevor and J'non at table. J'non had excused herself with her customary smile of hospitality, just as though nothing untoward had occurred or the primary conversation between marquess and solicitor would not be about her.

Lloyd clinked his cup against its saucer. "Shall we adjourn to your study?" His eyes flicked to the footman.

With a longing look to his plate, Trevor said, "I wish you had come with an appetite. I have at least three more helpings awaiting my attention."

Lloyd chuckled before they both left for the study. Only when the door closed did Lloyd speak again. "I assume the staff are otherwise informed."

Trevor offered Lloyd a seat by the hearth rather than at the desk. Despite the gravity of circumstances, Trevor wanted the impression of ease, if for no other reason than to convince himself this could be resolved without undue stress or heartache. This *would* be resolved. It had to be.

"Whatever rumors they share downstairs," Trevor said, "the understanding is Miss Whittington's arrival as Lady Pickering was a *mis*understanding, a jest on her part—at the expense of the staff—to surprise her old friend, who happens to be the real Lady Pickering."

"And they believe that rubbish?"

"Not for a minute, I'm sure, but what other explanation is there? I arrived with Lady Pickering on my arm, yet a woman claiming to be Lady Pickering sat in the parlor, only rather than escort the intruder out of the house, I invited her to stay as a guest. As ridiculous of a tale, what else would explain the confusion?"

Lloyd crossed one leg over the other. "Never mind Mr. Whittington has been touting the association for months. Who in London does *not* think his daughter is a marchioness?"

Trevor huffed. "Aside from our more pressing concern, that does have me ruffled. The truth is it'll do nothing more than brand him a liar—his word against mine—but I worry about any ripples, both for his daughter and him. I may not have cared for him as a person, but he has done nothing to deserve censure. I especially don't want Miss Whittington's name ruined."

Lloyd held out his palms in helpless apology. "However much faith in me you have, I don't possess all the answers. Shocking, I know. Best advice? Play it. Play the joke between friends you've already played. Once we settle the matter, see to it Miss Whittington receives a few of the same invitations, then take her as a guest of the Marquess and Marchioness of Pickering. Two friends, one who is a prankster, the other who enjoys a joke." Steepling his fingers, he said, "I shouldn't offer advice of that nature, to be honest. In the end, you're likely to be married to Miss Whittington, not her maid."

Trevor pierced him with a glare. "That better be pessimism and not legalese."

"Now, if you want the best advice of the day, I say remain married to Miss Whittington. As stunning of a beauty as was promised and marriage to her alleviates the whole debacle. Who cares if her maid played imposter since the motive was money?"

Pushing himself out of his chair, Trevor took three steps and towered over his old friend and solicitor. "How long has it been since I've cuffed you on the ear?"

Lloyd raised his eyebrows. "Since I was six. It wasn't a cuff but a punch, and it wasn't my ear, as I recall, rather my nose."

"Your nose looks straight enough. Shall I bend it this time?"

"I hear some ladies enjoy a more rugged look," Lloyd said with a grin. "Sit down, Lord Protector, and smooth your crest." Muttering, he added, "Next time I arrange a marriage, I'll escort the woman myself."

Returning to his chair, Trevor said, "Take it from personal experience: don't. If you had in this case, I'd have married Miss Whittington instead."

"Well, now, technically —"

Trevor shushed him with another look.

With an overly dramatic sigh, Lloyd said, "Right. Let's talk. I've no good news for you. In my defense, I've only had time to mull things over on the ride here. I've not had time to consult my files, split the spines of the old books, etcetera. I came the moment I received your note, so if what I have to say now isn't pleasing, which I don't believe it will be, allow me at least a day to sift through my office."

Circling his hands for Lloyd to continue, Trevor leaned forward, elbows to thighs, eager to hear the options.

"The most obvious," Lloyd began, "is to accept that the name in the register is that of Phoebe Whittington, and thus to acknowledge you're legally married to someone by the name of Phoebe Whittington. If so acknowledged, our two options are to divorce Miss Whittington so that you may marry Miss Butler, or to sue Miss Whittington on the grounds of bigamy, and then if granted, marry Miss Butler."

Trevor made to interrupt, but Lloyd held a staying hand.

"Allow me to do my job first before protesting." Lloyd laced his fingers, unlaced them, then laced them again. "Before proceeding with either option, we must first ascertain from Miss Whittington if she married the gentleman with whom she eloped or if she merely went on an extended lover's holiday. Do you know, by chance?"

Trevor shook his head. "I know she eloped with him but not if it was solemnized."

"Assuming it was a lover's holiday, then divorce is the best course of action. You can divorce her on the grounds of adultery. It's a wee complicated, but nothing we can't accomplish. First, I'd need to find the lover, Mr. Whateverhisnameis, who would need to testify that yes, he had engaged in illegal intercourse with the Marchioness of Pickering. The difficulties include a long trial, the need for him as a witness, the exorbitant cost, and the scandal, as the trial would be transcribed in the newspapers. It's also unlikely divorce would be granted after all our efforts. If we took this route, you would have to acknowledge the marriage as valid and Miss Whittington as your wife. To proceed, you would need to submit for legal separation on the grounds of adultery while also suing Mr. Whateverhisnameis for criminal conversation and alienation of affection. *If*, and I emphasize *if*, he is found guilty and you are awarded damages, then and only then can you petition Parliament to end the marriage."

Trevor slumped forward, cradling his head in his hands. "No."

"That was a short conversation. Next?"

"Next." Trevor grunted the word.

"Onto bigamy, then. If we confer, after confirmation from Miss Whittington, she married the lover rather than going on holiday, we can explore charges of bigamy. I've seen bigamy cases go quickly with a petition filed and granted all without fuss, and conversely, I've seen these cases drag out with more pain than they're worth, including full court proceedings.

Regardless, there will be a bigamous charge against Miss Whittington. If it's quick, then the marriage will be annulled immediately. If it's painful, then it will involve a trial, be printed in full transcript, and be included in the Old Bailey proceedings. The charges, either way, for Miss Whittington, will be six months imprisonment in Newgate along with a fine of one shilling."

"No," Trevor said again, running his hands through his hair with a tug. "Why did you waste our time with those options?"

"They're viable options. You're assured to marry Miss Butler afterwards, legally."

"She's *not* Miss Butler. She's Lady Pickering. She's been Lady Pickering since we exchanged vows at the altar, our ceremony officiated by the Reverend Obadiah Harvey. The whole of North Yorkshire knows J'non Gaines, née Butler, is the Marchioness of Pickering. You expect me to return with her as my *second* wife and explain to them she was not my legally wedded wife all that time but is now? No, *she* is my wife. I will not acknowledge a marriage with Miss Whittington because there is no marriage to acknowledge, no marriage to end. I had never laid eyes on her until three days ago."

"An annulment, then?" Lloyd offered.

Trevor looked up. "Explain."

Lloyd stretched his neck and shoulders before continuing. "It's nigh impossible. An annulment needs relief from the Episcopal Consistory Court of the Bishop of London. Only the Ecclesiastical Court can make and unmake a marriage. What we need to do is petition to nullify the marriage on the basis of having entered it fraudulently. A Decree of Nullity would then be granted by an Ecclesiastical Censure."

"Why didn't you offer this first?" Trevor asked. "This is exactly what we need. File the petition, have marriage-to-the-erroneous-name nullified, then I'll marry J'non by special license. No one will be the wiser."

"Not so simple, my friend. Not so simple. For starters, the petition is expensive. More importantly, a decree will not take effect until six to twelve months after granted."

"*A year?*" Trevor stood in outrage. "Not to be indelicate, but my *wife* could at this moment be carrying my heir."

"Sit down. I'm not finished. There's more."

"Superb." Trevor sat, returning his head to his hands and resuming his hair strangulation.

"If we pursue this route, you—the petitioner—would bring the case before the Ecclesiastical Court to have the marriage annulled on the grounds of misrepresentation of person of having contracted marriage with someone else. It's possible you would be required to pay back the dowry, but we could include in the petition wording about damages owed to the petitioner, and the dowry would then serve as damages paid."

Trevor groaned. "I already don't like the sound of this. The challenges?"

"We need burden of proof, which would be in the form of witnesses to verify the woman at the altar is not the bearer of the name on the register. Now, the good news is that you're a peer. Lucky you. With a peer as petitioner, the court should accept your petition with the burden of proof already proven, thus negating the need for witness testimony. The bad news is peer or not, there will be an investigation and involvement of Canon lawyers. Yes, the litigation would appear in all legal publications, including those oh-so-elegant pamphlets printed on superfine and priced at two shillings and sixpence apiece. Oh, yes, and the transcription would appear in the Old Bailey proceedings. Did I mention I would not be allowed to represent you at trial, rather the Court Council would? Your parish vicar would still have to testify regarding not only the name on the register, but which woman stood at the altar; although, again, we might be able to avoid the burden of proof testimonies since we're not suing anyone."

"No."

"Your reduction in vocabulary via monosyllabic responses is not helping, my friend. You asked for legal options. I have presented them."

"*Those* are the options? Those and only those? I can divorce the woman I did not marry. I can charge the woman I did not marry with bigamy. Or I can sue both women for committing fraud, and in doing so annul the marriage."

"Now, I never said anything about suing the women," Lloyd defended. "That was what I was avoiding. I said since we are *not* suing anyone."

"Then how am I to petition for fraud if there is no finger pointed at the conspirators? No. I don't want anyone to know about this. No scandals, no testimonies, no trials. I will not have any of our neighbors think she was part of some underhanded scheme or questioning her right as marchioness. I understand the register reads a different name, but I stood at the altar with *my wife*, and that's that. There is no fraud or divorce. There is a name error."

"A significant error, I'd say."

"What of the license?" Trevor looked up in horror at the realization there was no hiding from the legalities. "Her name is on the license, as well." With a strangled cry, he added, "And the application."

Lloyd waved a hand. "None of those are filed. By now, they'll be in a rubbish bin, used as privy paper, or warming someone's bum from the hearth. Are there clerks or clergymen who keep meticulous files? Yes. Are they the minority? Yes. The license application is only kept on file for four months, then it's destroyed since the license has expired. The license, once given to and agreed by the clergyman to conduct the ceremony, is of no use once the parish register is signed, and thus binned or put to more useful purposes."

Trevor leaned back, letting this news sink in. "That *one* signature in a parish book has all this power?"

Lloyd pressed his lips into a grim grin of confirmation. "Don't give up hope. I'll investigate more options. If all else fails, I'll slip coin into someone's purse to nudge them in the direction of the register, and they can change the name by hand." At Trevor's look of incredulity, Lloyd said, "Only jesting. I *will* investigate further. At least we've sorted what options not to explore. I find it encouraging to eliminate options, don't you? Now, shall we put a few pointed questions to Miss Whittington?"

"To what end? I already know I'll not be divorcing or suing her."

"No stone unturned, I say. We'll question her about the, er, holiday, and then I'll escort her to the old Tidwell house. Unless you'd like to do so yourself? No? Didn't think so."

Rising again from his chair, Trevor tugged at the bellpull.

When Bainbridge opened the door, Trevor nodded in greeting. "Bring Miss Whittington. Oh, and if you could arrange for a tea tray, as well, I believe our guest would be appreciative."

Miss Phoebe Whittington took it upon herself to prepare and serve the tea.

There was no denying for Trevor that she and he would not have rubbed well together as a couple, but he did find her pleasant enough company under the circumstances. The resemblance between father and daughter was unquestionable in terms of confidence and conversation dominance, but otherwise, she was feisty rather than vulgar, spirited and opinionated but not so bold as to be indecorous.

He maintained his guard, ears perked for signs of manipulation. Unnecessary by his estimation. She spoke genuinely as far as he was concerned and appeared as chagrined as any woman ought to appear after having jilted her betrothed, and then circled back with a new scheme and upset a happy marriage in the process. As for Lloyd's perception of her, the solicitor groveled at her feet and all but drooled, enamored by a pretty face and dynamic personality. Unfortunately for Lloyd, she did not look twice at him.

"I can't apologize enough," Miss Whittington said, continuing in what had been a long line of apologies. "I've made a royal mess and nearly spoiled a marriage from my selfishness. If I had never shown up, no one would have known."

Trevor accepted the cup of tea she offered and leaned back in his chair. "On the contrary. I'm pleased you *did* arrive, for in doing so, you removed the weight from my wife's shoulders. We can resolve many problems now before they become greater problems later."

Lloyd set his cup and saucer on the table, leaning in with interest. "But why did you come here of all places?"

Two red spots blossomed on her cheeks. "I had nowhere to go. I never dreamt my lady's maid would follow through with the silly idea, never in my wildest dreams. I thought she would confess I had eloped. When I returned, I assumed Lord Pickering would be unmarried and jilted, my father would be raging angry that I had eloped with Mr. Wilkins, and the lady's maid would have been sent back to the employment agency where we found her."

"But why didn't you return to your father?" Lloyd prompted.

"You've met my father." She pinned him with a stare. "Would *you* return to face his wrath after jilting a marquess to elope with a libertine? I thought to right the situation by coming here and convincing Lord Pickering to marry me after all."

Trevor took his time to sip his tea before saying, "The more pressing question is if you are Mrs. Wilkins or Miss Whittington."

"For bigamy charges?" she asked.

His cup rattled in its saucer.

"I'm more practical than you would give me credit for," she said. "I'm ashamed to say it was all a sham. He knew my father would never allow us to marry, so he thought to force my father's hand by compromising me. Don't flinch. We're all adults here. The problem was, I refused to play his game once I realized he was the worst sort of liar, only after the dowry." She scoffed when she said, "All his words of love were a lie. Typical. Naïve of me. It took time to return to London. I had a friend with whom I could stay for a short time, thankfully, to devise a plan of how best to approach Papa, but when her maid heard from one of the footmen that the marquess was soon to return to his London residence, I thought this would solve all my problems. I will confess I considered the other gentleman who had wanted to contract marriage, an earl in Shropshire, but Lord Pickering seemed the more viable option. How easy to continue with that plan since the settlement had already been signed?"

Trevor grunted.

Lloyd asked, "Could you not return to your friend?"

"My stay was temporary, unfortunately." She stared into her teacup before adding, "I only thought to save myself. I never dreamt I would hurt anyone in the process."

Trevor said, "Let us focus on the problem at hand. As we've established, *your* name is on the register, and yet you are not my wife. This is the problem we must resolve."

"I'm thankful it's worked out this way, that you've found love. What's a marriage without love? I've had enough of a loveless life. Not that you gentlemen care. I'm rambling. I'll do whatever is needed. Do I need to testify that I didn't sign the register?"

Lloyd said, "We're still considering possibilities. Your assurance is most welcome."

Setting his teacup aside, Trevor stood and paced before the fireplace mantel. "What of Mr. Whittington? There can be little doubt he's been bragging about the connection for the length of the marriage."

Miss Whittington looked up, her expression one of confusion. "I didn't return home because I had assumed my maid had already told him. Since she didn't, he would *believe* I married you, but he has no verification of that. He has no way of knowing you married someone else or that the name on the register is mine. Had I gone to my father first instead and confessed, I would not have discovered the truth, either. One word of confession from me, and he'll know I eloped with Mr. Wilkins instead."

Relief washed over Trevor. As quickly, he grimaced in realization of his error. "I called on Mr. Whittington in November."

Miss Whittington groaned. "Did you admit we were married? Did you give any indication we had exchanged vows? Perhaps I could spin your visit to be you wanting to question my whereabouts and why your contracted betrothed did not show for the wedding."

Trevor thought back to his conversation with Mr. Whittington. "I'm afraid I don't have a satisfactory answer. I did not have much opportunity to speak, and I did not divulge information since Mr. Whittington made it abundantly clear he did not care to hear about his daughter, his concern only that of being introduced to the right people. I can't be certain, however, that I didn't mention Lady Pickering. I don't believe so, but there's no guarantee."

Miss Whittington waved a hand. "I'll spin it anyway, say you came to put the question to him as to why I jilted you, but after meeting him, you didn't wish to pursue the arrangement further. It's his problem that he's been bragging about the marriage, is it not? He's the fool. I hate to say that of Papa, but there it is."

An unflattering portrayal of Trevor to have sought to confront a man only to leave him believing his daughter was a marchioness. In a way, he pitied Mr. Whittington. So much of his dislike for the man had been in blaming him for J'non's past, which he knew now was far from the case.

"What of the dowry?" Trevor asked.

"I assume you've used it well?" Miss Whittington asked with a laugh. "I would not have had it after confessing my elopement anyway, so I'm happy it's being used. It's my sacrifice for a poor decision. I will inform Papa that I wrote to you with full permission to use the dowry to assuage my guilt. He will not attempt to regain it. How humiliating if he did! You could, after all, sue him for breach of promise. Ooh, that's another point I can add. That I gave you full permission to use it as payment *not* to sue. Yes, he'll see the business sense in that. He's nothing if not business minded. In the end, my father will be angry that I eloped and didn't inform him, leaving him without the association he sought and with the embarrassment of having bragged about it. He won't cause a fuss."

Another notch against Trevor, now the acceptor of bribery. Alas, needs must.

Trevor said, "I won't have you put yourself in danger. If you feel he is a threat to your safety or that he will force you out of the house—"

"Would you offer me some of my own money, then? How kind." She batted her eyelashes. "Fear not, Lord Pickering. I will handle my father. I avoided going to him because I hoped to resolve the problem to my satisfaction rather than admit my folly. It would seem I must face my decision head on."

"For now, stay at my other London house, at least until we can sort the signature. After that, it will be your decision where to turn, be it to your father or otherwise. Come to me if the reunion is unpleasant. Regardless, I would like to extend my continued hospitality and, if it would be pleasing to you, invite you to join Lady Pickering and me to a few events, as our guest."

"Hmm. We'll see. For now, as you said, the signature. I was most certainly in Scotland at the time, and witnesses can attest to that, should we need them."

Feeling more confident than before, Trevor bowed to Miss Whittington, eager to conclude the interview and return to J'non.

Chapter 31

With the house to themselves again, they made use of the drawing room for their after-dinner enjoyment, although it was not the same without Gunner.

"All I'm saying," J'non continued, "is we should wait until matters are settled."

Trevor leaned back and stared at the ceiling. "Must *everything* wait? I've listed a dozen tasks for us to complete, all of which I'm ready to move forward with as early as tomorrow, yet you've said no to the lot."

"I recall you being the responsible sort at one time. Where did that gentleman go? If I might have him on loan for the next couple of weeks, I promise to return him."

He rolled his head forward to smirk. "Lord Responsibility left his duties on the home farm in Yorkshire."

"At least let me have Lord Reasonable. Until matters are settled, it's too risky."

"It can only help our case from my perspective." Propping an elbow on the arm of his chair, he rested his cheek in his palm. "The court dress, calling on

Lord and Lady Roddam, reconnecting with Lady Collingwood, attending a soiree or five..." His brows rose when his list trailed off, as if to continue on his behalf.

"You're thinking wistfully rather than practically. What if this isn't sorted tidily? What if we must go to trial to annul the marriage register, then remarry with a new entry? I think it would do more harm than good to introduce me to everyone as Lady Pickering when, presently, I'm not."

"You *are*. The vicar married *us*, not a name. I have faith all will be sorted. Lloyd is nothing if not a genius, however much he denies it. Besides, if there is a trial, would it not be better for everyone to know in advance you're the rightful marchioness?"

J'non harrumphed. He was not seeing reason. Part of her thought he might be teasing, but the part that knew he would jump to any and all activities if she said *yes* reminded her that he was ardently serious. What she would not admit, lest she encourage him, was her temptation. Only three days ago, she would have thrown herself into all these activities, but now, she wanted to ensure she did so as the *legal* marchioness. How dreadful to parade with confidence only for matters not to go as they hoped and it all be ripped away, this time permanently? No, she would rather look forward to matters being settled when she could enjoy London. Even meeting Lady Collingwood again held a new level of excitement, for while the baroness would not know the story of how J'non transitioned from maid to marchioness, the story would be true, and the husband in full awareness of her past.

Trevor drummed his fingers against his temple. "And if there is a trial? A scandal at best, not granting me an annulment at worst? Then what? We return home with you as my traveling companion? My mistress? No, there is only one way for this to end, and I want us to prepare for that eventuality by establishing you as my lawfully wedded wife."

His overconfidence made her nervous. She believed if anyone could find a way, Mr. Barmby could, but the reality of the situation was that she made an error grievous enough to make marriage legally impossible. There was the probability that Trevor would remain married to Phoebe Whittington's name, or if an annulment were possible, the scandal of a trial would ruin their matrimonial chances. He was not losing sleep over this, though; he was confident all would be resolved. But how?

If only she had signed her own name. In hindsight, it was foolish not to have — who would have looked at the register to know she had not signed Phoebe Whittington? Alas, when there was a vicar, a husband, and two witnesses, the latter with the sole purpose of overseeing the signatures, she would never have thought *not* to sign as Phoebe Whittington. Not even with sloppy handwriting could she have made a passable resemblance between names. The curious part was the only record of their marriage was in the parish register, and as such, could happily go ignored for eternity, no one ever knowing what name she signed, at least if Trevor were not a marquess and their first-born son not the heir, assuming she bore a son one day. When inheritance was at stake, when the legitimacy of their future children was at stake, one did not take risks.

"If you won't humor me," Trevor continued, "then at least grant me permission to find your aunt."

J'non snapped to attention. "My *aunt*?"

"Aside from whatever comeuppance I feel she's owed, I wish to restore your inheritance, the inheritance they stole from you. While you were led to believe nothing was settled on your care, no dowry set aside, nor dividends from the house sale, I would wager your parents had your best interest in mind. A certain aunt was greedy."

She closed her eyes and focused on her breathing. Just the thought of her aunt raised the hairs on the back of her arms. Living with her had been a nightmare. The woman had never laid a hand to J'non, but she did not have to. Her words cut deeper than any hand or instrument could. As if living with her were bad enough, living without her had been a new nightmare, one J'non would rather not recall for the second time in a single week.

"Is it about the money?" she asked, eyes remaining closed.

"It's the principle. She stole from you, and not just money, but we can't replenish all you lost under her roof or after. We can, however, regain as much of your inheritance as possible."

Opening her eyes, she studied him. No, it was not about the money. She could see that, hear it in his voice. Throughout her stay with her aunt, she had suspected the financial issues to be a lie, for her father was not a poor man and would have done all he could to see to her comfort and safety. That he was not wealthy, either, breathed possible truth into her aunt's narrative, as did J'non's refusal to believe ill of her aunt despite the poor treatment. It was one more unfairness J'non could not handle. Better to believe blindly than feed hate, or so she had told herself. Besides, what could she have done if true? She was at her aunt's mercy.

"Please don't," J'non said. "I know she is not a good person, and I believe you're right about the inheritance, but this is a wound I cannot reopen. Let it be. Whatever she stole from me, let us consider it as payment towards my future as your wife, for without the sequence of events as it was, we would never have met." When he scowled and made to respond, she said, "If I compare it to your not wanting to find your mother, would you understand?"

He leaned back, hand inching towards his heart. So quiet was he, she worried she had wounded him by mentioning his mother. That had not been her intent. Did the two not parallel in a way?

To her relief, he nodded, saying no more on the subject. Instead, he proposed, "A concession? We could go to The Pot and Pineapple for ices, walk Hyde Park in the early dawn, take a ride during a not-so-fashionable hour? There are things we can do and places we can go to enjoy all that London has to offer without bumping into people who would initiate introductions. While I'm champing at the bit to introduce you to all and sundry, my loyalty is only to you and your happiness. Let me show you London. If you need more convincing, be assured by this little fact: I'm not well known. I would never go so far as to say I've lived the life of a recluse, but I've spent little time making myself known beyond those few people who have been in my life since my youth. Few know me, and fewer still know me as Lord Pickering."

J'non narrowed her gaze. On the tip of her tongue was to ask how he would introduce her should they manage to bump into the one person in London who did know him. Since his answer would undoubtedly be unsatisfactory, likely something to antagonize her, such as introducing her as his ideal wife — wicked man that he was — she resisted the urge.

"I'll agree only on the condition you stop grinning at me like a madman," she said.

His smile widened as he pantomimed a cheer. She could not keep from returning the smile — she had never had ice cream, after all.

"What we need is to *void* the marriage," Lloyd said two mornings later. The solicitor sat in what was becoming his usual chair in the study. "What we will accept but would rather avoid is a *voidable* marriage. To void the marriage will mean it never took place, never existed, poof, obliterated from history. If deemed voidable instead, then the marriage is acknowledged as having taken place and was a legal marriage from the period of time between the ceremony and the annulment. Once annulled, you are *un*married from that point forward. Make sense?"

"Clear as the Thames." Trevor stood at the window, looking out onto the street.

It would not be long before callers descended. The tray in the vestibule was already collecting cards, ones he needed to reciprocate sooner rather than later. Being unknown gave the advantage of not being sought upon immediate arrival to the capitol, but there were those who had known the previous Lord Pickering and would be eager to meet who had taken the mantle after his passing. He could not avoid society for long. It was a wonder he had done so for nearly a week. Time was not on his side.

"What we ought to do," Lloyd continued, "is petition to *void* the marriage in order to circumvent an annulment altogether. There's nothing to annul if there is no marriage, see? There are, however, some complications."

"Of course." Trevor leaned a shoulder against the corner of the bay window.

"To end the marriage without annulment, we need the Courts and the House of Lords to declare the marriage void, which requires legal proof that the marriage doesn't or shouldn't exist, i.e. Miss Whittington was in Scotland at the time in which the supposed marriage was to have existed."

The benefit of living on a side street rather than on one of the squares was the relative quiet. Only one curricle had passed since he had moved to the window, a curricle driven by a fellow with a jaunty hat and too-wide grin, on his way towards Hyde Park to be seen. Would have been faster to walk to the park, only a few streets away, and far less traffic.

Trevor said, "I'm not certain I understand." Was *void* not the purpose of annulment and *voided* the result of divorce? He was not following Lloyd's terms or meanings well. "Regardless, continue. How do we accomplish this *fait accompli*?"

When Lloyd did not answer, Trevor glanced over his shoulder. The solicitor stared back, eyebrows raised and expectant.

"Ah." Trevor turned back to the window. "Since you don't have a plan for the wonderous *void* marriage scheme, any other possibilities to explore?"

"Short of bribing someone to forge a change, I'm running low on bright ideas. One of several issues with my bribery plan is we don't know where your vicar keeps the register. We could hazard a guess, but I'd rather know with certainty before I send someone rummaging around a church in search of records. The vicar could keep it in the vicarage for all we know."

"We're not bribing someone to change the register."

"Why you ask for my advice when you're quick to pooh-pooh the best, I'll never understand."

Turning his back on the view, Trevor joined Lloyd, his shoulders rounded. However confident he appeared for J'non's benefit, he was increasingly more disheartened.

He slumped into his chair. "At this point, I feel I should request an audience with the Archbishop, have a heart to heart, seek his advice. I'm not a marquess for nothing."

In slow time, Lloyd sat up, leaned forward, spread his palms, then whooped. "That's *it*!"

Trevor canted his head. In a single morning, he had driven his solicitor to madness.

"You don't see it?" Lloyd asked. "Right. Here's what we know. His Grace, The Most Reverend and Right Honorable Archbishop of Canterbury is nothing if not a devoted family man. I suggest you make a *social* call. Take tea with him. He loves to entertain.

Go on an empty stomach. He's more devoted to family than to ecclesiastic matters, to anything really, known even to make administrative decisions based on family, so devoted I believe we can use that to our advantage. This is not a *legal* matter we're facing. This is a *family* matter. See it now? No?" Lloyd huffed with exasperation. "Where's your imagination? Your creative spirit?"

"Is that not why I pay you? So I don't need one?"

"Fair enough. Where was I? Oh, yes, this is a *family* matter. You fell in love with a baronet's daughter. You exchanged vows with said baronet's daughter. You're beginning a family with same baronet's daughter. But then — "

Trevor sat up, a smile spreading.

"You see it, yes?" Lloyd rubbed his hands together.

Chapter 32

The State Drawing Room at Lambeth Palace was six windows long and minimalistic in décor, its attention on three details: a collection of gifts received by past Archbishops, the ornate plasterwork ceiling, and the view of lawn and gardens below. Used to entertain even the Royal Family, it devoted its humblest days to serving as Dr. John Moore's primary living room, Dr. John Moore being His Grace, The Most Reverend and Right Honorable Archbishop of Canterbury.

"You've not tried the ratafia cakes. Here, I insist." His Grace helped three of the little cakes find their way onto Trevor's plate. "I was heartily impressed by your part in the canal petition yesterday. Congratulations to its success. I find it remarkable you've achieved so much in such a short time since inheriting."

"Thank you, Your Grace. I couldn't have accomplished half without my wife. She's the fuel to my fire."

"Hear, hear." The Archbishop moved his attention to the Charlotte Russe cake. "How is your nursery looking?"

"Sparse at present, as we've only been married since August, but mark my words, I'll have an heir before the next opening ceremony of Parliament."

"Good man. My first wife, may she rest in peace, was unable to know the joy of motherhood, a regret I feel in my breast to this day, but my second wife has been most fortunate. It's our gift to them as much as their duty to us. Now, who is the Marchioness of Pickering, hmm? When may I have the pleasure of her company?"

"It would be our honor to call on you again," Trevor said, wanting to shake his head to the offering of a slice of sponge cake but not wanting to be an ungrateful guest. Grimacing a smile, he allowed His Grace to add it to the collection of other sweet and sugary bellyaches.

"I knew I could tempt you." The Archbishop savored a bite from each sweet on his plate before making a second round, again with one bite each.

"My wife is the daughter of the late Sir Julian Butler, a baronet from Surrey, who, as far as I'm concerned, revolutionized farming techniques."

"You favored her for her father's farming techniques?" The ratafia cake stilled on its way to his lips.

Trevor chuckled. "Not precisely, but those same techniques have made a significant difference to the state of my home farm and the flood-prone terrain surrounding. Hence the canal petition, to aid in flood prevention."

"Let us not mention the profits to be earned on those canal waters, hmm?" He waggled his brows. "Profits to line the purse of the marchioness, fill dowries for all the daughters you'll have, and spoil the boys. You needn't deny. I know what a family needs and make decisions accordingly. You've a good head on your shoulders, Lord Pickering."

Trevor nodded in gratitude.

"Will you bring her to my birthday celebration? In two weeks, I'll be sixty-six. A feast like you've never before seen."

"I'm certain my wife will be honored." Trevor grimaced again when it dawned what the guest list would look like for His Grace, the Lord Archbishop of Canterbury. J'non would strangle Trevor by his cravat. "This is her first opportunity to tour London and enjoy its entertainments. What a privilege it will be for her to see Lambeth Palace."

"Sir Julian of the revolutionary farming techniques didn't arrange for her come-out season in London?"

"She was young when he passed, both he and her mother, too young for an introduction to society," said Trevor before gulping down a bite of the least sugar-coated biscuit in the collection. His Grace was two plates ahead of him.

"If not in London, how did you meet this fuel to your fire?"

"Through a series of acquaintances. Someone she knew also knew my solicitor, and thus the network of associations began."

His Grace nodded sagely. "A trustworthy way to meet a spouse, credibility outweighing dance skill." He set down his plate, dabbed his lips with his napkin, then changed his mind and reached for his plate again. "Now, then, Lord Pickering, why don't you take another bite of the sponge cake then tell me what's troubling you. I can read in your expression you're wanting to broach a topic. A crisis of faith, is it?"

This was the opening he needed, the transition he had not expected but had been watching for as a way to press his suit. Caught unawares, he hesitated. He did not wish for his friendly social call to appear deceitful. This had not been a call on business, a request to meet His Grace in the Doctors' Commons. This had been purely social, a peer wishing to take tea with the Archbishop for idle talk.

Toeing the line of politeness, and as casually as he could, as though discussing the weather, he said, "Your perception does you credit, Your Grace. There *is*, as it happens, a matter about which I would value your perspective."

"Ecclesiastic? Social? Political?"

"Legal."

The Archbishop raised his eyebrows. "Piqued. Continue." He tipped another slice of sponge cake onto his plate as he listened.

"I have become aware of an error on the parish marriage register, an error with my wife's name. I'm uncertain how to proceed. My wife is my wife, the same woman with whom I exchanged vows before God, the vicar, and witnesses. But I'm concerned about the error, as you can understand, given we hope to fill the nursery soon. I would not want there to be any question over the legality of whom I married and who is heir apparent."

His Grace nodded, intent, his bites slow.

Since no comments were forthcoming, Trevor continued, "The irony is with the vicar, the two witnesses, and me all gathered around the register to sign our names, not a single one of us spotted the error. My wife, you see, so caught up in the moment of matrimonial vow taking, signed the wrong name."

The Archbishop's chewing stopped. He swallowed. He blinked. He took another bite and continued chewing.

Trevor cleared his throat. "You can appreciate my dilemma. As absurd as it sounds to me, is my best course of action to annul the marriage to void the register, and then remarry?"

His Grace nearly chocked on his sponge cake from laughing. His eyes watered as he set down his plate and reached for his handkerchief. "Annul the marriage to your wife to remarry your wife? The same woman? That *is* absurd. No man need marry their wife more than once!"

Trevor laced his fingers over his knee to keep from fidgeting.

The Archbishop dabbed at the corners of his eyes. "Go on, finish your sweets," he prompted Trevor. "Womenfolk are an adjective unto themselves. There's no reason to describe a woman as not being the swiftest arrow in the quiver when one need only say the word *woman*, and everyone understands. Their response? 'Ah, bless.' I love my wife to distraction, Lord Pickering, but the fact of nature is, she's a woman.'"

"Bless," Trevor said.

"See? It's a natural response. It's a peculiar thing to do, sign the wrong name, but womenfolk, being what they are, well… it's any wonder they know the right end of a quill." He was in no hurry to continue, pausing to enjoy another sweet. "There's no end to clerical errors when it comes to marriages, especially those by license. Bane of my existence, licenses. But I'm rambling. It sounds to me, my lord, your parish clergyman is in need of a new register. Personally, I cannot abide an untidy ledger. I'll send a new register straightaway along with a note that the marquess and marchioness will be renewing their vows in the new register due to a clerical error in the original. He'll know what to do with the original entry. Leave the pertinent information with my clerk. Now, why have you not finished your slice of the Charlotte Russe? Prefer the sponge cake?"

Chapter 33

J'non's arm was threaded with that of Baroness Collingwood, the two standing at the back of the room, awaiting Trevor's return. The warm May air was stifling inside the drawing room. The evening's entertainment was a soiree, hosted by a countess whose parties were known to be great squeezes. While J'non had never attended a soiree, much less one that could be considered a squeeze, she would assume the crowded room affirmed the countess' reputation.

Lady Collingwood patted J'non's hand. "Are you nervous for the curtsy? Only three days hence."

"Not remotely," J'non admitted, nodding to a group of ladies who passed, ladies who had been introduced to her an hour before. "I only want it over so I never have to worry about stepping on a train again."

"You say that now. Afterwards, you'll be vying for the opportunity to demonstrate your newfound talent."

Trevor returned, wearing a frown and puckered eyebrows. "She's surrounded by every eligible gentleman at the soiree. Try as I might to shoulder my way to her, they've tightened ranks."

J'non tried to spy Phoebe in the crowd, but she was too short to see above the guests. "She'll find us when she's finished being flattered. You know how she is."

Trevor grunted, then said to Lady Collingwood, "Too soon to call on Lord and Lady Roddam? I know it's been almost three weeks since Miss Colette was born, but I do not want to intrude on their domesticity or Lady Roddam's recovery."

"Oh, Lord Pickering, your thoughtfulness does you credit, but you and Lady Pickering are welcome to call any time. They would be delighted. In all likelihood, you'll have the opportunity to meet *two* new babies, for Lady Roddam and her sister brought their new bundles into the world only hours apart. Since I remain the overseeing midwife — thank you for not being squeamish about this, my lord — they arrange to be in the same place at the same time when I call. Thoughtful is it not?"

"Indeed," Trevor said. "I hope we'll luck into your being there, then, as well as her sister and family, although personally I'll look forward to seeing Baron Collingwood again and your son. Where is the baron this evening, come to think of it?"

"He promised to take my mother-in-law for a game of cards. In truth, I was supposed to join, but since I had already accepted this invitation to accompany Lady Pickering, I left him to his devices. I'm positive he's kicking up his heels in freedom."

J'non hushed them. "Here she comes. She has an older gentleman with her."

They all turned to witness Phoebe's walk across the room. J'non could appreciate the confidence of

Phoebe's carriage and the remarkable beauty of her person, but J'non no longer considered herself inferior, for her looking glass reminded her each morning of her inner strength, the glow of her personality, and even the understated beauty she possessed but had never recognized. What defined beauty, anyway? To J'non, it was happiness. Sheer happiness.

Phoebe approached with the opening words of, "Why are you all hiding in a corner?"

The older gentleman bent low. "What was that you said, Miss Whittington?"

Trevor caught the man's attention. "Lord Ascot, a pleasure to see you here."

"Well, well, if it isn't the Admiral's son, all grown up by the look of it." Lord Ascot took Trevor's hand and pumped it. Without another glance to Phoebe, he eyed J'non with a twinkle in his eyes. "Is this your wife, then? Your father would have approved." He leaned in to say to J'non, "I see the sunshine in your soul, my lady. Beautiful. Simply beautiful."

J'non had no idea what he was talking about, but she blushed at the unexpected compliments.

Trevor slipped a hand against J'non's back, something he had done all evening when he introduced her to someone new, a sort of imbuing of strength in case she was nervous. It worked every time.

"May I introduce a friend of my father? Lord Ascot. I've known him for as far back as my memory goes." Turning to the gentleman, he said, "This, as you surmised, is my wife, the Marchioness of Pickering."

Lord Ascot accepted her proffered hand and bowed over it. "A vision of goodness and beauty, my lady."

J'non, quite taken by the gentleman, said, "Do call on us, will you? I would love to hear stories of Lord Pickering as a boy."

"Wait, I didn't agree to this," Trevor protested with a laugh.

Lord Ascot said, "Expect me as early as tomorrow. How are you enjoying London, Lady Pickering? Finding the entertainment to your liking?"

J'non looked at Trevor then back to Lord Ascot before saying in a hushed tone, "I'm on a mission, an espionage mission. By order of Lady Osborne, I must gather as much information about London diversions as I can so I have an accurate point of comparison when she takes me to York. I have it on good authority, you understand, that York is superior."

Lord Ascot and Trevor both chuckled, although she could not say if they chuckled at her little joke or the thought that any city could be superior to London.

After a few more exchanges in conversation, Baroness Collingwood led Lord Ascot away, the two having launched into deep conversation about something of mutual interest, their destination the refreshment room from what J'non could see.

Phoebe slipped between Trevor and J'non, hooking her hands into the crook of their arms. "At last. Alone."

Trevor looked at J'non from over Phoebe's head. "Do you ever feel as though there's someone between us?"

"Yes, I do, rather," said J'non.

Phoebe tutted. "Don't be so quick to get rid of me. It's not as though you can't enjoy your tête-à-têtes at home. I'm your special guest, remember? I demand attention." She looked back and forth between Trevor and J'non. "This is important. No woolgathering. I'm off to Shropshire next week."

"Shropshire!" J'non exclaimed.

"Yes. Shropshire. I've an earl to snare."

Trevor and J'non exchanged glances again.

Phoebe continued, "I should have mentioned this sooner, but it slipped my mind." She laughed shallowly. "The only reason Papa has not had me drawn and quartered is on the condition I reconsider the suit from the Earl of Collumby. Only, there's a teeny, tiny caveat. He'll not be arranging the match for me. I must travel to Shropshire and use my cunning to convince the earl to marry me. No dowry to use to my advantage. Not that I need one, and not that Papa couldn't equal the previous dowry — which he accepted without question had gone to assuage my guilt, keep *you* mum about the breach of promise, and even aid in the marriage of a dear friend of mine to the very man I jilted — but he refuses to on principle."

J'non listened, her mouth slightly agape. At least she never had to face Mr. Whittington again. The man was far too intimidating for her. "What if you can't, as you say, 'snare' the earl?"

Phoebe laughed a single *ha*. "As if I couldn't snare him. There's no question about it. I will. The earl is *ancient* but still needs an heir. What does he care for a dowry? His priority is on establishing an heir. Apparently, there is some drama as to the person who would inherit should the earl fail to produce an heir apparent. He's desperate. I would have thought he would have found some poor girl by now, but Papa did his due diligence and assures me he's still available. Lucky me."

J'non shuddered. This did not sound like a love story with a happy ending by her estimation, but perhaps it was what Phoebe needed.

"I'll write, of course. Oh! Is that the sixth Earl of Bramley? I do believe it is. Speaking of espionage, did you know he comes from a family of spies? Or maybe not. I might have misheard. Either way, if you'll both excuse me, I must ascertain if there's a Countess of Bramley." She slipped away to make for the unsuspecting peer.

Trevor's hand found J'non's lower back and proceeded to make tantalizing revolutions with the thumb. "Alone. At last."

J'non giggled. "Had she not said it first, I would have found that endearing, if not flirty."

"Consider it both, my love."

He leaned closer, the warmth of his body causing sweat to bead along J'non's side. She inched closer still to inhale his cologne, a heady mixture of rose water, musk, and spices.

He said, "I've been wanting to have you to myself all evening."

"Yet when you had me alone for a full week, you were dying to take me to soirees and parties and operas and all the things."

"Men can be daft. Can we be alone for a full week again?" His lips were inches from her ear.

"You'll have me to yourself soon enough. For now, enjoy the party. You've only managed to introduce me to thirty people tonight. There are at least seventy more to go, I'm positive."

"You'd rather be home," he said, mistaking the sigh on her lips. "I can see it in your thoughts. I can read them, you know. Transparent as the night is warm."

"I don't believe you know what I'm thinking, but go on, hazard a guess."

"You're thinking," Trevor said, keeping his voice low, "our little problem has not been resolved until we return home to sign the new register and ensure the old one has been ripped out, blacked out, or whatever is to be done with it. You're thinking that although the problem has a resolution that will be implemented, it lingers still."

J'non laughed so heartily, she took Trevor by surprise, if his expression was anything by which to judge. "No, actually, that was far from what I was thinking. Quite the opposite. I was thinking to myself that I should do an extra-stellar job of establishing myself as Lady Pickering so there's no doubt whatsoever you'll change your mind between now and the renewal of our vows. During this wee little window of opportunity, you could break free."

He leaned away from her with an expression, this time, of dismay. "Wait. What? Why would I change my mind? Good heavens, J'non, do you fear I'm still—"

She shushed him with a finger to his lips. "I merely want to ensure that once you hear you'll be a father sooner rather than later, you won't become faint of heart and run while you have the chance. Fatherhood is a daunting prospect for some, you know."

Trevor paled, his eyes widening. His jaw worked open then closed, a fish out of water.

"You look faint. Should we sit?" J'non offered.

With slow precision, Trevor shook his head and reached his hands to cup her cheeks. "You tell me *now*, in a crowded soiree? You are a cruel woman, J'non Gaines, for I want to howl at the moon right now, draw you into my arms, kiss you like today is the beginning of forever... but all I can do is stand here and gaze upon your loveliness."

"I hadn't intentionally waited until this moment, but—"

"Never mind. We're leaving. Now. Forget your curtsy. Forget London. Let's go *home*."

J'non laughed. "You'll have to do better than that to convince me to leave after having such fun at this so-called squeeze."

"Gunner will want to know."

J'non's lips spread into a giddy smile. *Home.*

Epilogue

October 1799

The fête stretched across the village green, the largest festival yet with vendors, stalls, and guests from across Yorkshire.

Trevor led both his sons by hand to the juggling tent. To one side, J'non walked with him. To the other, Gunner heeled, but it was not to Trevor that he heeled but to Daisy the greyhound, waddling from her ungainly state of late-stage pregnancy. Just what his sons wanted, and just what Trevor and J'non had not planned for — puppies. At least two were promised to Lord and Lady Roddam, thankfully. Now only to convince Roland and Siobhan to adopt a puppy or two. Obadiah would want at least one, but Gwen may have other plans.

Out of his periphery, he saw J'non lean to accept the extended hand of their youngest son, a hand that had been denied earlier since he had wanted to walk with Papa like a big boy, or so he had informed them when J'non had tried to take his hand.

"I see them across the crowd," J'non said.

He assumed she meant Lord and Lady Roddam, who were due to meet them at the festival, followed by the traditional dinner at the Court. The crowd beneath the juggler's tent was too dense to navigate. He held his family back from the crowd for safety, then hoisted his eldest on his left shoulder and, with J'non's help, propped his youngest on his right. His shoulders primed to take the weight of those he held most dear.

"We could move closer," she offered.

"I'd rather remain here so we can make a speedy escape at our leisure."

"I like how you think, Trevor. No, no, stop squirming or you're going to kick Papa in his head."

The juggling show was nothing spectacular, but the boys enjoyed it. Trevor's attention wandered throughout, though, mostly to J'non's profile as she smiled and laughed with unadulterated joy at the juggler's antics. To most, it would appear she enjoyed the show. Trevor knew better, for they were of like minds. The joy was multilayered and reflected in all they did no matter how much time passed since the renewal of their vows — the joy of having found each other, of being together, of building a family, of developing a prosperous march, of surviving adversity and fighting for what mattered most.

Their joy was one of loyalty, truth, inner beauty, and the deepest of love, a love that could turn a maid into a marchioness and a marquess into man worthy of a maiden.

A Note from
the Author

Dear Reader,

Thank you for purchasing and reading this book. If you're interested in exploring some of the research that went into this book and others, check out my research blog: https://www.paullettgolden.com/bookresearch

Supporting indie writers who brave self-publishing is important and appreciated. I hope you'll continue reading my novels, as I have many more titles to come.

I humbly request you review this book on Amazon with an honest opinion. Reviewing elsewhere is additionally much appreciated.

One way to support writers you've enjoyed reading, indie or otherwise, is to share their work with friends, family, book clubs, etc. Lend books, share books, exchange books, recommend books, and gift books. If you especially enjoyed a writer's book, lend it to someone to read in case they might find a new favorite author in the book you've shared. Including the author's book in a Little Free Library is a terrific idea.

Connect with me online at www.paullettgolden.com, www.facebook.com/paullettgolden, www.twitter.com/paullettgolden, and www.instagram.com/paullettgolden, as well as Amazon's Author Central, Goodreads, BookBub, and LibraryThing.

All the best,
Paullett Golden

About the Author

Celebrated for her complex characters, realistic conflicts, and sensual portrayal of love, Paullett Golden writes historical romance for intellectuals. Her novels, set primarily in Georgian England, challenge the genre's norm by starring characters loved for their flaws, imperfections, and idiosyncrasies. Her plots explore human psyche, mental and physical trauma, and personal convictions. Her stories show love overcoming adversity. Whatever our self-doubts, *love will out*.

Connect online
paullettgolden.com
facebook.com/paullettgolden
twitter.com/paullettgolden
instagram.com/paullettgolden

.

Printed in Great Britain
by Amazon